On Frogs and Princes

by

Tess Marset

1 LONE CROW MEDIA

Book and Cover Design: Vladimir Verano, Vertvolta Design

Revised 2020

PUBLISHED BY

1 Lone Crow Media

www.1LoneCrowMedia.com

ISBN: 978-1-7333609-3-7

To Mom,
who indeed, has always been there for us.

On Frogs and Princes

Chapter One ~ The Introduction

"Gidge? It's me, Stazie. Okay so now with this stupid blackout, where is everyone going to meet? . . . But you told me that we were all going to meet at the Dive. Besides it's out . . . No, I'm positive it's out. I just drove by there . . . Uh huh. It's totally black. No lights, no action, no one. So where? Has everyone decided? Wait! Oh poop. You're breaking up. Stupid cell phone . . . Okay I can hear you now—can you hear me? Uh huh. Mars 'n Venus? Why there? But that's where all the transients hang out . . . No, I'm not kidding! Well, didn't you hear what Marcus said happened there last week? You didn't? Well remind me to tell you as soon as we meet up . . . Me? I don't know where I am right now. I must've taken a wrong turn off 107th . . . No. I don't know how to work that nav thing on my phone. Listen, make sure you guys wait for me. I can't stand it when you ditch me . . . No. I can barely make out the street signs . . . Wait—I think I just past Josh's . . . No, I guess that wasn't his place. Let me take this corner . . . Huh? Wait! Oh . . . I think I just hit something . . . I don't know, I think it was a dog . . . I'm not kidding, Gidge! I hope it didn't do any damage to my car! That would really suck. Hold on . . . Holy bunnies! It wasn't a dog, it's a person!"

Rey couldn't believe he had just been run over. Riding home from the supermarket, he was navigating his mountain bike around the large puddles on the street trying to avoid getting soaked. Next, the blackout plunged him into darkness. He was finding his way toward the sidewalk when he heard the squeal of tires behind him as they took the corner. His shadow loomed before him, quickly growing in size as the headlights from the oncoming car lit up his path. He was trying to get out of the way when it felt as if a fast moving wall had plowed into him. The force sent him sailing off his bike and crashing into a row of garbage cans that lined the curb. Reduced to a crumpled heap, dazed, and panting heavily from having the air knocked out of him, he listened to the sickening crunch of metal as his bicycle fell victim to that same moving wall. His only relief was that he wasn't the crunch beneath those wheels.

Still too stunned to move, he could only turn his head towards his attacker. He squinted against the glare of the car's bright headlights. Next, he heard the car door open and close and then the distinct click of high heels on the asphalt. Silhouetted in the halogen beams of the headlights, a pair of long, shapely legs led up to tight miniskirt. The sight wasn't totally lost on him although at the moment, he couldn't fully appreciate it.

Next, he heard a high voice say in the darkness, "Oh poop! Are you okay?"

Considering the question, Rey took a quick assessment of himself. *Ankle is hosed up. Elbow is bleeding like a son of a bitch in my sleeve. Left knee—completely screwed. Damn shoulder got it again . . . I'll be feeling this in the morning.* He counted himself very lucky that his head was still intact and realized how stupid it was that he hadn't worn his helmet.

"I said, are you okay?" the voice repeated, accompanied by a jangle of bracelets. She came closer and crouched down for a better look. "Are you, like, injured?"

A cloud of perfume wafted over to Rey's nose. He groaned and sat upright.

"ARE—YOU—IN—JURED?" she said, annunciating slowly. Then she said to herself, "Maybe he's like, deaf, or mute, or something . . . ?"

Grumbling, he said, "I'm okay, considering that I've just been flattened by your car. What the hell do you expect me to say?"

The outline of his attacker against the headlights indicated to Rey that she was slender and had long loose curls that fell to her shoulders. The steady rain drummed off the small umbrella she held over her head.

"Well, excuse me!" the woman said. "If you hadn't popped out on me, this wouldn't have happened. With this blackout and rain, I couldn't see you and–"

"I was getting onto the bloody curb when you hit me from behind. If I remember right, you had me in your headlights easily for at least fifteen seconds. Were you really watching where you were going or were you just trying to rack up kills tonight?" Rey shot back as he slowly rose to his feet. He craned his neck, reached back, and pulled on his shoulder, wincing. Staggering, he tested his battered knee and then his ankle.

He didn't look intimidating when he was slumped against the overturned garbage cans. Now on his feet, he easily stood a head taller than her. Trying to remain brave, Stazie remembered her father advising never to admit any guilt or wrongdoing unless it could be proven in a court of law.

Rey hobbled to the car. Taking off his muddied daypack and placing it on the hood, he fished around inside of it.

"Aw nuts," he griped as he withdrew his hand and shook it. Something runny flew from his fingertips. "My eggs . . ." he said woefully.

He stuck his hand back into the bag and this time withdrew a slimy flashlight. Wanting to wipe the yolk off and seeing nothing available, he cleaned his hands and the flashlight on his soaked khakis. Then, hanging onto the bumper of her car, he dropped to one knee to peer underneath while shining the light on the wreckage.

"Oh, this is just frickin' great. My bike is totally trashed!"

He reached under the car and gave the bike frame a tentative tug. The bike was securely pinned. He swore some more under his breath and furiously swung at the air with a clenched fist. Stazie hung back. The strange guy she had just run over with her car looked very angry. There was no telling what he would do. She secretly crossed her fingers that he wasn't some kind of psychopath. If he happened to go berserk, there was no other person on this dark street to help her. Turning, she decided it was best to sneak away while he was preoccupied.

"Hey, where do you think you're going?" he said as he straightened up.

She froze and then slowly turned back around. Now it was her turn to face the bright headlights. As he approached her, Rey saw the startled look in her eyes. Her glossy red lips formed a small 'o' as she peered up at him from under the edge of her umbrella. She appeared fearful as she took a tenuous step back and held her hand up defensively, bracelets sliding and jangling down her slight arm. Seeing her reaction, he decided to bridle his anger although at the moment he felt like running over something himself.

"Would you mind backing your car off of my bike?" he said through clenched teeth.

She flinched a little. "I—I guess. Um, does my car have any damage to it?" she asked.

"From what I could see of my bike, I'm sure there's got to be something 'scratched up' under there. Geez, how fast were you going?"

"I wasn't going fast. Well . . . at least not that fast."

When she didn't budge, he pointed to her car and repeated, "Would you *mind?*"

Giving him a wide berth, she got in and started it.

"Okay, now back it off easy," Rey ordered as he motioned her back with his hand.

Stazie put it in gear and slowly pressed on the gas pedal. When the car wouldn't budge, she pressed even harder. There was another loud crunch from beneath the car.

"I said easy!"

"Okay! Okay! I don't know what difference it makes anyway. You said your bike was trashed," she said as she continued to reverse.

The car rolled back to reveal the twisted carcass in the headlights. Rey just stood there looking at it in silence. From where she was, Stazie watched the muscle in his jaw clench and tighten like a stiff cable. Her fear mounted and she prepared to whip her BMW around, drive off, and leave this jerk and his broken bike behind. At the last moment, she reconsidered it. Her father's numerous stories about penalties people endured from leaving the scene of an accident sounded in her mind. Instead, she hoped he wasn't going to call the police. If she got another ticket, it would mean attending traffic school again. Stazie swallowed hard and took a deep breath, fighting her instincts that begged her to flee.

Rey would have called the police, but he was tired and sore, and the thought of standing in the rain on a blacked out street while waiting for a cop to show and fill out a report was something he did not want to hassle with. As long as she was willing to pay him for his bike and the lost groceries in his pack, he'd be willing to call it good. He was banged up a bit but he knew his injuries were nothing serious. He had suffered worse from wiping out while mountain biking or snowboarding.

He watched her chew her bottom lip and motioned for her to get out of the car. She hesitated, then finally opened the door, got out, reopened her umbrella and stood under it. Since she wasn't going anywhere near him, Rey sighed and approached her.

"Listen, I'm willing to not press any charges if you would just make amends to replace my bike. Oh yeah, and my groceries too," he said, pointing to his pack.

She couldn't believe her ears. It was a lucky break. There was no talk of the police or lawsuits or insurance. But as she reached for her wallet, the slow burn of outrage ignited in her.

Wait a minute. He was going to press charges on me? she thought.

Stazie was amazed at his audacity—it wasn't even her fault. And he hadn't even mentioned the damages his bike did to her car. It was enough to make her stop fretting about any psychopathic potential on his part. She placed her hand on her hip and faced him.

"*Excuse* me? What about my car? If you hadn't been out for a joy ride on your bike in a rainstorm in the middle of a blackout this wouldn't have happened! Any moron would know that!" she said.

"Joy ride? I was shopping for groceries!"

"Well, why aren't you driving like everyone else? Or can't you afford a car?"

His eyes opened wide in amazement. This chick was unbelievable.

"You know, I'm not even going to substantiate that with any kind of response. Like I told you— replace my bike and my groceries and I will not press any charges. That's my final offer."

"And what if I don't?"

"Have it your way. I'm calling the cops."

By the tone of his voice, Stazie knew there was no more argument. She tried to stand her ground for a few minutes more but the stranger stared her down. Rolling her eyes, she pulled out her wallet. She gave the bike a quick once over and started counting out cash.

"Okay then, how much? A hundred bucks? Two hundred?"

He looked at her incredulously. "Are you kidding? That's an Aero Zentorini!"

"Whatever. Three hundred? If it's more than three hundred, I'm going to have to find an ATM."

"That's a three *thousand* dollar mountain bike, so you had better start looking. I don't see any ATM's around here."

"Three thousand dollars! Seriously? For that? It's just a, a bicycle."

Rey glared at her.

"Whatever. I can't believe anyone would pay that much for a stupid bike," she said. "It's not even a fancy bike. You think you would get yourself a car or something instead."

"Listen, if you can't cover it—"

"Who or what do you think I am? Of course I can cover it! I just don't have my checkbook on me. Or if you'd give me your email address I can just send you a payment."

"Uh huh. And what do you make me out to be? Oh that's right, you think I'm some kind of idiot loser because I ride a bike."

"You said it, not me," she said.

He felt like slugging her. "Then, give me the name of your insurance carrier. You do have insurance, right?"

"Of course I do." She stalked off to the car, searched around and returned.

"Well?"

She averted her eyes. "I don't have my insurance card with me. And I can't remember the name of the carrier. I wasn't the one who made the policy."

"Unbelievable. Listen, you are going to give me a lift to the nearest ATM and get me the money for my bike," he said.

"I will do no such thing. You think I'm going to give a ride to a total stranger? How do I know you're not going to do something terrible to me?"

"Look around. Don't you think that I've had plenty of opportunity and motive to do that by now? It's not like there is a crowd of witnesses standing around in this frickin' rain. Besides, I'm not a stranger anymore. You introduced yourself to me with the front end of your car, remember? Now we can drive to whatever rock you call home for your checkbook or we can go to an ATM. Your choice."

"Or what?"

"Or like I told you before, I am going to call the police and press charges. Maybe they could pry my restitution from your tight little ass," Rey said, running out of patience.

In the fifteen minutes she had known this man, Stazie had developed repulsion to him. Completely irritated at how he had ruined her evening, she turned up her nose with disapproval but he seemed undaunted by her dirtiest look.

Relenting, she said angrily, "Oh, all right. Get in."

"Wait. Pop your trunk, I'm going to get my bike," he said.

"What? I'm going to get you your precious money. What do you need that piece of junk for?"

"Just open the damn trunk."

Stazie got into her car and released the lock. He had no right in ordering her around. With annoyance, she watched him in her rearview mirror as he secured the bike. When he opened the passenger door, she scrutinized him under light. It was her first good look at him up close. He was soaking wet, grimy and muddy, and his pack continued to leak slime.

She grimaced. "Ewww! Can't you dry off? These are leather seats. And your pack is dripping. What is that?"

Rey plopped down inside the small car. "Sorry, don't have a handy towel on me. And this?" he said, holding up his pack, "This was dinner until it was run over."

He tossed his pack onto the backseat and slammed the door.

"Oh, my seats . . ." she whimpered. Wrinkling her nose, she said, "What is that smell?"

Rey looked about him and then sniffed the fresh stains on his shirt. It smelled as if he had been dumpster diving for a week.

"Oh, so you like my new fragrance? I just started wearing it tonight. It's called 'Pulverized at Midnight.' You want to get this thing moving already?"

Stazie determined this man no longer repulsed her. She despised him. As she proceeded to drive, a loud scraping noise came from beneath the car followed by a vibration through the floorboards. The gearshift didn't feel right under her fingers.

"Oh my goodness," she said as she slammed on the brakes. "What is that?"

"I don't know. Probably a damaged cowling or something hanging underneath. Let me check." Rey got out with his flashlight and hindered by some pain, bent over to take a look. He could see a twisted piece of metal hanging from under the chassis. More than likely it had been bent out from running over his bike. He tried pushing it up out of the way but it wouldn't budge. Using his flashlight, he started hammering at it.

"Hey! Hey! Stop that! What do you think you are doing?" Stazie yelled out of her window.

He straightened up to face her. "There's a piece of bent metal dragging on the street. I was trying to get it out of the way so you can drive," he said. "Don't worry, I'm only using my flashlight."

"No! You don't hammer anything on my car with anything! Understand?" she said.

It was bad enough that her car was already broken; she didn't need some ape doing even more damage to it before her mechanic could take a look at it.

"But how are you going to drive—"

"Don't touch it."

Rey shrugged. "All right, I'll leave it." He got back in the car. "So what are you going to do now? Call a cab?"

"What? And leave my car here? In this neighborhood?" she said with amazement.

"Uh, yeah? It's trashed anyway, remember? That is unless you want to get out and push it to a higher-rent district. Besides, what's wrong with this neighborhood? I happen to live here."

"This is a brand new car! The paint alone is worth three of your bike. I'm not leaving it here!"

"*Whatever*," he said, mocking her for her earlier lack of concern for his bike. "I guess you better call a tow truck then."

Stazie mumbled something under her breath and looked out the window.

"I'm sorry, I can only hear in the human range. What was that?" he said.

She sighed impatiently and then admitted, "I said I can't call because I accidentally dropped my cell phone when I got out of the car." She held up a dead phone that was obviously missing a battery and cover. "It fell into a puddle. Do you have a phone I can use?"

"Nope. Sorry. I don't have it on me."

"Oh. What? Why not?"

"Because I don't."

"I've never met anyone who doesn't carry their phone on them. First no car, next no phone. I don't believe this . . . Wait a minute, I thought you said you were going to call the police on me."

"You want to walk to a pay phone?"

She shook her head.

"Okay then. What do you propose we do?" he said with feigned patience.

She sat for a moment, pondering. Then breaking down she said miserably, "I don't know. This night has been total poop. I was supposed to meet my friends and we were going to have a good time because it's Lindsey's birthday. I was all stressed out from the week and I just needed to relax and now I'm really stressed out!"

Squeezing his eyes shut, Rey pinched the bridge of his nose trying to keep his cool. *Was this nightmare going to go on all night?* His head was beginning to throb and his stomach growled. If life hadn't decided to be a bitch tonight, he would have been home already eating his dinner and watching the game, safe from stressed-out bubble-headed chicks with bad attitudes.

"And . . ." she said and hiccupped, "And . . . now my car is wrecked and you're being mean. And I don't know what to do!"

"*I'm* being mean? At least I'm trying to cooperate."

Big tears started to fall one by one, snaking the mascara down the rouge on her cheeks. Her lip quivered in restraint until a whimper escaped. She hiccupped again.

He shook his head and looked out the window. "Oh great."

She opened up and cried even more as she grappled in her purse for a tissue. He tried not to look at her but hearing her sniff and mew and hiccup he couldn't help it. *Oh geez. Why did she have to start crying?* The men in his family generally had a soft spot whenever a woman started to cry. He looked at her closely. Despite her red nose, puffy eyes, and heavy makeup, her face had potential. And her body was not bad either. A little on the skinny side, but nice rack. And those legs . . .

Whoa. Hold the phone. This is the chick that just ran you over with her car, he reminded himself. But still, she was crying. She looked like an orphan waif with nowhere to go. He told himself time and time again not to fall for a woman's tears but he never listened to himself.

"Okay," he said a little more patiently this time. "Why don't I try hammering up that piece again, just enough so it won't drag? It's already damaged and will probably have to be replaced anyway. Then you can at least drive your car home and call the shop in the morning."

Stazie hiccupped again. What he suggested sounded reasonable. Besides all she wanted to do was get home and get away from this dirty, smelly, rude, loathsome jerk.

"All right," she finally said.

Rey got back out and tapped up the piece of metal as far as he could. When he returned, he was surprised to find her sitting in the passenger seat.

"Would you mind driving? You do know how to drive, don't you?" she said.

"Me? Of course I do. But why would you want *me* to drive?"

"It's just that, I don't know what's wrong with my car and when I go to shift it, it doesn't feel right and well, I'm kind of scared to drive it now until my mechanic could take a good look at it. I don't want it to blow up or go out of control or—"

"I don't think it's going to blow up."

"Oh please! I'm in no mood to drive and I'll probably just get into another wreck. I told you I'm totally stressed out and I have a headache now.

If you just get me home, I'll write your check. Oh, and pay for your groceries too!" she said as she looked up at him with teary eyes. Her chin quivered and it looked like she was preparing to start the water works over again.

Oh brother. There was that waif-look again. I hope I don't regret this, he told himself. A small voice inside of him argued, *maybe she isn't so bad, just scared. Or maybe she's just a ditz or something. After all, she is entrusting me with her car. And it wouldn't help if she got into another accident or hit someone else.*

Ray weighed the possibility of another victim or two crammed into the small car with them, nursing their injuries after being run over by her if she drove him back. Despite what had happened, he had trouble refusing her. If he could just get her home, get his check, and call a cab, he'd be happy to call it an evening.

It took them forty-five minutes to wind through the darkened streets, keeping the speed down on the damaged sport coupe that continued to rattle and shift oddly. The car still handled remarkably well, and Rey imagined what it would be like to drive it in top condition. Stazie didn't say much except to give him directions and to hiccup occasionally. He knew by her address that she resided in an upscale part of town, so it was no surprise to him when they pulled up in front of the double glass doors to a luxury high-rise condominium. The complex was all lit up.

Apparently blackouts never affect the affluent, Rey noted.

A valet approached the driver's side and opened the door.

"Good evening sir," the valet addressed him. He frowned at Rey's appearance and odor. "Shall I remove the, uh, bike from the trunk for you?"

Stazie leaned across Rey and said to the valet, "Hello John. Yes. Take it out and leave it on the curb, thank you."

As they got out of the car, the doorman arrived.

"Good evening Miss Royale, have you had a bit of a problem?" he asked, looking at the twisted metal the valet had pulled from the trunk.

She nodded her head in Rey's direction. "Well *he* did. Would you please call him a cab, Alfredo? I must get something for my headache," she said.

Without another word, she marched through the double doors, crossed the lobby, and out of sight. Rey made a step to follow her but felt the arm of the doorman against his chest blocking him.

"I'll call you a cab, sir," the doorman said firmly.

"But she is coming back, right?"

The doorman arched his eyebrow and gave him a warning scowl, then without another word returned to his station. In the meantime, the valet disappeared with the car to the garage. Rey found himself standing out on the curb with his mangled bike.

At least the rain let up, he thought.

While waiting, he surveyed the neighborhood. It was lined with more luxury condos, boutiques, fine restaurants, and upscale businesses. A stylish young couple speed-walked by him without giving him a second glance. He turned, expectedly when he heard the door open behind him. But it was only an older man walking an over-eager Bichon Frise. While the man reached for his umbrella, the dog ran the length of its extension leash and sniffed at the bike. Then it started sniffing Rey's leg.

"Don't get any ideas," Rey said under his breath.

The owner looked to see who was addressing his pet. When he saw Rey, he eyeballed him suspiciously, reeled his dog in close, and walked away. Rey suddenly became aware of how he must look.

I'd be lucky if these stiffs don't call the police on me just for sitting here, he thought.

He examined his scraped elbow peeping out of the new hole in his jacket sleeve. It stung like hell. The near-freezing rain had begun to fall once more. He was soaked through and a chilly stream of water started to trickle under his collar. Still there was no sign of her.

"I've called a cab for you sir. It should be arriving shortly," the doorman called out to him. He closed the doors behind him, returning to the warmth of the dry lobby.

Rey checked his watch. She had been up there for over fifteen minutes already. How long did it take her to get a lousy aspirin and write a check? All of a sudden, he was dumbstruck with a realization that hit him like a bulldozer. He had been duped.

"Shit!" he said under his breath and shook his head.

That so-called bubble-headed waif had ditched him. She had no intention on ever coming back down with his check. And he was stupid enough to fall for it. He walked up to the doors and tried them. They were locked. He knocked on the glass and peered inside. The doorman gave him a glance but then returned to watching his TV.

"Shit shit shit!" Rey said out loud as he stepped out into the street and looked up at the imposing building stretching upwards twenty stories before him.

She was up there, somewhere, probably drying her eyes, reapplying her mascara and laughing her ass off at him. She had played him good. The tears, the big eyes, the promises—he had fallen for it completely just like the idiot she thought he was. *Idiot loser, wasn't it?* In his own defense, he reminded himself that he had just been run over and must be suffering from some kind of concussion. *Or brain damage,* he harshly corrected himself. And here he was, out on the street like so much garbage with a hosed-up bike, no dinner, and no check in his hand. He didn't even have a license plate number or her name.

Wait a minute—"Miss Royale" the doorman had said. There was a chance yet.

Just then, the cab pulled up. Rey loaded his bike and climbed in. It was then he was struck with yet another realization. His pack was still in her car. It wasn't so much the groceries he missed but the designs that he was bringing home to work on that evening. They were still sealed in their plastic sleeve next to the crunched eggs and milk. She probably would have the valet throw the entire mess out tomorrow without even looking at it. Months of work pitched in the trash. He glanced back at the lobby, the locked door, and the doorman. There was no way he was getting in there without an invitation. He dropped his head into his hands. *What a night.*

"Where to?" the cabbie said as he eyed Rey with disdain.

"Anywhere but here," Rey grumbled.

But he knew he would be back tomorrow.

✼

Stazie rose, stretched, and crossed her room to look out at the city spread before her in the morning light. It looked like it was going to be a pretty day. Opening the French doors wide, she walked out onto the balcony and to the rail where she looked to the street below. The memory of him standing down there prompted a giggle. If Alfredo hadn't called the cab, that jerk probably would still be sitting at the curb this morning holding onto that stupid bike. It had been so easy to give him the slip; much easier than getting out of the breaking and entering charge from the restaurant in Mazatlán where her friends dared her to break in for tequila at three in the morning after the place had closed. Or that other time she had to ditch the Paris playboy who had stalked her for two days. She couldn't wait to tell Gidge about her newest adventure in close calls.

She wandered back into her bedroom making plans for the day. Hearing a baritone voice in the kitchen, she smiled. Her father was home this morning. Now they would be able to have breakfast together. Most mornings, she spent alone with nothing to keep her company but her phone. Her father's successful defense practice kept him either at the office, in court, or traveling six to seven days of the week.

An only child, it seemed that she had always dined by herself. It had been that way for as long as she could remember. The maids they had were always too busy to sit with her. They would place her meal in front of her and retreat to their housework. There had also been an endless succession of nannies, too many for her to remember. Eventually each of them had left for one reason or another. Rarely had one ever stayed on for any length of time, much like her own mother. But that was long ago. Her last nanny left over twelve years ago when she was fourteen.

Stazie slipped into a pink kimono and ambled out to the kitchen. She snuck up behind her father and wrapped her arms around his neck while he was engrossed in reading a document on his laptop.

"Morning, Daddy," she said kissing his cheek and giving him a loving squeeze.

"Good morning, Pumpkin," he said distractedly giving her arm a pat.

He spent the next minute or so reading the screen while she patiently waited. Stazie eyed him as he worked. He was still handsome and debonair for fifty-eight, with his graying temples, trim tummy, and tennis tan. At least she thought so. He typed a couple of lines into his laptop, closed the lid, and then looked up to where she was seated across the table from him, as the maid served her espresso, diced papaya, and croissant.

"Sleep late this morning?" he said.

"It's not *that* late Daddy. It's only, let me see, nine forty-five. Still before ten," she said as she buttered her croissant. "Hey, are you going back to San Francisco this week? If you do, would you mind picking up that little handbag I saw at Bellacio's? You remember the cute one I showed you with all the buckles and straps? I knew I should have gotten it when I saw it there last week. It's probably been sold by now." She stuck out her bottom lip in a cute little pout.

"Actually, I have a flight to San Fran this afternoon. Will that be quick enough for you?"

She smiled indulgently as she sipped at her espresso.

"By the way, I hear there was a blackout last night. By the time I got home, all the power had been restored. Was it bad? And how's your friend, Gidge?"

"No, it wasn't anything. And I don't know how Gidge is. I didn't get to see her last night."

"Your message said the two of you were going out clubbing."

"We were, but—"

The sound of the lobby intercom interrupted her. The maid went to the foyer to answer it. Stazie tried to finish her train of thought but was curious about who would be calling at this time in the morning. They seldom had visitors.

"Go on," said the counselor.

"But, uh, something came up."

"Oh? How so?" her father said.

Just when Stazie finally had her father's full attention, the maid entered the room.

"Excuse me, Mr. Royale. There is a man downstairs who wants to speak with Miss Stazie. I tried to tell him that she was having her breakfast but he demanded to speak with her. He even mentioned the police," Beatrice said, raising her eyebrows.

"What? Did he give a name?" Doug said, mildly ruffled.

"He says his name is Rey Natal. And he insists on speaking with Miss Stazie."

The older woman eyed her young mistress as Doug joined her, looking stern. Being placed on the spot, Stazie couldn't help but feel somewhat annoyed. She kept her eyes lowered as she nibbled her croissant, trying hard to ignore their inquiring stares.

"I don't know any Natal. Is he someone you know Stazie? And why is he mentioning the police?" her father said.

She couldn't evade them much longer. She knew she had to say something as the intercom buzzed again from the foyer.

"Um, no. Well, I mean yes, I think—kinda," she said, hedging.

"I think you had better start explaining immediately," her father said. Then turning to the maid, he said, "Beatrice, tell him we will be with him in a moment."

"Well, as you know I was on my way to the club and it was raining. And then there was the blackout you had mentioned. All the street lights were out and it was very hard to see and . . ."

"The condensed version, Anastasia. I don't have all morning."

"Okay." She sighed and rolled her eyes. "This guy—Rey 'whatever-his-name-is'—rode his bike out in front of me and I . . . I accidentally hit him."

"You hit him? With your car? Was he injured?" her father asked with alarm.

"I told you it was dark! I couldn't see him! If he hadn't been out riding during a blackout this never would have happened!"

"But was he injured?"

"No. Well, kind of. Not bad, really. He could walk and everything and he didn't have to go to the hospital if that's what you are asking."

"Did he call the police? Or our insurance company? His insurance company?" her father said as he interrogated her.

"No, he didn't call anyone. Well, at least not right there. He said that he was all right and that he didn't want to press any charges, so I really don't know what he wants," Stazie lied, trying her best little girl face.

"And you are absolutely sure he said that he didn't want to press charges?"

"Yes! He said that he was all right."

"Well, apparently he's changed his mind. Now that he's seen where we live, he's probably contemplating a nice fat lawsuit," her father said more to himself than to anyone else.

He crossed his arms and pondered. She had seen this look before when she had visited court to watch him. It usually surfaced when a district attorney got the better of him or his client threw him for a loop.

Suddenly, he looked up and called out to the maid, "Beatrice, tell Mr. Natal that we can meet with him right now. In fact, have him come up."

Stazie sat up at the edge of her seat. "What? You want him to come up here?" she said. "But why?"

"I don't need some messy drawn-out lawsuit on my hands right now. I have enough with the Everett case this week and station WBAM's liable suit next month. I think I'll be able to persuade him to settle this matter out of court."

"But I'm not even dressed yet! Do I have to see him?"

"Don't be ridiculous," he said.

Hearing this, she instantly brightened up.

He continued, "Of course you do. You're the reason he is here. And I need you to verify the details he tells me. Now mind you, I don't want you to say anything. I will handle it. But be sure to listen very carefully. Now go get dressed."

Stazie's spirits sunk when her father ordered her off. Reaching her room, she slammed her door shut. She had never anticipated this happening.

What could Natal be doing? How did he figure out her name? And Daddy wants him to come up! What would he say happened last night? she worried.

She considered throwing herself down on her bed and stubbornly refusing to appear. But she thought otherwise. Her father would not be in the mood for those kinds of antics. He may not even pick up her purse if he grew angry enough.

Oh why did he have to show up now? And how did he ever get past the morning doorman?

She hadn't showered yet, so she quickly scooped up her long hair into a sloppy knot and pulled on some velour sweats. He would be up here in no time and her father would not like it one bit if she dawdled.

Within five minutes, Rey Natal was standing in the hallway staring at their massive front door, wondering how it ever fit it in the service elevator. He had never imagined that luxury apartments were so . . . luxurious. Beatrice showed him to the living room where, after refusing coffee and the offer to sit, he stood waiting for the residents to show. He noted the marble floors, expensive furniture, and impressive artwork. It all made sense now. The girl last night was no airhead bimbo. She was a spoiled rich brat.

"Mr. Natal? Hi, I'm Doug Royale, Stazie's father. Sorry to keep you waiting," the counselor said amiably as he entered the room and shook Rey's hand.

"Excuse me, *The* Doug Royale?"

"Why yes, unless there's another? How do you know of me?"

"Well, let's see, you defended Kip Gaffney, the ball player with the drug violation, and Buck Jameson, the quarterback with the domestic violence charge last year, and didn't you also defend the pro-golfer Dick Abernathy with that gun charge?"

"You scored on all three. Tell me, do you practice defense law?"

"Nah, just follow sport news. Actually, I am an architectural designer."

"Is that so? With what firm?"

"Uh, not any right now. I'm kind of freelancing at the moment."

"I see. Well, I understand that there was a bit of a problem last night."

Stazie approached the room and warily surveyed the uninvited guest through the doorway. She had expected to see the same scowling, smelly guy still dripping with mud and garbage, holding his twisted bike. Instead, she saw a friendly looking young man with short wavy brown hair, dressed in a clean pair of jeans and a pullover shirt. Scanning his tall frame from head to toe, she had to fight the urge to admit that he looked rather normal. *But in a rough sort of way*, she corrected herself. Last night, he seemed so old and grouchy. She could see now that he was not more than a few years older than her. *Maybe it was wrong of me to have ditched him like that?*

All of a sudden, she became self-conscious about her casual attire and thought about ducking back into her room to change. She caught herself and held firm, making herself envision him as she first found him: wet, slimy, angry, and repulsive, piled up against a stack of garbage cans. With that picture firmly implanted in her mind, she entered the room.

"Oh and here she is now. You two have met, I am sure," her father said.

"Oh, we've met all right," Rey said with a smirk as he eyeballed his attacker. The side of his face bore a bruise from the night before.

"And how are you this morning, Mr. Natal?" Stazie said.

"Well, I've got to say that I have been better."

"Would you like a seat? How about some coffee?" Her father quickly intercepted as he showed Rey to the plush sofa.

"Thanks. But I'm good."

"Can we get you anything else? Some fresh squeezed orange juice? Or perhaps some carrot juice with wheat germ? Whatever you'd like. Beatrice!"

"Uh, no sir, that's—"

"Please, call me Doug."

"Okay, Doug. But thanks again. I've already had breakfast this morning. What I'm really here for is—"

"Oh, I know what you are here for," Stazie said, narrowing her eyes at him.

"Anastasia," Doug said.

Her father only had to speak her name for her to button up. She knew she had crossed the forbidden line. Put in her place, she sat back petulantly and crossed her arms.

Rey looked at her. *Anastasia? Now that's appropriate,* he laughed to himself. Seeing her in the morning light with her hair carelessly pulled up and her face devoid of makeup, she looked less the queen bitch than she did the night before. He studied her large brown eyes, fine nose, and full lips and thought that she would look a lot better if she would leave all of the façade behind.

"I'm sorry, Mr. Natal. Stazie is feeling a little out of sorts this morning," her father said.

"Please, call me Rey."

Doug chuckled. "Sure, sure. Listen, I just want to extend our sincerest apologies for any inconvenience you have incurred. It certainly wasn't my daughter's intent to maim an innocent pedestrian. And we are determined to do whatever it takes to make things right. Which brings me to ask, *is there something* we can do for you, Rey?" her father asked delicately but with a look that smacked of negotiation.

Rey considered the question carefully. It was apparent that this man was willing to cut some kind deal right here and now. Looking at their condo and mindful of the counselor's successful career, Rey knew Royale would probably offer anything just to settle out of court. It didn't take genius to see that he most likely was used to getting Anastasia out of scrapes with his checkbook. With a twinge of revenge, Rey contemplated how she did make him the butt of her joke just the night before. He also had had a lousy night's sleep, trying to get comfortable with an ice pack on his ankle, a pulled shoulder muscle, a headache, and an empty stomach. At the moment, it was very tempting to soak them. When Rey thought about his one bedroom apartment, his convertible futon bed/sofa, and his bare walls and cupboards, he tallied a handsome dollar amount in his head almost immediately. But something inside of him made him change his mind.

"What I really came for today, Doug, is my pack. I think I accidentally left it behind in Anastasia's car. I have a client's prints in it that I am working on and I really need them back. And if possible, I need some kind of restitution to replace my bike that was damaged in the accident. I rely on my bike for transportation to work. Your daughter was going to write a check last night but she did not have her checkbook with her," he said.

Both father and daughter stared incredulously at him. Stazie couldn't believe that he didn't exaggerate the incident and play up his injuries, or that he wasn't yelling lawsuit and hit and run. He didn't even speak of the way she had left him stranded on the curb without payment. She immediately grew suspicious of this strange person. What was he up to?

The elder Royale was amazed at the young man's simple request. In his world of cut-throat deals, plea bargains, and people out to make a buck on someone else's misery, he found Rey's humbleness quite refreshing. It took a moment for him to speak.

"Why of course! Stazie, why didn't you get Rey his check immediately when you got home? Or even withdraw funds from an ATM?" he scolded.

"I—I—" was all Stazie managed to say.

Rey laughed inwardly at the expression on her face. It was worth all of the bruises and knots he felt this morning just to see her at a loss for words. Her father was up on his feet immediately and left the room. While he was gone, Stazie stared dumbfounded at Rey. Perplexed, she cocked her head at him, questioning him with her eyes. He just smiled back.

Oh, he's definitely up to something, all right, she determined.

Doug returned to the room with his checkbook in hand. "Okay sir, how much should I make this out for?"

"Well, the bike I lost was an Aero Zentorini."

"Ohh! That's a sweet bike," her father remarked as he put his pen to the check. He scribbled out an amount and handed the check over to Rey. "And there's a little something extra for any trouble or inconvenience you may have had."

The check was written out for fifteen thousand dollars. Rey read it again to be sure.

Then he swallowed hard and said, "But Doug, my bike wasn't worth—"

"Nah, don't worry about it. I only hope that it can reconcile for my daughter's lack of judgment."

Stazie's cheeks flushed red and her eyes flashed fire as she looked at her father. What did he mean, *lack of judgment?* She felt humiliated to be admonished in front of the stranger. No one considered how she felt or if it was even her fault. Opening her mouth to protest once more, at the very last second she exerted extreme control to close it. To do so was definitely in her best interest; her father would skin her alive if she botched up this deal. She recalled the time when she and her friends had trashed out a booth at a nightclub and restitution was owed. Just when her father had cinched a reasonable deal, she threw in that the Board of Health should have shut down the place anyway. Doug Royale had to pay triple the amount just so the manager wouldn't press charges.

"Now, if this is all settled Rey, I was wondering if you wouldn't mind possibly signing a 'receipt' for your check. It's just for my records," the older man said with a smile.

Rey knew exactly what he was driving at and decided to comply. "No, I don't mind at all. I told Anastasia that I would not press any charges and I mean that. All I needed was to replace my bike and your compensation has been more than adequate. But I do need my pack."

"Right! I'll have Stazie run down right now and get it for you."

Her eyes opened wide with indignation. This request was too much for her to keep her mouth closed. First the reproach and now she was to fetch and carry.

"But, why can't Beatrice get it?" she complained.

Her father looked at her sternly. "It wasn't Beatrice who got herself into this mess, now was it?"

Stazie stomped her foot in anger. She was about to tell them both where to get off but once again, she held her tongue. Pointing her nose upward, she walked past them haughtily without saying a word. As she went out the front door, she could hear her father say to their visitor, "So Rey, I'd like to hear more about what you do. It just so happens we're in the middle of a project . . ."

In the elevator going down, she fumed. Angrily, she pounded the wall panels, growled out loud, and jabbed the buttons. Mrs. McMurtry got in on the second floor and glanced over at her young neighbor's beet red complexion.

"Are you feeling all right today, Stazie? You look a little flushed," the older woman asked with concern.

"I'm okay, thank you," Stazie said and sighed heavily. She rolled her eyes as she jabbed at the buttons once again to get the door closed.

"Mrs. McMurtry, have you ever had those days when you wake up feeling great and everything is going fine and then some creep comes along and messes it all up?" she said.

The woman contemplated her question for a moment and without losing the pleasant look on her face replied, "Why no, dear. I can't say that I have. I'm sorry. I hope your day gets better."

Reaching the lobby level, the doors opened and Mrs. McMurtry exited the elevator. Stazie pouted once more and continued down to the garage level. When the doors opened, she peered out cautiously. The unfamiliarity of this place was enough to momentarily squelch her anger. In all the ten years they had been living in their condominium, she never had to go to the garage. The valets always brought their cars curbside for them. And if she forgot anything in her car, she would send Beatrice for it. Looking at the vast parking garage, she wasn't even sure where her car was. Within a minute, she recognized Tommy, the day valet, walking towards her. She breathed a sigh of relief.

"Is there anything I can help you with, Ms. Royale?" he asked.

"Um, yes, Tommy. In my car, there is a pack. Would you mind getting it for me?" she asked.

"Sure thing."

Stazie watched as he disappeared around the corner and then returned shortly, holding a pack out away from him. It was soiled and the bottom was obviously wet.

"It looks like you're going to have to get your seats and carpet cleaned, Ms. Royale. This leaked all over your back seat. What happened to it?"

She looked at the pack with disdain and hesitated in taking it from the valet. When he continued to hold it out to her, she gingerly accepted it, barely holding onto it with two fingers.

"It's not *mine*. It belongs to someone else. I have to return it to him," she said.

"Well, you might want to empty whatever is leaking in it before taking it into the building," Tommy said helpfully. "There's a trash can right over there."

Stazie looked at the dripping mess and turned towards Tommy, hoping that he would do it for her. But he had already taken off, responding to another resident's call on his pager for their car. She went to the trashcan. Feeling a sudden coolness across her toes, she could see that the contents had dripped across her designer flip-flops.

"Ohhh poop!" she shrieked in disgust.

Lifting up the pack, she felt like throwing the entire thing away and telling them that she couldn't find it. But the pack was part of the deal. If she didn't get it back to him, Stazie anticipated seeing a lot more of Rey Natal in the next few days. No, it was better to get this over and done with and him out of her life.

She wrinkled her nose and undid the buckle up front. Fighting her gag reflex, she opened the pack wide and peered inside. She immediately withdrew the offending crushed carton of eggs and the dripping half-gallon of milk, while squealing at the gooiness on her fingertips. Then she extracted a spoiled steak that had leaked blood through a hole in its wrapper and a soggy squashed box of donuts. Last, she pulled out a packet of drawings that were sealed in a clear plastic sleeve. These caught her interest for a moment as she looked at the intricate and complicated designs that were present on the top page.

Did he really draw these? She doubted it. Rey Natal looked too stupid to have accomplished anything like that. *Must be what his client gave him. Architectural designer? Yeah, right. He probably is a messenger. That's it! He was <u>delivering</u> these drawings. It explains why he was so insistent on that dumb bike. What a line of bull he is feeding to Daddy.*

After turning the pack upside down to let the last of the fluids drain into the can, she tossed the drawings back into the pack and buckled it up. When she returned to the apartment, she was surprised to hear laughter and talk when she entered. She stopped only briefly to rinse her hands and then quickly went to investigate. The French doors in the living room were ajar and her father and antagonist were sitting out on the balcony under the patio heaters, each with a cold imported beer in hand while Beatrice served them some hastily prepared hors d'oeuvres.

"Here she is! We were starting to wonder what was taking you so long, Honey," Doug said to his daughter. "I was just telling Rey here about some of your other 'little' fender-benders." He chuckled and winked. Rey smiled up at her.

What could he have possibly told him? Stazie worried. She returned a grimace to their guest, then turned to her father and narrowed her eyes.

"Oh, don't get so uptight, Stazie. No slander was committed."

"Yes, well, I'm sure Mr. Natal has a lot more to do today than sit around here drinking beer and listening to old traffic stories." She turned to Rey. "Since you are leaving, here is your pack. I took the liberty of emptying out the mess inside," she said as she tossed the bag roughly at him.

The gesture didn't go unnoticed. "Hey, thanks a million. You didn't have to do that. Really," he said, smirking once again at her.

She scowled back at him and then rolled her eyes. He was absolutely revolting.

Doug redirected to Rey. "Yes, so getting back to what we were talking about before my beautiful daughter came in, the place is a complete mess and the job, a total waste of time and money. That's why I was wondering, in your expert opinion, could something like that be fixed or should I just write the place off and start from scratch?"

"Well, from what you've told me, I wouldn't go as far as writing it off. Given a solid foundation, just about anything can be salvaged. But I think I know what you are after. In fact . . ."

He opened the pack and inspected the contents, then withdrew the designs. He carefully wiped off the plastic sleeve with his napkin. Opening it up, he thumbed through a few of the prints and after seeing they weren't damaged, selected one.

". . . I was wondering if this is what you had in mind, something with an open view but with a bit of drama to it. It just so happens that my client had requested something similar on these plans," he said, handing over the drawing to Royale. It was apparent that he and the counselor had been talking about much more than traffic in her short absence.

"Yes! This is brilliant. Exactly what I was thinking of! What firm did you use to work for, son?"

"Schuster and Mohlen."

"Schuster and Mohlen! Of course. Only one of the best in the country. I know because one of my clients had his family compound completed by you guys and he loved it."

"I recall that project."

"You do? How so?"

"I was on the design team for it, and let's face it, there's not very many billionaires who request family compounds every day."

Doug laughed, shook his finger at Rey, and said "Good point! Ha! So, how about you call my office and we can set a time to discuss your rates?"

"Sure, Doug. Since I'm freelancing, I can assure you there's a lot less overhead to worry about," Rey said tactfully as he extracted a business card from his wallet and handed it to the senior man. "Here's my number and email if you have additional questions before we meet."

"What?" Stazie said. "Wait a minute, you aren't suggesting—"

"Excellent! Let's set an appointment for next week. I'm eager to get started." Doug took a moment to look at the prints once more. "These are great. Except would it be possible for the roof edge to have more of an arch? Yes, and replace these pillars here with posts?"

"No problem. Actually, I always thought this would look better with more of an arch, but this client wanted something with a lower profile," Rey said.

"All righty then. It's settled. When I get back from San Francisco this week, I'll give you a call."

Stazie's look of contempt turned to puzzlement. It appeared that her father was planning on doing business with this creep.

Doug Royale glanced up to see his daughter's confusion. "Hey Staze, isn't this great? I've been discussing with Rey the improvements needed on our cottage. He thinks he'll be able to correct that botched-up mess from that incompetent asshole I fired," he said triumphantly. "*And* we'll get that sweeping view of the lake that we've been after."

Stazie's expression was smoldering. Rey returned fire with a confident smile and another swig of his beer. Then he let his eyes scan over the cityscape before him, ignoring her. For some reason, he liked the counselor. Although Royale was obviously powerful and wealthy, he seemed practical and down to earth. In fact, it was surprising how he could have ever raised such a brat. But all of that aside, Rey needed clients and Doug's design requests weren't anything too difficult. If it all worked out, he figured he could withstand a temper tantrum or two of hers if he had to.

In the meantime, Stazie wanted to push his smug face in. The thought of having to interact with him more in the future was inconceivable to her.

"But Daddy, I thought that you already contracted with another designer," she said.

"I want Rey to do it. He knows exactly what I am looking for," her father said, clapping Rey on his shoulder. "And you can't beat a Schuster and Mohlen man."

Rey said, "Well, I'll do my best."

"That's what I like to hear." Royale handed back the prints.

She thought she was going to puke. Natal couldn't have been any more of a kiss-up. Now she knew how he had won her father over. Doug had always been a sap for those atta-boy can-do lines.

The young man looked at his watch and stood up. "Hey, I'm sorry to have to run but I need to get hustling on these. Thanks again for the check and the beer."

"Right. Here, let me see you to the door," Royale said.

The two men walked to the foyer with Stazie tottering behind. She was still reeling with shock that this idiot had wormed his way into her father's good graces. The criminal defense attorney wasn't an easy one to win over.

"Hey Rey, while I'm thinking about it, we are having a get-together at the end of the month. It's just a little thing Stazie and I put on every year. Nothing formal but a lot of fun. We'd like it if you can come. I can introduce you to some people. Bring a date if you like."

His daughter's head snapped towards his direction. He couldn't be talking about their Spring Fling, *could* he? It was an annual tradition that father and daughter cleared their schedules for, no matter what. They took special pains to get the theme right, the exact menu catered, and the location picked. Then they invited no more than two hundred of their closest friends, clients, and acquaintances to join in on the fun. Each year the fling grew in their efforts to outdo the previous one. This year, they decided on a beach party at their vacation home in Florida. It was one she was particularly looking forward to.

That was, until now. Having Natal there would ruin everything. Just his very presence would conjure up memories of the accident, her damaged car, and disgusting gooiness across her toes. On top of that, her father would probably take special delight in telling each and every guest how his daughter ran him over. And Natal would be there with that smug look on his face, downing drinks and eating food that she had so carefully chosen for their guests. It wasn't fair. Less than twenty-four hours ago, she had no idea he even existed. She deeply resented that it hadn't remained that way.

She tried her hand at diplomacy. "Are you saying that you are inviting Mr. Natal *for dinner* when you get back from your trip?" she said, hoping her father would get the hint. "Beatrice and I can go over the details while you're away."

"No, no. Stazie likes to call it 'The Spring Fling.' I hope that you can come, Rey. We have a blast. This year, we're holding it near Sarasota."

"Well, I'll have to check. . . You did say *Sarasota*?"

Royale studied him for a moment and then understood his hesitation. "Oh, yes. Actually it's at Longboat Key, about thirty minutes outside of Sarasota. But I see that you may be a little concerned about the distance. Not to worry. We charter a plane for any of our guests who need a flight. Let me see, you said your email is on your card?" He pulled out Rey's card from his breast pocket. "Right here, great. I'll send the date, time, and flight info to you. All you have to do is show up and bring your appetite." He winked and tapped the younger man's elbow amiably.

"Daddy, may I have a word with you for a moment?" Stazie said tersely.

It was obvious to Rey that she was uncomfortable with the invitation. But on the other hand, Rey couldn't afford to turn Doug Royale down either. He needed as many contracts as he could get if he was ever going to get back on his feet again and Doug was gracious enough to offer. It also seemed like it could potentially be a good place to network and meet celebrities and other well-paying individuals who might need some design work of their own. Besides, this exclusive event sounded like it would be fun, and Florida! Lately he could do with a little diversion and it would be great to get out of New Jersey to somewhere warm for a bit.

Stazie had to think of something quick before her father ruined everything. She managed to stammer, "But Daddy, didn't you know that um, the final guest list has already been submitted to the caterer? And also, the head count for the charter flight. We couldn't possibly fit him in."

"Why sure we can. I'll call them this afternoon. What difference will one or two more people make? That is, if you'll be there?" he asked, looking at Rey.

"But Daddy-"

"Anastasia."

Rey glanced at the flustered daughter. It looked like she was about to pitch a fit. With resolve, he extended his hand towards her father.

"Sure thing. I'll be there. But listen, I really must be going. It's been a pleasure to meet both of you," he said politely as he shook Doug's hand.

When he offered his hand towards Stazie, she eyed him evilly and crossed her arms. He let his hand drop. Daddy's little girl was definitely upset.

As he left the building, Rey mused over the surprising turn of events. Last night he had been run over and thrown into a garbage heap, then forgotten on the curbside and duped. Today, he had money to pay the rent, a new contract, and a flight on a private plane with an invitation to an exclusive bash. It was as his Grandma Evora had advised him not long ago: "Don't be so fast to give up on life until you get to see what the next day has in store for you."

Right on, Grandma, he thought as he pulled the check from his pocket and took another look at it. Although his shoulder complained and his knee still hurt like hell, things were definitely looking up.

Chapter 2—The Bash

For over sixteen years, Antonio Oliveras was the owner and operator of The Au Claire Boutique of Fine Footwear. Au Claire was known for being one of THE places to find the right shoe to accent any wardrobe. Antonio took special pride in serving and getting to know his exclusive clientele, committing to memory their tastes, their fitting needs, their ingrown toenails, their bunions, and unfortunately, their moods. *And this particular customer was always sure to bring her moodiness and worse yet, her friends,* he thought to himself as he pulled five more boxes of various size seven espadrilles, mules, and pumps from the shelf. She looked unhappy today, sadder than other times when she shopped by herself. These were the days in which nothing seemed to please her and that usually meant more work for him. It was the third time she had sent him to the back room in search of a fantasy shoe of happiness that only existed in her imagination.

He tucked the stack of boxes under his chin and strode out to the showroom floor where Miss Royale and her friend sat waiting. Her friend had a worse disposition but at least she kept her conversation limited to Miss Royale. She wasn't a customer of his and didn't appear to have the means to ever become one. To Antonio, the girl with the jet-black and electric-blue dye job reminded him of those small suckerfish he had seen on Animal Planet; those hanger-on's that followed the shark's every move, scrounging for any morsels that fell from the mouth of their powerful host. Although he wracked his brain, he couldn't remember the name of those little fish at the moment. As he perched on his fitter's stool before his customer, he opened the first box and waited patiently for the shark to address him. *Miss Royale,* he corrected himself.

"And I said to him, 'No, you can't mean the Spring Fling.' But he went ahead and invited him anyway. I don't know *what* he was thinking. I bet he was getting back at me somehow for getting into another accident."

"No! Really? You mean that creep is coming to the Fling? Ewww!" Gidge said.

"Is this what you were looking for, Miss Royale?" the shoe salesman said, interjecting.

If he waited for these two to finish a thought, he'd be there all night. He slipped the shoe onto her foot for her inspection.

"Well, yes and no, Antonio. This is the color I am looking for but I need a higher heel. I'm only talking like a quarter inch more. And the buckle should be in platinum, not silver. Do you have anything like that?" Then she turned to her friend and continued, saying, "*Yes!* Daddy's driving me absolutely crazy. And there wasn't any way of convincing him not to invite that free loader. Not with him standing right there and all. I tried to drop enough hints for Natal to back off but the moron was too dense to get any of them."

"So after he left, did you tell your dad to blow off that creep?"

"No, once he makes up his mind, there's no way to change it. It's pointless."

"Oh, I think I could find a way to change your father's mind." Gidge giggled and then smiled to herself. She took a sip from the complimentary mineral water that was provided for each guest to Au Claire. "God, I wish they served espressos here. Why don't we go to that other shoe place that does? All they got here is this dog piss," she said, looking displeased.

Antonio slipped another pair of shoes onto Stazie's feet. She barely glanced down at them.

"I've been coming to Au Claire's for years. Besides, I hear too much espresso is not supposed to be good for the complexion. No, not these, Antonio. I'm sorry, but these are awful," she said as she finally got around to examining the shoes.

"Okay, so let me get this straight. Not only is this dork coming to the Spring Fling, he's going to do work for your dad too?" Gidge asked.

"Yes! That's what I've been telling you! Now I'm going to have to contend with him and those irritating expressions of his. Every time I see him, he always has that stupid smirk on his face. I just want to run screaming from the room . . . Hmm. Maybe I can convince Daddy to send me away to Venice until the work is done on the cottage. That way I don't have to deal with all of this."

"You think that he would let you go after what happened in Monte Carlo last year?"

Stazie thought about it for a second. "We both know that Monte Carlo was entirely Trish's fault. I just got blamed for it. But you're right, probably not," she said and then frowned at the next pair of shoes on her feet. "Antonio, these aren't going to work either. Don't you have any others? They are just not doing it for me. They are not very exciting."

I do my best to match the shoe with my client's personality. The salesman swallowed his comment as he reached over to pick up another rejected shoe.

"Well, I'm going to split. This is getting boring anyway." Gidge rose to leave.

"No Gidge, don't go yet."

Stazie's father was away on his trip and there was nothing to do or anyone else to hang out with for the rest of the day. Even Beatrice had the day off. She couldn't bear to return to the silent apartment alone.

"I thought you were looking for a pair of boots," she said enticingly.

"I am, but I can't afford anything *here,*" Gidge said and snarled.

"Oh don't worry about it. Just pick out something. I'll take care of it."

"Really? Okay!" Her friend immediately sat back down. Then turning to Antonio, she said, "Go get me those in a size eight."

The shoe salesman looked to where she was pointing at a pair of fine Italian leather boots, the most expensive ones he carried.

Remoras. That's what those little suckerfish are called, he suddenly recalled as he got up to fetch the footwear.

"So what am I going to do, Gidge? Rey Natal is absolutely repulsive. I hate his face, his smile, and that drippy little pack of his. If I could, I'd run him over again," Stazie said with a petulant growl. "Did I tell you his stupid bike did fifty-eight hundred dollars' worth of damage to my car? Daddy was not happy, to say the least. I don't know if my poor car will ever be the same again. I may just have to get another one."

Gidge admired the soft Italian leather now hugging her ankle. "I don't know. What can you do? It doesn't sound like he's going away anytime soon," she said distractedly as she snapped her gum.

"Well, you've got to help me think of something. The Spring Fling is two and a half weeks away. Maybe he'll get sick and die or something." Stazie sighed and pointed to a pair of shunned shoes. "I guess I'll just have to make those work," she told the salesman as she rose from her chair. "And I'll take the boots, too. Put them on my bill, Antonio. I hope you'll have a better selection next week." She gathered up her other shopping bags.

"And maybe you can work on getting an espresso maker too. I'd say your quality is slipping," Gidge said snidely and trailed out the store behind her friend.

The salesman watched them depart. He ran his hands through his frazzled hair and straightened his tie. "And what exactly would a remora know about quality?" he said out loud as he looked at the boxes of shoes, wrappings, half-empty bottles of mineral water, and loose footwear lying about his once-tidy showroom.

***

Rey wheeled the brand new Aero inside the entry of his apartment just as Jack Tate ran out from the bedroom. As his master set the kickstand and slipped out of his pack, the dog barked and turned happy circles.

"What's up with you, little man?" Rey asked the wiggly dog. "You dig the new wheels? Yeah, I'm pretty stoked about them myself. It sure beats trying to fix the trashed one." He looked the bike over, made a slight adjustment to one of the cables, and then stood back to admire it some more. "It's just like my old one," he said to Jack. "Only it's newer. And yeah, there's a few sweet upgrades too."

Things were definitely looking up. Whereas the bike shop he frequented usually had to special order bikes such as these with a shipping period of about two weeks, this one was waiting for him when he walked into the shop. The right tires, brakes, suspension, and color. *It's serendipity, Baby,* sport announcer Dick Vitale's voice sounded in his head as he rolled the bike over to the wall rack and hung it up.

He glanced at the prints lying on the big drafting table that occupied the corner of the room by the window. Just a few more hours on the Mitsui account and it would be finished. It was the second biggest account that he had handled in a little under five months. As soon as he put that one to bed, he'd be able to start on Royale's improvements. A twinge of anticipation hit him as he thought, *And who knows how many more projects I'll get from hobnobbing with the rich and famous at the party?* He made it a goal to deliver a working draft to Royale before Longboat Key.

With his newfound cash, in addition to the bike, Rey decided to go for broke and get a bigger TV to replace the small ancient one he had bummed from his sister, and a sofa and a real bed to do away with the worn-out futon he had been sleeping on. They were all being delivered this afternoon. The rent was paid up for three months on his one bedroom apartment and his cupboards and fridge were filled. With all of this, he still had money left in the bank. He had forgotten how easy things were when you had an ample cash flow.

Rey looked about his living room and although it was sparse, he knew he should move some things to make room for the deliveries. The drafting table, file cabinet, plotter, and rolls of vellum and plotter paper could stay where they were in the corner. He scooped up scattered vinyl LPs, books, and more papers from various piles about the floor and kicked some shoes and socks that were strewn about into another corner. The only thing that remained in the middle of the living room floor was his stereo cabinet positioned in front of his work area. When he moved in, he hadn't been too particular about where he placed it since he had so few furnishings, so it stayed where it had been unloaded from the hand truck. With the arrival of the furniture, the cabinet would have to be moved up against the wall.

Not wanting to take the time to empty it, he tackled the cabinet by grasping it and sliding it across the wood floor. A few scoots later, a small crash of breaking glass caught his attention and stopped him in his tracks. Searching to where the noise had come from, he spied a picture frame lying on the ground littered with shards of glass. Unnoticed, the frame had toppled off a shelf in the cabinet. He stooped to pick it up.

"What the—? Aww, crap," he said softly.

It was a shot taken of him and a friend against the backdrop of Hunter Mountain. Both were dressed in snowboarding gear and holding their boards. They were grinning with their arms across each other's shoulders.

Rey's thoughts flew back to that moment almost a year and a half ago. He and his best friend Ivan had caught some awesome snowfall that day and some of the best snowboarding, ever. They had challenged each other to bigger and higher jumps in the backcountry and whoever lost had to buy the winner a case of imported beer according to their tradition ever since their high school days when cans of soda were the victor's gain. That afternoon, Ivan clearly beat him on the board by at least two more feet of air and three more feet in distance. The promise of Guinness, pizza, and a side of Buffalo wings had fueled those grins in the photo.

That Ivan was always a crazy air-dog mother, Rey thought as he smiled and shook his head. *God how I miss him . . .*

Against his will, a hard knot formed in his throat and his vision became blurred with tears. He carefully shook the glass fragments from the photo and studying it, walked to the kitchenette. He took a deep breath to ease the tightening in his chest and placed the photo on the counter.

It just isn't fair, goddamnit. He could feel the anger building once again. Surprised at the intensity of its resurgence, he knew he had to act quickly before he succumbed to it as he had so many times before. Rey reached for the phone. *Should I call Rick? No, probably still at work . . . Mei-Lin?* Just as he was about to dial, he took another breath. *No. I can do this,* he coached himself as he hung up.

He went to the refrigerator and pulled out a beer. He knew he shouldn't be drinking, not while he felt like this, but he popped the cap off and chugged heavily, downing the contents of the bottle. He reached for another. Swiping the photo up from the counter, he returned to the living room where he plunked down on the floor with his back against the wall and the photo in his lap. Jack Tate eagerly ran over to him but he pushed the little dog away.

"Not now, Jack. Go lie down."

Not easily dissuaded, the dog sat and cocked his head, questioning with his big watery eyes. Then he balanced, ungracefully, on his back haunches and begged. Rey knew he was trying to garner any attention his owner could spare, but searching inside of himself, he didn't have anything to offer the little dog. As he looked down at Ivan looking back at him, he felt spent, his anger converted into a sluggish depression that wouldn't permit him to move much more than lifting the beer bottle to his lips.

Rey's eye caught his new bike hanging on the wall rack. He watched as its front wheel spun slowly on its precision bearings as it caught a breeze from the open window. The excitement of the bike's purchase was gone. It had become like any other object in this room: stereo, chair, drafting table, LPs. *He who has the most toys, wins. Wasn't that the way it went?* Although he felt far from being any kind of winner.

He couldn't even recall any of the thrill of receiving Royale's check a couple of days ago when it felt as if he had won the lottery. Now, only emptiness presided there. With his back against the wall and a discouraged Jack Tate curled up beside him, Rey couldn't bring himself to do anything else.

The gulls dipped and swooped in the late afternoon sky, hoping to glean a bit of food from the banquet being served below. The sound of white canvas tents rippling in the ocean breeze mingled with conversation, laughter, and live music. Clouds of smoke and water vapor rose from the huge pits dug into the sand as the caterers lifted the wet greens and sorted through the steaming racks filled with clams, lobsters, chicken, and mussels.

The dining was held on the expansive patio that looked out over the low rising dunes and the sparkling Gulf waters beyond. Each table was flanked by rows of wooden folding chairs and bedecked with floral linens, crystal glasses, tea lights, birds of paradise, and fresh fruit garnishes of plump grapes and bright citrus. Guests strolled and mingled while caterers kept busy serving hors d'oeuvres of chicken spring rolls, muffuletta hearts, and caviar on buckwheat blinis. Bartenders kept an ample supply of champagne, cocktails, and spirits flowing at the open bar. Everything was perfect.

A shake of the hand. A pat on the back. Doug Royale moved about his two hundred guests with hospitality and confidence, addressing each person by name and casually asking just the right question, paying the right compliment, and telling the right jokes. Rey watched how the older man operated. *So that's the way you do it,* he thought, making a mental note on how the counselor made sure to include some kind of body contact to put each guest at ease. The young architectural designer had been raised to be cordial and polite but he knew there were certain social elements missing from his working class upbringing. There was conversational timing, of knowing when to speak and when not to. Poise in carrying oneself confidently. Last, appearing to be in control in all situations. Here was an art form being played out right before his eyes and he soaked it in, wanting to make sure he learned from an obvious master.

Mindful of his social inadequacies that had plagued him for most of his twenty-nine years, Rey surveyed the other guests and wondered what he would say to them. He spotted a couple of well-known sport figures right off and if he wasn't mistaken, more than a few celebrities in the crowd. He suddenly became self-conscious of how underdressed he was. It was supposed to be a casual fling at the beach. This morning, after spending almost a half hour going over what he should wear when rubbing elbows with the rich and famous, he had settled on a pair of jeans, a navy blue button-up shirt, and a tan tie. The tie was a last minute decision when he considered that he could be meeting potential clients, although his brother Rick thought that he had overdone it when he came to pick him up to take him to the airport.

However, these people before him were decked out in linen suits and silk and the latest in high fashion. The women flaunted dresses that his mom or sister would wear to a wedding or graduation or some other significant occasion. *I thought this supposed to be a beach party,* he pondered, wondering where the cutoffs, flip-flops, and bathing suits were. After more observation, he realized the guests found it amusing to run around barefoot in their fine clothes, carrying their shoes, and turning up the cuffs on their expensive trousers. *Huh. Must be a rich people thing,* he figured.

Soon Royale made eye contact with him and crossed the sand, his hand outstretched.

"Rey! So glad you can make it! Have any trouble finding our little beach?" he asked amicably as he pumped the younger man's hand and clapped his shoulder.

"No, not really," he fibbed.

In reality Rey wasn't sure if he was ever going to make it. A traffic jam due to a rollover on I-95 caused a forty-five minute backup. It then took him and Rick another twenty minutes to find the strip where the private jet was waiting. He was the only passenger on board. The rest of the guests had left on an earlier flight on time. Then the only hotel he could afford at such a short notice was in Tampa, an hour-and-a-half drive from the beach. Next, he had to contact a ride-share that would get him there in time to catch at least *some* of the party. Arriving at Longboat Key, the driver got lost trying to find the private beach to the Royale's vacation home that was located in an exclusive gated neighborhood. So far, his invitation to this 'little beach party' was costing him a small fortune. But half-driven by prospects, half-driven by curiosity on how the one percent lived, Rey was determined to be there.

"Thanks again for inviting me. I'm sorry I'm a little late," he said.

"Nah, you haven't missed anything. We're just getting started. You know, I was looking over those drafts you dropped off and I think they are very do-able. There are just a few more things I'd like to add if I can while we're still in the planning. We can go over them next week if you're free. But in the meantime, grab a drink and some chow. Dinner is in another half hour. I'll be back around in a bit to introduce you to some people," Doug said and winked, knowing full well that Rey was hoping to score some more clients. Then he added, "Stazie's around here somewhere . . . oh there she is."

Royale pointed to his daughter at the shoreline where she was laughing with her friends and wading in the water. Rey had almost forgotten that she would be there. The last time he dealt with Doug Royale, he had brought the drafts to the counselor's office for review. He hadn't seen Stazie since the morning after the accident and hadn't given her much, if any, thought at all.

Seeing her laugh and cavort, and then splash her friends with water, he wondered if he had gotten the wrong impression of her at the start. It was easy to see how it could have happened. They both were on edge from the accident, giving neither the chance to be seen at their best. But out there in the surf and afternoon sun, she looked friendly enough. It occurred to him that he hadn't seen her smile before. It brightened her face and made her even prettier. And those legs . . . he scanned down to the soaked hem of her short lace dress clinging to her. There was no mistaken first impression there. She definitely had knockout getaway sticks.

He contemplated apologizing to her for getting off to such a lousy start. Maybe they could let bygones be bygones and try again. Grabbing up two flutes of champagne from a server who had approached him, he set off across the sand to see if he could make amends. After all, her father was now a client of his and it only made for better work relations if all who were involved were happy.

Rey made it about halfway when he caught her eye. He could see her squint trying to make out who he was. But once recognition kicked in, he saw that pretty smile of hers fade rapidly. A somber look came over her face as she stopped splashing, straightened up, and started exiting the water. She whispered something to the dark-haired girl beside her. The girl nodded and she too, turned to stare.

Seeing Stazie's dark expression brewing, he wondered whether he should take a quick right and avoid the situation all together. But after a quick debate with himself, he opted to press on. It would be better to get this settled and out in the open, regardless of the outcome, he determined. She couldn't stay mad at him forever.

Stazie couldn't believe he would have the nerve to come, invitation or no. After the party had gotten underway and time had passed without him showing up, she had relaxed. Now he was walking towards her, with the intent to intrude on her event that she had worked so hard to put together. Apparently, it was completely lost on him that he wasn't welcomed and this occasion was for *friends* only. Or was he that obtuse?

As he drew closer, one of the guys in her group said, "Hey dude, nice tie."

Ignoring him, Rey walked up to Stazie.

"I see that you managed to make it after all," she said.

"Yeah. And let me tell you, it wasn't easy," he said in a friendly tone.

"Then why didn't you just stay where you belong?" she said coldly.

He could hear a snicker from one of her friends. They had formed a loose semi-circle around them like vultures awaiting the outcome of a death match. Watching the scene unfold, they hung on every word, apparently having been informed about him.

"I don't give up that easily." He forced a smile back.

"I see. Especially if there's any chance of free alcohol, I suppose?" Stazie eyed the two flutes in his hand and then returned her steely gaze to him.

Rey could hear a couple more snickers. This was going to take some effort. *Patience and tolerance. That's what Mei-Lin said,* he reminded himself.

Stazie continued, "I don't suppose you ever heard the saying, 'A drop of champagne will not ruin a turd but a single piece of turd will ruin a whole vat of champagne.' Why don't you take the hint and realize that you are ruining everything. You don't belong here."

There were audible claps, whistles, and cheers from her sideline.

Rey stared her in the eye. "Well then, I suggest you stop playing with turds like a child and learn to drink your champagne like an adult."

Her crowd grew silent. Stazie's mouth grew round with indignation as she tried to muster up a stinging comeback. None was forthcoming, adding to her frustration.

"You . . . I . . . you . . ." she sputtered.

"Listen, would you mind if we took this somewhere else? Just the two of us? For a minute?"

"Why? What's wrong with here?" she said. He stood there, waiting. She sighed impatiently and rolled her eyes. "I guess."

Stazie crossed her arms and strode a few paces away from her crowd. It wasn't as far away as Rey had hoped—they were still within earshot—but he knew it was all he was going to get.

She whipped around and faced him. "Okay. What?"

"Listen, it seems that somehow we got off on the wrong foot with the accident and all," he said.

"You know, you really do show true genius."

"Hey, what exactly is your problem? In case you haven't noticed, I've been trying like hell to make amends here. This champagne is for you, in hope that we can at least call a cease fire?"

"Oh nice. Champagne that I paid for. And if you want it exactly, *you're* my problem. Why did you insist on being here?"

"I usually respond to invitations."

"Do you? Or just the ones in which you need to kiss ass in order to get a job? Why don't you get a real job somewhere, go back to where you came from, and leave us alone?"

He couldn't believe the hostility emanating from this woman he hardly knew. "You know, forget it. I don't know what I was thinking in believing you could be civil. You obviously have some emotional issues that are none of my concern. Right now, I'm going over to that side of the beach and I'll try my best to stay out of your way. But don't think that I am leaving any time soon. Your father is the one who invited me. Not you. As for this champagne, I am inclined to believe that he was the one who footed the bill." He turned to walk away but suddenly swung back around. "And don't you ever forget, for one minute, you were the one who hit *me*, sweet cheeks. So if there's anyone here who should be pissed, it should be me," he shot back. Without giving her a chance to respond, he stalked off, carrying both glasses of champagne with him.

Some of the guys in her group chimed in a chorus of "Ohh, that's cold!" while covering their mouths and snickering.

Stazie's jaw could have hit the sand. The audacity of him to address her like that and at her own event! Just exactly who did he think he was?

As soon as Rey walked off, Gidge and the rest of her friends clustered around her.

"Are you going to let him talk to you like that?" Gidge said, incredulously.

Stazie was still too flustered and angry to respond. "You—you jerk!" was all she was able squeak out. She watched him as he walked away without giving her another glance. There was no way he was going to get away with this—come to her party, eat her food, and insult her in front of all her friends. She would find a way to get even, although at the moment, she didn't know exactly how she would do it.

Rey retreated to the shady side of a secluded dune to cool off. He downed both glasses of champagne. *Patience and tolerance my ass*, he thought bitterly. *It's not working. It didn't back then and it certainly isn't now.* He didn't like to believe that she held the power to get to him like that. Her constant attitude was completely baffling. *I don't need this shit . . . Well, actually I do*, he corrected himself as he thought about it some more. True, there were well-paying job prospects here, but he also knew he deserved whatever treatment he got. He watched a small pink crab picking its way around the debris that littered the shore. With disdain, he realized he wasn't doing much better than that.

The dinner bell rang out over the sound of the surf. Racks of seafood and chicken were arranged with side dishes, drinks, and appetizers as servers readied to begin service. The guests assembled and then seated themselves at the rows of tables. Rey spotted Stazie at the head of a table by her father and made sure to take the farthest seat away from her but his head turned at the sound of his name being called. Doug was waving and beckoning him over. *Oh Christ. Here we go again,* he thought as he rose from his chair and hesitantly obeyed.

"Rey! Come sit here by me. I saved you a seat. They go quick around here!" Royale laughed as he pulled out the chair next to him. "Where did you take off to? There are some people I thought you should meet."

Unwillingly, Rey took up his station directly across from Stazie. She coolly averted her eyes and made small talk with the woman seated next to her. The dinner commenced and Rey tried his best to act indifferent. The dramatic twilight skies and the delicious food were somewhat of a distraction and Doug made sure to introduce him to key people sitting near. Still, he couldn't help but feel that the blonde facing him would take his heart out with her lobster fork in a moment's notice.

At the end of the main entrée, Doug tapped the side of his wine glass with his fork calling for his guests' attention. Upon this cue, a server brought him over a microphone.

Taking it, he stood up and announced, "I want to thank all of our guests for coming to our little Spring Fling. We hope you are enjoying yourselves."

There was a round of "Here! Here!" and tapping on water glasses from the attendees. Doug held up his hand, smiled, and nodded. It was obvious he knew what their reaction would be.

He continued, "And for any of you who haven't had a chance to come to one of our previous fiestas, this is a moment of great significance for Stazie and me. At this time, as is our tradition, we always like to propose a toast to our friends."

The food servers fanned out to place down trays of champagne at each table for guests to help themselves. At the head table, the tray arrived holding several filled crystal flutes. Among them were two polished silver chalices set out for the host and hostess. The vessels appeared to be some kind of family heirlooms. Rey ducked as a server reached past him, causing his napkin to drop to the floor. He bent down to retrieve it and when he sat back up, only the two chalices remained. Apparently, the server had overlooked him. Doug scooped up one of the chalices and since Stazie was busy talking to the woman beside her, he offered the other one to Rey.

"Here, Rey. Take this. I'll have the server get another one for Staze," Royale said.

"Uh no, Doug, I couldn't. I'll wait. Really, it's not a problem."

"Don't worry. She doesn't care. I'm the one who likes all the traditions. Here. I insist," he said placing the cup in Rey's hand. "Sir, we're short one champagne here," Doug said to the server.

Laughing at a joke, Stazie turned from the woman and looked to the tray for her chalice. When she didn't spot it, she looked about the table confused. Her eyes immediately went to Rey and seeing her vessel in his hand, they flashed fire.

"That's my chalice!" she said indignantly. "What do you think you're doing?"

"I didn't chose it—your father insisted—" he stammered. "Here, you can have it back," he said, quickly placing it down in front of her.

"Stazie, it's been taken care of. I already told the server to bring you another glass," her father said calmly as he picked up the chalice once more and handed it back to Rey.

"But Daddy, it's *mine*. He doesn't have the right to use it! These are *our* chalices, remember? Just for you and me?" she said, fuming.

"Stazie, Rey's our guest."

"No really, Doug. Seriously, she can have it. I'm sorry," Rey said as he returned it to her.

"I can't drink from that now," she said with disgust.

Doug picked up the chalice and placed it back in his hands, "Here, son. Take it. It's no big deal. Next year, I'll have to make sure I get some more made, that's all."

Then he raised his own to make the toast before too much attention was drawn to this unusual little dispute. The server arrived and placed a crystal flute down in front of Stazie.

She wouldn't pick it up but instead glared at Rey.

"Stazie," her father said with an unmistakable firmness under a seemingly loving tone, "Pick up your glass. It is time for the toast."

Stazie wanted to scream. It was her party, her tradition, her chalice. And this toad was ruining everything!

"Anastasia. It is time."

Begrudgingly, she held the crystal barely within her fingertips with the pale liquor dangerously near the lip of the tilted glass.

"To our honored guests here tonight, to each and every one of you for making our lives even richer," Doug said, giving a nod to Rey, "Health and prosperity to you all. May your windfalls be plentiful and may I never see you at the opposite end of a courtroom."

There were some more "Here, here!" and laughter as everyone drank up. Everyone, except Stazie. She got up and left the table, upsetting her flute, and letting the champagne stain the tablecloth. Out of courtesy and protocol, especially with Doug's eye upon him, Rey took a sip from the chalice, but the champagne left a bad taste in his mouth. He put the chalice back down and didn't touch it again.

He continued to avoid Stazie for the rest of the evening, although she seemed to be making herself scarce as well. The discomfort he felt over the disputed chalice was quickly left behind as he was introduced to many of the other guests. In hindsight, he wished he had brought his business cards. At the last moment, he had left them behind, thinking that it would be cheesy to bring them. Aside from that, he scored two definite contracts and three maybes, including one from the alternate third baseman on the Red Sox. *Rick isn't going to believe it when I tell him,* he thought happily. It had certainly turned out to be worth his time and aggravation thus far to come to this "little beach party."

As the evening grew late, the gathering became less formal and thinned out. Bonfires were started and people broke off into smaller, more intimate groups. Couples were scattered across the dunes. Rey decided before he called it a night, he would check out the live guitar music being played at one bonfire. When he approached, he noticed that most of the people present were comprised of Stazie's gang but a quick survey showed that she wasn't among them. He seated himself on the fringe with his last beer for the evening and settled back to enjoy the music. Before he could get into it, the quiet easy atmosphere was broken by the sound of gossip erupting between Stazie's friends.

"And can you believe she wore that dress? You know the way she went on and on about that rag. I don't see where it is any hot shit. That was so last year in Milan."

"Really. It makes her ass look huge. She's such a cow. I think she better lay off scarfing down the crab puffs, if you get a clue."

They giggled wickedly, downed some beer, and passed a joint between them.

Rey tried to ignore them and concentrate on the guitar but they continued with their loud trash talk. It was clear they couldn't care less about listening to the music. Their subject of scorn was much more entertaining. He was about to give up and go home when what they said next caught his attention.

"Yeah, and wasn't it a crack up the way that deadbeat took her down? I just about died laughing."

"Oh you mean that loser with the tie? Yeah, I couldn't believe it. I've never seen ol' Staze with her mouth open like that. She's so pathetic. She looked like a fucking fish."

The girl opened her mouth over and over again in fishlike mockery. The other two cackled and howled.

A guy sitting next to them laughed and chimed in, "Wasn't that awesome? I wish I had thought about video-ing it. Why didn't you guys remind me? It would have gotten, like, a million hits by now. Daddy was probably off hitting on some chick so he wasn't there to cover her ass like always. Hey, where is Stazie anyway? I haven't seen her since dinner."

"I don't know. Probably off screwing someone, or getting shit-faced, or both. I haven't seen Gidge either. Sometimes I think those two lesbos have something going on. What do you think?"

"Fucking A. Anyway, I don't think I'm coming to another one of these lame-ass Spring Flings. They are getting sooo old and I've got better things to do. Hey, has Josh come back yet? He was supposed to be out getting some good shit right now. Liven up this sorry snooze fest."

"Haven't seen him yet. But yeah, right. I'm sure you're going to miss out on these things. If I know you, as long as there's free booze, free ass, and the chance to be seen, you'll be there."

"You got that right."

They sniggered some more and passed the joint again.

It was apparent they didn't see Rey sitting there on the sideline or they just didn't care. What intrigued him more was that they were supposed to be her friends. These were the same people she shared that bright smile and easy laugh with, the ones who huddled around her in the surf, defending and comforting her after she and he had had their confrontation. He studied each of their faces in the firelight and watched their cruel mouths twist in insults about their hostess. At first, he couldn't help but feel vindicated. However, as they went on, it no longer felt so justified. None of it was right. They were nothing more than shallow, backstabbing moochers. He was almost moved to pity her, until he reminded himself that it was none of his concern. It made sense that someone as mean-spirited as Anastasia would chose similar people to hang out with.

Suddenly, he was grateful for not having these kinds of 'friends' in his life. His buds were fewer in number and some were pretty rough around the edges, but he knew they had his back. He could trust them with his life if he had to.

Rey had had enough of the Spring Fling. Whereas the food was incredible and racking up clientele a boon, it wasn't enough to counteract the weariness he felt over the day's events and the present company. He rose from the sand, stretched, and threw his empty beer bottle into the fire. What little he was able to hear of the music wasn't that good anyway. The thought of another hour and a half of travel to his cheap hotel room near the Tampa airport made him feel even wearier. Most of the guests were lodged at a nearby resort for the night. But unless he drained even more money from his carefully accrued savings, it was time to leave.

Rey searched for Doug to thank him for the evening but wasn't able to locate him. There wasn't anyone left by the tables or bar and the caterers were packing things up. The remaining guests were disbursed to the various dunes, campfires, or surf. As he walked on, a naked couple, dripping wet from a swim, streaked past him giggling as one pursued the other. He stopped short at the sound of heavy breathing and moaning in the dark just a few feet off to his right and decided to veer left. With only the light from the campfires and the moon, it was hard to see where to step without accidentally stumbling upon someone or something hidden on the sand and in the beach grass.

He was just about to call it quits and contact Doug in the morning when he heard yet another noise by a patch of shrubs. At first he thought it was another couple getting it on but then he distinctly heard the sound of a woman crying. That is, until she started vomiting. Against his better judgment, he decided he would investigate just in case the person was in serious trouble. As he came around the shrubs, he could make out a female on her knees and doubled over on the sand. She retched and coughed miserably. As far as he could tell in the dim light, she was alone. He didn't want to startle her.

"Excuse me, miss? Are you all right? Do you need any help?" he called out before he approached.

She didn't answer but cried some more, held her stomach, and vomited again. Crouching by her and looking at the headful of curls, Rey realized it was Stazie.

Holy shit. I don't need any more of this, he thought as he immediately rose to leave.

However, looking about, there was no one else nearby. He considered seeking help but felt that she might get worse. She sounded pretty sick. Despite it all, he couldn't just abandon her there.

All right, I've already endured plenty of headaches today. What difference would one last one make? He finally decided. At least he could make sure to get her to her father or one of her so-called friends.

Stooping back down, he asked again, "Are you okay? Can you walk?"

Stazie looked up at him in the faint light, swayed, and then steadied herself. "Oh no. Not you. Not you. Oh poop," she managed to say before she succumbed to dry heaves.

Coughing and wiping her mouth with her hand, she fell onto the sand. Lying there she groaned.

"What's the matter with you? Are you hurt or something?" Rey asked.

"No. I'm drunk. Stinkin' drunk. What d'ya think? . . . Oh, why did it have to be you? You ruined everything . . ." she slurred as she lie there. "I don't like you. Or your bike. Or your pack. Or your face. You're like . . . *everywhere.* Don't you ever go away?" She groaned some more.

Here we go again. Doesn't look like she's going to give it up. Rey sighed. *Big mistake—again.* "Here, let me give you a hand up. I'll get you to your father." He tugged at her hand but she lay there uncooperative.

Pulling her hand away, she said, "No. Leave me alone. I'm always alone. Go and talk with everyone . . . Have some more champagne. They all like you better anyway . . . My own father likes you better." Stazie rolled onto her side and started crying again. Rey could hear the bitterness in her sobs. For a moment, he thought he heard her say "Why?" in her lamentation.

He didn't know what to tell her. Besides, he didn't know how much she would comprehend in her state of extreme intoxication anyway.

"This was my Spring Fling! It was for me . . . Daddy promised me. Just for me . . ." she whispered.

"Okay. That's cool. Listen, I was on my way out of here, okay? I'm leaving and you can have the whole thing to yourself again. But let's get you back to your dad now," Rey said, trying to console.

Not paying him any attention, she went on, "Fourth grade, those girls didn't come to my pool party. Sasha and Brenda and Anna-Lisa and all the others. They told me they would come . . . Everything was ready . . . food and cake and games . . . But no one. They didn't show up! They were all laughing at me . . ." She curled up tighter and cried even more. "Nobody ever came to any of my parties and I don't know why . . . Why? I'm fun, right? Why doesn't anybody like me? Why am I always alone? You know I have to buy people things to get them to like me? That's all they ever want from me."

Rey couldn't make sense of her inebriated rambling. "Come on, I don't have all night," he said as he reached down and pulled her upright.

"So this is my Spring Fling! Ever since then, we showed them! Every year . . . and everybody comes . . . My daddy makes sure they come . . . But they are supposed to like me. *He's* supposed to like me . . . Isn't he?" She turned her tear-streaked face up to him and pulled on his shirt. "No, he likes you better. You're his favorite."

The mingling smell of hard liquor and vomit on her breath made him recoil reflexively.

"See? You don't even like me," she whimpered.

Seeing that she wasn't going to get up and walk on her own, Rey scooped her up in his arms and started making his way back to the fires.

"No! Put me down! I just want to stay there . . . stay there forever. I don't want to go back . . . I don't want to be forgotten anymore," she mumbled as she nuzzled her head against his chest and passed out.

As Rey came back around the shrubs, he spied Doug Royale by the edge of one of the campfires having a drink with Gidge. Both were laughing until he walked up. Seeing his daughter being carried, Doug dropped the smile and ran over to Rey.

"What's going on? Stazie, honey, are you all right?" he said with concern as looked her over.

"I found her over there by the bushes. I think she's all right. She's just really drunk," Rey said as he handed her over to the counselor.

Stazie's head fell back and she mumbled some more. Doug lowered her carefully to the sand and then smoothed back the hair from her face and fixed her dress. Gidge looked over his shoulder.

"Yup. She's shit-faced all right," her friend confirmed. "Stazie, girl, you never know when to quit." Gidge giggled.

His worry put at ease, Doug straightened up and shook Rey's hand. "Thanks a million Rey, for looking after her. It looks like my little girl has had enough for the night. Hey, are you sticking around? There's still some more beers on the way and fireworks."

Rey looked at Stazie lying on the sand like a crumpled lace handkerchief. Oddly, in the firelight she looked a lot younger than she was.

"Huh? No, no. I'm calling it a night. Thanks though. And thanks again for inviting me. I, uh, had a great time," he lied.

Back at his hotel, he leaned on the railing of the tiny terrace of his room and breathed in the cool sea breeze, feeling relief. *What a night,* he mused to himself as he looked out across the swaying palm trees that surrounded the building, thinking about everything that had transpired. He decided that in the upcoming months, he would make sure to deal with Doug Royale only at his office and over the phone. With any luck at all, he could complete the plans on the cottage without ever having to intrude in Stazie's world again. *That should alleviate at least one of her perceived problems in life,* he determined.

As for any more beach parties, he felt he had had enough to last him a lifetime.

Chapter 3 ~ The Crash

"Hey, you want to drive?"

"Nah, I'm good."

"Are you sure? I don't mind."

"No really. I'm good," Rey said as he and Rick walked up to the fully restored '67 Fastback Dodge Charger and climbed in.

After wrapping up a day at the annual auto show, they were heading off to their favorite crab shack for a bite to eat. Rick started the engine and sat for a moment, listening to the smooth rumble of the finely tuned V8. He nodded his head and smiled with satisfaction.

"All those bells and whistles are nice on the new ones but nothing can compare to that now, huh?"

"No shit," Rey agreed and grinned.

He treasured the time spent with his brother, his elder by six years. It had always seemed to Rey that the entirety of his younger years were spent waiting for Rick to come home whether it was from school, football practice, and then a part-time job. The small boy would patiently watch the clock and when the time drew near for his big brother to come through the door, he would find multiple ways to waylay him in the form of a superhero leap, karate kick, or ninja jump, and as he got older, wrestling moves. Rick always obliged with a quick match, a well-placed noogie, or tickle torture.

And since he outweighed Rey with his maturity and heavier build, it was always the younger brother's challenge to try to take him down.

Then Rey hit his teens as Rick started working fulltime as an auto mechanic and suddenly the younger brother was too busy with his own friends and then college studies. When he graduated, they finally stood on equal footing. It was then they were able to form a true friendship around the strong sibling bond they already felt for each other.

They drove to the crab shack with the windows rolled down and the music turned up. Hard rock cranked on the stereo, reverberating the speakers. Howling to their favorite songs, they cruised through the Newark streets where they had spent all of their lives.

"Hey, how's Marcie doing?" Rey said, knowing it was a tricky question to ask about Rick's live-in girlfriend of four years.

He could never understand why his older brother just didn't marry her. She was smart, funny, compassionate, and practical, and very much in love with his brother. Rey knew if he were faced with the choice, he wouldn't be wasting time. However, Rick always seemed to be holding out for a supermodel to show up instead.

"She's doing good. Why?"

"Just wondering. I haven't seen her in a while, that's all."

"She's been busy. Still working at the State. She should be finishing up her online classes this summer. But she's good."

When Rick finished with 'she's good,' it usually meant that he wasn't in a mood to further discuss his relationship, especially regarding any matrimonial goals.

"Cool."

"So when do you work for the Red Sox?" Rick asked while they waited at a light.

"I told you it wasn't the Red Sox. I said I *might* do some work for the alternate third baseman, Tony Atwater. He hasn't called to let me know yet."

"Same difference."

Rey chuckled and shook his head. "I hope you haven't been telling everyone that I work for Atwater."

Rick shrugged. "Maybe a few people."

The younger brother threw a punch at his sibling's brawny arm. "Asshole," he said and laughed.

Rick grinned back.

"So in the meantime, are you still working on that lawyer dude's place?"

"Yeah. The previous designer and contractor he had really hosed things up. It's been a nightmare to get it all sorted out and have it come out halfway decent without tearing it all down and starting over. The plans he gave me from the last designer are a real headache. They are so vague, a lot of the dimensions are missing. I may have to take a ride up there to check out the site in person."

"What about that chick? You know, the one that ran you over? Is she still around?"

The last memory of Stazie passed out cold on the sand flashed through Rey's mind. He looked out the window.

"Yeah. As far as I know. I try not to deal with her at all if I can help it. In fact, the last time I saw her was at that thing in Longboat Key. I work directly with Royale at his office if he wants to discuss or look something over but most of the time, we handle everything through faxes, emails, and phone calls."

"Oh," was all Rick had to say. He never lingered long on any subject. They drove for a bit more. "Ma tell you that Glo is coming into town this weekend? She wants all of us to get together for dinner with her and Pop on Sunday."

"Gloria? Cool. It'll be good to see her. Man, when was the last time she was in town?" Rey asked of his sister that was eight years older than him. During their childhood, she was more like a substitute mother when his own mother couldn't tend to him. Gloria loved her baby brother to pieces, and though there were times she was great fun, it was only when she wasn't being bossy.

"Let's see . . ." Rick scratched his chinstrap beard in thought. "It was right before she broke up with Harry, so it was right after your acci—Um, it's been a while."

He gave a sideways glance to his brother hoping he hadn't been paying close attention. But Rey had caught it and returned his gaze out the window.

"Hey, it'll be great to see the munchkin too," Rick said, trying to redirect. "Seely? Sweet! How old is she now? Three or four?"

"No way, man. She just turned five. Can you believe that?"

"That little squirt?" Rey said. *Had a year flown by already?* "She must be getting big."

"Yeah. I guess she's in kindergarten this year."

"Damn."

The two uncles nodded in contentment at the thought of seeing their little niece again as they continued their way to dinner.

After the crab shack and a few beers, Rick watched Rey as he walked to the stairs leading up to his apartment over the storefront, waved, and then went up. He knew he didn't have to wait to make sure his brother was secure but old habits died hard. He had been watching out for him all his life. And as he drove back home through the city streets, Rick's thoughts remained on him.

He worried that Rey still seemed depressed. Sure, it had been a while and his brother had gone through all that counseling. He had even started back to work. But Rick knew that something was still missing. His brother, the brother he knew before—the jokester, wise-ass, daredevil kid with the happy-go-lucky confidence—was gone. He wondered whether he should call Mei-Lin and clue her in. But Rey had said that he wanted to get through this on his own. In his opinion it didn't sound too smart but he wasn't going to get into it with him. Instead, he decided to keep his eyes open just in case the kid should slip again.

Why did I have to mention the accident? Rick kicked himself inwardly. Out of all the events that took place that fateful night eleven months ago, the thing that stood out foremost in his memory was the floor tile. In fact, anytime he saw it anywhere, whether it was in a restaurant, a hotel, in an ad—it always took him immediately back. *That frickin' green and white linoleum floor tile in the waiting room.* And for just cause. He had stared intently at that floor for the nine hours Rey was in surgery. He had paced over it, spilled his coffee on it, and watched as his parents' tears fall upon it.

He recalled how that ordeal had started. The phone ringing in the pre-dawn hours jolted him from a heavy sleep. After having put in a twelve-hour day at the garage, he was exhausted. He grappled with the phone on his nightstand and was barely able to hold it to his ear as he fought against lapsing back into slumber.

"Please Ricky, come quickly. Your brother's been in an accident."

The sob in his mother's voice woke him in an instant. He focused his eyes on the clock that read three a.m. while Marcie asked him groggily what was going on. All he answered was, "It's Rey," as he dressed quickly, kissed her, and dashed out the door. The Charger wasn't fully restored at that time and he almost panicked when the engine wouldn't turn over. A few more frantic tries got it started and he was able to race to the hospital, blasting through red lights on the empty streets.

Rick hated hospitals and was very impatient with the front desk clerk. His heart gave a jump when she finally located Rey in surgery. Not waiting for the elevator, he took the stairs, two at a time. He grabbed the first nurse he found and asked her where the operating room was. She was able to calm him down long enough to get the details and then lead him to the waiting room where his mother was crying in his father's arms. It shook him to see them look so old and shrunken when he entered and sat down beside them.

"Pop? What's going on?" he asked, almost too scared to find out the answer.

His father turned to him. Rick could see that he had been crying too.

"The police said there was some sort of rollover. We don't know yet. There's not much information. They think that he may have been drinking. We just got here right when he went into surgery," the elder Natal said.

"Do they know what's wrong with him?"

"They said he has a skull fracture and a punctured lung. But they also said his left shoulder has been severed and the joint is dislocated. There's a lot of bleeding from the main artery under his arm, the doctor said the subclavian or something like that. They're trying to stop it. It doesn't look good."

When his father ran his hand through his thinning gray hair, Rick could see it was trembling.

"Ricky. I'm so glad you are here," his mother said as she reached out to hug and kiss him.

"It's gonna be okay, Ma. All right? It's gonna be okay."

She gave him a little smile of gratitude but the tears continued to run down her cheeks.

"Did you call Glo?"

Carmen Natal nodded. "She can't find anyone to watch the baby and Harry's out of town. She's coming as soon as she is able."

Rick recalled the many cups of coffee, a rerun of *M*A*S*H* playing on the waiting room's TV, talking to Marcie on the phone, and taking turns comforting his mother through the seemingly endless hours, but most of the time was spent sitting and praying. Their wait was broken up a bit when Marcie showed up at five in the morning with donuts and fresh coffee, but no one could eat. Gloria joined them at eight telling them how Seely had kept her up most of the night. But after that, they settled back to their anxious vigilance.

Finally, the surgeon came out to let them know that Rey had pulled through. He had lost a lot of blood but other than that, he was stabilized. Rick remembered entering Rey's room in the Intensive Care Unit to see his baby brother unconscious and hooked up to monitors and oxygen. Both of his eyes were blackened and there was dried blood and bits of glass still in his hair. The kid looked like he had been through a grinder.

Although it was nearly a year ago and Rey was healed and functioning, the memory of it dredged up the same anxiety he had felt for his brother that night. Rick also knew it was why Rey had waited over a month before sharing with him that he had been hit on his bike by that woman, knowing all too well that the family would worry and fuss over him again. Yet Rick couldn't help but feel annoyed that he hadn't told him immediately. If only the kid realized what they had been through. But that was what you did when you loved your brother, wasn't it?

❧

The elevator doors opened and she strutted out onto the polished mezzanine of the seventh floor. Stazie was feeling good. She knew she looked fantastic in the snug new angora outfit she was wearing and lifted her chin a little higher. A cute guy getting off on the fifth floor had just verified it by paying her a compliment on her appearance complete with pickup line. In addition to the flattery, she was going out to lunch with her father and had been looking forward to it all week. If only every day could feel like this.

Judy, her father's receptionist, greeted her. "Hello Stazie. How are you dear? My, that's a cute ensemble you have on."

Stazie beamed back at the older woman. "Thanks Judy. Is my father ready to go? He remembers that we're having lunch today, doesn't he?"

"Yes, I believe he has it marked here on his schedule . . . Yes. Here it is. But let me see if he's finished yet. He's busy with someone right now."

"Oh, that's okay. He won't mind if I went in. Maybe it'll remind him of our lunch date," Stazie said, heading for his office door.

The receptionist tried to intercept. "But he's right in the middle of a meeting, dear. Maybe you should wait. It should only be a few more minutes."

"Oh, you worry too much, Judy! I'll stay out of the way. Besides, you said it would only be a few more minutes. If I don't go in now, Daddy will never take lunch." With that, she turned the knob on the door and let herself into her father's office.

Doug and Rey looked up from the conference table where they sat, the plans for the cottage scattered between them. Stazie froze in her tracks. Out of all people to be there in that office, she didn't expect to see *him* sitting there. A confused mix of self-consciousness and embarrassment flooded her. Although she had been extremely drunk that night on the beach, she knew that he was the one who had found her. The man had a real talent for being at the wrong place at the wrong time.

"Oh, I didn't know you were busy," she stammered and started backing her way out.

"Stazie! Come on in. Rey and I were just going over some of the final details," Doug said as he turned back to the drawings.

She noticed that Natal had initially nodded at her but then turned his attention back to what they had been doing without saying a word. It probably was his attempt at ignoring her. Or maybe he was just trying to snub her. As Stazie took a seat by the large picture windows of the corner office, she desperately tried to recall what she had said to him last when she was puking her guts out and showing him that she couldn't hold her liquor.

Rey didn't anticipate seeing Stazie there. He had come to think of Doug's office as a neutral ground where he could conduct business with the counselor without having to tangle with her emotional ups and downs. Not wanting to provoke her, he felt it wise to say nothing to her at all. A mere greeting on his part most likely would set her off. He would conclude this meeting as quickly as possible and get the hell out of there. There were only a few more details left.

"Babe, come over here and see what Rey has worked out. It's brilliant. We should be able to have everything completed by this summer," Doug said to his daughter.

There was an audible sigh from her as she rose and sauntered over to the table. She took a seat across from Natal and pulled herself in as close as she could to her father. She stole a peek to see if Natal was staring at her but his eyes remained glued to the plans.

Royale continued excitedly, "See, he's made this big bay window over-looking the lake. And look, he's even worked in a balcony so we could sit outside of it. It'll cantilever off of the cottage with a dramatic drop below. I've also asked him to add a fireplace in the family room, redo the north wall on the master bedroom to add more windows, and enlarge the guest bathroom to accommodate the walk-in shower."

Stazie tried to act bored while glancing at the drawings. But in reality, when she studied what was before her, she was amazed at the transforma-tion of the dull cottage. *Was he really capable of all of this?* Before she could feel completely impressed, while she now knew he wasn't a bicycle messen-ger, she wondered if somehow he was playing some elaborate con job on her father. After all, the designer they previously hired promised them the moon but had absconded with the down payment, leaving them with an unworkable mess. Her father was still having him tracked down by a private investigator and the attorney general's office was involved.

Considering her hypothesis some more, she eyed her nemesis. He was still avoiding her gaze. Although it was obvious he had some design talent, he was up to something, she determined. She had felt that way about him since he first set foot in their apartment, asking for nothing more than restitution for his bike. Now that she had him figured out, she was no longer self-conscious or befuddled by his presence. She would see how this whole scheme played out.

Oh, you trust him so much, I can't wait to see the expression on your face when you find out what he's really up to, she thought as she looked at her father. And she could add with great satisfaction, *I told you so.* It would be just what he deserved for so foolishly believing in Natal.

"So Rey, when can you get the finals to me so I can send them off to the general contractor?"

"I would've been able to get them to you by the end of next week, but there are quite a few inconsistencies and dimensions that are off on the original plans. I guess your former designer felt that they weren't important but I think they are."

"So what do you have to do?"

"Well if you don't mind, I'd like to get up there and check things out myself. I know others who draft everything right off the CAD but I like to see things first hand. There are a lot of details and nuances that are missed in the two-dimensional plane. Besides, I want to get an overall feel for the environment and space before I make the final adjustments. I like to make sure the design integrates well with the existing building and the surrounding area as much as possible. It gives it a sense of unity," Rey explained, keeping his eye trained on Royale.

"Sure, that's no problem. When do you want to go?"

"Anytime soon. The sooner the better, if I'm to get them to you by next week."

"Do you plan on taking the bus or riding your bike?" Stazie said, looking at him smugly. "Or have you finally broken down and gotten yourself a car? My father has certainly paid you enough to afford even a small one by now."

Rey surmised, *she's still up to her games all right.* He was really hoping to get through this encounter without any bloodshed. Unwillingly, he directed his attention to her.

"A cab or rideshare will get me there, no problem," he said matter-of-factly.

"Either of those will run you a fortune! Listen, if you need it, I'll just rent a car and have it delivered to your home on the day you want to go. That way you can take your time and come and go as you please," Doug said.

Now it was Rey's turn to feel embarrassed. "Thank you for the offer, Doug. And I would take it, except I currently do not have a driver's license."

He made sure not to make eye contact with the perfumed vixen across the table from him. She would be there with a big smirk on her face, if he knew her at all.

"Hmm, that is a problem," Doug said as he reflected on the situation. Suddenly he struck upon an idea. "I would drive you except I'll be in Detroit for the next several days. But Stazie here could drive you."

Stazie gasped and turned to her father. "What! Are you crazy? You expect me to chauffeur—"

"Sure, Honey. Weren't you just nagging me the other day that you had forgotten your favorite something or other up there and you wanted to try out the color swatches the interior decorator gave you for the den?"

"Well I can't. I'm just too busy. And you can't expect me to drop everything just to drive him there."

"You? Busy?" Doug laughed out loud. He turned back to Rey and said, "She can drive you."

"Daddy," Stazie hissed under her breath, "I cannot. My car is going to be in for servicing. And I hate driving your car. He can just wait until you get back. Or maybe you can hire a driver for him or something."

"I want this done now, Staze. And if Rey says he has time this week, then we're going to do everything we can to get him up there. You can get your car serviced next week. It still runs right? C'mon, Honey, you know you want this cottage finished more than I do. And didn't you say you wanted to spend Fourth of July there?"

"But what about hiring a driver?"

"I am not throwing away good money on things that are absolutely unnecessary. You wanted to go to the cottage. Well now you are and you are taking him with you."

"I'll get my own ride. It's no problem, really," Rey said, barely able to interject.

"No. It's taken care of. Anastasia will drive you."

Rey was beginning to recognize the courtroom tone in Royale's voice. Apparently it was the one he used when there was no more debate.

"Now, how about some lunch, Rey? Stazie's here because we had a lunch date. Care to join us? You two can discuss when you want to go upstate."

Even if he had been starving for months, Rey would have refused. There was absolutely no way he was going to get in-between these two. Not after what just went down. He couldn't believe that Royale was forcing his daughter to drive him to the cottage. And if that wasn't bad enough, he did not want to imagine the scene that would ensue at the restaurant should he tag along on their lunch date. Rey decided it was in his best interest to pack his things, politely decline lunch, and make a hasty exit immediately after telling them he would be ready to go the day after tomorrow.

As he pedaled down the street after the meeting, a very familiar gold sport coupe tore past, narrowly missing him. It was so close he caught the draft from being sideswiped and the grit from the road peppering his face. He could see her lone blonde head through the back window as the car raced down the street. Apparently she was no longer in the mood to have lunch with her father. Rey groaned. This next trip with her was certainly going to be one he would never forget.

A couple of days later, she arrived in the morning and pulled up in front of his apartment. Surveying the working-class neighborhood, Stazie double-checked to make sure her doors were locked and her windows were rolled all the way up. She couldn't believe she was actually going through with this. Her father had no right in forcing her to do it. But after he threatened to cut off her allowance for two months, she acquiesced. Recalling this detail irritated her even more and she impatiently laid on the horn. Rey instantly appeared down the stairs and walked out to her car, while she contemplated leaving the door locked and ditching him once again.

Stazie was not a morning person and this ludicrous suggestion of his to leave at eight o'clock to give them plenty of time at the cabin made her even crankier. Her father told her that whenever Rey wanted to leave, she was to be there, on time and ready to go. No excuses.

Natal could have told Daddy to have me drive an ice cream truck here in my underwear at midnight and he would have made me do it, she thought resentfully.

Well, maybe she *had* to do this but she did not have to be happy about it. In fact, she was going to make it a point to be downright miserable.

Rey had been waiting up at the top of the stairs where it was warmer. Mornings were still chilly, but on this first day of April, it felt colder than usual. The morning weather report confirmed his intuition that a storm front was moving in. When he had looked out his window as he ate his breakfast, he noticed the skies were laden with heavy dark clouds as a front made its way south.

He was sure to have everything ready to go and not leave her waiting knowing she would drive off at any excuse to do so. He depended upon this opportunity to see the cabin and push onward with this project to be done with it once and for all. When Rey saw her pull up, he wasted no time in gathering up his stuff and went quickly down the steps. He approached her car and tapped politely on the window to be let in. She glanced at him and hesitated for a few seconds as if contemplating something and then finally unlocked the door.

It is not quite eight o'clock yet and she's already brewing, he thought as he shook his head.

When he considered what potentially lay in store for him, he knew this two-and-a-half-hour drive would probably seem more like a week by the time they got back. Summoning his courage and resolve, Rey climbed in with his pack and closed the door.

"Good morning," he said cordially.

She ignored him and instead put the car in gear and floored it, pulling out into oncoming traffic. A car from behind slammed on its brakes in a hard nosedive to avoid hitting them. The frightened driver laid on his horn and yelled a few obscenities at them as they drove off. Rey braced himself for the impact and then looked out the back window with relief at the near miss. He almost said something about her dumb-ass maneuver but decided that they were only five seconds into their trip. There was no telling how she would drive should he criticize her.

They drove on in silence for the next hour. The car was well-insulated so there wasn't even the sound of road noise as a distraction. To Rey, it felt as if they were trapped in a vacuum bubble where no one else could reach them. The only occasional sounds were the clatter of her bracelets as she turned the steering wheel and the quiet hum of the engine.

The city fell way to suburbs and then small towns. The naked branches of the dormant trees were only starting to bud. The day grew colder as they journeyed north. Clouds continued to roll in and the sky grew dark, casting a dismal gray glum over the landscape. Feeling the chill in the air, he would have never believed they were on a warm sunny beach in Florida a few weeks earlier.

Rey observed that Stazie was not much of a driver. He considered her merely an operator of a vehicle, more like a trained chimp who knew the basics but showed no judgment or skill. Her braking was brutal and she tailed other cars too closely. She wove from lane to lane erratically and tore past drivers to get in front of them, only to slow down. He wished she would set the cruise control to even out the constant speed changes but she gave no indication that she was going to bother. He wondered if she even knew where it was and how to use it. When he stole a sideways glance at her, she appeared to be lost in her thoughts and not fully engaged in what she was doing. It was as if the car was cruising on autopilot with her along for the ride. It was definitely a waste of a fine driving machine.

Oh well, as long as we get there, he concluded.

The silence was getting to Stazie. She was becoming bored and restless. As far as she was concerned, she may as well have been driving a houseplant to the cottage instead of the uninteresting jerk in the seat next to her. Picking up her cell phone from her cup holder, she scrolled for a number to dial, her eyes intent on the tiny screen instead of the road, never having bothered to figure out the app for hands-free talking. She would have texted but she had already received two tickets for it and Daddy would not have any patience if she got hit with another one. A car horn and an "Oh shit" muttered from under Natal's breath brought her attention back to driving. She veered the car sharply back into its lane and avoided a near collision just in time for Gidge to pick up.

"Gidge? It's me. Thank bunnies you are awake. I was going out of my mind with boredom. Hey—what are you doing up so early? I thought you would be sleeping but I just had to try you anyway . . . Huh? What's that? . . . You're catching a flight to see your grandmother? Which grandmother? I thought both of them were dead . . . Uh huh. Okay. Sorry about that. It's just that I thought you said . . . Me? I got stuck driving you-know-who upstate to the cottage . . . Yes! Daddy had an absolute hissy fit and told me that I had to . . . I know. I could have killed him . . . That's what I told him—hire a driver, but he said it would be a big waste of money . . . No. I doubt *he* has any money to hire a driver. I suggested he take the bus . . . No. He refused to go on any other day when Daddy could have driven him instead . . . Nah uh. He doesn't have a driver's license, so he has to be driven everywhere. And I guess this was too far for him to ride his bike," Stazie said and snorted, casting a sideways glance towards him.

Rey rolled his tongue inside his cheek and looked out the window. He knew what she was trying to do. But he determined that he wasn't going to give her that opportunity. He was going to be in control of the situation regardless of what little control he had over getting to the cottage. *Choose what you are capable of handling,* he reminded himself of Mei-Lin's advice.

"No. He says he has to measure something at the cottage because he can't figure it out on the plans . . . I don't know, maybe he doesn't know how to use a calculator. I wouldn't be surprised . . . Huh? What was that? You want me to *tell* him that? Okay, hold on." Giggling and turning to him, she said, "Gidge says 'Hi Dick.'"

Rey looked at her unaffected. She could have been telling him the contents of her refrigerator for all he cared. He returned his gaze out the window.

"Nah. He didn't do anything. That's because I've told you before his name isn't *Dick* . . . No. He just acts like one . . . Um hmm . . . No. Thank our fuzzy bunnies, we're only spending the day up there. Even less if he knows how to use a ruler." Turning to him once more she added, "You do know how to use a ruler, right?"

There was no response.

"Nah. He's no fun. I don't think he wants to play anymore. He's so boring anyway . . . Uh huh. No, I can't say he possesses any real conversational skills . . . What? Really? She said that? No! I told her that I thought Josh was kind of cute . . . No! He was the one coming onto me . . ."

Trying to shut out the babble, Rey inserted his ear buds, switched on his MP3 player, and settled into the comfortable seat, resting his head back. This trip was quickly becoming tedious. He may as well catch up on some much needed sleep. A few days ago, he had started on another smaller account and had spent all evening working. Within a few minutes the combination of his favorite playlist, Stazie's mindless chatter, and the steady hum of the engine lulled him to sleep.

She talked for a few minutes more until Gidge had to go. As she reluctantly hung up her phone, she pondered whom she could call next, knowing it was still too early for any of her crowd to be awake. She dialed Josh but he didn't want to talk. Then she tried Tab but all she got was her answering machine. And Lindsey cussed her out for waking her up. Feeling put out, Stazie chucked her phone back into the cup holder and sped up.

After a few more miles she was restless again. She had been over this route so many times before, there was nothing interesting left to see. She looked over at Natal, who seemed to be peacefully asleep. His mouth was even slightly open. Feeling wicked, she decided to veer her car from side to side in the lane to watch his head wag back and forth. It was fun at first but grew tiresome within a few tries. Then she sped up and slowed down, sped up and slowed down, but that didn't wake him either. Stazie pouted. It wasn't fair. He got to sleep while she had to get up early to be his stupid chauffeur.

Her mind went back to their tiff on the beach and how he had addressed her that day. Suddenly, a diabolical plan occurred to her. And the best part was that he couldn't retaliate. Having the opportunity to see how he lived over the storefront, she knew he was dependent on the money her father was paying him. She doubted he was going to do anything foolish to cut off his lifeline. Now she understood why he had been so tolerant and conniving all along.

Looks like its payback time, sweet cheeks. She grinned evilly, recalling his pat little term.

Stazie reached over and carefully pulled his ear buds out. Then she turned on the radio, selected an acid rock station, and turned it up, hoping to see him spring awake. To her dismay, he continued sleeping. She turned it up even louder but he slept on. By then, she grew impatient and slammed on her brakes, plunging the sports car into a hard nosedive. Rey's eyes sprung open. Letting out a small cry, he sat straight up in his seat, gripping the armrests. Seeing the terror on his face, Stazie was delighted that one of her little pranks finally worked. It took Rey a second to get oriented when he became conscious of the extreme head-banging music that was blaring over the car's ten different speakers.

His hands went up to his ears. "Will you turn it down?" he yelled.

She pretended not to hear him and kept driving. Rey turned the volume down himself.

"Hey! I was listening to that!" she protested as she cranked it back up again.

This time he turned it off. "For the love of god! That's enough!" he snapped.

He slumped back in his seat and rubbed his face hard, trying to gather his wits about him. Meanwhile, Stazie giggled and playfully hummed the melody from the song that had been turned off.

"Are you purposely trying to be obnoxious?" he said.

"Daddy was the one who said you were brilliant, not me."

"What exactly is your problem? I've never met anyone like you—always rude and impossible. Daddy doesn't give you enough attention? You don't have enough stuff? It's got to be something."

"Nothing," she said petulantly. "Shut up."

"Then what happened in your pampered charmed existence that makes you so damned unhappy? Was it the girls in the fourth grade that didn't come to your party? Do you ever stop to think it might have been your behavior?" He was feeling grouchy and had had enough.

It was now apparent what she had divulged to him that night on the dunes.

The unexpected words had a sting to them, causing tears to gather in her eyes. "I said, shut up. I don't want to talk about it. Did I ever tell you how much I dislike you?"

It wasn't supposed to turn this way. His candor shook her up, leaving her feeling exposed and vulnerable.

He said, "Listen, I may work for your father but that doesn't mean I have to put up with any nonsense from his family members. If you have a beef about driving me, then talk to him about it. From the very beginning I wanted to arrange my own means to get there since I had no intention on having either one of you drive me."

She abruptly pulled over to the shoulder of the highway and stopped the car. Turning to him, her cheeks were flushed and her eyes were glistening.

"Okay, then. Get out. Call yourself a cab or whatever. You'll be doing us both a favor."

He gave her one last look, opened the door, and climbed out. Swinging his pack onto his back, he started walking down the road. She watched him go, his long strides taking him far in just a couple of minutes. Stazie knew they were miles from the nearest town and she figured he would be walking for quite a bit before he got there. The skies were growing more stormy and the wind had started to blow.

She wiped her tears and checked her mascara. At first, she was somewhat satisfied with her accomplishment. It certainly would teach him not to talk to her that way. Being relieved of her loathsome chore, she could now go home and try to salvage something of her day. Maybe she would get a spa treatment just to relax. One of the things she hated most about Natal was his ability to always make her feel in knots.

Soon, a little voice in her head started to gnaw at her like it always did. *What if Daddy finds out? He would be furious.* She couldn't risk that Natal wouldn't tell either. Especially if her father called tonight to ask him how everything went. After she had hit him with her car, Natal hadn't told her father about her ditching him, she reasoned. But then again, that was before Natal got to know her father. Lately they were acting like long lost buddies.

Rey was already a small figure in the distance. He never looked back and didn't give any indication of stopping.

"Oh poop."

She put her car in gear and raced down the road after him. She pulled up alongside of him expecting him to be relieved at her arrival but to her dismay, he kept walking. Keeping up with him in the car, she rolled down the window.

"Hey! Come on. Get in."

He continued his pace, not breaking his stride.

"Come on. Get in already. I'll give you a ride. It's a long way to the nearest town."

Rey kept his eye on the road ahead of him.

"It looks like it's going to ra-ain," she sing-songed in a cutesy voice.

He stuck his hands in his jacket pockets and kept walking.

"Will you quit being so stubborn? You're not proving anything to me."

No response.

She hated what she was going to say next but she had to think of something quick. If he made it all the way to town, he'd probably end up being really pissed, and her father would surely hear about it. It could spell real trouble for her if he decided not to finish the cottage.

"Please. I'm . . . I'm sorry."

Rey couldn't believe his ears. It almost sounded like an actual apology coming from this girl. Or more than likely just another one of her ruses to manipulate him. If he reached for the door, she'd probably drive off and spray him with a rooster tail of gravel from her tires, laughing her ass off for the next fifty miles or so. He kept walking.

Stazie saw no other recourse except to stop ahead of him and get out of the car. She was blasted by a gust of wind that swept across the highway and her high heel boots did not give her a good footing on the shoulder gravel. She stumbled ungracefully as she walked towards him, holding out her hands in effort to stop his progress.

"Please, I mean it. I am sorry. Really. Will you please get in the car?"

Rey brushed passed her. For a moment she felt defeated and out of options, until he walked up to the driver's side of the car and opened the door.

Is he thinking about stealing my car? she thought with alarm.

He turned to her and waited, obviously holding open the door for her. Relieved, she trotted as best as she could on the loose gravel and climbed in.

He slammed her door shut, came around, and then got in beside her. She looked at him but he didn't say a word, only stared straight ahead. So she started the car and resumed their trip.

"Golly, I was only kidding with you," she said in a small voice. "I guess you took it wrong."

He would not respond. They drove on for another mile. When curiosity got the better of her, she was compelled to ask, "So, what made you get back in the car? Was it getting too cold out there or did you finally realize how far away the town was?"

"You said please," he said.

"Oh."

The cottage perched atop a high hill nestled in the rolling mountains near the Sproul State Forest. It was a secluded location, flanked by mixed oak and hemlock trees, and overlooked a crystal blue lake below. Compared to most homes, it was no 'cottage' by any sense of the definition. They pulled up to a sixty-five hundred square foot, two-storied rustic contemporary home. The vague building plans that had been provided him apparently were in error of the full square footage. By his estimation, he figured it was going to be big but he didn't know it would be like this.

Rey had always wondered what it would be like to live like this. He had seen similar sized vacation homes when he would hike or go snowboarding with Ivan but he could only fantasize about what it would be like to own one. And it would only be as a result of winning a huge lottery or something equally as unlikely. His average paycheck could never afford it. He gazed with wonder at the breathtaking scenery across the mountain range. From atop the hill, they had a commanding view of the valley and lake below. The heavy clouds that had been accumulating all morning seemed so low at this altitude he felt he could reach out to touch them.

Stazie didn't stop once to take in the view as she marched nonchalantly to the house and opened the door. Inside she threw down her keys and purse and looked about while Rey caught up. It was obvious the cottage was undergoing major renovations. Drop cloths and plastic were draped and stapled up everywhere and the east wall that overlooked the lake below was only a skeleton frame shrouded by more plastic teased apart by the breeze. Rey walked to the exposed wall and looked out and then down, amazed at the drop before him. The steep bank below extended for a few hundred yards. This is where his proposed balcony deck would cantilever. He startled when he felt her at his shoulder, looking down the embankment with him.

"Yeah, those imbeciles tore out this wall and then took off. It's been left like this for over six months already. It's pretty far down there, huh?" she said and then turned away. "Let me show you where everything else is."

As they turned towards the expansive living room with vaulted ceilings, Rey's eyes were drawn to the smooth curves and fine legs that peaked out from beneath a canvas drop cloth in a corner of the room. Although Stazie had started for the hallway, he headed straight for the object in sight. Drawing back the dusty drop cloth, he revealed the ebony elegance of a Steinway baby grand piano. The sight of it made him draw his breath.

"You keep *this* up *here*?" he said incredulously.

"Keep what?" Stazie turned back.

"A Steinway. You keep a Steinway baby grand *here*? At the cottage?"

"Oh, that old thing. Yeah, we felt we had more room to store it here. Daddy keeps thinking it would be fun for parties or something."

"May I?" Rey asked, nodding toward the instrument.

"Huh? Sure, whatever."

He stroked the rich wood grain of the fallboard, then opened it and ran his fingers lightly over the ivory keys. The piano's full mellow tone filled the room. He realized he was holding his breath.

"But aren't you afraid of something happening to it? The walls are open to the weather right now and what about theft? And the dust and construction?"

"It's fine. Nobody comes up here anyway. One of Daddy's clients gave it to us. I think it was in lieu of some debt he owed to Daddy or something. It's not like either of us play piano or anything. To tell you the truth, most of the time, it's just in the way," she said with a bored sigh. "So do you want to see the rest of the house?"

Rey stroked the smooth keys once more, then slowly closed the fall-board and pulled down the drop cloth with care, reluctant to leave the instrument behind.

The rest of the morning passed quickly as they toured the house with Stazie pointing out features and explaining the ideas that she and her father had. It was the first time she conducted a normal conversation with him without any attitude or hostility. He began to wonder if she truly was sorry for her roadside behavior or if it was something more. The way she described the color plans and window treatments for each room, it was as if he were dealing with another person entirely. If he wasn't mistaken, she seemed to have an interest and flair for it.

He carefully measured all the needed dimensions and took digital pictures of each room. Then he meticulously jotted down notes, made sketches, and double-checked and corrected the existing plans.

While she waited, Stazie busied herself with her color swatches in the kitchen and bathroom and made lists for the decorator but after a while she had run out of things to do.

When she entered the living room, Rey was engrossed in his work. He barely noticed her there. It made her secretly wish she had some special skill in life to call her own that made her look important and occupied her so fully. Although she had had her choice of the best colleges in the country, there wasn't any one subject that ever caught her interest long enough. A semester at Smith and then a half-semester at Barnard was all she could muster before she called it quits.

"How do they even get wood to, you know, bend? I know they saw it and use hammers and nails and all that stuff but not all the edges are straight and sometimes," she said as she pointed to the rounded doorway above her head, "there are curves, like that."

She looked genuinely interested so he explained, "Well, they can cut curves with a special saw called a jigsaw or they can build up edges to make them look more rounded. They can also steam planks of wood to get them to bend. Why do you ask? Do you like carpentry?"

"Not really . . . I guess, a little. I was just wondering if curves like that can be added to the tops of the built-in bookcases over there, you know, to tie everything all together, that's all."

"I don't see why not. In fact, it's a brilliant idea," he said.

"It is?" She looked surprised.

"Have you ever thought about trying carpentry?"

"Who? ME? You're kidding right? I'm a girl just in case you didn't notice?"

"So? There are plenty of women who are carpenters. If it interests you, do it."

"I'm not smart. I'd just screw things up."

"You can learn how, I'm sure."

"Yeah, right," she said, rolling her eyes and walking away.

Too busy to stop, Rey continued working right through lunch. Stazie on the other hand, always thought about eating, as long as food was provided and prepared for her. She and her father usually drove down to the lakeside grill for meals since they hadn't stocked the cottage with food during the renovations. Her stomach was not use to doing without and rumbled loudly. She decided to approach Rey while he worked.

"Um, excuse me? Are we ever going to eat today? I mean, you are going to take a break, aren't you?"

He looked up from his calculations. "Huh? What did you say?"

"I asked if you were going to break for some lunch? There's a grill down by the lake that isn't too bad."

"No. I'm not hungry. Go on ahead, if that's what you are asking."

The truth was Stazie did not want to eat at the restaurant by herself. The quiet solo mealtimes at home were difficult enough most of the time but the thought of having to spend one in a public setting seemed dismal, even if she had her phone. No one wanted to talk with her today anyway. Looking at Rey working on his notes she thought if she acted pleasant enough, she could possibly persuade him to dine with her. After all, even his company would be better than none.

"Well, you see, we don't keep anything here with the cottage being unfinished and all. The grill is not very far."

His eyes never left his notebook and he punched a few more numbers into his calculator.

"I just need to finish up one last room. You can pick me up when you are done," he said, sounding a bit distracted.

She didn't anticipate his response. Her stomach let out a loud growl.

As a last resort, she made up an excuse. "No. It looks like it might storm soon. I'd rather not be out driving if I don't have to."

"Well, if you don't mind bologna and cheese, you're welcome to the sandwich I have in my pack. There are some chips and a soda in there too."

"Oh. Are you sure?" Puzzled that he'd be willing to give up his lunch to her after the way she had treated him, she didn't know what else to say except for a quiet, "Thanks."

He shrugged. "No problem," he said and crossed into the next room.

Stazie rummaged through his pack and pulled out an insulated lunch bag. Removing the ice pack to get to the sandwich, she couldn't help but think, *He's a regular Boy Scout, isn't he?*

Then she called to him, "What kind of bread is this anyway? Didn't you have any bruschetta or brioche? And why is this cheese so . . . so orange? And so square?"

He didn't answer.

Having never had bologna and American cheese on white bread before, she sniffed it first, then took a test nibble. She didn't know if it was her growling stomach, the late lunch hour, or the mountain air, but she found it delicious and took a bigger bite. Next, she dug out the soda and potato chips and made short work of them as well.

Afterwards, Stazie tried to keep herself occupied while he worked. She texted a couple of friends she was able to get through to. Then she played solitaire on her phone just to pass the time. Within another hour, Stazie was restless. She made it a point to droop about any area in which he worked, sighing loudly and looking bored.

Rey was finished and started to pack things up. He felt he had everything he needed not only to complete this job but also to make the cottage one of his better remodels. If Royale was satisfied and entertained guest here, Rey's hope was that the counselor would endorse his handiwork as he showed off the transformation of his "little vacation home."

"Why does it take so long for you to write down a few numbers and take a few pictures?"

"To make it all come out right, I've got to be as accurate as possible. See, the last guy really screwed things up by—"

"But don't you have enough already?" she said.

Taking the hint, he wrapped it up, not wanting to be subjected to another one of her changing moods and subsequent attacks. It had been fairly peaceful since they arrived and he very much wanted it to stay that way. He buckled his pack and they were headed for the door when a strange noise made them stop. At first it was a random popping sound. But it grew louder and more thunderous. They tracked the sound to the large plastic sheet that hung against the open wall of the house as a fierce wind rippled through it.

"I guess we finished just in time. Looks like its picking up. We'd better go," Rey said as they exited the cottage.

Feeling the drop in temperature, Stazie stood for a moment outside the front door, watching sleet start to fall from the black storm clouds above. She cowered, looking anxious.

"I hate storms," she said.

A sudden gust of wind blew against them. "Come on, let's go before it really gets bad," he said as he nudged her from behind.

They made a dash through the increasing torrent. As they ran, they were stung on their heads, faces and hands by the frozen drops. By the time they covered the short distance to the car and climbed in, they were both soaked with bits of ice stuck in their hair and on their shoulders. They sat for a moment in amazement as the sky opened up and the rain pounded down.

Rey noticed that Stazie's teeth were chattering as she rubbed the goose bumps covering her arms. Her outfit consisted of a suede miniskirt, a thin tight-fitting top that exposed her midriff, and a short shearling lined vest to match her boots. It wasn't much to keep her warm.

Why do chicks like these always have to wear the skimpy stuff when it made the least amount of sense? Rey wondered to himself.

He and Ivan had met plenty of attractive snowboarding girls that always made sure to dress appropriately for the weather regardless of how "un-sexy" it made them look. He had dressed in a pullover sweater, jeans, and his leather jacket and was feeling pretty comfortable despite the sudden change in temperature. Stazie, on the other hand, continued to shiver.

"Did you bring any other clothes with you?"

She shook her head. "No, I wasn't expecting to be outside."

"Do you have anything in the cottage?"

She shook her head again.

"Why don't you start the car and get the heat going?" he suggested.

"Right."

She pulled out of the long driveway still hunched over and trying to get warm, the rain-sensing windshield wipers and headlights turning on. The frozen rain alternated between BB- to pea-sized pellets, the wipers piling the slush onto either sides of the windshield.

"Man, can you believe this?" Rey wondered out loud. "They forecasted a storm but I don't think they were expecting anything like this."

Stazie tried her best to drive in the relentless weather. The daylight was fading fast under the cover of storm clouds and towering trees. The mountain road was dark and had many blind turns, forcing her to drive slowly. As they turned off the forest service road and onto the two-lane road that led to the interstate, within a half a mile they came upon amber lights on construction barricades flashing through the pouring sleet. A large sign blocking their path loomed above them and wobbled in the wind, reading ROAD CLOSED. Off to the side, a portable LED sign confirmed: "Road closed for repair 4/11, 4 pm – 6am."

"The road's closed? What are they talking about? We just drove through here on the way up," Stazie said, confused.

Rey vaguely remembered a road crew preparing some heavy equipment parked on the shoulder on the way up. "Well, it looks like they want to work on it tonight. I don't know how they're going to accomplish that in *this* weather. They must've closed it sometime today after we passed."

"But why are they working on this road? There isn't anything wrong with it."

"Who knows? Did you call ahead for any road closures today?"

"No." Stazie started to get irritated. "This road has never been closed before. How was I supposed to know that they were going to do any construction up here?"

Rey held his tongue. He reasoned that she couldn't have known this would happen. The frozen rain kept coming down and although it was warm inside the car from the heater running, he could feel a cool drift off the windows. The external temperature display read thirty-four degrees. The temperature had dropped at least eighteen degrees since they had arrived at the cabin this morning.

"I doubt they are even working in this rain. Ohhh, I hate it when they do this!"

"How much gas do you have left?"

"A little less than half a tank."

"Do you know of any other routes out of here?"

Stazie bit her lower lip. "Um, I'm not sure."

"Did you bring a map with you?"

She shook her head and looked out the window. "No. But I've been up and down this road at least a dozen times before. There are other turnoffs. I just wasn't expecting to have to take a detour."

"Do you have a map app?"

She picked up her phone. The screen lit up with only one bar indicating power left. She rolled her eyes and sighed, anticipating what was he going to say when he found out her battery was running low.

"My battery is too low to pull up the web. I'm not getting a strong signal here."

"Maybe you can call someone on your phone and see if they have a map of the area. They can guide us out. That doesn't take as much juice."

It sounded plausible. She decided to give it a try. It would help to defer for at least a couple of minutes more before Natal started interrogating her again. She scrolled through her phone's directory. Out of all the people listed there, it was hard to figure who would have a map. Worse yet, which one of them would even care to take the time to help her. At the last minute, she called Beatrice. She could hear the phone connect and ring but just as the maid answered, the power went out. Stazie tried again, but the phone was dead. She let her hands drop in her lap.

"What happened? Did you get through?" he asked.

"The battery is dead."

"Can't you put it on the car charger?"

"I didn't bring one."

"Okay, how about calling your Navistar?"

"I don't subscribe to them anymore. I didn't like the snotty way they gave directions."

They sat for a few moments more, the windshield wipers keeping a steady beat clearing the ice. Finally she said, "I think there's another road but it's a round about way to get to the highway and it winds up on the other side of the lake."

"And you're sure you know how to get there?" Rey couldn't trust Stazie's memory or common sense.

"Yes! Will you quit giving me the third degree? Did you do this and did you do that. You must really think I'm stupid or something, don't you? Just because you're Mister Math Whiz and can design houses and things, you think you're all that. I wish you would just keep quiet and let me think," she said defensively.

Actually Stazie was feeling fearful. Not only of the encroaching night and ice storm and having to find her way off of this mountain but more so that she was the one they were relying on. This predicament was foreign to her and made her uncomfortable.

"I didn't say— Listen, never mind." He shook his head. "I guess we better try that other route. We're running out of light and the road is going to start icing over. Man, this is one helluva storm."

The temperature now read thirty degrees. She turned the car around and headed back to where they came from. She went for the first turnoff, steering the car down an unmarked road. The heavy downpour made it hard to see even with headlights and made it appear as if they were traveling through a tunnel of sleet. Within a couple of miles, the pavement ended. She came to a complete stop.

"Oh poop," she said under her breath.

"What are you doing?"

"What do you mean, what am I doing? Don't you see there isn't a road?"

"Of course there is still a road, it just isn't paved."

"I'm not taking my car on any unpaved road!" she said indignantly.

"It's not going to hurt it. It looks like it's been graded so you should be fine. You just have to take it slow because of your low ground clearance. This car is fully capable."

"I don't think so. This car has never been off the pavement."

Except when it was parked on my bike, Rey thought to himself.

"Well then, what do you propose we do?" he said.

It was an all-too-familiar scene for him, a déjà vu in a way—rain, the dark, Stazie at a crossroad of decision. The first time had gotten him into plenty of trouble. He hoped this time wasn't going to cost him dearly.

"I don't know. I'm thinking."

Rey rubbed his jaw, took a deep breath and looked out the window. He was finding it hard to maintain patience with this dimwit next to him. It seemed she never considered anything besides which shoes matched what outfit. He saw her when she was talking on the phone and playing games on it all day. Did it ever occur to her that she might need it later?

"Don't get angry with me. Where's your phone, Boy Scout?"

"It doesn't have coverage up here."

"Oh, that's great."

"Is there any other road you know of?" he said.

"No. This is the only other one."

The storm did not look like it would abate for a long while. Rey weighed all of their choices. It seemed they were only left with two. They could possibly drive through the construction site if it was passable and back to the highway. Their only other option would be to stay at the cottage until the storm passed.

"How about going back to where the road was closed and slip past the construction site? I doubt they've gotten much done over there yet and with all of this rain—"

"Sure! And I would be the one ticketed, not you. So I don't think so. I'm beginning to see why you don't have your license anymore."

"Okay, then how about we turn back and go to the cottage? We can wait out the storm, and if worse comes to worst, stay the night there."

"The cottage? Are you crazy? You know how cold it will be?" she said with alarm. "There's nothing there! No heat, no food, no electricity, nothing. It's also missing a wall."

"If we stayed in an interior room, closed the door, and kept together, we should be okay. It will be cold but it shouldn't be too bad. Then we can drive out when the road opens in the morning."

"No. There's no way I'm spending the night freezing in an unfinished house. I want to go home to my own bed."

"Well then, I guess you better be prepared to get your car tires dirty because there is no where else to go but that way," he said pointing to the dirt road ahead of them.

"I've told you before I am not taking my car down that road."

"Then what the hell do you propose to do? You don't want to go to the cottage, or go by the construction, or drive your car down a dirt road. Unless you want to sleep in this car overnight, you're going to have to make a decision. This isn't something that Daddy can get you out of. Even if he was in town, he'd be down there and you would still be stuck here. Make up your mind already because there are no more options left."

"All right already!" she said.

She wanted to slug him. Instead she gritted her teeth, put her car in gear, and floored it. It leapt off the pavement and hit the gravel of the dirt road, peeling out in serpentine, and spraying rocks and mud out from under its tires. The needle on the speedometer climbed as she raced down the mountain road, skittering around turns and bottoming out her car on dips and ruts.

"Goddamnit! Will you slow down?" he yelled.

Stazie was intent on showing him she knew how to handle her own vehicle and her own life. He wasn't going to tell her what to do. And the way he kept questioning her —why did she have to make all of the decisions for the both of them? She told him that she didn't like storms or driving in them. All she wanted to do now was to get home as quickly as possible and dive in under her bed blankets away from the cold, rain, and being depended on.

The beam from the headlights bounced crazily on the bumpy road ahead of them. There appeared to be an opening in the trees up ahead. Rey wondered if it was the lake and hoped that she wouldn't drive them straight into it. Just then he could feel the back end of the car break loose as it fishtailed on ice and rock. At the last second a sharp turn came up, surprising her. She slammed on the brakes but the car skidded and went into a spin. She tried to save it but wound up over-correcting instead. Suddenly the car tipped to its side on two wheels, struck something hard, and toppled over the shoulder's embankment. The front and side airbags deployed with a deafening explosion, engulfing them in the billowy dusty fabric. Stazie screamed. They were definitely going over. Panic seized Rey as they tumbled twice, his mind flashing an instant recall of the horrific night of his own accident.

After a metallic crunch like the amplified sound of a can being crushed, the car rolled onto its side, and with the very last of its momentum, settled down on its wheels. The built-in crash sensor clicked on the interior light, popped open the locks, and set the hazards. The wipers continued to beat, smearing mud into the frozen rain that drummed down on the cracked windshield. He sat, panting for a few seconds and concentrating on getting his white knuckles to release their terror grip on the armrests. Then, catching his breath, he said, "Are you okay?" as he quickly unbuckled his seatbelt and pushed his airbag away.

There was no sound from her. In the dim circle of the interior light he could see her face down in the deflating bag on her steering wheel, her arms crossed in front of her. She made a short jerking motion and then started to emit a low strangled noise from her throat.

Oh shit! his mind cried. *She's choking on something!*

He grappled to undo her seatbelt.

"Hey? Are you all right!" he said, as he carefully pulled her back by her shoulder.

She was crying.

"Are you hurt?"

"Are we still alive?" she said and then hiccupped. "I'm SO scared."

"But are you hurt?" he asked again as he scanned her over. She didn't appear to have any cuts or bruises but her breathing was strained.

"I think . . . I need my inhaler." She pulled in another breath with effort and hiccupped again. "My purse. Do you see it?"

Rey quickly looked at everything that had been thrown about the car. Finally he located it behind his seat. He handed her the bag and she fished around in it until she extracted an inhaler. She shook the device, put it to her mouth, and drew a deep breath while depressing the button. One more puff and then she settled back in her seat, staring straight ahead while working on controlling her air intake. Rey had never considered this aspect of Stazie. It was an unexpected revelation to her otherwise bristly personality.

"Are you okay now?" he said as he studied her carefully.

"Better. But what are we supposed to do now? This was such a bad idea. It's really dark out there." Hiccup.

Rey slumped back and took several deep breaths himself, then swore softly, closing his eyes. His heart continued to pound, feeling the jump of adrenaline pulsing through his veins. His memory summoned the sound of sirens from that night when he wasn't able to see anything because of the blood running into his eyes, and pinned, he couldn't move. He had been gasping desperately for air as the sirens grew louder and louder. Then he had blacked out.

Here out in the woods, there was nothing but the sound of the frozen rain drumming on the bashed-in roof of the car, the blink of the hazard lights, and the pitiful mewing and hiccups of Stazie sitting beside him. He tried opening the car door but it was jammed. Ramming it hard with his shoulder, it only budged a crack, having been buckled from the collapsed roof above. He swung around in his seat and using both of his feet, started to kick at the door.

"What are you doing!" Stazie said, startled by the sharp sound.

He gave one last forceful kick. The door swung open, squealing on its hinges. He climbed out. Immediately, his trekkers sunk into the loamy wet earth as the wind gusts stung his face with ice pellets. Eerily, the forest was pitch black, lit only in flashes of yellow by the hazard lights, the headlights broken. He had read somewhere that these cars came equipped with a flashlight in their glove boxes. Reaching inside the car, he found it where it should be.

Thank God she didn't decide to get rid of this, he thought.

He turned it on and spotlighted the car. The gold sport coupe was totaled. Shining the light back to the roadway, he realized how lucky they had been in only tumbling down a forty-foot embankment. Some of the other shoulders in the vicinity ended abruptly in cliffs hundreds of feet high.

Rey ducked his head back into the car. "Are you going to come out of there?" he said.

She had righted the rearview mirror and was wiping her eyes and blowing her nose.

"Why? What's out there?"

Good question. Rey shone the light past where they were and could see nothing more than trees. He climbed back into the car and closed the door. It would not shut all the way now and with each gust of wind, ice-cold air blew in. Water came through the cracks in the windshield and dripped off the dash.

"Did you try the engine?" he said.

"Do you really think it's going to start now? After being smashed in?"

"You can always give it a try. You never know."

Stazie pushed the fabric of the airbag out of the way and turned the key. The engine fired up. She opened her eyes wide and yelped with joy but then the engine stalled. Trying it a couple of more times resulted in the same thing. The bright smile faded quickly.

"Pop the hood. I'll take a look."

"Can you get it to start?"

"Maybe."

She reached down for the hood release but it failed to engage.

"Must be broken. In fact, I think my whole car is broken," she said sadly. "We shouldn't have gone down that road."

Rey held his tongue about her reckless driving, seeing no sense in discussing it any further. He knew he was the last person to point a finger at anyone. His best recourse right now was to stay calm, think rationally. He couldn't afford to use energy in getting angry.

Stazie didn't know whom she was mad at but she had to blame someone. And Natal sitting there was a perfect target. If he hadn't wanted to come up here in the first place, this never would have happened. But as she stared out her side window, the inky black surroundings swallowed up her anger. The rain pouring down the glass distorted the view, making it look like a surrealistic watercolor painting. She was reduced again to feeling small and helpless.

"I guess we better see if there's somewhere close we can walk to."

"We're on the other side of the lake. There's nothing over here. Not for miles around," she said.

"Well, maybe there's something we can take shelter in. If it were just me, I'd walk out of here and try to find it."

"Maybe it's better to stay right here."

"Here? In the car all night?"

"I'm not going out there. There could be, you know, *things* out there."

"Okay . . . Water's coming in and the windshield is bashed in," he said logically.

"I can see that."

Seeing her start to shiver again, Rey slipped out of his leather jacket and handed it over to her. "Here take this. You're going to need it."

"What for? I'm fine. Keep it."

A few moments later, the wind howled through the doorjamb. She shivered violently and clasped her arms around herself.

"It's going to get cold in here pretty quick. This door doesn't close anymore, so we're losing heat rapidly."

Another blast of cold air and she held out her trembling hand for the jacket and said, "Okay, I'll take that now."

He dug around in his pack and produced a wool beanie. "Here, take this too. You lose a lot of heat through your head."

"Thanks," she said quietly as she reluctantly accepted the item. When she put the jacket on, she wrinkled her nose at the smell of the wet leather but inside it was warm and cozy. Then she said, "At least my hiccups subsided."

"Good."

They both fell into silence.

Within twenty minutes, the car was freezing inside. The water stopped trickling on the dash and started to seize up. Stazie's teeth were chattering again, despite the warmth of the jacket. Rey felt cold but he could still manage in his sweater. He knew there was no way they would be able to stay there for the remainder of the night. It was only early evening and they would have another ten or more hours to go before the sun came up. If it did anything; this storm, depending on its size could last well into the next day.

"Listen, as much as you'd like to, we're not going to be able to stay here tonight. I'm going out to take a look around to see if there is anywhere close we can get to. I thought I saw some lights out there on the way down."

She didn't want to leave the security of her car but she couldn't argue that it was getting too cold. She had his jacket zipped all the way and the collar turned up. The stockings on her legs weren't enough to keep her warm. She couldn't stop shivering.

"You're going out there? But what if there's animals?"

"It'll be okay. I think any animals out there would be hunkered down in this mess. It almost looked like there was a clearing to the west. It might have been the lake's edge. If that's the case, all we would have to do is follow it around to the other side where the cabins and tackle shops are."

"Do you know how far that is? We won't be able to make it."

"All we can do is try."

"But what if someone comes along while you're gone?"

"If they do, just point them in the direction I am going, if you don't mind."

"No, I mean like a killer or someone dangerous. You never know who could be out there."

"On this night? I don't think even a psychopath is out in this weather. They're probably hunkering down with the animals," he said, trying to joke a little to lighten up their situation.

She looked at him, her eyes growing a little wider. It was apparent she either didn't get it or wasn't in the mood for jokes.

"Seriously, I think most people are decent and we need all the help we can get right now," he said.

"Can't we just light a fire or something?"

"Everything is too wet."

She hesitated for a moment and then finally caved in. "Don't go. Please don't leave me here alone."

"I'll be back in fifteen minutes, tops, okay? You'll be all right." With that, he grabbed the flashlight, pushed open the door, and stepped out.

The wintery gale tore at him. He pointed the flashlight west and started walking, picking his way around boulders and tree roots. Within a few minutes, he could feel the frigid wet soak through to his skin as his sweater and jeans became drenched in the downpour. It made him walk even faster.

Back at the car, Stazie was more frightened than she had ever recalled in her life. She had asked him not to leave, yet he left anyway. What if he didn't come back? She had no idea what to do out here by herself and didn't know how to protect herself in any way. Wiping the condensation off her window, she peered into the dark. It was so complete and vast, as if it could swallow her up at any moment.

It was like looking into the blackness of the hallway at night after she had been put to bed as a child and expected to stay. At four years old, she wanted to be with her parents, not in her bedroom on a sleepless night with no one to keep her company except for lifeless dolls and plush animals. She had longed for someone to cuddle up with or talk to until she could fall asleep.

One night she would always remember, she had been frightened by something she had seen on TV earlier in the day and couldn't sleep. She thought she heard noises coming from the closet and imagined a big ugly something lurking in there. Stazie climbed out of her bed and tucking her favorite toy frog Hoppy under her arm, toddled down the hallway looking for her parents. Their bedroom door was closed and a dim light shone from underneath the door. When she reached up to try the doorknob with her small hands, it was locked.

"Mommy? Daddy? Can I sleep with you?" she called to them as she knocked on the door.

They did not answer. Turning away dejected, she went only as far as the end of the hallway, but the dark living room stopped her. The big ugly something could be out there waiting for her to come back. She didn't want to go back to her bedroom, so she returned to her post by their door, rubbing her eyes and yawning.

She could hear some strange noises coming from their room. Her father was breathing hard, like he did when he would go jogging. Her mother was making groaning noises like she had a tummy ache. Stazie was about to knock once more when she heard her mother cry out and her father yelling back. She thought they were having a yelling match to see who was louder. Then it was quiet.

The child put her ear to the door to find out what had happened, when she heard low voices at first, too low for her to understand what they were saying.

Then she heard her father say plainly, "Aw, babe, not that again. What's the matter now? You have everything. Money, clothes, this place. You wanted a kid, you got one. You wanted a career, you have one. I don't understand what it is you want."

"I want my happiness. I want a life. I want my freedom. Being with you is all a sham. I've told you that! I've put up with it for more than four years already. I can't stay here anymore," her mother said.

"But what about Stazie? Don't you care what happens to her?"

"Doug, this is all shit. It just isn't working. You know it isn't. I'm not even going to pretend it is."

"But she's only a baby. What am I going to do with her?"

A few minutes later, there was some more talking in low voices. She thought she heard Daddy crying but that couldn't be right because her daddy never cried. Stazie decided that he was telling Mommy a story so she could sleep even if she had a tummy ache. She wished they would let her in so she could hear the story too. By that time, she had grown very sleepy and decided to curl up on the floor outside of their door to get comfortable. In the morning, she would ask them all about the story and why they were using their outside voices inside when it was bedtime.

When she awoke, she was in her bed once more. She found her father sitting at the kitchen table by himself with his head in his hands. Her mother was nowhere to be seen. When she crawled up into his lap, she remembered how he had held onto her so tightly that she told him she couldn't breathe.

Stazie pulled the leather jacket around her and blew into her hands, trying to warm them while she pushed away the painful memory of that time long ago. She briskly rubbed her legs that were covered in goose bumps. It was hard to see out the window. The frozen rain had formed an ice sheet on the windshield now that the wipers no longer worked. She never thought she would admit it, but she wished Natal would come back.

⁂

Rey stumbled about in the darkness for more than thirty minutes. It was hard going with no trail to follow. At first, the exertion from the hike had kept him from feeling the cold. However, after a while, he started to feel a chill and next a coldness seeping down to the bone. It had been over eleven hours since the orange juice and bagel he had for breakfast and his stomach was empty. His shoes were soaked through and freezing, numbing his feet to the point in which he couldn't feel them anymore. He couldn't stop his teeth from chattering loudly and his body trembling uncontrollably.

Just when he decided to turn back, he spied a structure to his right through a clearing in the trees. Feeling lightheaded, he blinked hard again to make sure he wasn't imagining it and when he turned his light toward it, he could make out a small fishing shack. Panning to the left, he saw that he had reached the lake's edge. Across the wide expanse of water, he spotted some distant lights on the opposite shore. Nothing else was visible on the bank along the way.

There was no way Stazie would be able to walk to the other side tonight, he determined. As for himself, he had to warm up soon. From his experiences on the hiking trails and snow runs, he was familiar with the symptoms of hypothermia and knew he had to keep moving before he got worse.

He returned his attention to the shack resting by the bank. It was nothing fancy by any stretch of the imagination, probably just a little getaway for a fisherman. The way the temperature felt, he doubt even an avid fisherman was occupying it tonight. He tried the door to find that it was locked. When he peered through the single small window, he could see there were a cot and chair inside, but more importantly a propane heater and what looked like a rolled up sleeping bag in the corner.

This is going to have to do, he decided.

He kicked the door in. The old lock gave away easily. Although he felt odd about breaking and entering, his actions were determined by a question of survival. He would pay for any damages as long as they had a place to stay, safe from the elements.

Immediately, he went to the propane heater but discovered its fuel tank was empty. They would have to do without heat. Nevertheless, it was shelter and a helluva sight better than a bashed up, freezing car on the side of an embankment. He was tempted to stay for a few minutes to warm up before going for Stazie. But if he felt this cold, how was she doing back there? He had to go back.

When he stepped outside, it took him a few seconds to get his bearing. He knew confusion could set in easily when a person got too cold and he strained to keep his wits about him. Concentrating, he carefully made his way back to the car. *It should be quicker on our return to the shack*, he told himself now that he knew where he was going.

Stazie was startled by his sudden appearance from the darkness, although she was relieved to see him. The door opened and he climbed in. His hair, eyebrows, and sweater were covered with ice slivers and his nose and cheeks were crimson red. She could see he was shivering violently.

"I-I found a shack d-down by the l-lake," he struggled to say over his chattering teeth.

"Is it far?"

"N-not t-too far. Y-you'd b-be able to m-make it if-f- y-you k-keep m-moving."

"I was thinking, what about the cabin? Could we make it back there?"

He shook his head.

"What about the bait shops?"

"A-across the l-lake. T-too f-far . . . Hat?"

"What? Oh, I can't wear that thing. It flattens down my hair too much."

Blinking at her in disbelief, he decided not to make the stuttering effort to tell her what he was thinking at that moment. Instead, he took the hat from her and put it on himself.

"G-got to g-get going. C'mon," he said, grabbing up his pack.

He opened the door and hoisted himself out once more, summoning extreme effort from his sluggish muscles. Holding her purse, Stazie climbed across the seats and pulled herself out for the first time. She squealed as the wind blew against her legs. Then she reached for the flashlight he held in his hands and shone it on her car.

"Ohhh my goodness. We were in there?" she said incredulously.

"C'mon. Th-this way," Rey said, not wanting to linger much longer.

The sleet was starting to lighten and they were able to see more clearly as they walked. Stepping over dead branches and sinking her heels into the freezing loam of the saturated earth made the trek difficult. More than a few times, wind gusts nearly blew her down. Not wanting to risk losing sight of him, Stazie made sure to stay right on his heels. It wasn't a problem to keep up because he was moving slower than usual. In fact, she thought he looked like a shuffling old man. It was a stark contrast to the confident Natal striding easily down the road earlier today.

Once the bitter cold settled around her head and her ears started to sting, she said, "Um, excuse me, I think I'll take the hat now, please."

Begrudgingly, he handed it over his shoulder to her.

They reached the fishing shack in almost half the time it had taken him to find it in the first place. He was relieved to see the humble building. Once they got inside, Stazie pushed past him and plunked herself down on the cot. She curled up in his leather jacket, holding onto her legs to keep warm. Rey searched about the shack and found a small battery powered lantern. He tried to turn it on but his fingers were too stiff and numb with cold. Holding it out to her, she just looked at it.

"What?"

"T-turn it on," he said.

"Can't you?" she asked, not wanting to expose her hands.

He shoved it at her. She did as she was told, put the lit lantern on the cot, and went back to curling up. He handed her the sleeping bag and then turned to the task of looking for an alternate heat source.

"Uh, excuse me."

Her voice behind him sounded so far away, he wasn't sure if he was starting to hear things.

"I'm sorry. But I can't seem to find my inhaler. I think it may have dropped out of my purse when I got out of the car. Is there any way you can get it for me?" she said.

Perplexed, he could not fathom how she dropped it. *She probably forgot it on her lap.*

"I know you probably think I'm an idiot and I wouldn't ask but the way things are going tonight I might really need it. So . . . would you?" she implored.

"It-it's all r-right," he said, shivering uncontrollably.

Once again, Rey debated whether to warm up first or go out now while he was wet and miserable. He decided to get it over and done with so he could come back to dry out and stay warm for the remainder of the night. Now that they had established the route to the shack, it shouldn't take him anytime at all. Although his body instinctively fought against it, he forced himself to go back outside. About halfway, he realized he wasn't thinking clearly and should have had Stazie cover up with the sleeping bag while he took his jacket back. It would have provided some warmth. But he wasn't about to turn around and lose more time. He would just press on, get the inhaler, and get back.

Stazie thought that Natal looked a little on the cold side when he left but most guys she knew were fine with the cold. She inspected her surroundings. There wasn't much in the small nine-foot-square building. Just the cot she was sitting on, a chair, the heater in the corner, a couple of buckets and cooking pots, a toolbox, and a pile of fishing magazines. Opening up the sleeping bag, she wrapped it around herself, jacket and all, and covering her head, snuggled down to wait.

When Stazie finally felt warm enough to drop the bag from her head, it occurred to her that Natal had been gone for quite some time. Even if she doubled the amount of time it had taken them to walk to the shack, he had been gone for longer than that. *Maybe he was lost?* She thought about it some more, then her eyes narrowed with suspicion. *Or maybe he found someone on the road and is now on his way to dinner and hotel in a nice warm car.* He probably would leave her here out of spite and fetch her in the morning.

A thump outside interrupted her escalating thoughts. It was an odd sound and close by. She hesitated for a moment, straining her ears. She wished that Natal would come back already. There was no lock on this door and who knows who or what could come in. Summoning up some courage, she got up and cautiously peeked out the little window by the door. There wasn't anything out there in the blackness. Stazie returned to her spot on the cot and glanced about the dreary little shack. *There's probably spiders all over this place*, she thought with a shiver.

She picked up a magazine and idly thumbed through it. Uninterested, she tossed it back down, feeling restless. Again her mind chewed on the possibility that Natal was long gone by now and she started to grow impatient. Thoughts of various movies she had watched where people were attacked out in the middle of nowhere and their bodies never found ran through her head. In another twenty minutes, she started to panic. Throwing back the sleeping bag, she went to the door, flung it open and peered out into the night. *Where IS he?*

"Hey! Hey Natal! Are you out there?" she called out.

It was silent except for the sleet coming down again.

He left me here. How could he? Now what am I going to do?

As she started to turn away, a faint patch of light on the ground caught her eye. It was an odd light and she couldn't figure out what it was. Suddenly it occurred to her —the flashlight. She sensed movement near the flashlight and went back in to get the lantern. Shining it out the door before her, she could just make out the top of Natal's head. He was lying face down on the frozen ground about fifteen feet away, the dying flashlight clutched in his outstretched hand before him.

She shone the light around, cautiously. *Oh no! Was he attacked by some kind of animal or . . . a killer?*

"Hey, are you okay?" she called out.

He continued to lie still.

"Oh poop."

She reluctantly stepped outside. The sleet stung her dry face and neck. Reaching him, she stooped down and shone the lantern in his face. His eyes were closed and his mouth was open. Then she moved the light down the rest of him. It didn't look like he had any injuries or bites taken out of him and it looked like he had tripped over a tree root.

She shook his shoulder. "Hey, what's the matter? Are you okay?"

Stazie could see the faintest flutter from his eyelids. Although she couldn't tell what was wrong, a dormant instinct within her told her that she should get him inside and out of the frozen rain. Bending over, she tried hoisting him up by his shoulders but ended up dropping him. Her mini-skirt restrained her movements, making it difficult for her to get a good footing in her heels. She shook him hard.

"Natal! Wake up! I can't move you," she yelled in his ear. "You're going to have to get up. C'mon, GET UP!"

He started to stir. She seized the opportunity to grab his arms and start tugging him toward the door as his legs kicked in a sluggish crawl. It took almost ten minutes to reach the shack and shut the door behind them. She was panting heavily by that time and fell back onto the cot, trying to catch her breath. Then she sat up and looked at him lying on the floor. He had stopped moving.

Something didn't look quite right. She rose off the cot and knelt down beside him. Seeing his exposed neck, she reached out timidly and felt it. Her hand recoiled immediately at the feel of his skin. It was ice cold. She wrung her hands, not knowing what to do. She listened for any breathing and held her hand up to his nose to feel him exhale. There was no breath.

Oh my goodness! Is he dead? she thought with alarm.

She thought about when she had first heard the thump and estimated that he had been lying out there for almost thirty minutes. Putting her ear to his chest to listen to his heart, the icy wetness of his sweater against her cheek made her pull back. She wasn't expecting that. Trying again, she forced her ear against his chest once more. There was no sound.

He is dead! I'm alone here with a dead guy!

Pressing her ear hard to where she guessed his heart was, she listened carefully and heard a faint beat. Then she heard another faint beat a couple of seconds later. He was indeed alive but she knew his heart was beating way too slow.

What should I do? What should I do?

The first thought was to get him warm. She lifted his hand and started rubbing it vigorously. It remained limp. Dropping it, she tried rubbing his cheek and neck instead. Still, no response.

Oh please, you better not die on me.

She glanced around, feeling frightened. There was no one to call, no one to help. Everything was entirely up to her. Her eyes fell on the sleeping bag that kept her cozy just minutes before. She placed it on top of him. A few minutes later, he still hadn't moved. Checking his heartbeat she noticed its pace had not picked up. Stazie was growing increasingly agitated. All she had wanted was her inhaler. She never intended on killing anyone over it.

Wracking her brain she remembered another movie she had watched a while ago. The guys in the flick were on a rafting trip and had gotten stuck somewhere freezing. They ended up taking off all their clothes and huddling together for warmth in a cave. Although the movie was a comedy, it seemed like it could work.

Grabbing up the cooking pot and a cigarette lighter that she found by the heater, she figured she could start a small fire in it. Then tearing off pages from the magazines, she crumpled them into balls, and lit them with. She placed the pot by him. The paper burned quickly and created a lot of smoke, but she kept adding pages.

She plucked off the sleeping bag. Tugging at his soggy sweater, she pulled it up as high as it would go around his neck. Then she stretched out his limp arms to get the garment over his head and off. Next, she tackled the wet tee-shirt that clung to him. It was much more difficult to get off than the sweater but when she finally pulled it off, she was surprised at what she saw.

By the combined light of the fire and lantern, she was able to see that his body wasn't anything like she had expected. She always thought that he would be an underbuilt nerd, doughy and soft. But in fact, his torso was quite built with well-defined pects, shoulders, and abs.

Where has he been hiding _this_?

She wondered what else she would find. The frozen trekkers and socks came off next. Then she unbuckled his belt and pulled down his zipper. Going back to his ankles, she tugged hard at the cuffs of the uncooperative wet jeans. After a fight, she finally worked them off, exposing his muscular thighs and calves, and leaving him only in his boxer briefs.

I guess all that bicycle riding pays off, she thought as she was forced to acknowledge what was before her.

Giving into her curiosity, she let her eyes travel up his legs to his clinging briefs. She caught herself and immediately grew embarrassed for him over the vulnerability of his unconscious state. Feeling ashamed at her behavior, Stazie covered him with the sleeping bag.

As she gathered up the wet clothing, she found her inhaler tucked safely in his jeans pocket. Once more, her face burned with shame as she studied it and then the man who risked his life to get it. She couldn't recall anyone who had ever done anything so incredibly kind for her.

Looking around she felt she had to do more to get him warm. Her eyes spied the cot. She knew she would never be able to lift him onto it. But what if she moved the mattress to the floor? First feeding more crumpled pages to the pot, she then pulled the dusty thin mattress to the floor and laid it beside him. Next by pushing, pulling, and rolling, she maneuvered him onto it.

Taking a moment to catch her breath from all the exertion and taking a precautionary puff from her inhaler, she watched him carefully in the dim light. She thought by now, he would be moving about and snuggling in under the bag like she always did when she was cold. However, he remained lifeless. Sensing that something was still not right, she pulled back the sleeping bag. His skin continued to feel icy and in the firelight, he looked gray and stiff. She returned her ear to his chest. Although his heartbeat had picked up in pace, it was still slow and weak. Until now, it hadn't occurred to her that he might not survive the night. The severity of the situation shook her. The overwhelming responsibility scared her like nothing had ever before.

After spreading out his clothes to dry and throwing a couple more magazines into the pot, she crawled in under the sleeping bag with him but her own wet clothes made it feel even colder. Rethinking things, she stripped down to her bra and panties. Last she pulled the hat on his head, spread the leather jacket over the top of them, and settled in close. Despite all that she had done for him thus far, she couldn't help but be repulsed at the cold clammy feel of his skin. So she rolled him up on his side away from her, and then settled down as best as she could with her back against his.

There, Stazie lie in the small firelight, tired and hungry, the evening's events running through her head. She had been in an accident, her car was totaled, and she was out in the middle of nowhere, struggling to keep warm, with someone's life depending upon her. She always had so much in her life, never having known hardship of any kind. Yet with all her wealth, here she was, huddled under a smelly sleeping bag with a frozen half-dead guy that she didn't like in a tiny shack by the lake, hoping that he would survive.

In time, the shack started to feel a little warmer although her feet were still cold. At least she and Natal weren't freezing anymore. She could hear the wind outside and the frozen rain pelting the tin roof. It suddenly struck her—she had handled a crisis all on her own. It was her very first and she had come through. A newfound sense of pride filled her. Although she was physically uncomfortable, the moment was exhilarating like nothing she had ever experienced.

That was *if* he made it.

Aware of her charge once more, she turned to him. His skin was now dry but still cool to the touch. She listened against his back. His heartbeat had picked up its pace. Reaching around him, she laid her hand on his chest and felt it rise and fall with deeper breaths. It looked like he was going to be okay. Or so she hoped. She would have to make sure she kept track of him during the night just in case he took a turn for the worst for some reason.

The lantern's light dimmed to an orange glow from the low battery. The paper in the pot completely burned out, leaving nothing but smoldering ashes. Stazie was settled in under the bag and jacket, not wanting to get up to feed it and feel the cold again. Exhausted, with little left to hold her attention in the darkness, sleep finally caught up with her.

When Natal twitched and called out in the early hours, Stazie was awake in an instant although her head felt fuzzy. Turning over, she couldn't see him in the dark. He remained his side but he finally felt warm and was mumbling something. Listening closely, she barely made out a few words.

"No . . . Sorry . . . I'm sorry . . ." he murmured.

His improved condition encouraged her. Making sure the jacket was pulled up on them and the sleeping bag covered him completely to keep out the draft, she returned to sleep.

The stillness of a new day permeated the tiny shack. The morning light entered through the small window. As Rey turned onto his back, he jostled Stazie awake. He felt toasty next to her now, his body putting off a lot of heat. He stuck an arm out from the sleeping bag and draped it over his head.

Although Stazie felt hung over, she couldn't get back to sleep in the strange environment. However, she wasn't ready to leave the warmth of the covers. It was too early and the shack was still cold. Stiff from sleeping on her left side most of the night on the thin mattress and hard floor, she rolled onto her right. There before her, lay Natal. For the first time since she met him, she made up her mind to take a good look at this man who perplexed and aggravated her.

His normal coloring had returned, making him look tan and healthy. Her eyes wandered from the long fingers on his curved hand, to his muscular arm resting above his head. They lingered on the features of his face, his straight nose, his parted lips, the shadow of a beard on his lean cheeks, the small faded scar over his left eyebrow. Curiosity prompting her to continue her assessment, she gently tugged the beanie off his head without disturbing him. His face was framed by wavy brown hair and sideburns flanked his square jaw.

According to the standards of the women in her group, he was unrefined, and not at all like the pretty, metrosexual primps they were used to. Instead, here before her was a *man,* and truth be told . . . an attractive one. She blinked hard, not believing her eyes as if it were all a clever illusion.

Has he always been this way? And if so, how could I have possibly missed this?

Carefully she pulled back the sleeping bag to reveal the rest of him while he slumbered on, undisturbed. As she let her eyes browse over his well-defined neck, chest, and biceps, she noted that his body was hard and fit on his medium frame. She wondered how she could have never noticed. Even the hair on his arms and chest intrigued her. All of the males she knew were plucked, waxed, and shaved clean.

It was hard to imagine that this was the same annoying Rey Natal from yesterday. He looked so completely different this morning. She felt funny inside all of a sudden as if her core were filled with electrical pulses. An analysis from within told her what was amiss. There was no denying it — strangely, she found herself attracted to him.

Although he looked peaceful, the circles under his eyes indicated he had been through a rough night. In an instant, she was filled with remorse, recalling how he was always willing to be kind and civil to her despite her being rude, snotty, and unforgiving. She thought about how he had refused to indict her over the first accident, tried to apologize on the beach, rescued her when she was drunk, offered his sandwich to her, and even gave up his jacket last night. His very last act of retrieving her inhaler when he was obviously freezing and in trouble had almost killed him.

He could have died last night trying to help <u>me</u>.

Guilt enveloped her. What was it about this man that had made her behave like she did towards him? She needed to sort through all the confusing and conflicting thoughts that flooded her head and being this close to him was terribly distracting. She pulled back up the sleeping bag to cover him and then slipped out so he wouldn't awake. Putting on his leather jacket, she zipped up her boots, grabbed her purse, and stepped outside, quietly closing the door. The air was frigid and clear, and the wind blew the icicles on the tree branches above like wind chimes. Although the cool air helped clear her mind, the implication continued to resound. He had always been up front and genuine. She on the other hand . . . just what kind of person was she?

Ice lay in sheets on the ground where puddles froze. The sky was overcast but it looked like the storm had abated. The cold air hit her legs and floated up under the jacket, reminding her that her bladder was full. Against every fiber of her being, she finally resorted to going behind a tree. When she reached down to retrieve her tissue and hand sanitizer, she was surprised to find her purse had frozen fast to the frigid ground. After she pulled it free, she hurried back to the wood structure, knowing it would be much warmer in there than out here. They were lucky they had found the shack.

He had found the shack, she reminded herself. There was no telling what would have happened to them last night if he hadn't.

Rey remained where she had left him. She took another close look at him, just in case the cold air had cleared her head enough to show that she had been dreaming and he had mutated back to his old repulsive self when she was outside. But as she gazed at his face, she had to admit with a sigh and a flutter from within—he was incredibly fine.

She couldn't wait to get back under the covers to his toasty warmth. More so, this would be the first time she had ever woken up with someone. There had been only two physical encounters in her past, however neither of the guys she had slept with stayed until the morning. The encounters were brief at best and mostly one-sided, favoring his needs. Although these would-be lovers were quick to get her into bed, they were equally as quick to leave afterward, leaving her to spend the remainder of the night alone. The next day, she would wait to hear from them but they never called back.

Even the last one who told her he was in love with her had left. It hurt too much to admit to herself that they were simply one-night stands.

She huddled up close to Rey, soaking in the heat radiating from him. His skin gave off a light scent that was inviting but unfamiliar to her. As she settled in, he turned onto his side away from her, much to her disappointment. In the increasing daylight, she spied a large scar that ran beneath the curve of his left shoulder blade. It wrapped around to the side of his chest a couple of inches under his armpit, marring his otherwise perfect back. It shocked her.

Where could he have gotten such an injury? She wondered.

It looked recent and she could almost count the marks left by the hundred or more stitches he must've received. Curious, she reached out a timid finger to touch the scar.

Rey opened his eyes. At first he didn't know where he was. Last he knew, he was stumbling almost blind through the freezing rain, trying to reach the small square of light that shone from the shack's window through the dark stands of trees. Now his eyes focused on a metal cot frame and a dusty wood floor. He blinked hard.

How did I end up here? And . . . where are my clothes?

Feeling her touch, he flipped onto his back and looked at her. Startled, she let out a small gasp and pulled back her hand. It was the moment she had been waiting for; he was awake. But then again, he might be angry with her for almost losing his life to retrieve her inhaler that she had dropped. She braced herself.

"What happened? How did I—?" he said, groggy and confused.

She contemplated his eyes, completing her survey of him. They were dark brown, almost black, and brightened by a certain spark that danced in them. She gulped, not believing how she could have overlooked those eyes before. Even more preposterous was the fact that she had *disliked* this man. She searched for the resentment she had harbored inside for him only yesterday but it was no longer there. With his eye upon her, she caught her breath as that funny feeling filled her again. It was as if he had been magically transformed over the course of a night.

"You must've tripped and fallen outside last night in the storm. I found you on the ground," she said quietly, finding her voice.

"So you . . . ?"

"I pulled you inside." She added quickly, "I'm sorry about taking off your clothes but they were all wet and cold. You had to get warm."

He rubbed his face, trying to wake up. "No, no. I understand. You did the right thing."

"I *did?*" Inwardly, she beamed at his affirmation. "You were icy cold and hardly breathing. I listened to your heartbeat and it was really slow. So I put you on the mattress and covered you up and lit a fire, there in that pot." She was eager to tell him all that she did. "Even then, you were still so cold and not moving, so I thought I could share some of my body heat with you to warm you up. I saw it in a movie once."

He held the sides of his head and closed his eyes. "Oh shit," he muttered.

His response puzzled her. She fretted, "What? Did I do something wrong?"

"No, not at all. You did great. I screwed up. I can't believe I was dumb enough to let myself get hypothermic that's all."

Although she wasn't sure what 'hypothermic' was, she knew he still approved of what she did. She swelled with pride.

Rey faced her, propping his head up on his arm. "Thank you. For giving me a hand and for, well, basically saving my life. I would've been a goner last night, for sure," he said, his voice filled with gratitude.

Stazie gobbled it up, enjoying his gaze directly on her but then immediately felt sheepish. Although relieved that he hadn't mention anything about having to return to the car for her inhaler, she knew that if it weren't for her, he would have never gotten into trouble in the first place.

He returned to lying on his back, yawning and stretching. The hypothermia had worked him over and he still felt tired. Looking at the ceiling he couldn't help but be amused at the thought of Stazie in her miniskirt and high-heeled boots trying to move him at all. It must've looked like something out of a comedy. He was surprised she had even attempted it in all of that sleet. But she did. If anyone would have asked him just the day before if she was capable of something like this, he would have said 'No way. She's too soft.' Or worse yet, 'Her? She's too coldhearted.' He wondered why, after the way she had been acting towards him, that she didn't just go to bed last night and leave him outside.

It suddenly occurred to Rey that Stazie was stripped down next to him under the sleeping bag. The sight of her clothes lying on the cot frame confirmed it. It was an odd position to be in, to say the least. He was going to have to play this cool. If he so much as comprised her modesty in any way, even unintentionally, he would probably be facing charges and a massive lawsuit. It was definitely time to bail out of that bag.

Rey stretched his arms above his head one last time, then sat up. A pain shot through him making him reach over and massage his scarred shoulder, moving his arm joint slowly to work out the morning stiffness. Wondering how he was going to get up to get dressed, he figured he had to be discreet to avoid embarrassing her. Although she obviously had seen him the night before, he was unconscious then. She might pitch a fit if he paraded around in his boxer briefs when he had his faculties about him. This morning started out quiet enough and he wanted it to stay that way. Picking up his jacket off the sleeping bag, he slipped it around his waist to cover up, pulled back the sleeping bag, and stood up. Still feeling the effects from the abuse his body had endured, he was overcome with dizziness and subsequent head rush, making him hold onto the cot frame to steady himself.

"Are you okay? Do you need to lie back down?" she said, a bit worried.

She let her eyes roam over the hard contours of his back.

He blinked hard again. "Seems like the side of my head caught part of your dashboard last night when the airbag deployed. But I'll be fine."

"Are you sure? Maybe you should lie back down," she said as she sat up, covering herself with the sleeping bag.

Rey spotted his clothes and thought it curious the careful manner in which they were laid out to dry. He would have expected her to leave them in a pile on the floor. Instead, they were smoothed flat, side-by-side across the top of the cold propane heater. His shoes were neatly placed beneath them and his socks laid out flat on the floor. He would have never taken her for one to be tidy with anything, especially things belonging to him. Yet her things were hanging haphazardly on the cot frame.

"Are your clothes dry?" she asked.

"Yeah, well, pretty much so. Thank you for laying them out."

He didn't have the heart to tell her that they were still very damp.

"Uhh, you might want to close your eyes. I have to, uh . . ."

She looked at him puzzled. Then her eyes widened.

"Oh sure. No problem," Stazie said as she lay back down and pulled the bag over her head.

Seeing this, he turned his back to her and dropped the jacket. With a shiver and recall of being so incredibly cold the night before, he slipped on his chilly jeans.

"Okay, you can come out now." Then he stepped barefooted into his trekkers and put his jacket on without his shirt. "If you'll excuse me, I have to see a man about a horse," he said politely with a slight wink.

That certain spark in his eye she now recognized as one of mischief. He opened the door and left the shack.

Arrrgghh, why did he have to do that? She squealed inwardly, treasuring that tiny wink and feeling giddy. She had to catch herself once more. *I've got to stop being so goosey. It's only Rey. I mean, Natal . . . No. It's <u>Rey</u>.*

She couldn't believe the way she was behaving this morning. What had gotten into her? She touched around her forehead wondering if she, too, had somehow knocked it during the accident and didn't know it. She couldn't find any lumps or bruises, nothing there to explain this crazy feeling. Anticipating her period in another week and a half, she hastily concluded that it must be a hormone thing. Although she knew she had never felt this way about anyone during any of her cycles. She couldn't wait to get home to soak in a bubble bath. There, in her own environment, she could gather her wits about her and act herself again.

Stazie got up, dressed, and tried to smooth out the wrinkles in her clammy clothes. She fished her mirror out of her purse to check herself over and gasped when she spied the puffiness about the bridge of her nose, complete with light purplish bruise from the accident. Her hair was limp from the rain the day before and matted flat on the side where she had slept. Mascara smudges under her eyes like dark half moons accentuated the bruising, making her look ghoulish. She looked like a wreck.

He saw me like this? she thought and panicked.

In desperation, she squirted hand sanitizer on a tissue in an attempt to rub off the mascara. It worked only marginally as the fumes stung her eyes. Her comb didn't do much to liven up her limp hair. She checked her breath and since she couldn't brush her teeth, she popped a breath mint instead. She couldn't do anything about her bruised nose, so she dabbed foundation on it, brushed some blush onto her cheeks, and applied lipstick.

Springing into action, she returned the sleeping bag and mattress to their places on the cot frame. Tossing the remainder of the magazines under the cot, she stowed the pot back in a corner. She was debating whether she should be sitting or standing when he entered, when suddenly he walked in catching her off guard. Her heart gave a jump when she saw him.

This can't possibly be the same guy, she thought as she saw how incredibly sexy he was with his bare chest, open leather jacket, and jeans.

"Wow, you've got everything put away in here already," he said.

He noticed.

"Boy, that was a helluva storm, wasn't it? Everything's frozen over out there. I saw the place where I did the face plant and I could even see the drag marks leading up to the door. You really got a work out, didn't you?" he said admirably, flashing her a grin.

He has dimples. Her heart pounded.

"Oh, it was nothing," she said and blushed. "I'm just glad I was able to do it."

"So what do you want to do now?"

"I don't know, Rey. I'm fine with whatever you want to do."

REY? She called me Rey?

Of all the insults and spats she had hurled at him over the past couple of months, he couldn't recall if she had ever addressed him by his first name. In addition, she had never wanted to hear any of his ideas before. He couldn't help but wonder why she was being so agreeable and cooperative this morning. And then she was blushing and smiling so much too. It was odd. He felt on guard, knowing that a sneak attack should be in store for him at any moment. This might all be just the set up.

"Well, I was thinking that if you felt up to it, while the weather is clear, we could try walking around the lake to the other side. Find a phone and call for a ride and a tow truck. Maybe get something to eat while we wait?"

"Sure. But that's if you feel up to it. You're the one who almost died last night, remember?"

Is that what this is all about? I must've really scared the hell out of her, he realized. It made sense. He decided to put her fear at ease.

"I feel fine. Don't worry, I don't expect to keel over anytime soon."

"I hope not," she said shyly and then averted her eyes.

He smiled nervously. She definitely was acting bizarre. This was the woman who would have gladly torn his head off just the day before. He tried to shift the attention onto her.

"Hey, how are you feeling? I'm sure sleeping on that cot mattress couldn't have been too comfortable for you. Are you sore from the accident in any way? How's your nose?"

She fought hard to control the tremor in her voice, "I-I'm fine. Really." She blushed again.

Rey studied her hard for a moment.

"Well, that's good . . . Before we go, is there anything else you need from your car before we leave it there all day? Your registration or insurance or anything like that?"

"No. Nothing."

"All right then. How about you wear this." He took off his jacket and handed it to her. "It's still chilly out there."

"No Rey, you should—"

"Nah. I'll be fine. I've got my sweater and as the sun comes up, it should warm up in a bit."

She accepted the jacket and slipped into it, savoring his lingering body heat and knowing he was just there. Her eyes trained on his well-defined torso and arms as he went to the heater and started pulling on his shirt.

Shaking herself, she remembered to say, "Thank you. Oh and thank you again for getting my inhaler for me."

When he nodded and smiled, she thought she would faint.

Before they left, Rey made sure everything was as they found it. Next, he tore a page from one of the magazines to write his name and number on it for the owner so he could pay for the damage to the lock. If the shack hadn't been there, they would have been in a world of hurt.

They spent all morning trekking around the lake to get to the bait shops on the other side. Stazie tried her best to keep up with Rey's long stride. Her feet were killing her in boots that obviously weren't designed for hiking cross-country. Gratefully accepting his hand anytime he helped her over a log or rock or incline, she came to long for the feel of it in hers. She wished that they could talk while they hiked along but the going left her breathless although she wasn't quite sure if it was the exertion or the small smiles of encouragement he offered her along the way.

Rey, on the other hand, felt sluggish and slow. All he could think about was having an extra-large sausage, mushroom, and pepperoni pizza when he got back home. He also took into consideration Stazie's ill-chosen footwear and made sure to slow his pace. However, he was surprised that he hadn't heard one argument or complaint from her yet. This had to be a record.

At the bait shop, they called for a ride and tow truck. The lakeside grill was closed but they were able to get some chips and cookies from the vending machine outside the boat rental place. They found a bench to sit down to eat. As they waited, neither one of them could find anything to say. Yet every time he looked her way, Rey couldn't help but notice her stealing glances at him. She even insisted on sharing the cab ride home.

In the back seat of the cab, she drowsily laid her head against his shoulder and with a sigh, fell immediately asleep. Looking at her curls, Rey felt that something had definitely changed between them. He wasn't sure how long it was going to last or if it was for the better. But at least he didn't have to stay on guard for the impending attack anymore. Before he knew, he relaxed and soon was asleep too.

She continued to snooze when the cab reached his place first. Rey got out quietly and paid the driver for his and Stazie's fare, and let her sleep on still curled up in his jacket.

His apartment was empty when he opened the door. A note on the counter read:

> *Rey,*
>
> *Got your mutt after it got late and I stopped by with tickets to the Game and you weren't home. Call me.*
>
> *R.*

After a long shower and a hot pizza, Rey lay across his new bed, exhausted. Too tired to sleep just yet, he puzzled over Stazie's polar behavior. There was something up with that chick. He hadn't met any person who was more erratic. Rey had dated a few women in the past and while some were moody at times, it was nothing like this. Had women gone crazy since the last time he dated?

Before he closed his eyes, he remembered Rick had wanted him to call. He knew it was just his big brother checking up on him but he was willing to oblige him so he wouldn't worry. He dialed and waited for him to pick up.

"Yo."

"Hey Rick, it's me."

"Rey! I've got Jackie here. Where've you been, man? I've been trying your phone but all I keep getting is your voicemail."

"Don't ask. Believe me, I'll tell you later. I'm too tired right now. And thanks for taking Jack."

"No prob. Good to hear you're home."

"Thanks. Good to be home."

"All right."

"And Rick? One more thing . . ."

"Yeah?"

"Marry Marcie. Don't let her get away from you. You don't know what you've got there."

"Wha–?"

"You've got to trust me on this," said Rey as he drifted off to sleep.

There was a moment of silence, and then Rick answered, "Uh . . . sure, Bro."

Chapter 4 ~ The Crush

Carmen Natal loved it when her children came together, filling her and Joseph's home with their laughter, jokes, stories and adventures, and teasing of each other. She would do her best to scold them and act as if she didn't approve of all the teasing but they knew laughter was hidden behind her merry eyes. She was the ultimate straight man.

Now that Gloria was coming to town, they would all take time from their busy lives to see each other. Family time together wasn't as regular as when the kids were still at home. Rick and Marcie had them over for dinner about once a week. Gloria stopped by whenever she could, bringing their precious grandbaby Sela with her. And their own baby boy, Rey . . .

Carmen sighed when she thought about her youngest son. So smart—there never was a doubt that he would be the first one in the family to go to college. And he was a good boy, and sweet, kind to others and helpful. But he had always been so daring and impetuous too, constantly on the move with his biking and hiking and throwing himself down the mountain on that board, almost to the point of being reckless. When he lived at home, Joseph and she would lie awake many nights wondering if and when he would come back safe and sound.

Nonetheless, he got through it all in one piece, graduated summa cum laude, and hired on with a big architectural engineering firm. With relief, Carmen and Joseph saw that there was a bit of an improvement and settling down as he matured, although he never gave up his restless nature. And Rey always came around to visit regularly, dragging friends along to sample his mother's Portuguese home cooking.

His friends were loud and boisterous and always quick to eat anything that was offered. Carmen not only took pride in preparing the food, but satisfaction in knowing her meals pleased them. Often she heard, "Mrs. Natal, that was the best meal I ever had in my life," and "Mrs. Natal? Can I live here?" Joseph sat by quietly during these times, taken aback by their vivaciousness and volume. But she knew by the pleased look on his face, he enjoyed the rabble as much as she.

Her memory turned to Ivan. He was the one with the biggest appetite and smile out of all them under that unruly mop of black hair. He often confused her with his vernacular when he would say something like, "Mrs. N. that bacalao was tight," or "Pass those doinklets over there, please. They look gnarly." But she knew it often meant that he was satisfied. Even more confusing was when he would praise their hospitality by quoting Eliot or Shakespeare. She and Joseph would exchange perplexed looks until Rey translated what he meant. Ivan was their most frequent visitor and her favorite.

Lately within the past year, Rey hardly ever came around anymore. And when he did, he never brought any friends with him. Whereas mealtimes use to be lively and entertaining, now when he dined with them, he was quiet and introspective. So much had changed since then. She prayed every night for all of her family but she always put in an extra prayer for her Rey, hoping that he would find happiness and peace once more in his life. Although she got much more sleep these days knowing that he was safe and settled, she would trade it all just to hear him laugh out loud the way he used to.

Atop of the step stool, she stretched her plump figure up on tiptoes to reach a platter in the high cupboard, yet it still escaped her grasp.

"Joe?" she called to her husband who was reading *The Daily News* with his afternoon cup of coffee in hand. "Would you please get the platter down for me?"

Having not paid attention to what she was doing, he looked up from his paper and gave a start. "Carmen!" he said, "What are you trying to do? Kill yourself? Here, get down and let me get that for you."

He waited patiently for her to get off the step stool, offering her his hand as she stepped down and then he climbed up there himself, his arthritic knee giving him some complaint. He was only a couple of inches taller than she but he knew his wife depended on him to get anything out of her reach now that their tall sons no longer lived at home anymore. He lowered down the platter to his squat wife.

"Anything else you need up here?"

"The gravy bowl, the carafe, and the big salad bowl."

"What is all of this for?" he asked as he retrieved each item.

"I told you already. The kids are all coming over tomorrow night for dinner. Gloria and the baby? Rick and Marcie?"

"That's right! Rey too?"

"Yes, he should be here. Ricky said that he told him."

"Good, good." The old man smiled. "Is he bringing his friends too?"

"I don't think so, Joe. We'll have to wait and see."

It had already been a couple of days and she knew she should return it. By now, she was familiar with every crease and wrinkle on its water-stained surface. She knew there was a ballpoint pen and a couple of folded clean tissues in the right pocket, and a subway token, an auto show ticket stub, and a wrapped toffee candy in the left. She ran her hand over the leather jacket hanging on her bedroom chair. *He probably needs this,* she mused, cherishing the feel of its worn shoulders and sleeves. Still, it was hard to let it go. To do so, might end the reverie that she was in.

All of her life, she had never felt this way, dreamy, light and giggly. She would slip on the jacket, wrap its arms around her and think about those eyes and that smile. She had tried—really tried—to get Thursday morning in the shack out of her mind. But there was no escaping it. When she arrived home from their ordeal, she had soaked in her favorite French bubble bath. And on Friday morning, she had gone shopping and then to the spa for the remainder of the day. Yet nothing she did was enough of a distraction. She found she couldn't eat, couldn't sleep. She couldn't stop thinking about *him.*

Stazie fretted. It puzzled her as to why her feelings for Rey were so strong now. After all the loathing she had had for him, what had changed in her? She thought if she gave it a day or two, she should be back to normal, reasoning it was all due to the emotional roller coaster of being in the accident. But it never did go away. In fact, her thoughts of him only grew more intense as the days passed. And that funny feeling she had first felt at the shack only returned in force, bouncing between her stomach and chest, alternating between butterflies and heartthrob.

The change must have been apparent because even Beatrice noticed. The very next day, when Stazie was sitting there, wondering what he liked to eat for breakfast while waiting for her own, the maid asked her why she was in such a good mood. Beatrice seldom asked that of her, never having a reason to.

Am I that obvious? Stazie questioned herself.

And after breakfast, when she sat staring off dreamily with her food untouched, Beatrice studied her carefully as she removed the plates before her and asked her if she was feeling all right.

The most difficult time about this new predicament was when she was in bed. At night, the only way she could get to sleep was to put one of her pillows against her back to pretend he was there. In the lonely morning light, she propped up another pillow facing her to imagine him sleeping beside her. She didn't know which was worse—having such dislike for him before or having such longing now. Either way, Rey Natal still had the ability to make her feel in knots.

And there was so much she didn't know about him! Why had she wasted all this time? Counting back to their first accident together, she already would've known him for three whole months. She dismally recalled every harsh word, every snotty tone, and every dirty look she had ever given him and wished beyond anything that she could take it all back. There was a good possibility that he would he have liked her by now if she hadn't acted that way, or at the very least, she would have stood a much better chance.

"Oh poop," she sighed with heartbreaking regret.

Stazie thought about calling him. But when she finally built up enough nerve to do so, she realized she didn't have his number and he was unlisted when she called the operator. An internet search on him yielded the same results. She knew her father must have his number but he was still out of town and he would question why she wanted it. Rey hadn't called her but she had to remind herself, *why would he?* There wasn't any reason to, especially if he was trying to avoid her hostility and wrath. *If only he would call about his jacket . . .* However, she figured he most likely would ask her father for it or else do without.

The spacious apartment began to feel like a cage. She grew restless in looking out over the cityscape, wondering what he was doing at that very moment and if he ever thought about her. Stazie wished she could talk to someone about her dilemma but there was no one to confide in. All of her friends would be uninterested because he was not in their social circle. Moreover, they didn't have a good opinion of him largely in part because of the things she had said. Gidge was still visiting her grandmother and she seldom brought up subjects like this with her father, so it wouldn't help even if he were home. Besides, he would only want to grill her over the details of the accident.

By early Sunday morning, after another long day and sleepless night of tossing and turning and heartache, Stazie had had enough. She decided that she would go to him. She knew where he lived. Returning his jacket would be the perfect excuse to go there. He should be home on a Sunday morning, especially if she showed up early. Who didn't sleep late on Sundays?

Fueled by excitement, she flung back her comforter and hopped out of bed. She showered, styled her hair, and moisturized. Taking extra pains to pick out just the right outfit, it had to be one that showed off her figure but complemented her eyes, her best feature in her opinion. *Showing a little cleavage wouldn't hurt either* she thought as she slipped on a push-up bra. She carefully applied her makeup and checked her fingernail polish and toenail polish. Then she chose her finest perfume and amply doused herself in it. Bracelets were slid up her wrists and chandelier earrings dangled from her earlobes.

Last, she picked up his jacket and held it to herself, hugging it, and wishing he were in it. She opened it one last time and put it on, smelling the leather and the lining, hoping to catch his scent and wondering what his arms would feel like around her. Then reluctantly, she slipped the jacket off, folded it carefully, and placed it in one of her big tote bags.

She startled Beatrice when she entered the kitchen. The older woman was reading the newspaper and enjoying some tea and didn't expect to see her mistress so early in the morning.

"Oh, uh, good morning Miss Stazie. I'll get your breakfast started."

"No, relax, Beatrice. There's no need to. I'm not hungry."

The maid nodded with relief. She didn't recall her mistress telling her she needed breakfast early and was worried about becoming forgetful.

"You look like you're off to somewhere special," she said, seeing that Stazie was in yet another good mood.

"Oh, I am. Hope you have a good morning, Beatrice."

"Why, thank you, Miss. I hope you do too."

"I most certainly will," Stazie said, grinning.

Rey flew down the big grassy hill and leaned into a low turn that led under the footbridge. This was the best time of day in the park, when there were no pedestrians in the way or police on patrol to tell him to stay on the bike path. He switched gears, climbed another lesser hill, and then coasted down the other side, testing his skill on some of the flat boulders that were piled up on its bank. As he made it back to the path, he glanced at his watch. It was time he headed home.

Through the quiet Sunday morning streets, he hunkered down, shifted gears, and started to pedal hard, hoping to beat his best time yet. He breathed deep the cool crisp air untainted yet by exhaust. He wove in and out of parked cars, down alleyways, and through light traffic until he reached the final corner on his route.

By the time he reached the storefront of the Three Fortunes Asian Market that stood beneath and to the right of his apartment, he became aware of a sweet odor in the air. Its presence seemed strange on such a cool morning. Not thinking much more about it, he swung off his bike and came to a stop. The stopwatch on his watch read fourteen minutes and forty-eight seconds. That was four seconds better than his fastest time.

Yes, he thought, *this has been a good morning.*

Hoisting his bike and resting the frame on his shoulder, he started to ascend the stairs. He noticed that same sweet odor was even stronger in the stairway, almost to the point of being nauseating. He wondered if Li Zhu had gotten in a bad shipment of kumquats again at the Three Fortunes. As he neared the top of the flight, the smell was overpowering. It was then that he discovered the source.

Looking up, there stood Stazie. Rey froze in his tracks. *What was she doing here? And why so early on a Sunday morning?*

She was decked out to the max like she was ready to go clubbing and beaming down at him with her brightest smile. He was momentarily at a loss for words.

Stazie jumped when she heard someone at the bottom of the stairs. She hoped it would be Rey after being disappointed when no one answered the door. She was pretty sure it was the right apartment. These were the stairs she had seen him emerge from when she came to pick him up. Besides the only other apartment had an Asian name in its name holder on the door.

Unless he was a heavy sleeper or in the shower, she assumed that he was not at home, or worse yet, he wasn't answering the door. She had waited and knocked for fifteen minutes and was about to leave when she heard him on the stair below. Without a sound, she watched him as he started to climb. He wore a helmet and kept his gaze down, watching his step as he carried his bike on his shoulder but she would recognize him anywhere. Her heart went into an instant flutter. And when he looked up at her and stopped, she thought it was going to beat out of her chest.

"Hi," she said shyly with a small wave.

"Uh, hello . . . ?"

He reached the top stair where she stood on the small landing that served his apartment and the apartment next door. There was no way he would be able to squeeze past her and unlock the door while carrying the bike. He hoped she would get the idea to step down so he could get past but she continued to stand there, grinning.

"Um, you're going to have to—ah, move. I can't get to the door with you—"

It suddenly occurred to her what he was politely trying to get at.

"Oh!" she said as she scurried down a couple of stairs, hugging the wall so he could get past. She felt like a fool and blushed deeply.

"Thank you. Hold on just a minute . . ." he said as he set the bike on the landing and fished around in the rear pocket of his riding jersey for his keys.

He unlocked the door and opened it. When he looked down at her, she looked back at him, her face expectant.

Reluctantly, he said, "Um, would you like to come in?"

"Yes, thank you," she said, wasting no time in getting back up the stairs.

Rey placed the bike inside the entry and pulled off his helmet. He glanced uneasily about his place. As always, he had drawings, clothes, books, and LP's everywhere.

"Come in. I'm sorry. I've got kind of a mess here. I wasn't expecting anyone."

"Oh, it's okay. I know I came around unannounced."

She surveyed the tiny apartment. It was his home after all and she wanted to take it all in.

"It's cute," she said. "It's got a lot of potential."

"Well, thanks."

Just then Jack Tate came running out of the bedroom, barking and growling. He reached Stazie's feet and held his ground, jumping and barking in his fiercest manner. Startled, she took a few steps back from the small dog.

"Hey! Hey Jack! It's okay," Rey said.

The little dog stopped barking and promptly lapsed into a combo sit and beg. His bulgy watery eyes peered up at Stazie from his squashed little face.

"Oh, a dog," she said. "Its name is Jack?"

"Yup. This is Jack Tate."

"Jack Tate? Okay . . . And why do you call him that?"

"What? Jack Tate? I had to call him something."

"No, what I mean is that he has, like, a full name. I've heard of dog names like, I don't know, Patches, Fluffy, Spot . . ."

"Right. Same old same old. I figured that a dog has just as much right to a surname as anyone else. Would you like to go through life being called by your first name and getting confused with other Stazies? Or worse yet, how about being named after one of your physical attributes?"

She pondered it for a moment and then said, "Oh. I guess I never gave it much thought."

"Nope. Not too many people have."

It was an old game he and Ivan used to play, one in which they liked to perplex the general public with preposterous ideas. By the confused look on her face, it appeared that it was working on Stazie.

Oh well, so much on attempting to break the ice with a bit of humor, Rey thought.

Jack continued to sit and beg, facing her. He gave a couple of snorts through his pushed-in nose.

"What does he want?" she said.

"It looks like he wants you to pet him. His 'begging-for-food' face is much uglier."

"Oh."

She gave a few tentative pats to the dog's head and then discreetly wiped her hand on her skirt.

Rey unzipped his biking jersey and reached back to pull it over his head. Her eyes riveted back to him. Dressed only in a sleeveless tee and road shorts, he started untying his trekkers and kicking them off.

Yes, she thought with satisfaction. His physique was everything that she remembered it to be as she scanned his arms and legs that were still pumped from riding.

He hung his bike up on the wall rack and then stooped to gather up a few discarded socks, shirts, and a pair of underwear that were strewn about. Embarrassed, he tucked the briefs quickly under the other clothes in his arms.

"Uh, make yourself at home. I'm going to change and I'll be right out, okay?" he said, grabbing his trekkers and heading off to his bedroom.

"Sure. Take your time."

With the bedroom door closed, Stazie felt free to investigate this place he called home. She wandered over to the big drafting table and printer in the corner by the window and perused some of the drawings he had out. She even peered out his window to see what kind of view he had as he worked all day. She took notice of the things hanging on his walls: the few abstract art prints, a couple of Ansel Adams prints of Yosemite and Yellowstone, the full-page ad torn from a magazine featuring a motorcycle, a calendar of scheduled work projects, and a few family photos. One photo was of an older couple, a plump woman and a thin man that she guessed must be his parents. She immediately recognized his features in theirs, noting that he had his mother's eyes. Another photo was of a husky bearded man with two brunettes and a little girl. She was relieved to see that there were no photos of single women in sight.

But then again, she thought, *I haven't seen what he has in his bedroom yet.*

Aside from that, there wasn't much else in the living room except for the sofa and a TV perched on top of a steel milk crate. Stazie went to his stereo rack full of complicated equipment, hundreds of old vinyl LPs, and a few CDs. Her eyes fell upon a photo frame that was missing its glass, sitting on top of the rack. The photo showed Rey and some guy with their arms across each other's shoulders and holding snowboards. What caught her attention was Rey's face. She studied his relaxed, open, happy expression and his bright mischievous eyes. The expression was novel to her, making her long to have him look at her that way one day.

The guy beside him looked like a snow bum and she wondered why Rey would hang out with that sort. Stazie recognized the type from when she and her father would go snow skiing. They were the ones that typically cut them and other skiers off with their hot dogging snowboarding tricks and irreverent attitudes, thinking they owned the slopes.

While she waited in the living room, Rey quickly changed into jeans and his old college sweatshirt. He usually liked to shower after he rode but he had no time with her sitting there, so he just splashed water on his face and brushed his teeth. He made his bed and stowed some of his things should she need to use the bathroom.

He still couldn't figure out why she was here. He tried to recall if Doug had said he would be sending some work over but there was no recollection of anything like that. Maybe she dreamed up some kind of lawsuit against him about wrecking her car because she had to drive him. He hoped not but couldn't be too sure. There was no telling what Stazie's mood was going to be like from one day to the next.

And why was she dressed like that? Her makeup, outfit, and jewelry were reminiscent of the time she had hit him when she was on her way to some kind of nightclub. He planned to open the windows to air out the perfume after she left.

So much for a good morning, he said to himself.

He should have stayed out just a bit longer on his bike. If he hadn't tried to beat his old time, he might have missed her altogether. When he re-entered the living room, he found her scrutinizing the photo of Ivan and him.

She looked up at him. "There you are . . . Who's this in the photo with you?"

He crossed the room and took the frame out of her hands. Returning it to its place on top of the rack, he said plainly, "My best friend, Ivan." Then walking to the kitchenette, he said, "I'm sorry I didn't offer but would you like something to drink?"

Stazie took one last glance at the photo and then joined him by the breakfast counter. She pulled up one of the bar stools. It seemed to be the only place to eat in the apartment. Jack Tate got up from where he was resting and sat by her to beg once more. She eyed him warily and then turned back to Rey. "I would love an espresso right now," she said.

"I've got instant, if you don't mind that. Instant coffee, that is."

Instant coffee? It was another first for her.

"Uh, sure."

She watched him as he filled an old chipped enamel kettle from the tap and set it on the stove. Then from the sparse cupboard he took down two mismatched mugs with company logos on them and heaped some coffee granules into them from a plastic container.

"Do you take any sugar with that?"

"Please. Demerara, if you have it."

He set an open box of plain white sugar in front of her with a teaspoon. She smiled politely at him again as she gingerly pulled them closer.

"I'll take some cream too, please," she said.

He placed a gallon carton of milk next to the sugar. "Will this do?"

"Uh, sure."

An awkward silence developed between them. Feeling he was lacking as a host, he struggled to be cordial.

"So, how have you been since the accident? No hidden injuries or anything that showed up the next day?"

"Me? No I'm fine. Even my nose feels fine. See? The bruising went away."

"Well, good."

"And how about you?"

"Nope. I'm good."

"Good."

Back to the silence once more. Rey was grateful when the kettle started whistling. It would be something to keep him occupied. He poured out the water and mixed the coffee. Then he opened the other cupboards.

"Would you like anything with that? I've got granola bars, power bars, bagels, and I think I even have some cold cereal left . . . I guess that's about it."

She sipped the coffee and fought hard not to make a face. It tasted brackish and was not very smooth like the fresh roasted whole bean coffee she was used to. And none of the food fare he had mentioned sounded even remotely appetizing.

"No thank you. I've—I've already had breakfast," she lied. After months of humiliating him, she was trying her best not to now.

"Well, would you mind if I eat something? I'm starving."

"No, go right ahead."

He shook out a couple of granola bars from their box.

They sipped their coffees for a few minutes more. Then trying to sound casual, he finally asked, "So, were you just in the neighborhood?"

"In the neighborhood? Oh no, I came to return this."

She got off her stool and fetched her tote. From it, she extracted his leather jacket and held it open.

"I thought you might need it especially if the weather acts up again," she said, hoping that he would notice the fact that she was thinking about his wellbeing.

"Hey thanks. You know, I almost forgot about this," he said as he took it from her.

His nose was instantly hit by her perfume emanating from his jacket. *Geez, does she drown everything in that stuff?* He thought as he folded the sweet-smelling jacket and laid it on the sofa arm. He wasn't sure if he'd ever get that smell out.

"You're welcome. I just don't want you to end up like you did out there again. You know, with what did you call it? Hypertheria?"

Hypothermia. He forced a smile. "Nope, I hadn't planned on it."

The conversation lapsed once more but Stazie continued to linger and leisurely sip her coffee. *Okay, what else could she possibly want?*

Rey had a busy day planned centered around his drawings, catching up on laundry, food shopping, and weight training. His parents also expected him at their house by two o'clock for the family dinner at four. He glanced at the clock. It was already a quarter past nine. *There must be a polite way to tell her to leave after she finished her coffee.* Maybe he could say that he had to go help Rick with something. Or something like he had to go to Mass. *It was Sunday morning after all*, he reasoned. But he knew it had been years, much to his mother's shame, since he had last been to a church.

He figured the best thing would be to tell her the truth. He had a ton of stuff to do. She would just have to accept that. For the time being, he would give her until she finished her coffee. Maybe she'd leave on her own accord to get her hair done or hang out with friends or do whatever it was that she did. That would make it easier than, well, basically kicking her out.

Stazie wasn't going anywhere. As far as she was concerned, she was perfectly comfortable where she was. Oh, she knew she was imposing but there were two very good reasons. First, there was absolutely nothing to do at home and no one to do anything with. Reason number two was much more pressing: there was no one she would rather be with than Rey. Just the sheer proximity to him in his tiny apartment was enough to keep her rooted to her chair. She wanted to get to know him, what he was *really* like—his habits, tastes, likes, dislikes. She had wasted so much time already she wasn't going to let any more slip by. Most of all, she wanted to show him, more than ever, that she wasn't as horrid as he probably thought. If she stuck around long enough, he would have to see it.

"What is all of that?" she said, pointing to the stereo cabinet.

"Would you like to listen to something?" he said, hoping that music might help fill the awkward gaps. He picked up the remote from the counter, aimed it at the stereo, and turned on the components.

"Okay."

"How about some Lady Day? I think she's just about perfect for Sunday mornings. But I've got others if you like."

It wasn't a matter of liking to Stazie. The music she was most familiar with was the dance mixes at the clubs and only a few of the pop forty on the streaming. For the most part, music was background noise to her. She never considered making a selection.

"No. Play whatever you like," she said, trying to sound agreeable and not screw things up. "What's-her-name, uh Lady Day, would be fine."

"Okay."

He started his playlist. After the muted trumpet lead-in to *Good Morning, Heartache*, Billie Holiday's sultry voice started to croon about romance, heartache, and longing at the break of day.

Stazie was immediately transfixed. This Lady Day person knew exactly how she felt this morning. Or perhaps Rey somehow guessed what she was experiencing and chose this particular song. Stazie studied him as he drank his coffee and munched on his granola bar. He didn't seem to give any indication that he knew.

She wondered what it would take to see those dimples. Better yet, maybe he would beam like he did in that photograph. The thought filled her with anticipation but she realized she should be making some conversation. Otherwise he might think she was dull.

She heard a snort below her. Jack Tate had given up trying to beg for anything and decided to lie down where he was.

"So what kind of dog is Jack Tate?"

"To the best of my knowledge, Ol' Jackie is part pug, part Chihuahua."

"Oh. Was that intentional?"

"Huh? Nah. I found his litter in a dumpster when he was just a pup. The vet said he was about four weeks old. Some heartless son of a bitch literally threw the entire bunch out. I couldn't find the mother. Yeah, I've had Jack for seven years already."

"Seven years? That's a long time. How long do dogs last anyway?"

"Depends on the breed and their own health. But he'll probably be around for another six or seven more years."

"Oh."

"Do you have any pets?"

"Me? No."

Rey took another sip from his mug.

"Not that I didn't want one. My father just thought that they were too much trouble. I wanted a pony once, so he signed me up for riding lessons. When I fell off, I realized that I didn't want to do that again."

"I see. More coffee?"

"Oh, no thanks."

Rey picked up their empty cups and set them in the sink. The time had come and gone. Still she did not give any sign that she was ready to leave. Dealing with Stazie seemed like a tricky proposition, similar to making friends with a pit bull. One had to handle them with caution or risk losing a body part.

"Yeah, well, I'm kinda slammed today. I'm sure you have things to do, too," he said.

"No. Not really. I just thought I'd hang with you today."

Dumbfounded at her candidness, Rey did a double take. "With me?"

"I won't get in your way. Do you need any help with anything? I can give you a hand."

"Nah, its boring stuff—you know, food shopping, laundry, working on accounts. Nothing I need any help with."

"That's no problem. I'll just sit there on your couch. If you're working on something, I won't disturb you, I promise," she said.

"But I'm not going to be home all day. I have to go somewhere around two."

He knew it was a mistake when it left his mouth. He should have said ten.

"Really? Where?"

"A family get-together. My sister and niece are in town," he said, hoping to dissuade her.

"Great! Can I come?"

She was like a little child who wouldn't take no for an answer. He felt flustered.

"I-it's just a family thing," he said, shrugging.

"Well what do you guys do?"

"We talk, catch up on things, eat dinner. Really, it's just family—"

"Sure! I'd love to come and meet everybody. Sounds like fun."

He was astounded. Short of being overtly rude to her, there was no way to get her to leave. He honestly did not know how to handle this. This was a person who went clubbing and clam baking with the chic and famous. Why would she want to go to a simple family get-together with him whom she absolutely detested? At least that was up until a few days ago.

She looked at him with an innocent stare and flashed her prettiest smile. He sighed inwardly, thinking about her nasty habit of throwing temper tantrums. He couldn't imagine what he would do if she pulled that in front of his family. But she remained firmly rooted to her chair. Aside from bodily picking her up and throwing her out, she was there to stay. He thought about his deal with Doug and knew he really needed this contract. He concluded that he would just have to see how things turned out. If anything, he knew his family could handle themselves.

Rey tried to stick as close to his schedule as possible, hoping she would get bored with his dull average life and go home. After all, what could be more tedious than going to a laundromat? By her own admission she had never set foot inside of one, let alone doing her own laundry. He figured that she probably would split by the time the first load was finished.

To his consternation and ensuing headache, she stuck it out through the first, second, and then third load, while looking about the place and its occupants with half curiosity, half disdain. Every time he rose from his seat, she jumped up, ready to leave, not understanding that there was much getting up and down while laundering.

"Can I help?" she asked, when he got up again, not wanting to be left sitting next to the woman in curlers reading a magazine.

"Sure. If you want," he said. He handed her a basket. "Here, go get the load from dryer number two."

She strolled down the aisle, trying to appear confident but viewing the machines flanking either side of her with uncertainty. She paused in front of a washer that had stopped. Hesitantly, she reached for the door.

"Stazie?" Rey said. He pointed to the dryer behind her.

A few minutes later, Rey couldn't help but eye her curiously as she attempted to fold one of his shirts. Although she tried her best to imitate the folding motions of those around her, she finally rolled the shirt up into a ball and hid it among his folded stacks.

The few other people present were just as curious about the overdressed girl with the expensive jewelry and heavy perfume inside the Sudz 'n Dudz on a Sunday morning. And there were more than a few stares when Stazie broke a nail on Rey's laundry bag and cried, "Oh poop!" followed by a full minute of lamentation. It was time to clear out of there.

This must be my lucky day. Thank you, God, the paunchy middle-aged grocer thought to himself as the attractive young blonde approached his register.

One look at that bosom squeezed into that tight top and those legs, he knew she was put together well. He straightened up his sloop shoulders and tried to suck in his gut, at least to get it level with his belt line.

"Good morning, miss," he said brightly, "How may I help you?"

"Are you the manager?"

"Yes I am. Do you have a concern?"

"I sure do. We have searched and searched your so-called 'coffee aisle' for over five minutes and still cannot find where you keep the Sulawesi roasted whole bean. While I don't expect you to carry Kopi Luwak, you should at least have a basic Sulawesi. In fact, we couldn't find any other recognizable coffee fit to drink either."

A man standing beside her averted his eyes, looking somewhat sheepish, and trying to act as if he were intent on the lottery scratch ticket display. The grocer thought he recognized him as one of his regulars.

Momentarily distracted, the grocer redirected his attention back to her, "And you were looking for . . . ?"

"Sulawesi roasted whole bean. You've had to at least heard of it?" She eyed him.

Not wanting to appear ignorant in front of the attractive woman, he nodded, "Oh yes, yes."

He tried to keep his eyes from straying down to her cleavage but he was weak and he knew there was no point in fighting it.

"Okay, so if you've heard of it, why isn't it on your shelves?"

"Where's what?" His eyes snapped up again.

"Oh, this is impossible." She tugged on Rey's shirt pulling him close and then pointing to him. "*He* needs a suitable coffee in his kitchen. And how about some demerara sugar, organic cream, or fresh croissants? We couldn't find any of those either." She cocked her head and placed her hand on her hip.

"Actually, I'm fine without any of those," Rey piped up, apologetically.

The grocer suddenly recognized him. He was the clown who was always trying to pass off expired coupons.

"Don't listen to him. Of course he needs them. What kind of so-called 'grocery store' are you running here anyway? I don't recognize half of the things you pass off as food here. Maybe if you spent more of your time managing properly instead of staring at women's boobs, I wouldn't be standing here asking you where you keep the Sulawesi. Now how do you intend to correct this matter?" Her eyes narrowed.

Rey knew it was mistake number two taking her to a grocery store. It was obvious that she had picked up a thing or two about arguing from her attorney father. Outside in the parking lot, she was back to being chipper and helpful after the run-in with the manager.

"Is something wrong?" she said as she watched him empty the groceries from the cart to the trunk of her rental Mercedes.

"I really don't need 'Sula-whatever it is' coffee. Hell, I don't even know what it is."

"Sulawesi. And that's not the point. The point is he should have it stocked. And he calls himself a food manager?"

"Yeah well, Jerry's been the manager for longer than I've lived here. I think he knows his clientele."

"Not from what I can tell. Doesn't he care anything about his customers? I could hardly call what you put in your cart, food. "

"But I don't think you changed his mind by insulting his store. And I think he was a little worried when you mentioned the possibility of a civil suit for fraud and public endangerment."

"Oh, he deserved it. I'm glad that Beatrice does all the shopping at my house. I don't think I'd have the patience to put up with that kind of nonsense every week. Maybe I can ask her where she shops if you like. She never has a complaint."

"And I was just getting to where he was letting me slide on expired coupons," Rey said under his breath, shaking his head.

Back at the apartment, things didn't get much better. After the groceries were put away, he attempted to work on his accounts. Just as he was making progress, he found her either peering over his shoulder at his computer screen or handling his drafting tools. He thought it would be easier keeping up with Seely and her friends. She wanted him to explain what it was he was doing whether it was designing or drafting. Although he answered her questions, he kept it brief, trying not to encourage conversation and hoping that she would get the hint. Eventually, she retired to his sofa and paged listlessly through his *U-Bike* magazines.

Knowing that wouldn't keep her very long and she would be back to plague him, he wracked his brain to find something to keep her occupied.

He said, "Hey, I have an old laptop. It's not very fast anymore but it'll at least get you on the Internet. You want me to get that for you?"

She looked up, "Huh? Oh no, that's okay. I hardly ever use a computer if I can help it."

"What? Seriously?"

She shrugged. "I have my phone. That's all I need. It's not like I have to pay bills or check emails. I don't mess with any of that. And I don't like shopping online."

He would have laughed out loud if he knew she was kidding. But he was quite sure she wasn't capable of putting on a poker face.

After a while, Stazie went over to his stereo where he had been playing his playlist of blues and jazz while he worked. She browsed his racks of vinyls. Hundreds of albums later, she still hadn't recognized any thing.

"Hey, don't you have any good stuff?"

"Like what?"

"Oh, I don't know. Like the stuff they play at the clubs."

"No. I like my 'stuff' better."

"Who are all these people anyway?"

"Huh?" Rey said distractedly. His eyes remained glued to the screen as he reviewed data.

"These singers—Miles Davis? Vince Guaraldi? Marvin Gaye? I've never heard of them before. Eartha Kitt? Bobby Darin?"

"Uh huh," he muttered.

Wondering what was inside the LPs' colorful covers, she opened one up and shook out the contents. The record slid out and nearly dropped to the floor.

"Ooh. They have all of these little lines on them."

He had barely glanced up to find her scratching her nails back and forth across the vinyl's fine grooves.

"Stazie! No, don't!" he said as he leapt from his seat to take it away from her.

He held it up to the light from the window, inspecting its surface carefully. Luckily he had gotten it away from her with only a few smudges.

"Holy bunnies, what is that thing?"

"It's an LP record. C'mon. You've had to have seen these before."

"Nah uh."

"Your dad? He must still have some somewhere."

She shook her head.

"Well, they are like a CD, except that they are more fragile and you need a turntable to play them on."

She looked at him quizzically.

"Here, I can show you."

He placed the record on the platter and set the needle. The music started.

The motion of the record going around was enough to divert her attention. Rey returned to his computer, glad to have something to occupy her.

"Who *is* this?"

He continued working, not hearing her.

"Rey? Who is this singing?"

"Huh? Oh, Dinah Washington," he said as he typed away.

The song's lyrics had caught her ear. "Why did she write this song?"

He wouldn't answer.

Stazie propped up a pillow on the sofa and snuggled in, transfixed by the words that reached out to her. For her, they rang absolutely true—about the difference one day could make after you met that perfect someone. This was the second time these singers he listened to pinpointed to exactly what she was feeling. The music at the clubs never did that before. Mostly they were pulsating loud and hard to understand. It was as if this Dinah person had been spying on her and singing about her every thought, and with such feeling that Stazie was surprised to feel a longing stirring within her.

❧

By the end of side two, she had dozed off. When Rey looked up to find her asleep, he let out a sigh of relief and sat back in his chair. It was only a little past noon and he was feeling weary. He determined that Stazie was nothing short of an energy sink, a black hole that sucked the life out of you if you merely stood in its presence. It wasn't that she was doing anything in particular. She was cooperative, friendly, and cheery. *And constantly there.* There had been more than a few times this morning that he had bumped into her because she was standing so close to him. He imagined if he stopped short, she'd run right up his ass if he weren't careful. It took some getting used to.

With her zonked out, he thought it was an opportunity to sneak into his bedroom to do some weight training as planned. He wanted to stick to his regimen of physical conditioning to restore his shoulder and didn't need her chattering away and getting into everything. It was a bit terrifying to contemplate bench-pressing one hundred fifty pounds while lying flat on his back with her hovering about. He closed his door, slipped off his shirt, and warmed up.

Twenty minutes into some reps, the door opened a crack and he caught her bright eye spying in. He placed the weights on the stand and sat up, cursing himself for not remembering to lock the door.

"What are you doing now?" she asked.

"I was getting some lifting in while you were snoozing," he said, breathing heavy from the workout.

"Well, don't let me interrupt you," she said as she opened the door all the way and let her eyes drift across his bare chest.

"Did you need the restroom? Something to eat? Or did you decide to take off?"

"Me? No. I'm fine."

He felt awkward. "I can put these away. It's not that important. I can do it tomorrow."

"No!" she said, a little too emphatically and then caught herself. "Please, stay with your plans. I told you that I wouldn't get in your way. But would you mind if I watch? I've never seen anyone lift weights before."

He eyed her skeptically. "Right. First LPs and now this? C'mon, you must've been in those workout rooms or gyms at all the resorts you stay in. Or how about those friends of yours? A lot of them look like they are in pretty good shape."

"Those people I hang with? Unless being born practically perfect to begin with, their bodies look that way from steroids, plastic surgery, liposuction, and implants. And I've been to some fitness centers but mostly everyone just stands around and chats about diets or politics or investment portfolios. Nobody ever really works out. It's too . . . I don't know, *sweaty*," she said, wrinkling her nose.

"But isn't this too *sweaty*?"

It was obvious that he was perspiring. She blushed at her stupid choice of words.

"No, this is different. It's the real thing. Not someone pretending to work out or posing just to be seen."

Rey considered it. Tomorrow he wouldn't have the time and tonight would be late after dinner at his parents. That would set him back by two more days if he didn't finish today.

Finally he said, "All right. But I really can't be talking while I do this."

"I understand. I won't say a peep."

"Are you sure you don't want to watch some TV or a movie? I can stream something. Or maybe there's stuff you have to get to at home?"

"No, this is much more interesting."

"O-kay." He sighed and walked over to his dresser where he pulled out a tank top and slipped it on.

"Oh, but why are you—?" Stazie said.

He looked at her and cocked an eyebrow.

"Never mind. I'm sorry. I won't say anything more."

He reclined and squared himself on the bench. She scampered over and perched on the edge of his bed by him.

He lifted his head and asked, "And you're sure I can't get you anything?"
"No, really. Go back to what you were doing."

He took a couple of deep breaths and lifted the bar off the stand, trying to concentrate on his sets. But within a few minutes, he started to feel self-conscious. Her unabashed stare was nothing short of predatory, hungrily sizing up her prey. And when he sat up, the way her eyes brazenly roamed all over his body suddenly made him feel uncomfortable, although he couldn't explain why. He quickly toweled off and headed to the shower, making sure this time to lock the bathroom door securely behind him.

Stazie sulked back to the living room to wait For her, the morning had been filled with novel and provocative experiences. And it was all Rey's world. The variety of people, places, music, sights, smells— it felt as if she were visiting another country as they completed his errands. Although some things were unpleasant, it certainly was surprisingly titillating and real with all the thrills of a fun house to her. She didn't know what to expect next. What's more, she desired that driving force that was so pervasive in him. By being in his proximity, she felt she could draw from it and become a part of it all somehow, even if she was merely hanging on the fringes.

Once she saw him on his weight bench in his bedroom though, she knew her girlish infatuation had taken another stimulating turn. It had now shifted to lust. Not only did she want everything about him, she now hungered *for him*. Rey was all male. There was no denying that. She found his very lack of refinement to be an exceptionally sexy quality. It was all she could do to keep herself from stripping off her clothes and seducing him when he was working out. Just to know that at this moment, he was behind that door, naked in the shower, and running water all over that body made her swoon. She would gladly pay anything to be in there with him. Her heart skipped a beat to think that soon, if she pushed ahead, she would be.

By two o'clock, they were standing on the stoop of his parents' modest tract home. Rey gave a quick once over at her bangles and cleavage and despaired. He wasn't quite sure what his family would make of her. If only she could've toned it down just a little bit. Instead, right before they left, she teased and sprayed her hair a little higher, reapplied her makeup, and spritzed on even more perfume.

Oh well, here goes nothing, he thought as he rang the doorbell.

His mother answered the door.

"Rey, sweetheart! Hello! There you are. Come in, come in," Carmen Natal said as she embraced her son warmly.

He bent down so he could kiss and hug her and she could plant a big kiss on his cheek. Carmen then turned to the visitor, who stood behind her son.

Taking in the strange girl before her, she hesitated for a moment before switching to her hostess smile and asking, "And who do we have here?"

"Ma, this is Stazie Royale. Stazie, this is my mother, Carmen."

"Hello Mrs. Natal," Stazie said as she shook the older women's hand. "It's a pleasure to meet you."

Rey sighed an inward sigh of relief. At least she knew how to conduct herself when it really mattered.

He said, "So Ma, I meant to call and tell you Stazie was coming to dinner but I kind of got sidetracked. I hope you don't mind."

Actually, after much thought, he figured it would be better to spring Stazie on his family than to give them a heads-up to avoid a lot of explaining and endless questioning.

His mother smiled more broadly, "No, no, not at all. It's like the old days. Come on in Stazie and welcome! Please, make yourself at home. It's so nice when Rey brings his friends over."

As Carmen reached out to hug her, Stazie stiffened at the unexpected gesture and her eyes opened wide. She timidly patted the plump woman's back. Then she immediately tucked in behind Rey who followed his mother into the house. In the living room Rick, Marcie, and Rey's grandmother were seated and Sela was playing on the floor with her dolls. Stazie immediately recognized the bearded man, the brunette and the little girl from the photo in Rey's living room.

Rey stooped down to his elderly grandmother in the armchair. She was a tiny wizened woman with a serious face that broke into a grin when he entered. She reached out her shaky arms to hug him.

"Vovó! How are you?" he said warmly, kissing the old lady's cheek.

Chuckling, she answered him in her native Portuguese and kissed him back, clasping his face with her frail withered hands.

Rick stood up to shake Rey's hand and clap him on the back while Marcie greeted him with a hug and a peck on the cheek. Rey scooped up a giggling Sela off the floor and held her high in the air. She squealed with delight until he lowered her to plant one on her cheek as well. Stazie watched it all with fascination. They acted like they hadn't seen each other in years. She gave a small wave, feeling a bit nervous when they finally turned to her.

"Stazie, this is my grandmother, Maria Evora Natal," Rey said, fluently rolling his 'R's. "My brother Rick and his girlfriend Marcie. And this munchkin here is my niece, Sela. Everyone, this is Stazie."

They all broke out into hellos and handshakes. Rick gave a sideways glance to Rey, his face a question mark as he lifted his chin. Rey shrugged in return. He knew his brother was fishing for an explanation already. By the time the evening was out, he'd probably have to do a lot of explaining to all of them.

Hearing Rey's arrival, Gloria and Joseph Natal had emerged from the kitchen followed by a beaming Carmen. There was yet another round of hugs, kisses, and joyous greetings. Gloria was in her most melodramatic form as she greeted her baby brother with a huge hello and outstretched arms. Stazie could see a slight blush in Rey's cheeks as his older sister rumpled his hair. Once more, his family turned to Stazie and she found herself the focus of the room. Feeling a bit overwhelmed by all the greetings, she was beginning to wonder how many more people were stashed in the corners of this house.

They converged on the living room, all taking seats wherever they could fit in the small modestly decorated room. With no other seats available, Rey offered the remaining seat on the sofa between his mother and Gloria to Stazie, and then plunked down comfortably on the floor where he propped up one knee and stretch his other leg out. Sela immediately cuddled up to him to show him her dolls. Stazie found herself wedged between the ample hips of Carmen and the husky frame of Gloria. The two women were animate and talked a lot with their hands, making Stazie envy Rey's space on the floor. She was tempted to join him there.

"So Rey, how is your design work coming along?" the senior Natal inquired.

"Doing pretty good, Pop. I just got another new account last week."

"Good, good."

"Rey was one of the top designers for the big architectural design firm, Schuster and Mohlen," Carmen said proudly to Stazie. "He was the youngest designer to win their top award."

"Oh Ma, that was so long ago. Seely here could have won that. It was no big deal."

"It was quite the honor and they don't give it to just anyone," Carmen insisted stubbornly. "Don't let him tell you any different."

Marcie rose from the loveseat. "Stazie, can I get you something to drink? There's wine, beer, soda, and fruit juice."

"Oh Marcie, dear, thank you so much. I've lost my manners," Carmen said with much embarrassment. "I'm just so happy to have everyone together. I'm sorry Stazie, what would you like?"

"Some wine would be great."

"All righty, one wine. Can I get anybody else something while I'm up? Rey?"

"Ah Marce, you read my mind. Can you read this?" He squeezed his eyes shut in feigned concentration and put a finger to his temple.

"A pale ale coming right up. No glass."

"You haven't lost your touch."

"You're darn right, I haven't," she answered with sass and a wink. Rey laughed.

Stazie watched their exchange closely as a bit of jealousy popped up unexpectedly in her. It was obvious that Marcie was quite at ease in the Natal household and everyone adored her.

"So Stazie, what do you do?" Gloria asked.

The question caught her off guard and brought her back to the conversation. No one had ever asked her that before and at the moment, she didn't know what to answer.

"What do I do? Um, what do you mean?" she said.

"Where do you work? Or do you go to school somewhere?"

"Oh . . . neither, actually."

"You don't work?"

"No. I don't have to."

Gloria looked at her for a second as if what she had said was incomprehensible. "Oh. Well, that's quite a luxury," she said, nodding.

"I started college but I decided it just wasn't for me."

"What was your major?"

"I didn't have one."

"Oh."

Stazie giggled nervously and said, "So I guess you can say that since I majored in nothing, I now have a career in it."

Gloria nodded slowly and decided to keep her lips pursed.

"Stazie's father is Doug Royale. You know the criminal defense lawyer who represented the pro-golfer, Dick Abernathy last spring? He also represented Kip Gaffney too. It was all over the news," said Rey.

His family answered a collective "Oh" as if that explained everything.

Stazie couldn't help but feel conflicted as to whether she should feel proud of having Doug Royale as her father or ashamed at her own lack of ambition. She decided to paste on a smile. It usually got her through most scrapes. To her relief, Marcie returned with the drinks and a small tray of chips, pretzels, and pickles that shifted everyone's attention off the subject. After more small talk, Carmen announced that she had to finish up dinner. She excused herself and went to the kitchen, followed by Rey's grandmother.

"Stazie, Marce and I are going to bail and let these guys talk cars like they're itching to do. Care to join us ladies in the kitchen? We have a lot more fun in there," Gloria said, getting up from the sofa.

Stazie smiled and shook her head. "No thanks. I'm fine. I like cars," she fibbed.

"Okay, suit yourself."

With that, Gloria and Marcie left, leaving Stazie behind with the men. Rey wished that she had followed them but she stuck around, situating herself on the sofa directly behind him while he remained on the floor. If he didn't know better, he'd almost say that she was hiding behind him.

The three men fell into an easy conversation discussing the matters at Rick's performance garage, the mechanics' union, and then onto the latest cars that were out. Stazie tried to keep up with the rpm's, gear ratios, torque, and horsepower, but she couldn't make heads or tails of what they were talking about. She resorted to sipping her wine and smiling if they happened to look in her direction. Sela continued to play with her dolls, snuggled on Rey's lap. The little girl would occasionally hold one up to him so he would make faces or funny voices that started her giggling and calling him silly. Stazie wished she could trade places with Sela. Not only to have Rey's attention now instead of having to listen to this wearisome topic, but to have had someone interact with her like that when she was that age.

Gloria leaned out from the kitchen doorway and called out, "Hey Stazie, I bet they're talking about horsepower right now, am I right?"

She nodded.

"Why don't you join us in the kitchen? We gab about a much, much broader range of subjects, I guarantee you. You won't find any talk of revs or what weight engine oil to use."

"I'm fine, really."

Rey said over his shoulder, "Are you sure you don't want to go? I'm sure this car talk must be boring for you."

"No, its okay."

"Okay. Well, dinner should be done shortly," Gloria said as she shrugged and ducked back into the kitchen.

Pretty soon though, the topic of discussion had moved onto car racing. Even little Sela picked up her toys and took off to join her mother. The guys glanced over in Stazie's direction from time to time, trying to make her feel included in the discussion but all she could do was smile and nod. Meanwhile, she could hear genial conversation punctuated with laughter and exclamations drifting from the kitchen.

On second thought, maybe I could just pop in there to refill my wine, she reasoned as she got up and smoothed out her miniskirt.

Then she cleared her throat and said, "I'm going to the kitchen for some more wine. Can I, uh, get anything for anybody?"

They all stopped talking for a moment and looked at her, surprised at her offer. They shook their heads.

Eyeing his empty bottle, she said, "Rey, can I get you another beer?" She tried the tone of voice that Marcie had used, hoping to illicit the same playful response from him. "Another pale ale, no glass?"

"No, I'm good. Thank you though."

"Okay. I just thought I'd ask," she said, disappointed that it didn't work for her.

As soon as she left the room, Rick glanced cautiously towards the kitchen and then slid closer to his brother.

Lowering his voice, he said, "So Rey, *that's* Stazie Royale? That's the chick that ran you over and rolled her M3 just a few days ago?"

Joseph also moved in closer to get the scoop on the odd girl his younger son had brought home. She wasn't typical of the girls Rey knew before.

"Yeah. That's her."

"Well what is she doing *here*? I thought she hated your guts and was waiting to ice you the next opportunity she got?"

"Yeah, believe me, it sure seemed like she wanted to. Beats me why she's here. She showed up early this morning to return my jacket I lent her."

"You lent her your jacket?"

"Yeah, up at the cottage. She was dressed kind of like she is today but during that big storm upstate and all. What was I suppose to do, let her freeze?"

"Okay, I can see that."

"The problem is she won't go away. Would you believe she's been hanging around all day? No matter what I do—laundry, food shopping, working on my accounts—she's there. I can't get rid of her."

"Why don't you just tell her to get lost?"

"Come on, get real. I can't do that. She's the daughter of my client. And she's also the one who saved my ass up there, remember?"

"Yeah, but you weren't the one who wrecked the car in the first place. And you were the one who saved both your asses by finding the fishing shack."

"I guess. But you know, she's not behaving like she was before. Since the trip to the cottage, she's been friendly. Too friendly, as a matter of fact. And helpful. And she keeps doing that smiling thing. I don't know what's up with her but it's kinda freaking me out."

"So what are you going to do?"

"I don't know. I was just hoping that she'd get bored and leave on her own."

"And what if she doesn't?"

"What do you mean?"

"She might want to stay on," Joseph said.

Rey hadn't considered the possibility of a long-term situation. Today had been long enough. What *if* she decided to return tomorrow and the day after that? He would have to address it sometime. Just then, Stazie came back into the room. The guys instantly clammed up.

"Your mother wanted me to tell you all that dinner is ready," she said, smiling prettily.

Plates were heaped with the delicious food Carmen had so lovingly prepared for her family. A generous portion was served to Stazie and before she could say that she didn't want seconds, more was added to her plate despite her protest. She had never eaten so much before. However, the evening was lovely and relaxed. Dinner was a lively affair, filled with jokes, laughter, and affection among the siblings. Stazie interjected here and there but mostly she just sat back and soaked it all in.

Is this what it would have been like to have brothers and sisters? she wondered as she watched their exchanges with each other.

Gloria pretended to give her younger brothers a hard time while they both ganged up on her in defense. Marcie laughed and took Gloria's side. And everyone took special delight in listening to little Sela tell her tales of preschool and classmates.

Stazie glanced over at the elder Natals. *They seemed to dote on each other,* she thought as she watched Carmen gently tell Joseph of a spot of gravy on his chin. She wondered if her parents would have ever acted like that if they had stayed together.

The only person at the table that made her wary was Rey's grandmother. Stazie didn't have any experience around old people. With their hazy eyes and feeble bodies, they always made her feel uncomfortable and for the most part, they scared her. This one was no different. The ancient woman sat across the table from her. She didn't say much and when she did, it was in her native tongue. From time to time, Stazie could feel her eye upon her and would smile sweetly back but the old lady continued to stare at her, stone faced. The younger woman did not know what to make of it.

She shifted her focus instead to Rey sitting beside her. He looked like a different person around his family. That spark was alight in his eyes and his laughter came easily and from deep within. She noted how lucky he was to have been raised in an environment like this, thinking back to her own solitary dinners or those quiet ones with her father. Whenever the Royales entertained, their guests mostly consisted of business associates, acquaintances, or people who only wanted to be seen in the right circles. Her own friends seemed to change as often as the flavor of the month. Rarely was there ever anyone present who really knew or cared for them.

As for relatives, most of them lived in other states and had few or no children. She had a distant cousin who was close in age to her but they had never met. Her paternal grandparents were deceased and she had never seen her maternal grandparents. Most holidays, Stazie and her father spent on the ski slopes or at resorts. Sometimes they would even take separate trips if there happened to be someone in her father's life at the moment. During those times, Stazie would round up a few of her most current friends and vacation on her own.

It wasn't necessarily a bad life; it was just different than this, she thought.

After dinner, while the dishes were being washed and Rey, his brother, and father slipped out to the garage to look at Rick's car, Stazie wandered into the living room to survey the family photos she had noticed there earlier. She was taken by the array of photographs that filled the wall before her: old black and whites of stern-looking ancestors; snapshots of family get-togethers; school portraits of Rey, Rick, Gloria, and Sela; and candid family moments. What the Natals lacked in artwork, they made up in a hodge-podge of faces and frames crowding the wall. In her own home, there were only two photographs displaying formal poses of her father and herself in matching frames, tasteful in size, and never competing for space.

Stazie delighted in locating Rey as a chubby, dimpled-cheeked baby and then watched him grow up before her eyes. He always had that mischievous look and charming smile. In one shot, he was a skinny first grader with a missing front tooth. In another, he was about eight and had his arms wrapped around a teenage Rick's neck. Another shot caught him jumping on a snowboard when he was a pre-teen. He donned a mortar and gown for his high school graduation picture in a younger, thinner version of what he looked like now. Stazie was surprised to see a snapshot of Rey in a military uniform sitting in Humvee, with his sleeves rolled up, sunglasses on, while flashing a peace sign. Last, she located another shot of him and that snow bum friend again, except this time they were dressed in suits and standing next to each other, shaking hands. It looked like it had been taken recently.

"A motley crew, huh?"

Her thoughts were interrupted as Gloria came up beside her.

Suddenly feeling shy, Stazie shook her head and said, "No. Not at all. I think it's a great collection."

"Did you find Rey as a baby? There he is. That little stinker," Glo said, affectionately. "He looks innocent and cute there but that kid was always on the go. He drove Rick and me crazy with all of his energy. And the questions! He had to ask about *everything.*"

Stazie blushed, wondering how much Gloria had caught of her studying her brother's photos.

"Do you have any siblings, Stazie?"

"No . . . but sometimes I wish I did."

"I always thought it would be great to be an only child."

"It's kinda quiet."

"What I wouldn't have done to have a little peace and quiet from two brothers. But I guess you're right. I don't know what I would have done without them either."

"Rey was in the service?" Stazie said pointing to the photo.

"Yeah, a short stint in the Navy. He was twenty-one and he and his best friend signed up without our parents knowing. It nearly gave our mother a heart attack. Luckily, he qualified to serve as a Seabee and mostly worked at building things."

"A Seabee?"

"Construction Battalion."

Stazie wanted to ask more questions but the rest of the family began returning to the living room discussing politics and the local race for mayor. They had started on pie and coffee, when Carmen Natal unexpectedly went over to the old upright piano in the corner. She lifted its fallboard and lightly tapped the keys. The conversation ended abruptly. Everyone knew what she wanted as she turned towards her youngest son. Rey, on the other hand, tried to pretend that he hadn't noticed.

"Sweetheart, would you? It's been so long since I've heard you play. It must be over a year already."

"Aw, Ma. I don't know if I remember anything anymore. Why don't you ask Rick?"

Rick held up two crooked fingers. "Sorry, Bro. Ever since these fingers got busted, I just don't have the dexterity."

Gloria chimed in, "Don't look at me. I left my violin at home—on purpose."

"Do you play, Stazie?" Carmen asked.

"Me? Oh no."

"All my children have had music lessons and I had always hoped they would continue to play throughout their lives. I thought it would bring such joy to them," Carmen said sadly while Joseph nodded in agreement. It was the guilt trip she always used. And for some reason, it always worked.

"Go on man, don't break Ma's heart," Rick said jovially, giving his brother a shove up.

Rey groaned and sulked over to the piano like a little boy and sat down on the bench.

"All right. I'm here. What would you like for me to play?"

"How about that Mozart piece? The pretty one that I like," his mother said with a pleased look on her face. She settled in next to Joseph and held his hand.

He stared at the keyboard for a few moments and half-heartedly tried a few keys. Then he started to play in earnest. As the melody continued to build and flow, the music coming from the old upright wasn't any mediocre attempt on his part. He was quite good. Stazie recalled how he had looked longingly at the grand piano at the cottage. At the time, she remembered thinking he was only considering its price tag, hoping to finagle even more payment from her father. Now that she saw he could play so adeptly, she realized what it must have meant for him to see that piano.

She became entranced with the live music, having to get up from where she was sitting to come around to the side of the piano to watch his fingers dance up and down the keys. It amazed her that this was the same guy who rode a bicycle and lifted weights. She would have never guessed it.

He fumbled a few notes, looked up, and grinned at her. "Sorry about that," he said.

Then he went back at it. She recognized that same concentration that filled his face when he worked on his designs. After the Mozart piece, he slowed down with a song that sounded so melancholy and haunting that Stazie was surprised to feel a longing ache from within.

"What is that?" she said, spellbound.

"From Godard's opera, *Berceuse*," he answered without missing a note.

The song's pensive tone touched everyone, his family aware of the depths from which it was coming from. When he finished, the room was silent, the final notes fading in the air.

Carmen Natal had tears in her eyes as she reached for her son's arm. "Honey, I didn't mean for you—"

Quickly cutting her off, Rey said quietly, "Somebody better get over here and help me or I'm calling it quits for the night."

Marcie pushed Rick out of his seat and egged him to go over. He sat down next to his brother and cracked his knuckles. Then he started to pound out a rollicking bass riff. Rey joined in on the treble clef and the two brothers hammered out one lively jazz piece and then another. The contrast in mood was obvious and everyone welcomed it with relief.

"Hey, how about one for your grandma?" Joseph called out.

The old lady clapped her hands and sang in her gravelly voice as Rey played the Portuguese folk tune she had taught him when he was small.

Then the brothers took turns playing a couple of tunes for their mother and then *Mack the Knife,* their father's favorite. The family joined in singing at different pitches, knowing they sounded pretty awful but nevertheless having a good time. The spontaneity and fun of it all got to Stazie; she only wished she could join in, but she didn't know any of the words or songs.

Then Rey turned to her and said, "Anything you'd like to hear? We know quite a few tunes and if we don't know it, we'll either make it up or massacre it."

She was taken back by his inclusion of her. She wracked her brain for a title but nothing came to mind. She smiled shyly and shook her head.

"No, please, play whatever you want. It all sounds wonderful."

She didn't know what the song was that he played next but she knew she would never forget its melody.

By ten o'clock, Gloria started to gather Sela's things together and Rick and Marcie were getting ready to leave. Stazie thanked the Natals for dinner and the evening and said good night. Then she waited for Rey out in front of the house. When he approached her on the sidewalk, she slipped her arm through his as they walked to her car. She was feeling free as a bubble, floating along, her head still swimming with the day's events. This was one of her best days ever, making her feelings for him intensify. Although she was sorry that the evening was drawing to a close, she looked forward to having him all to herself again when she drove him home.

Maybe he will invite me up to his apartment for one last drink and we could spend some time alone, she thought dreamily.

"So what do you think about my family? Crazy, huh?" he said as they walked.

"No, I thought they were all wonderful."

"Really? All of them together could be a scary bunch to someone who has never been over."

"No, it was great. The only one who scared me some was your grandmother."

"My little grandma? Scary? Why do you say that?"

"She just seemed, I dunno, angry or annoyed at me. I'm not sure which."

"I'm sure neither. The only time I've ever seen her angry is when she can't get the nurses at her senior care apartment to pluck her chin hairs for her. Poor thing can't see to do it herself anymore."

"Maybe you're right," Stazie said, but still feeling a bit unsure.

"Hey listen Stazie, Rick and Marcie are going to drop me off. I'm on the way home for them," he said as they reached her car.

Her bubble burst.

"What? I don't mind taking you home. In fact, you can even drive if you like," she said.

"Nah, it's late and it's out of your way. Besides, Rick's got to stop by to pick up something."

"But I really don't mind—"

"Nope, really. I'm covered. But thanks anyway."

She looked up at his face, lit softly by the streetlight. Her pulse started to quicken as she stared deep into his dark eyes. It would be the perfect moment for him to kiss her. She drew close to him and waited expectantly. Hoping to feel his mouth on hers, she tilted her head back, gazed at him invitingly and parted her lips, making sure to show him every indication that she was ready. He wouldn't be able to resist her if she looked so alluring.

"So, you should get going. You've got a ways to go."

"But wouldn't you like to . . ." she breathed, stepping in closer and reaching up with her arms.

"Like to what?" he said, pulling back and looking puzzled.

Her cheeks flushed red. She straightened up and closed her mouth. Obviously, he wasn't receiving the messages she was sending him now or all day long for that matter.

"Nothing. Never mind," she said, flustered. She hurried around to the driver's side of the car and got in. Then she drove off without saying another word.

"Good night?" Rey said perplexed, as he watched her drive away.

Stazie Royale was a hard one to figure out.

They were all waiting for him, squeezed around the table in the kitchen and hushing each other when he entered. He knew by the looks on their faces what they wanted. He was reminded of an old rerun where Ricky Ricardo sees his troublemaking wife and says, "Luu-ccyy, you've got some 'splaining to do."

"Okay, what's up?" he said.

"All I want to know, Honey, is if you had a good evening?" Carmen said, with her most sincere face.

"Sure, Ma. The food was great as always. Why do you ask?"

"Ah, you know what Ma wants. It's what we *all* want to know— is there something going on between you and her?" Glo said bluntly. She never believed in beating around the bush, no matter how sensitive the subject was.

"Wha—? With Stazie? No! Oh, *hell* no." Rey looked at them incredulously.

"See? That's what I told them. Would they listen to me? No!" Rick said defensively.

"It's none of our business, really. It's just that it was kind of a surprise when you brought her over," Carmen said trying to smooth things over. She poured out more coffee.

"I know I sprung her on you all and I'm sorry about that. Wait a minute—why is Grandma crying?" he said when he saw the old lady weeping.

"We don't know. She won't say," Marcie said. She placed her arm around their grandmother trying to console her.

"Vovó, what's the matter? Why are you upset?" Rey said gently, holding the old lady's hand.

In her heavy accent, she managed to say heartbroken, "You . . . breeng to home . . . una prostituta. No good."

"Huh?"

"She's upset because she thinks Stazie is a prostitute," Joseph said in a serious tone.

Rey almost laughed out loud and tried to contain himself despite everyone else breaking out into giggles.

"What? No, Vovó, she's not a prostitute. No. Don't worry. I won't ever do that, okay?" he said as he stroked his grandmother's cheek. She cried some more and kissed his hand. Then he said to his family, "Listen, I brought her over without saying anything because I didn't want to have to do a lot of explaining. Like I was telling Rick, she showed up this morning and for some reason, she just hung around all day and wouldn't go home. I told her I had this dinner to go to but she insisted on coming. And I didn't think you would mind an extra person."

"No, not at all, that's fine. It's just that Rick was telling us she was the one who had run you over with her car," Carmen said.

Rey flashed a look at his brother. *Thanks a million, Bro*, his eyes said.

"They wanted to know where you two met," Rick said apologetically and shrugged. "What was I suppose to say?"

Gloria said, "But wasn't she really evil to you afterwards? I heard she was a real bitch."

"Gloria!" Carmen gasped.

"Jeez, Rick, what else did you tell them?"

"Nothing! Just that you got that contract with her father and you both went up to the cottage and . . . well . . ."

"You didn't."

"They asked! Come on Rey, we're all concerned about you. And we don't want to see you get chewed up and spat out by some devil she-woman. We didn't think that you were ready—"

"Hey, I think I should determine how I handle my own affairs," he snapped.

"Why didn't you tell us that you were in another accident? And that you almost froze to death in that place?" Carmen said, checking over her youngest son and touching his face out of concern.

Joseph appeared just as worried, his brow furrowed. Seeing the expression on his mother's face diffused Rey's irritation at his older brother.

"It's just that I didn't want you to worry and fuss over me again, Ma. Like you're doing now. I was fine. I wasn't any worse for the wear so I figured, what was the point in putting you through all of that again?"

"And that girl, Stazie—she helped you?"

"Yes, surprisingly she did. She got me out of the weather and warmed me up. I was just a little on the cold side, that's all. The next morning I was fine," Rey said, oversimplifying the events. If his mother knew how truly close he was to knocking off, she'd probably never let him out of her sight again. "That's why she came over this morning, to return my jacket that I lent her when we were up there. And when she asked if she could come to dinner tonight, I thought it would be all right."

"Of course it was all right. God bless her. I've got to thank her the next time I see her."

Rey hoped there wouldn't be a next time.

"But if she was such a bitch to you before, why the change? I mean, she seemed pretty nice tonight," Gloria said.

"That's what I can't figure out. On the ride upstate, you should have seen her. She was totally hostile and difficult. In fact, we were arguing when we got into the accident. She was so pissed off that she lost control and ran off the road. But by the time I woke up the next morning in the fishing shack, she was acting completely different. You know—happy, helpful, sweet. If you could have seen how Stazie was before, you would think it was a real Jekyll and Hyde thing going on. At least that's what it seems like to me."

"Maybe she's psycho or something. One of those split personalities that will take you out in a heartbeat. Or even a stalker," Rick said and then laughed diabolically.

Grandma Evora looked up. "Quem é *psycho*? Essa garota?" she asked.

"Ricardo, watch your mouth. Your grandmother's here," Joseph scolded.

"Sorry, Pop."

"Nah uh. I'd say the way she was looking at you tonight, I think there's something completely different going on. Oh yeah, Ma, did you count your photos on the wall to make sure they're all still there?" Gloria said.

"What?" Carmen said, puzzled.

"Huh? What do you mean?" said Rey.

"It's really obvious she's got a thing for you," Gloria said.

His eyes opened wide. "What! *Me?* Get out of here."

"No, really, I'd know that look anywhere."

Marcie and Carmen nodded their heads in agreement.

"Aw, come on. I know she was acting weird, but that's a bunch of bullsh—" He stopped short when his mother raised an eyebrow. "—uh, bull."

Glo just grinned at her youngest brother and nodded her head definitively.

"But why on Earth would she? She absolutely detests me. Or at least she did. I thought she had hit her head in the accident, that's why she was acting so nice. Or maybe the fact that I got so cold that night was because I went back to get her inhaler that she had dropped outside of the car. I thought it was a case of the guilts."

"Actually, if she helped you out when you were an ice cube and totally dependent on her, maybe she's experiencing that Florence Nightingale Effect where caregivers fall in love with their patients," Marcie said logically.

"Oh, you mean like in that old movie, where Helen Hayes is a nurse that falls for Gary Cooper who is a soldier?" said Gloria.

"Yeah, or Tristan and Isolde where she falls in love with her enemy after she nurses him back to health."

"Oh, the ending was so sad. I couldn't stop crying."

"Wasn't it? Me neither."

"And the guy who played Tristan in the movie version was such a hottie."

"Oh, geez!" Rick said disgustedly at the turn in the conversation.

"Wait a minute, wait a minute!" said Rey reeling them back in, "Before you go off on Florence Nightingale and hotties and all of that, what should I do?"

"What do you mean?" said Carmen.

"About Stazie. I can't keep having her hang around all the time but I don't know what to tell her. Even though she was or still is psycho—," he glanced at his grandmother when his father cleared his throat disapprovingly and nodded his head in her direction. "Uh, I mean, *needy* before, I don't necessarily want to hurt her feelings. She's already got a lot of emotional baggage."

"And you don't want to be her skycap?" Rick said and snickered. The rest chuckled along.

"No, seriously. She's very temperamental and sensitive as it is. And I still have a ways to go before I finish the plans on their cottage, so I will see her from time to time. I can't just avoid her, especially if she shows up unexpectedly on my doorstep like she did this morning."

"See? What did I tell you? *That* is stalking," said the older brother.

"All I can say is, if anything, treat her with kindness, Honey. There's something fragile about her, I sense. And if you have to be honest with her then so be it but just remember to always be kind," his mother advised.

"And if I can't?"

"You're a sweet boy. You've always been. And smart. I know you'll figure out what to do, I don't doubt it."

Rey felt tired. Although well meaning, his mother's advice wasn't concrete enough to guide him through this dilemma. As for the rest of the family, his predicament was as entertaining as a soap opera. Though he would never admit it to them, he wasn't ready to handle something like this right now. He had enough trouble getting through most days. Sighing, he recalled what his counselor had told him last year. He would just have to take it one day at a time. That was something he could stick with.

It was late when Doug Royale entered his darkened penthouse apartment. It had been a long trip, much more difficult than he had expected. He left his luggage in the foyer, threw his keys down on the credenza, kicked off his shoes, and headed straight for the liquor cabinet. Some fifteen-year old Scotch neat would be just the ticket right now. Seeing no lights on in the apartment was promising. Stazie must be out with her friends or asleep. He could sit and gather his thoughts in solitude and let the Scotch work its magic.

Pulling up the ottoman in front of the overstuffed armchair, he plopped himself down and put his feet up. Soft city light from the balcony shone in through the French doors. He loosened his tie, wriggled his toes in his socks, took a whiff of the heavenly liquid in his glass, and put the tumbler to his lips.

"Hi Daddy," said a teary voice from a darkened corner.

He nearly spilled his drink.

"Stazie?"

She turned on the table lamp. The brightness of the light blinded Doug momentarily. The peacefulness snuffed out by the glare.

Resignedly, he said, "How are you, Sweetie?"

He had really, really hoped to be alone.

Stazie's cheeks were wet with tears and her eyes were puffy and red. She dabbed at her nose with a tissue. His eyes adjusting to the light, Doug could see more crumpled tissues all over her lap and on the floor.

"Stazie? What's wrong, Baby?"

While he was concerned for his daughter, he learned from numerous past episodes to take it slow. Stazie was prone to emotional outbursts and it was best not to get excited unnecessarily. Besides, he had hit his comfort zone on the chair and did not relish the thought of getting up. He sipped at his Scotch.

"Oh Daddy. I don't know. I can't figure it out. I mean, I'm pretty aren't I?"

Bingo. Nothing serious.

Doug patted himself inwardly for remaining in his chair. He rewarded his good judgment with another sip.

"Of course you are. In fact, you're beautiful. Why?"

"And I'm fun to be around, right?"

"Sure. And cute too."

"And I'm smart and sexy and rich and—"

"Stazie, what is going on?"

"It's just that . . ." A sob caught in her throat. "It's just that I can't seem to get a certain someone . . . a certain guy to notice me."

"A guy not notice you? Where? At the club? Are you sure he wasn't gay?"

"No, not at the club. And no, he isn't."

"Well, then. Anyone I know in particular?"

"Rey," she whispered and pressed the tissue to her nose.

"What was that? Rey? Rey who?"

"Rey Natal."

Doug had just taken another sip and upon hearing this news, he almost spat up. The fiery liquor went down the wrong pipe and he coughed spasmodically for the next few moments.

Getting it to clear, he finally managed to squeak out, "Rey Natal??"

She nodded pathetically and then started tears anew. Clutching a throw pillow, she buried her face in it.

Doug was dumbfounded. Rey Natal would have been the last person on Earth that he would have guessed. He was all too aware of his daughter's contempt, if not pure dislike for the young architectural designer. He had witnessed her verbal attacks, insults, and humiliation she imposed upon him, although he could never figure out what the deal was. Natal seemed like a nice enough fellow.

Something obviously had happened while he was away in Detroit. He recalled how Stazie had phoned him to let him know of the accident they were in on the way home from the cottage. However, she had told him that everything was fine, no one was hurt, and that he should finish his business trip, so it didn't give him much concern for worry. Royale had even anticipated his daughter launching some kind of lawsuit against Natal regarding the accident. She typically had to blame someone or something when things went wrong.

But he wasn't expecting this. Not in the least. It piqued his curiosity.

"You do mean Rey Natal?" he asked once more, just in case he misheard.

She slowly lifted head. Tangled strands of her long hair stuck to her wet cheeks. "Yes! It seems no matter what I do, or what I say, I can't get him to notice me."

"Well . . . have you tried acting nice to him for a change?"

"Daddy!" she wailed and threw her hands up in despair. "Of course I have! I returned his jacket, and dressed up for him, did my hair, and smiled pretty. I even patted his ugly dog. He acted like I wasn't even there!"

"What do you mean? He ignored you?"

"No. He made me coffee and took me to his parents' house for dinner and asked me if he could play a song for me on the piano," she said miserably.

"Okkaayy . . ." said Doug, confused. He seemed to have lost her somewhere along the way.

"But don't you see?"

"See what? Apparently I'm missing something here."

"If he did all of that, why wouldn't he kiss me? I gave him every chance to. He acted like I was a nobody he had just met. Not someone he has been in two accidents with already."

What __had__ happened up at the cottage? Doug started to wonder, a father's protectiveness kicking in.

"Okay, but he didn't do anything to you, did he? I mean before, when you went upstate or anything?"

Stazie's face crumpled. "No," she said despondently, barely above a whisper. "And I don't know why he won't."

She rose up and toddled over to him seeking comforting and consoling like she did when she was four. She plunked down and squeezed in next to him on the oversized chair and draped her arms around his neck to soak his shirt with more tears.

Doug had to put his drink down in order not to spill it. He stifled a groan when shifting his tired legs off the ottoman so he could move over to give her room. He had been standing in airport security for three hours in Detroit and his legs had fallen asleep on the flight back. Daddy's 'little girl' certainly wasn't little anymore, he thought to himself and then quickly dismissed it. His daughter needed comforting right now, not any mention of her size. He patted her arm.

"It's just that, I can't stop thinking about him, Daddy. But I know he doesn't feel the same way about me and he probably never will," she said.

Doug was surprised to hear the pain in his daughter's voice. Apparently, this wasn't one of her typical pout and whines. This was deeper, more heartfelt—more genuine—and he was moved by it. The counselor loved his daughter more than anything but he knew perfectly well that she had always been somewhat shallow. It was a mistake of parenting on his part; too much indulgence, leniency, and coddling had led to her undeniable personality flaw. But he figured that with her financial endowments coupled with her physical endowments, most men would overlook it. And in the past they had.

Rey was different though. He knew it from the first day that he met him. The young designer was a far departure from the narcissistic pampered brats Stazie was used to dealing with. Doug could see right off that he was an independent operator, not reliant on anyone or anything to make his way. *A real guy in a real world*, he thought.

In a way, he reminded him of his own humble beginnings as a fledgling lawyer from a working class family. His privileged daughter would have a hard time understanding the rules in which he and Rey had to play by, and the world from which they came. Yet, maybe this was the exact thing his daughter needed in order to undo some of her upbringing. In the very least, it would be an abject lesson in learning who she could handle and who she could not.

"This all seems kind of sudden, don't you think? I mean, how long have you two been, uh, 'seeing' each other? I've only been gone a week."

"We're not *seeing* each other," she said, sighing. "He hasn't called or any-thing. I was the one who went to his place this morning."

"So, technically, it's only been one day?"

"Yes. But it was *all* day. I made sure to hang around him the entire day from morning 'til night to make him notice me."

"You did what? Why did you—I mean, why would you do that?" His mind quickly clicked through the implications and definitions of harassment.

"Well, I wanted to make up for all the time I wasted."

Doug knew when his daughter set her sights on something she was pretty tenacious. But he had never known her to react this way with any of the guys she had dated before. Usually, she played cat and mouse, let-ting them chase her until she caught them. Given all the indications, he realized with astonishment that his daughter must truly be smitten this time. Inwardly, he smiled. He patted his daughter's curls and then kissed her forehead.

"Aw, Baby. Give it time, okay? You've always been impetuous and impa-tient. You can't force this to happen, no matter how hard you try."

"But can't we do something? Can't you pay him more or make him spend time with me as part of his contract?'

"What? No, no. I can't do that. Like I said, something like this takes time and it's all been pretty sudden. Rey, himself, probably needs time to adjust to the fact that you don't want to rip his head off anymore."

At his remark, Stazie let out a pathetic squeak, shuddered, and hung onto her father's neck even tighter. Embarrassed and filled with remorse, she buried her face in his shirt once again.

Oops, I must've hit a sore spot, Doug corrected himself.

He tried again. "Listen Staze. Just be your sweet self, okay? And keep showing him that pretty smile. He'll come around eventually. No one I know can resist that smile of yours, okay? You'll knock him dead. And if he doesn't come around, well . . . we'll find something we can pin on him and then we'll slap him with a lawsuit."

He threw in that last line as a joke but he noticed that she wasn't laughing.

Chapter 5 ~ The Bite

It wasn't as bad as he had anticipated. He had prepared himself to see her on his doorstep the first thing in the morning on the very next day. It made for an almost sleepless night fretting about the unknown. He still hadn't come up with a plan on how to handle her should she show up again.

To his relief, there was no sign of Stazie on Monday morning. Maybe it meant that she had returned to her usual antagonistic, contrary behavior. Or perhaps it was further subterfuge in some ultimate plan of payback to keep her opponent off balance.

But could it be something else? he pondered.

Even if what Gloria had suggested was true, he couldn't imagine why Stazie would be interested in him now after the way they had started off. There wouldn't be any logical reason why she would. They didn't even have anything in common.

If by some remote chance in hell she was, it perplexed him even more to think of what he did last night to upset her. He recalled how she drove off without saying another word. All along, Rey knew this was why he did not want to get tangled up in relationships. *Any* relationship. It wasn't exclusive to spoiled, rich chicks. There were others in the past but nothing ever became of them because of one reason or another: too temperamental, too possessive, too neurotic. His track record wasn't encouraging.

It wasn't that he was a cynic. He contemplated marriage and starting a family one day but he was patient because he knew there was a special person out there for him somewhere. It would only take a matter of fate to meet her. And when that right someone came around, the relationship would be easy—as easy as breathing or eating. It would not be complicated.

That was why he knew damn straight, Stazie was *not* the person he was destined for. There was nothing uncomplicated about their interaction. It had been difficult from the start. In fact, it had been pure hell. And she still had a way of making him feel unbalanced and stressed. Her mood swings were over the top and if that wasn't enough, she was too needy. He did not have the time or emotional stamina to commit to someone like her and doubted they could ever establish even a friendship.

He reassured himself that she would get bored with 'slumming' and return to the social circles, tight cliques, and metrosexual guys she was accustomed to. For now, while he worked on the cottage he would do his best to get along with her and show tolerance. It would be in his best interest, both financially and mentally, to be allies rather than enemies.

Having the morning before him, he decided to treat his dog to a long walk. It felt good to get out from that tiny box they called home. Rey loved the outdoors and preferred spending as much of his time in the open air as he could. He counted the days until his driver's license was reinstated so he could escape the city once more. He missed hiking and snowboarding but more so the feeling of being unburdened. One day he hoped to move west to the big states with the wide open skies and towering mountain ranges. He had always imagined himself somewhere in Colorado or maybe the Pacific Northwest. He would miss his family no doubt but he would not miss the regrets and pain he left behind.

By the time he got back to his place, he felt re-energized and ready to get on with his day. It was the one thing he didn't mind about being self-employed. The ability to call one's own hours was definitely a perk. Where else could he have taken a long walk to clear his head during a workday? His agenda was full: a phone conference with a prospective client, finalize and email drafts of the Nova, Inc. account, and put some time in on the cottage plans. Although he had been stalling, he knew he should also call Rachel to see if she needed anything. It was definitely shaping up to be a busy day. Throwing a handful of kibble into Jack's bowl and selecting a playlist, Rey got down to work.

When Stazie's eyes finally opened and focused on her clock, it read nine forty-five a.m. As she rolled onto her back and stared up at the ceiling, she realized she wasn't feeling much better than the night before. Not only did she have a throbbing headache, her heart was heavy beneath her baby doll pj's. She knew that what her father had told her last night was true. Maybe she had pushed things along too hard, too fast. Maybe this was something she couldn't force, no matter how much she tried.

When it came to Rey, why was she always making such stupid, foolish mistakes? She could've just dropped off his jacket and had coffee with him. After a breezy chat, she could have strolled out of there. That would have been cool and sophisticated. Instead, she acted like a dopey schoolgirl with a crush and stuck around in his face all day. No wonder he didn't want to kiss her. It was surprising that he didn't think she was stalking him. Or maybe he did, and was just too polite and kind to say so. Either way, she screwed up once again.

She was listless for the remainder of the morning, not wanting to talk to anyone. Gidge most likely was back in town but Stazie did not even want to commiserate with her. Anyway, her friend wouldn't understand. The only other time in her life she remembered feeling so sad was when she was very young, but that memory was old and faded. Usually, if Stazie Royale was unhappy, it was not for very long. Everything to ensure her ultimate contentment had always amply provided. However, this time she knew that neither Daddy nor his money could fix this. She wasn't sure if anything could.

Stazie sighed heavily and turned on her side. Hot tears soaked into her pillow. She knew her father had told her to take it slow and give him some space but that would take too long. What if she backed off and he slipped away from her completely? What if he met someone else?

She picked up the phone and dialed.

"Judy? This is Stazie."

"Oh, hello Stazie.

"Yes, hi. Could you—"

"Are you feeling well, dear? I hardly recognized your voice today."

"Yes, I'm okay. Listen, could you get me the number to Rey Natal? My dad should have it listed somewhere. He's our architectural designer."

"Well Stazie, you know I'm really not at liberty to give out any phone numbers from your father's contacts. But he's in right now. Would you like to speak with him?"

"No, it's just that I . . . um . . . I want to add a special change to the plans on our cottage, and I want it to be a total surprise for Daddy," she lied. "You know how much he would love a workout room. But I don't have Rey's—uh, Mr. Natal's number and I was wondering if you could give it to me?"

"I don't know. I'm really not supposed to," the secretary said.

"That's all I need. I won't ask you for any other numbers. I promise."

"And you said that this was for a surprise?"

"Oh yes. It's definitely a surprise."

"Well, I guess in that case . . ."

When Stazie hung up, her tears dried as she looked at his number with satisfaction. He was now only a phone call away. She had the ability to hear his voice any time she wanted. She started to dial his number but hung up at the last moment, her father's advice resounding in her head. After a few more agonizing moments she decided, *Daddy's not the one suffering through this. I am. He doesn't understand.* Clearing her throat, she tried out her voice. She certainly did not want Rey to hear the catch in it when he answered.

But when he picked up, she had to stifle a squeal when she heard him say,

"Rey Natal Architectural Designs."

Her heart was pounding. ". . . Hi. It's me."

"I'm sorry, who is this?"

"It's *me*, Stazie."

"Oh, hey. Uh, yeah . . . you're going to have to excuse me, I'm lousy with voices," he apologized.

By the sound of his voice, Stazie knew he was surprised. "It's okay, really." She suddenly she didn't know what to say, not having anticipated getting this far. Growing anxious she said, "Um, how are you today?"

"I'm fine, thanks. And you?"

"Oh fine. I . . . um, want to thank you for taking me to the lovely dinner at your parents' last night. I really had a good time."

"Good. I'm glad that you enjoyed yourself."

The conversation lapsed once more. *Why was this so difficult?* She agonized. She struggled onward. "Yes, it was nice to meet your family."

"Thanks. I'm sure they enjoyed meeting you too. Hey, was everything okay when you drove off last night?"

She hadn't expected his question. *Could it be that he cared?*

"Why do you ask?"

"I don't know. Never mind. Uh listen, Stazie, I've got a call coming in that I have to take. I'm sorry, but can you hold or can I call you back?"

"I'll hold."

It gave her the minute or more that she needed to gather her swirling thoughts. She hit her forehead with the heel of her hand. *I must sound like an idiot.*

On a better note, he had noticed that she was upset last night. What was confusing to her was the fact that he stopped there and didn't ask her more. *What exactly was it that I want from him?* She thought. But the answer was immediate. It was to see, hear, and be with him.

"Stazie, are you still there?"

His voice startled her back.

"I want you," she blurted out. "I mean, I, uh, want you to let me know if it would be all right for me to come over today," she salvaged. Then she rolled her eyes and hit her forehead again. *Total idiot.*

"I don't think that's possible. I am really busy today. Was there something you needed?"

You. And only you. "I . . . um . . . I lost my earring and I think it might be at your place." The lie sounded fairly reasonable to her, especially having made it up on the fly.

"I haven't seen it. But I can take a look around. Do you have any idea of where it might be?"

"Maybe in the sofa? Or at the counter?"

"I'll check. This place isn't big enough for anything to be lost too long."

"Maybe Jack took off with it somewhere?"

"Jack? No. I haven't seen him wearing an earring this morning."

"Huh? . . . Oh." She didn't get his joke at first but when she did, she kicked herself for being slow on the uptake. *Marcie probably would've had some cute comeback right off the cuff,* she thought miserably.

"Nope. I just checked everywhere. Are you sure you lost it here?"

"Yes. I remember when I was at your parents' place I noticed that it was gone. I . . . didn't get a chance to tell you. I must've forgotten to put it back on when I was fixing my hair at your apartment. So, yes, I'm almost sure it's there."

"I can send it to you when I find—"

"I'll just pop over there for one tiny minute and have a look around, okay? I promise I won't get in your way. You just keep working or doing whatever it is you were doing."

"It's just that I—"

"All right. I'll be over in about fifteen minutes. See you."

She hung up before giving him the chance to say no. It wasn't exactly fair on her part. But then when you needed to see someone as bad as she needed to see him, she didn't care about being fair.

"I don't know. I have a strange feeling that chick is up to something. And let me tell you, the feeling isn't good."

"I *know*. You've already said that, I don't know how many times last night?"

"Oh yeah? When?"

"Well, let's see. The entire drive back home, when we came in through the door, after we made love, and right before you went to sleep. And now, we're not even through breakfast and you've said it again."

"Okay. But I wonder what she's up to?"

"Ricky, why don't you just let it go? Rey's a big boy. I think he can handle it on his own," Marcie said gently as she patted her boyfriend's brawny arm. They were both enjoying a day off together and their morning had just started.

"I'm not so sure. He's always been a sucker around chicks. Did I ever tell you about the time he was in third grade? A girl named Veronica Patel used to sit next to him. Would you believe he gave her his lunch every day for two months straight?" He sipped at his coffee.

"Well, that's kind of sweet. Was it because she needed it? Or did he have a crush on her?"

"Nah. She told him that her mother never made her any. When the teacher finally caught on to what Veronica was doing, we found out she was giving her own lunch to another boy she thought was cute and then eating Rey's. See what I mean about gullible?"

"Yeah, but I'm sure he must've learned his lesson. He's a little older these days."

Marcie placed down a plate of hot fresh danishes she had just pulled from the oven. Rick immediately seized one.

"Oh, but not so quick. In high school, there was this other girl, Amy Korvitch," he said while he munched. "She went around telling everyone that Rey was her boyfriend, when he wasn't. She had given him some sad-sob story that no one liked her. So even though he had no interest in her, he let her say it just so she wouldn't feel bad, when in fact, she was only saying it just to make her real boyfriend jealous. Yeah, ol' Rey got his ass kicked good over that. Her boyfriend and three other members of the football team really worked him over. It cost him a bruised rib and three stitches over his left eyebrow."

"Okay, but then again—"

"Well look at what he's already done for Rachel. I mean, it's none of my business but if you ask me, I think he's gone a little too far."

"You're right. It is none of your business," Marcie said matter-of-factly. "Remember, she has the baby now to support."

"Yeah, yeah. That's what he keeps saying too. But I still think that he's done more than enough. He's got to move on." Rick grabbed up another danish.

"Guilt does funny things though."

"I know. But this Stazie, why he should feel any guilt over that bimbo? Okay, she helped him out some while they were upstate. But I also know Rey would've never let himself get into a dangerous situation like that if he had any choice in the matter."

"I'm not sure if I agree. You know all too well how wild he used to be. You used to say he was just having fun, or living it up, or some other excuse, when all along it was just plain recklessness. There's no other word for it."

"Yeah, but not like that. If someone's life was at stake, he never pushed it that far."

"Hmm, I think you should reconsider that statement and in the meantime make sure you don't say something like that to him, if you get where I'm going with this," Marcie said, looking at him in earnest.

Rick suddenly understood. "Yeah, you're right," he said insightfully while stroking his beard. "Yeah, that wouldn't be too good." Then he studied her illuminated from the morning light streaming in from the window. He loved the way her hair flowed around her face before she pulled it back for the day. "How did you ever get to be so damned smart anyway?"

"I've always been smart. It's just taken you a while to realize it, that's all," she said, giving him a peck. "If we're stopping by Rey's today, I think I'll bring him the rest of these danishes. He'll probably like these."

"Hey, those are my danishes!" Rick said in mock protest, scooting the plate possessively towards himself. "I thought you baked these especially for me."

"I did. And you've already eaten two, you big baby. Here, you can have one more. The rest go to Rey. He's looking a little skinny these days."

"Yeah. I noticed. Ma's gonna have a fit."

Rey hung up the phone and shook his head.

Somehow or another she had managed to worm her way in again. Just when he thought that Stazie was going to be a no show, she was on her way back over. It was a dangerous precedent that was being set. Okay, he had already screwed up by letting her hang around all day yesterday instead of showing her the door early on. But he was definitely going to have to put his foot down today. He simply had too much to do to let her loiter whether or not she liked him or hated his guts. At least when she hated him, she stayed away and life was normal.

Of all the people to have run him over that night, it had to be this odd, spoiled woman. Rey wondered why it couldn't have been instead an average moronic driver who would have just called the police, settle the sum, and be out of his life within a couple of hours. When he considered that in about fifteen more minutes Stazie would be walking through his front door on the pretense of a lost earring, he would have even preferred being the victim of a hit and run.

Rey tried to return his attention to his designs. He absent-mindedly clicked on his computer mouse and stared at the screen but his brain didn't register any of it. Annoyed, he forced himself to concentrate. He still had piles of work stacked up around his apartment but he didn't budge to tidy up. He wasn't going to disrupt his whole day again. And when she came, he would make sure she didn't linger this time.

❧

Naturally, they didn't find her earring in his apartment. Cleverly concealed in her pocket, the earring was ready for a quick plant should Rey start to doubt she had ever lost it in the first place. However that strategy didn't look like it was going to be necessary.

Stazie sat back on his sofa and folded her legs up under her as she contemplated his face. In it she could see that endearing mix of consternation and politeness at odds with each other. It was one of the qualities she found irresistible in him—his inability to get mean with her. She knew full well that he wanted her to leave. He had dropped dozens of hints about how busy he was today. Spying the prints, papers, and flash drives scattered all over, she knew he was telling the truth. But through it all, instead of yelling or getting angry or physically tossing her out, he refused to get rude and seemed to try everything to avoid hurting her feelings. This overwhelming act of kindness touched her.

Few people in her life ever had this much consideration for her. Even her own father had been known to forsake her feelings, especially if it meant coming between him and a certain someone he was seeing at the moment. Yet here was Rey—dear sweet Rey—raking his hand through his hair, his other hand jammed into his pocket, stumbling over his words and looking sheepish like a little boy who had been caught at being bad. It made her want to hug him. No, kiss him.

Maybe if he came a little closer or better yet . . .

She stood up and drew close enough to him to smell his aftershave, feel his warmth, and see the glow of his reddening cheeks. She could also see the look of panic that glazed his eyes as she puckered up.

There was a short rap on the door. Rey wasted no time in bounding over to it and with one last incredulous look at her, opened it with relief.

"Hey man, what is that sweet smell stinking up your stairwell?" Rick said as he entered. "God, it smells like a funeral hall out there. Wow, it smells like that in here too. It must be seeping in under your door. I was just telling Marce that's some pretty strong smelling shit—"

He stopped short when his eyes fell on Stazie.

She smiled and waved. "Hi guys."

Rick returned his gaze to his younger brother. Rey opened his mouth preparing to explain but then simply just shook his head and rubbed the back of his neck. There was no explanation for this and he didn't feel like inventing one.

"Hi Stazie, how are you?" Marcie said warmly.

"Oh fine."

"So are you plaguing Rey again today? Had nothing better to do?" Rick said bluntly with a pasted-on smile. Marcie got in a discreet elbow to his ribs.

"Rey, we brought you some danishes," Marcie said. "They're fresh. I just made them this morning."

Rey gratefully took the plate from her feeling relieved that she had interceded. There was no telling what a showdown between Stazie and his older brother would look like.

"Thanks, Marce! I love your danishes." He pulled back the plastic wrap and offered the plate towards Stazie. "Would you like to try one? Marcie makes the best danishes I've ever tasted."

Stazie shook her head politely. "No thanks."

"Are you sure? I'm not kidding. They're friggin' awesome." He plucked one off the plate and sunk his teeth into it. Munching happily, he said, "Marcie, your timing is dead nuts. I hadn't eaten anything this morning and I was totally starved."

"You know, I was just telling Ricky that you are looking a little skinny these days. I thought I'd bring them over to help fatten you up. Lord knows there are enough calories in them to do it."

Finishing up another bite, Rey gave her a peck on her cheek. "Thanks again. They're amazing. You're amazing." Then he went to the kitchen to get some milk.

Stazie's eyes turned cold at Rey's display of affection towards Marcie. She became conscious of her hand gripping her earring in her pocket so hard that it began to hurt. She eyeballed her new rival—the smart, self-confident brunette who always managed to steal his attention. *Isn't she just sooo sweet?* She angrily mused to herself.

Then her attention returned to Rey as he contently finished off his second danish. She pondered what she would have to do for him to ever be that happy with her. He didn't even seem as grateful to her for saving him from freezing to death as he was over those dumb pastries.

"Hey, can I get you guys anything?" Rey said.

Rick and Marcie both said, "No thanks, we're good."

Just then Jack Tate came trotting out of the bedroom, barking, whining, and dancing on his hind feet with excitement as he ran to the couple. Marcie stooped down to greet him as his curly tail wagged furiously and he wriggled and grunted to be picked up.

"Hey there, Piggy-Boy! Did we catch you off-guard, sleepy head? We could have come in and stolen Rey and you would have never noticed," she said. The little dog was beside himself with joy as he licked her chin.

Even the stupid dog loves her, Stazie fumed as the seed of jealously within her grew exponentially. *Great bunnies, does she have to be <u>that</u> good?*

"You should take the little runt home with you already. He prefers being with you guys anyway. I'm just his boring old roommate," Rey said seeing his pet's ardent display. "Besides, I'm tired of him drinking all of the beer."

"Oh no. We couldn't take this little stinker, could we, Rick?" Marcie said cuddling the grunting pug mix.

"This mutt? Nah," Rick said, but he affectionately rubbed Jack's ears and head.

Stazie reached out her hand to join in. "Besides, he's *your* dog, Rey. Not theirs."

At her touch, Jack Tate growled and snapped at her, narrowly missing her fingertips. Stazie gasped with surprise and withdrew her hand quickly.

"Holy moley! Did he get you?" Rey said as he bolted from around the counter. "Are you all right?"

"I don't think he got her," Rick said shrugging. "Although it was one helluva try. I gotta give him that."

"N-no. I'm okay," Stazie finally said, embarrassed and a little shaken.

Rey scooped Jack out of Marcie's arms. He stared into the pug-mix's face, as Jack tried to avert his weepy, worried eyes.

"What's gotten into you, you little rat? That is NO! You've gone too far, bucko. Just for that, you're on lockdown." With that, he shut the unhappy dog back in the bedroom. Jack whined and scratched at the door as Rey apologized, "I'm really sorry about that, Stazie."

"Wow, I wonder what was that all about? I've never seen him act like that," Marcie said. "Has Jack been feeling okay lately?"

"Yeah, as far as I know. I just took him on a long walk this morning. He seemed perfectly fine."

"Maybe it was the strange smell that set him off. You know, that perfume and all," Rick said, trying to sound logical.

Stazie cocked her head quizzically at him but Rey knew exactly what his older brother was up to. And he didn't need his help to chase her away. In another minute more, he would have gotten her to leave on his own. She just so happened to be there when they showed up and now Rick was looking at him like it was another Amy Korvitch scenario all over again. Rey loved his brother, but sometime or another he was going to have to back off. He was perfectly capable of handling his own affairs.

At that moment, it occurred to Rey that he had left Rachel's number out on the counter by the phone. If it was anywhere in Rick's line of vision, it could start yet another interrogation and argument. He gave a quick glance over his shoulder but couldn't spy it anywhere when Stazie let out a plaintive little sniff.

Turning his attention back to her, he said and motioned, "Here, let me see your hand. Are you sure you're okay?"

Jack had gotten nowhere near her hand but she gladly offered it to him anyway. As he gently inspected each one of her fingers and the front and back of her hand, she felt as if she were melting under his touch.

"Stazie? I asked if you are all right?"

The question woke her from her trance. She nodded. "I'm okay."

"Well, it doesn't look like he came away with any of your digits. Again, I'm really sorry for the way he acted. I don't know what's up with him."

Stazie locked eyes with him and stared deeply. "It's okay," she repeated breathlessly.

Rey caught her drift and dropped her hand. As she continued to gaze at him, he noticed that Rick was focused on her. Between Stazie getting moony over him and his big brother feeling protective, things were getting way out of hand. Rey wished that he could magically transport himself to a secluded mountain peak somewhere, away from everyone and these games they played. Colorado was probably not far away enough.

"So what are you guys doing today?" he said, trying to shift everyone's attention elsewhere.

"Marce and me both took the day off. But we haven't decided what to do yet. We might hang at the beach or maybe we'll drive up to the Catskills. I dunno. Anyway, that's why we stopped by today, to see if you have any guides or ideas."

"Hey, it's a beautiful day out. Why don't you join us?" said Marcie.

"Sure! That sounds like fun," Stazie said. "We'll go."

This time, both brothers looked at her in amazement.

"Well, I mean if Rey wants to, that is," she said when she felt their scrutiny.

"It's not that I wouldn't love to blow this place but I've got a ton of stuff I'm right in the middle of. In fact, I was just telling Stazie that when you got here." "Sure, I hear you, man. We'll catch you later." Rick hesitated for a moment. "We should *all* get out of your hair," he said, directing it at Stazie.

She stared straight ahead with an innocent look, ignoring Rick.

"So which guides do you need?" Rey said, intervening. If those two got into it, there was no telling how long they would linger to bicker.

Wisely, Marcie was just as eager to keep the peace in that tiny apartment. "How about the Poconos? Oh, do you have anything for the Hudson Valley? We might as well take it just in case."

"Cripe! You want to drive all the way up there? Day's about half over with already," Rick said.

"Why don't you just hop a flight? That's what I do when I don't feel like driving," Stazie said brightly.

"We would, except we gave our pilot the week off while our plane is in the shop having its wings rotated," said Rick.

Stazie glowered at him. *Why didn't he just leave her and Rey alone and take Ms. Perfect Danish with him?*

"Here are all my guides. Just take them all," Rey said. "But I really can't go with you guys. I'm swamped right now and I've got to finish up these plans and make some phone calls."

"Oh, you mean like to Rachel?" Rick said holding up the slip of paper with her number on it.

Shit. He found it, Rey thought.

"Rachel? Who's Rachel?" Stazie asked.

"Yeah, Rachel. What about it?" Rey said, challenging his older brother.

"Yes, Rick, what about it?" Marcie said. "Rey can call or help whomever he pleases."

 "C'mon, Bro, you know what I'm talking about," Rick said.

"No, I don't. But I have a pretty good idea."

"I don't want to start anything but haven't you done enough for her already? I mean, if you want to waste your time on a person like that, go right on ahead."

 "But who is Rachel?" Stazie demanded.

"We've been through this a million times already. I'm not going there anymore, especially with you." Rey said, pointing at Rick.

"All I'm saying is she's using you, man. You know she is. And you're too freakin' blind to see it."

"There's no way you can understand and I don't expect you too."

Rick said, "You've got to see that it's a bunch of bullshit."

"And if it is, it's *my* bullshit. I don't need any extra from you."

"Come on, Rick. Time to go," Marcie said, scooping up the books and then linking her arm through her boyfriend's while the two men glared at each other. "Thanks for the guides, Rey and sorry your brother here can't keep his nose out of your business. Nice seeing you again, Stazie."

Rick let her lead him out but not without mouthing the word, 'bullshit!' and pointing over his shoulder at his sibling.

"Thanks, Marce," Rey said as he closed the door.

Stazie stood there, waiting anxiously. "Rey? Who's Rachel?"

"Not now, Stazie. In fact, I need you to go too. I'm not lying when I say I've got a bunch of work I have to get to."

"But—"

"Goodbye Stazie," he said, opening the door once more. "I'll let you know if I find your earring."

"But you'll call me?"

"Sure, right. Whatever," he said as she exited. After a few moments had passed, he was almost certain that she was still lingering out there behind the closed door.

Maybe I should move to Colorado soon. Very soon, he thought.

It couldn't possibly be that hard to make, now could it? Any idiot who can read, can cook.

Or so she thought as the flour dust settled out of the air.

"Oh poop," Stazie said when pieces of eggshell fell into the mix.

As she tried to fish out the slivers with her finger, the cold slimy egg white made her scrunch up her nose in disgust. Frustratingly, the elusive shells danced around her fingertip. She decided to leave them in thinking that a little bit of eggshell shouldn't make any difference.

She could have had Beatrice bake the cake and then call it her own but Stazie was bound and determined to carry this through. After seeing Rey's delight over Marcie's danishes, she wanted to be the one who invoked that kind of pleasure in him. The possibility of one-upping the brunette had crossed her mind as well. But it wasn't as easy as she had envisioned. First, she agonized over the exact dish to make for him. She didn't want to make another breakfast pastry. He would be able to compare something like that directly to the danishes. Instead, she tried making cookies but the blackened flat disks were not fit for human consumption.

Finally, she asked Beatrice to round up every last cookbook in the house and when she still couldn't find what she was looking for, made the maid run home to fetch ones from her own kitchen. Beatrice was perplexed by her mistress' sudden interest in cooking. Stazie rarely ever set foot in the kitchen, hardly for a glass of water. However, she decided on a complicated recipe for a chocolate crème-filled cake. Beatrice offered to give her a hand and instruct her but Stazie adamantly refused and even resorted to barring the maid from the kitchen. She wanted this cake to be one hundred percent made by her alone.

She even went as far as purchasing all the ingredients herself. He should be proud to know that she went to the grocery on her own. And this time, she tracked down everything without having to confront a store manager.

It had been two days since she last saw Rey and even though he said he would call, her phone remained silent. Her heart ached thinking that he was more concerned about this Rachel person. It was obvious that he was definitely planning to call *her*. The cruel burn of jealousy ignited once again in Stazie, making it hard for her to concentrate on much else.

It was another reason why she had to get this cake right. She often heard her dad say, "The way to a man's heart is through his stomach." Now she was hoping there was truth behind the old cliché. To her frustration, the recipe called for heating the crème, letting it cool, whipping the butter and sugar, and slowly melting the chocolate. Looking at the clock, she grew impatient. Things were not moving fast enough. So instead of following the steps, she threw together the remainder of the ingredients, mixed them on high for a minute, dumped the mix into the pans, turned the oven on, and put the cake to bake.

Marcie said he looked a little skinny. Stazie thought Rey looked fine the way he was. But then, maybe she should start noticing details like that too. In retrospect, she supposed he did look thinner than when she first met him. In fact, the more she thought about it, she would have mentioned it herself except that Marcie had beaten her to it. She wished the brunette would focus on her own boyfriend and leave the younger brother alone.

It made Stazie wonder what it was about the older woman that put Rey at ease. Marcie wasn't exceptionally pretty or glamorous. She didn't even have big boobs. When it came down to it, she was on the plain side, wearing her hair back in a ponytail and keeping her jewelry and makeup simple. No designer clothes, perfume, or nail polish.

Looking at herself in the mirror, Stazie studied her own face and features more closely than she ever had before. With her fine nose, high cheekbones, and full lips, she beat Marcie in looks, hands down. Then she took a more objective look at her face. It was possible that she was scaring him off with all the glitz. She heard some guys didn't go for that, although all the guys she knew wanted the works from head to toe.

Hmmm, what if I gave it a try? she wondered.

Using her facial cleaner, she carefully removed all of her makeup, leaving her face unpainted, unfinished . . . natural. Next, instead of teasing and spraying up her hair, she gathered her loose curls and pulled them back into a ponytail like Marcie's. A few spiral tendrils escaped and fringed her brow and cheeks. The face staring back at her was new to her, but in a strange way, she was beginning to like it. She hoped that he would too.

A light rap on the door interrupted her thoughts. Beatrice called in, "Miss Stazie, Miss Martin is here to see you."

❧

"You? You baked a cake? I don't believe it. And what's up? You look kinda sick. You're not even dressed to go shopping yet," Gidge said.

"I'm not sick. I was just—Wait, I have to get the cake out of the oven before it burns. I think it's done."

"So you seriously did make a cake? This I've got to see."

Gidge dogged Stazie's steps into the kitchen. There, she made sure to position herself by the oven door, phone in hand, ready to video record the spectacle.

Stazie wished that Gidge hadn't showed up. However, she had forgotten all about their standing date to go shopping on the first of the month. Part of Stazie was jumping with anticipation over her first attempt at baking.

Part of her was wrought with anxiety that it would be a total disaster, and her friend would be there to witness it all.

Taking a deep breath, she opened the oven and impetuously reached in to seize the pans.

"OWWW!!" she howled as she withdrew her singed fingers and promptly put them in her mouth.

"Well, duh! That's what they use mitts for, stupid," Gidge said, heckling followed with a guffaw.

Embarrassed, Stazie looked around the kitchen with her fingers still in her mouth. She had no idea where Beatrice kept the oven mitts. In fact, she wasn't sure what they even looked like. But there wasn't any way that she was going to let on that she didn't know this and give Gidge even more ammunition.

Grabbing up a couple of dish towels she spied nearby, she bunched them up and went after the pans again. Feeling the heat soak through the towels to her sore fingers, she quickly tossed the pans onto the granite counter top. As one skittered precariously towards the edge, Stazie dove for it, catching it just before it toppled off. She realized then that she had just lain across the other pan and stuck her top into the warm chocolate cake. Straightening up, she looked at the gooey smear across the front of her shirt.

By this time, Gidge was laughing so hard she was doubled over. She caught her breath long enough to catch a glimpse of the lopsided disks in the pan, prompting hysterical shrieks of "I knew it! I knew it! Oh my god, look at those things." Then she checked her phone. "Ha! This is epic. I caught it all. I can't wait to post this! This is going to get, like, a million hits."

Stazie looked at the unusual cake she produced and was greatly disappointed. *How come it didn't look like the one in the cookbook?*

She had had visions of a sumptuous, perfect cake being extracted from the oven for her friend to see and admire. Her disappointment turned to humiliation as Gidge continued to hoot and snicker. *Oh why did she have to be here to see this?*

Finally catching her breath, her friend managed to say, "So whatever possessed you to even attempt this? Are you, like, on drugs or were you bored out of your mind? You can't even boil water without burning it! If you wanted a cake so bad, why didn't you just have Beatrice bake one for you?"

Her eyes brimming with tears, Stazie said dismally, "It's not for me. I was baking it for someone." The words had left her mouth before she realized it mistake to mention it.

"Seriously? Who? You didn't tell me about it."

"Just someone."

"A guy? Ooo, I know! It's Josh, right? I knew it! Well, I can save you a little time and trouble—he's probably not going to like it," Gidge said sarcastically, winking with mock confidentiality.

Stazie was growing indignant. "It's not for him. Josh is a total jerk. The person I'm giving this to would appreciate anything I tried."

"Not Josh? Then who? I can't think of anyone we know who would actually *appreciate* crap like this." Gidge grimaced and picked up the pan with the towel. She gave it a sniff and then tossed it down carelessly on the counter for emphasis. "He would have to be a goat or some kind of fricken' transient to eat this shit. So come on, who is it? And don't lie because you know I'll find out."

"No, never mind. You—you wouldn't understand."

"C'mon, Staze. I tell you everything."

"I don't want to."

"Okay then, be that way. But then maybe I'll just have to tell your Daddy about how you paid that guy in Dallas a grand and flashed him your boobs after you ran into his car just so he wouldn't report you to the police," Gidge said, trying extortion.

Stazie gave her friend a hard look. That little mishap had taken place over five months ago. She thought Gidge had forgotten all about it. After all, she had, and she was the one who did it.

"Oh, all right. It's . . . my dad's architectural designer," she said in a small voice, then sighed. Her secret was out.

"Who?"

"The designer who's working on the cottage."

Gidge puzzled over it for a moment and then her eyes opened wide. They immediately narrowed to two wicked slits.

"HIM? You mean that asshole you had to drive up to the cabin? EWWW!! I don't believe it! He's so gross. What was his name again? Dick? Dick something?"

"It's Rey Natal."

"Oh my god. Have you lost your mind? He's such a fucking loser! Why would you ever stoop so low?"

"Don't call him that!"

"Why not? He is. And you were the one who said it, not me."

"Oh, why don't you just shut up already, Gidge?" Stazie had had it—first the cake and now this. When her friend started to insult Rey, Stazie felt it as deeply as if she had been insulted herself.

Gidge looked at Stazie in shock. "What!"

"I said shut up. You don't understand."

"Well excuse the living shit out of me! Not three weeks ago, you didn't want anything to do with the prick and now you're like, little Miss Suzie Homemaker baking cakes for him. What a joke. And tell me, what in hell would make him 'appreciate' this? Does he even *like* you?"

At that moment, Stazie realized that Gidge always had the ability to make her doubt herself. She was beginning to resent it.

"Seriously. I bet you haven't even given it any thought."

"You don't even know him! In fact, I think it's time that you leave," Stazie said.

"Leave? I'm only, like, your best friend trying to clue you in to the big mistake you're making. I ask one little question about some jerk-off you don't know anything about and you want *me* to leave?"

"Yes I do."

"It's not like he's even part of our circle."

Stazie remained silent, her mouth a straight firm line.

"But what about our shopping date? Remember, the first of the month?"

"It's off. It's about time you spent your own money for a change. Now leave."

Gidge stared at her incredulously. Stazie had never spoken to her like that before. Opening and closing her mouth in indignation, she finally turned on her heel and left in a huff.

Stazie knew she had hurt her but she was angry enough not to care. Gidge did not have the right to say all those horrible things about him. But even more troubling was her friend's question still resounding in her ears: *does he even like you?*

She turned to the pitiful cakes before her. Determined to try even harder, she was going to salvage them. Although they didn't look appetizing, at least they smelled good. A glance at the clock told her that she wouldn't have any time to try another recipe if she was going to see him today. And she had to get this to him soon before he made even more calls to that Rachel person.

Poking around in the cupboards, she found a couple of cans of instant chocolate frosting towards the back of the cabinet. Turning the pans upside down and shaking them, the cake flopped out in pieces upon the plate. She spent the next half hour patching and gluing them together, trying to hide lumps, cracks, and other imperfections. The frosting was hard to spread on the top of the cake without peeling away the soft cake underneath, so she mixed in some water until it was finally smooth.

With some work, the cake pieces held together. For a topping, she dusted flour over it, mistaking the white powder for confectioner's sugar. Then she placed a bright fresh flower on top, just as she had seen Beatrice do on special occasions. With a last look at her handiwork, she knew it wasn't anywhere near as pretty as her maid's but she thought he would like it. After all, she had gone through all this trouble. He *should* be pleased. She couldn't wait to see the look on his face when he took his first bite. Maybe she would see that smile of his or better yet, get a kiss on the cheek like he did for Marcie.

Leaving the kitchen in shambles, she dashed back to her bedroom to get dressed. Out of habit, she immediately reached for her cosmetic cases and fragrances but caught herself. Forcing herself to put down the makeup and perfume, she fought against lining her eyes even a little. Before she could leave her bench, at the last minute she dabbed on moisturizer, covered the few freckles across her nose, and applied a light-colored lipstick.

A girl can't go out without something on her face.

After all, she didn't have to go totally overboard. Turning her head to view first one side of her profile then the other, she thought, *Now, how does Marcie do it?* while teasing out a few more strands of curls to frame her face.

Next, she selected one of her plainer sweaters and a pair of jeans. She felt so exposed and underdressed without her makeup and bangles. It was hard to imagine that he would prefer her this way. She couldn't see how because it did nothing to emphasize her looks or shape. Insecurity almost made her abandon the whole plan. Instead, she took a deep breath, and with her chin held high, she packed up the lumpy cake, grabbed her coat and purse, and was off. Veering her car through the streets while humming the tune he had played for her on the piano, her pulse quickened at the thought of being near him again.

Rey opened the door to maneuver his bike out into the hallway. Turning, he nearly ran into her.

"Oh, excuse me. I didn't see you there. If you're looking for Li Zhou, he's down at the store."

"Hi Rey."

At first, he couldn't see who was addressing him through the dark lenses of his sunglasses. There wasn't any trace of fragrance to help in identification.

"Stazie?" he said. Even after he removed his glasses and did a double take, he barely recognized her. Without all the paint and big hair, she looked younger and . . . prettier. He was taken aback for a few seconds.

"Is something wrong?" she said, feeling self-conscious. Worry clouded her bright smile and she lowered her eyes and nervously touched her hair.

He wanted to remark on how different she looked but wasn't sure if she would take it right. He said instead, "Huh? No! It's that I wasn't expecting to see you here today. I was just getting ready to go for a ride."

"I see," she said giving a nod to his riding outfit.

"So what's up? Was there something else you forgot?" He conceded, returning his bike to the apartment. Any visit from Stazie usually took some time. He would just have to get in some riding this afternoon after she left. *If she left,* he thought as she followed him in.

"No, nothing's up. I made something for you and thought you might like to try it," she said, holding up a container.

"You made this? For me?" he said, amazed. "Thanks. You didn't have to go through all that trouble."

He placed the container on the counter and lifted the lid to reveal the contents. There wasn't anything in its sagging shape or form that offered him the slightest suggestion to what it was.

"No, I mean seriously—Uh, what . . . is it?"

She beamed. "A chocolate cake, silly! And it was no trouble at all. I love to bake!"

"*You* love to bake?"

"Uh huh. I do it all the time."

"All the time, eh?" he said as he watched the top layer of the cake slide off, traveling on a landslide of frosting.

"Uh huh. Oh wait. This is supposed to be here," she said as she repositioned the top layer back onto the bottom layer.

As she daintily licked the frosting off her finger, he noticed a red burn mark running the length of it and across the tips of her other fingers. Next, he studied the disaster on the plate. Deep fault lines began to appear as the warmed frosting melted and the wilted flower followed the flow. He managed a polite expression.

"Uh, thank you."

She grinned back obviously proud of her accomplishment. Before Rey could put the lid back on, she popped the question he feared would be next.

"Aren't you going to try some?"

He swallowed hard. "Maybe not now. I . . . I, um, just finished eating before you came. Yes. Too full," he said, patting his stomach.

Stazie's bottom lip stuck out in disappointment. "You're not going to try any? At least one little bite? I wanted to see what you thought of it."

It occurred to him that this might be the one time Ms. Anastasia Royale went out of her way to do something kind for him, or anyone, for that matter. And it wasn't a matter of life or death as when they were at the cabin where she had taken pity on him and was perhaps dependent upon his survival in some way. No, this time, it was premeditated and purely intentional. Stazie had planned on, followed through and baked this cake, just for him.

Unless, he surmised by the look of it, *she is trying to kill me.* He couldn't help but wonder if it was all an elaborate scheme to lead up to trust and then poisoning. But he knew his imagination was running wild. At least he hoped so.

"Okay," he said, sighing inwardly. "Would you like some? Surely you'd like to try your own baking?"

"No, it's just for you," she said smiling once more.

Fighting off a shiver, Rey took out a fork and scooped up the goo. When the cake entered his mouth, his taste buds awoke to a battle of tastes. Unsweetened baker's chocolate clashed with bitter clumps of baking soda and unbaked flour. Pieces of eggshell mingled and crunched with the grittiness of uncooked sugar between his teeth. He fought hard to chew through it all without losing his breakfast.

Maybe she is trying to kill me. He tried to think where he had put Poison Control Center's magnet with its phone number.

"So, what do you think?" Her bright eyes looked anxious as she bit her lower lip.

As he choked the mess down, Rey found he didn't have the heart to quash her overture. He filled a glass with water and immediately chugged it.

Clearing his throat, he managed to say, "It's *different*. I don't think I've ever had chocolate cake quite like *that* before."

"Really?"

Rey nodded his head and said with a queasy smile, "Yes, really."

Stazie's worried face erupted into a grin as she giggled and clasped her hands. He had to admit, at that moment, with her genuine joy and the absence of all her makeup, her face was quite pleasing.

Before she could suggest he eat some more, Rey quickly packed up the cake and put it in the refrigerator, and said, "I'll just put away the rest of this for later."

Stazie braced herself, hoping against hope that he would give her a kiss on the cheek or something even better. She looked up expectantly but all he did was smile at her. Feeling awkward, she tried to hide it.

"Ooo, what are these?" she said, looking at the photos scattered on the counter. "Did you take these? Where is this?"

"It's the San Juan Wilderness near Durango."

"Durango? Where's that?"

"Colorado. I took those about two years ago."

"Daddy and I have gone to Colorado to ski a couple of times. But we only go to Aspen."

"Aspen? Sure. I've been up that way. I love it. I try to go whenever I can."

"Wow. They look like postcards."

"Thanks. But the scenery there makes it easy."

"Is that why you go? For the scenery?"

"No, I like hiking, biking, and backpacking in the summer. And if I'm lucky, I catch some snowboarding at Ouray in the winter."

"So are you planning another trip? Is that why these pictures are out?"

"Nah, I was just going through some files this morning and came across them."

"You should go. It'll be fun."

"I don't have the time or money to go. And it looks like it's gonna be a while before I can."

"You need to get out and enjoy yourself once in a while. I always make sure to go somewhere out of state at least once a month if I can."

He raised his eyebrows. "I'm sure you do. I would love to go but there's no way that I can swing it right now."

Stazie did not want their conversation to end on a bad note. She fished around for something else.

"So what do you do when you backpack? That's like, when you carry all of your clothes and food in a bag, right?"

"Yeah, kind of like that."

"But why?"

"Why what?"

"I mean why go to all that trouble when you can stay at a resort or hotel?"

"I do it just to get outdoors where it is fresh and clear and I'm completely dependent on myself and what I can carry. No one around. It's peaceful."

Stazie pondered it for a moment. "Wait a minute. Then what do you do when you want to take a shower? Are there some kind of special shower things out there?"

"Shower things? Uh, not really. I guess there are solar shower bags you can bring, if you don't mind hauling the extra weight. Sometimes I just jump in a lake if its available but that can be pretty cold."

"Are there at least bathrooms?"

"Nope. No bathrooms."

"What! But how about when you have to, you know, go?"

"Where do you think?"

Her mind flashed back to the fishing shack and the tree and the frozen air that blew up her skirt that morning.

"Great bunnies! All the time? I thought that fishing shack just hadn't added the plumbing yet. Oh, that's disgusting!"

He laughed. "You get used to it."

"I'm not sure if I ever could! So how about when you hike?"

"What do you mean?"

"I've never been hiking before. What's it like?"

"You've never been hiking before?"

She shook her head.

"It's kind of like when we were walking around the lake. You pick a destination and then you go for it."

Unconvinced of hiking's attraction, she said, "But what do you do once you get there?"

"I don't know, whatever you want—fish, explore, sleep, daydream."

To Stazie, it seemed like a whole lot of effort for something that sounded pretty uneventful.

"I guess you could always shop if you got really bored with all of that?"

"Shop? What do you mean? There aren't exactly a bunch of malls to choose from," he said and chuckled.

"Okay, well maybe not a mall, but how about some of those cute shops in the small towns or on someone's farm? You know, the ones that sell homemade butter and alpaca wool socks and things like that?"

He looked at her with disbelief, realizing she wasn't joking.

"What? There's got to be at least a little gift shop at a ranger hut or something, right?"

"There are no gift shops or ranger huts. We're talking miles out there. Like I said, nothing but trees, mountains, rivers, awesome views. And freedom. Fantastic freedom."

"Miles! But why would you want to go through all of that just to be where it's cold, wet, dirty, and full of bugs?"

"Well, why would you want to go through all of the primping and wearing uncomfortable clothes to pay money to stand in a loud, crowded club with drunk strangers trying to impress each other?"

"Oh." She hadn't thought of it that way.

Just then the phone rang. Rey picked it up.

"Oh hey, Rach," he said. "Listen, could you hold on a minute?" He turned to Stazie. "I'm really sorry but I have to take this. Will you excuse me?"

He immediately headed to his bedroom and closed and locked the door. When he entered, Jack Tate scooted out. Having been woken up, the dog looked up groggily at her. Not liking what he saw, he started to growl.

Rachel! Stazie's head sounded the alarm.

She went to the bedroom door and put her ear to it only to make out him saying, 'Okay, when's a good time for you to come over? . . . Uh huh. So when you get here, let's—"

The dog growled even louder, interrupting her eavesdropping.

"Shh! Quiet, Jack," she hissed under her breath, holding her finger to her lips.

At this, Jack erupted into a barking fit. She tried shushing him but it only made him bark and growl louder. The door cracked open. Stazie jumped back hoping that Rey couldn't see her hugging the wall. But all he did was poke his head out to check what was going on. Then he snapped his fingers and pointed at the pug mix. The little dog obediently stopped barking and sat, but he kept a wary eye on his adversary.

As soon as Rey closed the door, Stazie's ear went up against it once more. She stuck her tongue out at Jack who growled softly in return but held his position.

Then she heard Rey continue, "Yeah, it was just Jackie going off. He's been acting strange lately. Uh huh . . . Okay, so I'll see you Sunday? . . . Yeah, that would be good . . . Sure. That would be great if you could. All right, catch you then. It'll be good to see you."

Hearing him conclude his call, she quickly resumed her place by the kitchen counter, pretending to look at the photos. Rey stepped back out. His dog ran up to him wagging his tail.

"And what's up with you, little man? Stazie's not doing anything." He looked up at her. "Hey, I'm sorry about him. Seems like I'm always apologizing for my dog's rude manners."

"It's okay. Hey Rey, who is Rachel anyway?" she said.

"Just someone I know. So is this all you had planned for today? Dropping off cake to me?"

His answer didn't satisfy her and her gut started to churn with jealousy. She had to do something before this Rachel moved in. *Literally* she feared.

"Stazie?"

Breaking her train of thought, she said, "Huh? I've got to get going. I've got a really busy day." She gathered up her stuff and bustled to the door.

"Sure thing," he said as he walked with her. "And thanks again for the cake. It was . . . good."

She nodded and looked distracted. Then she hurried down the stairs and out onto the street without another word.

Before, Rey would have been puzzled by her sudden change in behavior but not anymore. He was growing used to it. As he watched her from the landing, he was reminded of a time hiking in the Rockies. It had been a perfectly beautiful June day with clear skies and mild temperatures. When he hiked up the trail and stopped for lunch, a cool breeze started to blow and dark clouds crowded the sky. By the time he had made it back to his rental parked at the trailhead, snowflakes fell from the sky. He had always been amazed at the unpredictable weather in the mountains of Colorado and never thought he would ever see anything else like it. That was, until now. Shaking his head, he went back in to retrieve his bike and get some riding in for the day.

Chapter 6 ~ The Flight

I've been shanghaied and now I'm on my way to Purgatory.

Skimming over the voluminous clouds, Rey couldn't help but wonder how he had ended up in the cushy leather seat of the private jet. He looked at his abductor, still amazed at her powers of manipulation. Apparently, he must not have put up much of a fight or she was very good at getting what she wanted. He pondered how it was that she had bested him and he cursed himself for being so stupid.

Catching his eye, she smiled and scrunched up her nose as if she were anticipating something thrilling. "This is fabulous that you were able to come along. Both Daddy and I are eternally grateful."

Attempting a smile in return, he controlled his mouth from twisting into a sneer.

How the hell did this happen?

Looking back, he recalled it started when he had noticed the approaching date on the calendar. Next, he found himself drowning in a pit of depression. The only way he treaded the surface was with a six-pack of beer, and multiple shots of tequila alternating with vodka. This was followed by tumbling face first into his bed.

He remembered somewhere in that alcohol-induced slumber, the phone ringing and his head feeling as if a bat had been taken to it. By the fifth ring, he barely managed to pick up the phone and hold it to his ear, as he lay with his face smashed into his pillow. Through a drunken haze, he thought he heard Doug running on with something that sounded like, "Stazie wanted to travel to Colorado and he was unable to go with her because of a business trip he had to attend to and he felt uneasy about sending his 'little girl' alone and if he could trouble him not as a business associate, but as a 'friend,' to accompany her, he would consider it a personal favor."

Rey's first thought was that Stazie could surely take care of herself. Not too many people were going to tangle with that chick. However, his inebriation had zapped any strength he had left to speak, let alone argue. Besides, Doug had been extremely generous, paying him more than half for the job up front without setting foot in the cottage. There wasn't a gracious way to say no to one of his best clients. The discussion was brief and futile, although somewhere in his intoxicated state, he regarded the timing of the call as highly suspicious.

Thinking more clearly now, he determined *drinking seriously does screw with one's judgement.*

Nevertheless, he was stuck in the company of an unpredictable storm cloud for the next two days. The only upside was getting to see Colorado again. Trying to console himself, he knew it would only be until Sunday evening—probably late Sunday evening if he knew Stazie at all. And then it was back to work, bright and early Monday morning, at least for him. She would be back doing whatever it was that filled her days—sleeping, shopping, stalking people . . .

Oh shit. Rachel.

He had totally forgotten about his lunch date with her on Sunday. She was even going to bring Tristan with her. There was no way for her to know that he was out of town and with the approaching anniversary, she needed him more than ever.

"Rey? Something the matter?"

"Huh?"

He was jolted back to thirty thousand feet.

"I was asking if something was troubling you. You seem so quiet." She studied him closely.

"Nah. I just need to make a phone call as soon as we land."

"Here, you can use my phone," she said as she handed hers over.

He was about to take it but then decided against it. It wouldn't bode well to have Rachel's number stored in Stazie's phone's memory as well as her hanging on his every word.

"Thanks. It can wait."

"No really, it's okay."

Rey thought it best to change the subject before she got too insistent and his hangover headache returned.

"So your father's also on a trip right now? Do you guys charter two planes?"

"Oh no. Not Daddy. He's much too practical to ever fly private. He always says, 'I'm not in the habit of throwing away hard-earned money,'" she said, mimicking her father's tenor. "Not me. I book these because they're quicker and you don't have to sit with who-knows-what next to you sleeping on your shoulder or hogging the armrest. So anyway, who do you have to call?"

"Just an appointment I had on Sunday that I forgot to cancel."

"An appointment on a Sunday? Well, I'm sure that your 'appointment' will understand that you were out of town on much needed rest and will reschedule, right?"

He didn't answer but returned to looking out the window.

Stazie felt vexed. There was no way she was going to let Rachel, or anyone for that matter, get between Rey and her this weekend. Wasn't that the whole point in getting him out of town? She wanted him all to herself for the next couple of days with no maybe-girlfriends, future sister-in-laws, bossy brothers, yappy dogs, or other distractions. Her thoughts shifted to hopefulness.

Maybe, just maybe, he will finally notice me.

She had booked rooms for them at a secluded resort and planned on brunch in the morning, candlelit dinners, long walks, and soaks in the hot tub. If she could persuade him, they might even get in a club or two. *But quieter clubs with intimate settings. Not the loud, crowded ones that he seemed to dislike.* And if all went well, she had packed her sexiest negligee, just in case. She felt giddy with anticipation.

When their plane touched down at Pitayin County Airport at six fifty-three in the evening, there was a rental car waiting for them. After Rey loaded their luggage, Stazie wanted to drive directly to dinner instead of stopping first at the resort. She noticed how he kept checking and rechecking his watch. Resignedly, he turned to her once more.

"Stazie?"

"Mmmm, yes?"

She loved it when he said her name.

"Would you mind if I borrowed your phone? I'll pay any charges. My cell doesn't have nationwide coverage."

"Don't be silly, I couldn't charge you! Here it is . . . Oh no. Looks like it's dead. You're going to have to wait until it charges up. I'll be sure to plug it in tonight when we get to the resort, okay?" she said cheerfully.

According to its tiny screen, her phone had plenty of charge but she wasn't going to hand it over it so easily. Not if it meant him contacting Rachel.

Knowing it was getting late on the East Coast, Rey had decided to risk using Stazie's phone, but it appeared that she was suspicious of his intent. That aside, he was excited to be in Colorado again. It was one of the few places that he felt totally at home and he always believed he was somehow meant to live here. The daylight was fading fast but just the smell of the evergreens and mountain air was comforting to him.

They turned into the crowded parking lot of Le Aubergè, an upscale hotspot for wealthy tourists. During the ski season, tables were booked weeks in advance but during the off-season, there was slim chance to land one on a walk-in basis. Like a shark she circled persistently around the lot for five minutes, waiting for someone to pull out. All the while, she chattered on about it being one of her favorite places to eat in the state, how she wished they had valet service in the summer, and how he was going to have one of the best dining experiences ever.

Rey felt doubtful. Looking at the line of people waiting outside, it seemed like it was going to take forever to get in. It was crowded and noisy when they finally entered the dimly lit restaurant. With a little convincing and a token fifty slipped to the maître d' from Stazie, they were accepted without a reservation but were told the wait time was going to be at least forty-five minutes. After ordering drinks at the bar, an awkward silence developed between them. Rey seemed distracted and fidgety, craning his neck to see around the dining room from where they were perched on the tall bar stools.

"So, what do you think about the 'Berge?"

He couldn't hear her above the din of voices and music.

"I said, what do you think about the 'Berge?" she asked once again, raising her voice.

"The what?" He leaned in closer in effort to hear her.

"This place? Le Aubergè? Daddy and I eat here every time we come to ski."

"I honestly can't say yet. Hey, which way to the restrooms?" he said as he rose from his bar stool.

She pointed and said, "That way."

With nothing more than a hasty "Excuse me," he took off. She quickly lost sight of him in the crowded restaurant. After about ten minutes of sitting alone, Stazie went to use the restroom as well. When she came back she had expected to see him waiting at the bar for her. He had not returned. Anxiety swamped her mind with questions.

Where was he? Could he have stood me up? Would he do that after she flew him all the way over here?

The bartender served her up another drink and asked her if Rey needed one as well. Distracted, she didn't answer him.

Maybe he was angry about the phone? she pondered as she looked about her and sipped her daiquiri. *I should have just given it to him.*

It was not until a few more agonizing minutes later, she could see Rey returning, making his way through the narrow aisles. She signed with relief.

"For a minute there, I thought you had abandoned me," she said, half-joking as he approached.

"Huh? No, I was just looking for a phone. I thought there would be one by the restrooms. It was out in the lobby instead."

"Were you calling your brother?"

"No, just Rachel," he said.

She raised an eyebrow. "Oh. I thought you said you had an appointment you had to cancel. So what DOES Rachel do for a living?"

He noted her innuendo but decided to let it pass. It looked like it was going to be a long enough weekend already without getting into a petty fight an hour after landing. He took a pull from his beer and looked around, not answering her.

"So, was she asleep already?" Stazie said.

"Yeah, unfortunately. I woke her but she was cool."

"Huh, too bad," she said nonchalantly. *Good. Maybe if Rachel got annoyed enough with him, she would drop him like a bag of dirty laundry.* "Did you let her know that you were here with me?"

"Yes."

"And?"

"And what?"

"It would seem that if I knew a guy and he was on a trip with some other woman, I don't know how well I would take it."

"It's not like that."

"But aren't you and she—?"

"End of subject."

Their table was wedged in the middle of the dining floor between dozens of other tables packed with people. The food servers squeezed in and out of the crowd, skillfully balancing large trays of food suspended over the heads of their guests. It would have been the last place Rey would have chosen for dinner, crowded and expensive, but Stazie seemed pleased.

Throughout the course of dinner, she disclosed the details of her plans for the weekend but to Rey, it all sounded like shopping and eating. Not once did she ever mention anything that involved the outdoors. He quietly picked at his food that he found unappetizing while she happily prattled on.

By the time they checked in to the Shadows Mountain Resort, it was close to eleven. Stazie asked if he was interested in seeing what was up at the bar but he declined. Another bustling, loud place was not what he had in mind for the remainder of the evening. At her room, she swiped her card to open the door, but lingered in the doorway. A coy smile tugged at her lips.

"Well, instead of a noisy bar, how about a nice long soak in the hot tub in here? Oohh, doesn't that sound good? I can get my suit on in a jiff."

"No Stazie, I'm going to pass."

"Well, then would you like to just come in instead?" she said suggestively. "We can call room service and have a few quiet drinks."

"It's been a long day. I think I'm going to hit the sack. Good night."

With a hungry look in her eyes, she lingered for a moment longer but he left quickly, not giving her much of a choice.

When he entered his room, he stood for a moment in awe. The suite was at least three times bigger than his apartment. He couldn't believe the size and luxuriousness of it. Even when he could afford more, he had never stayed in a place this posh. After checking out the cable TV and paging listlessly through the tourist magazines, he had enough. Rey stood in a hot shower, letting the water run over his head and course down his back, trying to erase away the day's events and the guilt of standing up Rachel. Regrets of ever being talked into coming here were beginning to resurface.

There has to be some way out of this, he contemplated as he opened the window wide to let the cool mountain air fill his room. *However, she did pay for this trip.* He inhaled deeply, wishing to be free of these traps that continued to snare him.

He was here, purely under duress but obligated to stay. As it stood, the futility in pretending this weekend might be enjoyable wasn't going to do either of them any good besides being a total waste of time. There had to be some other way to get through this. Her itinerary was going to require a few adjustments.

❧

The next morning he stood before room 314 with a plastic grocery bag in his hand hoping that what he prepared to do wouldn't lead to more regrets.

A man, wheeling a heavy duffle bag and loaded down with a overnight bag on one shoulder and a laptop case on the other, slowly shuffled by on his way to an early morning checkout. Rey gave him a brief nod and the man returned it. Baggage, in one form or the other, all felt the same.

Rey knocked. There was no answer from within but he didn't expect one. It would have been more of a surprise to him if she were an early riser. She certainly wanted to stay up late the evening before. And taking a guess at the type of person she was, he knew the two didn't mix.

"Not now. Come back later," said a groggy voice from within.

He shifted the grocery bag to the other hand and knocked harder this time, continuing a steady rhythm when the door suddenly swung open.

"Hey! Can't you see the 'Do Not Disturb' sign?"

Stazie looked cross until she saw him standing there. Obviously, she thought it was the maid knocking. She ducked back behind the door and sheepishly peered out.

"Oh Rey, it's you! Hi. Um, what are you doing up so early?" she said as she patted down her hair that looked like she had tangled with a cat and lost.

Rey stared at the two half-moons of smudged mascara under her eyes, trying to make out what they were.

"I just thought we should get going and make the most of our time while we're here."

"But brunch doesn't start until ten o'clock. What time is it now? Eight or so?"

"Six-oh-five."

A low groan escaped her.

"I can leave if you want to get back to sleep."

"No, no. It's okay," she said and yawned. "Uh, did you want to come in?"

"Sure. I brought breakfast, if you're interested." He held up the bag.

"Breakfast? Really? How sweet! Listen, could you hold on a moment while I fix my hair? I don't want you to see me like this."

"I'm sorry I woke you up. Besides, I've seen you like this before, remember?"

"I guess you have." Her smile was shy. "Okay, you can come in, as long as you promise not to laugh."

As he followed her in, although his eyes weren't on her hair, they couldn't resist admiring her bare legs underneath the short pink nightie as she padded barefoot to the living room.

She motioned to the sofa as he set the bag down on the coffee table. Then she crawled into the armchair and continued to yawn, trying to wake up.

"So what do you have in there? Let me guess, croissants and lattes I hope?" she said sleepily.

"Nope. Better." He slid out a package of cake donuts and a quart of orange juice with extra pulp. He thought he heard her groan again. "Do you have any glasses?"

As she shuffled back with two water glasses, she said, "We can get going early if you want but you know nothing is open at this time in the morning."

"What do you mean?"

"Well, most of the shops don't open until ten-thirty. I think there might be a few that open as early as nine but that's still another three hours away."

"Last I checked outside seems wide open right now."

"Outside? What do you mean?"

"The trails, the mountains, the lakes, they're open twenty-four seven. That's why I brought breakfast. We can eat quick, get on the road, and make the most of daylight." Rey said as he poured out the orange juice and opened the donuts.

She tried to look agreeable but his offer didn't sound appealing.

"Wasn't that why you wanted to come to Colorado this weekend? To see the places in my photos? At least that's what I think I recall the purpose was when your father called me on the phone. Well, I'm going to take you to see them up close today," he said, taking a bite of donut and chugging some juice.

Stazie looked queasy. "We're going *there*?"

"Well we won't be able to get to all of them today but at least maybe one or two. You said you wanted to go and I'm happy to oblige. So, do you still need to shower?"

"Yeah . . . But really, don't do all of this on my part. I am perfectly happy knowing that we are very close to the places in your photographs."

He smiled a Cheshire cat grin at her. "Nah. It's no problem at all. In fact, it'll be fun."

Stazie gave a slight nod and swallowed hard. Then she rose and toddled off, her donut and orange juice left untouched.

Going to the woods? Outdoors?

As she showered, she wracked her brain over what went wrong. It was the last thing she had in mind. Stazie had told her father that she wanted to see the forests in Colorado and that Rey knew all the best places. She suddenly wished that she had thought of a better excuse to come here at all. It was unfortunate that his photos weren't of Hawaii instead.

When she returned to the living room, he was staring out the sliding door at the scenery beyond with his arm resting above his head against the pane of glass and looking like an animal longing to be free of its confines. She knew he really wanted to go.

There's no backing out of this now, she thought. Taking a deep breath, she cleared her throat and said, "Okay, I'm ready."

When he turned around, he scanned her over to see what she was wearing, wanting to make sure she was prepared this time. She was dressed in a pink velour hooded jacket and pant outfit with flimsy sequined flip-flops on her feet and a matching beaded bag on her shoulder.

Oh well, at least her stomach isn't exposed, he thought with a sigh.

"I even have a camera to take some of those shots," she said, proudly holding up her cell phone.

"Right, but do you have any other shoes that are more suitable for hiking?"

"Why? These are fine. I walk all over in them. They are very comfortable."

"No, Stazie, I don't think you understand. Remember how by the fishing shack, we had to walk around the lake?"

She nodded. Then in the next moment, she grew wide-eyed with disbelief. "You mean we are going to go tromping all over the place like that again? There are sidewalks, right?"

He shook his head.

"Seriously? But aren't there plenty of other places with sidewalks we could go to instead?"

"Not if you want to see those places in the photographs although I won't take you to any of the ones that are really rigorous. For the most part, the trails I'm taking you to aren't rough but I do suggest proper foot protection. Let me see what other shoes you've brought with you."

She presented at least six other pairs of various shoes, slides, and boots. All of them were fashion footwear.

"No, it doesn't look like any of these are going to work," he said after inspecting them all.

"Oh well, too bad. Guess it looks like we're going have to stick around town today," she said sighing as she sunk down into the armchair. Her lip turned down in a cute little pout. "Maybe the next time we come to Colorado, I'll remember to bring the right pair of shoes."

He wished he could have given her an award for her performance. Instead he said, "Nah. Come on. We'll go anyway." He stood up, grabbed the remainder of the donuts and juice, and started for the door.

"Wait a minute! I thought you said I didn't have the right shoes," she said.

"You don't. But it doesn't matter."

He opened the door and stepped out. She scurried to catch up.

"But what about my feet? I can't go hiking in these. Don't you care what happens to me?"

"We'll stop somewhere along the way when we see a place that sells real boots. By the time we're down the road a bit, the stores should be open."

Amidst the frantic flapping from her flip-flops as she hustled down the hallway, he could hear her say, "Oh, poop."

"All I see are guns, coolers, and fishing rods. Are you sure they sell shoes here? And why do they have all those animal heads on the walls? It's creepy."

"They're hunting trophies. Boots are probably down one of these aisles."

Along the way they had pulled into a camping and hunting supply store. Stazie was excited at the prospect of shopping and pavement only to be immediately disappointed at the sight of tackle, bullets, and outdoor equipment.

"I just saw a sign saying 'live worms in a cup.' Why on earth would anyone sell worms, in a cup?" she said with disdain.

"They're great in coffee, especially when you're hiking. They generate a lot of energy from wriggling that you can use, like a hot caffeinated drink. And plenty of protein for muscle recovery. Should we pick some up?"

Stazie stopped short, her mouth wide with a mix of astonishment and disgust.

Rey laughed. "Nah. They're for fishing. It beats having to dig them up."

"Can I help you find something?" asked an attractive young salesclerk who filled out her 'Hunter's World' uniform tee in all the right places. She smiled directly at Rey.

"Sure. She needs a pair of boots."

"We're fine," Stazie said, as she sized up the clerk. Then she pointed to her flip-flops and said, "Rey, I think I'll be just fine in these."

"Where are you headed?" the clerk said.

"Ashurst Trail," Rey said.

"Oohh, I love that hike. Have you been there?"

"Sure. It's one of my favorites."

"Me too," the clerk cooed at him, while scrunching up her nose.

"Let's get going. We're wasting time here," Stazie said.

"Not until you get some proper foot gear. Believe me, you'll thank me out there."

The clerk nodded her head. "He's right. I wouldn't want to be hiking in those. They're cute, but your feet are going to be killing you," she said giving a glance at Stazie's flops. "We have several boots on sale right now. I'd be happy to show them to you."

"Sounds good," Rey said and smiled at her. The clerk smiled back.

Stazie felt her hackles rise. She hadn't seen him smile like *that* before.

At the shoe department, Stazie sat in one of the chairs, held out her foot and waited to be fitted. Instead, the clerk gestured towards the shelf.

"Our ladies boots are all against this wall. There are different sizes under each boot. Let me know if you can't find your size. We can always order it. I'll be back to see how you're doing."

When she left, Stazie said, "Just what kind of service do they have here?"

"What do you mean?" Rey said as he watched the clerk work with another customer down the aisle. "I thought she was *exceptionally* helpful."

She rolled her eyes and mouthed his words to herself with scorn. Then, trying to regain Rey's attention, she tapped him on his shoulder.

"So what am I suppose to do now?" she said, pointing to her foot.

"Well, I'd suggest you look at the boot on the wall, then look for the box beneath it with your size, take it out, and try it on. I'll go look for some socks."

Twenty minutes later, Stazie still couldn't find anything. Her complaints were many. All of the footwear was heavy and clunky. And they didn't come in fun colors like canary yellow or fuchsia, only ugly tan or olive drab. There simply were none that went with her outfit. And the heavy socks he had selected for her felt hot and scratchy. Suddenly she appreciated Antonio and the attentive service back at Au Claire.

Rey was beginning to wonder if it was all a mistake to have even attempted this. At the rate they were going, they'd never make it out onto the trails in time.

The salesclerk returned. "Having any luck? I can show you some others."

"I'll take these," Stazie said abruptly, holding up an olive drab boot.

"But you just told me that you didn't like those," Rey said, confused. "She said there's others on sale."

"I like these."

"Are you sure? They go with your outfit and all of that?" he said with a sigh.

The salesgirl snickered. Stazie shot her a dirty look.

"Yes. They're fine."

"All right. Might as well put them on now with those socks and start breaking them in. There are a few other things I need to pick up. Miss, where do you keep your topos?"

The young woman brightened as he rose to his feet. She held out her hand. "My name's Emily. Right this way."

"Sure thing, Emily," Rey said as he shook her hand and their eyes locked.

"Wait, I've got to get these on. How do you even lace this thing?" Stazie said trying to divert him. "Just a sec . . ."

Rey had already disappeared down the aisle with Emily. Stazie hastily laced the boots whichever way she could and gathered up her flops and purse. Next, she searched aisle after aisle looking for topos although she had no idea of what they even were. When she finally caught up with Rey and Emily by the checkout counter, they were both laughing over something they had been discussing. A hot jealous fire ignited within her as she watched him grin and the girl flirt. She also couldn't understand why he had loaded up on water bottles, maps, trail snacks, and other things she couldn't identify.

"What is all of this?" Stazie said, pointing to the small pile. "How long are we going to be out there?"

"Just for the day but these are a few things we need to bring along with us."

"Did *she* suggest all of this?" Stazie said, raising an eyebrow in Emily's direction.

"No, he knows what he's doing. He doesn't need any help from me," Emily said, exchanging looks with him. "Don't forget to call me with that backpacking website when you get home, okay, Rey?" She jotted down her number on the back of the store's business card and handed it to him.

"I will. Man, I wish I could remember what it was called again, but it's fantastic. You'll like it."

"And be sure to let me know the next time you're in town?"

"You bet I will, Emily," he said with a wink. "Hope to catch you on the hiking forums."

"Rey, don't you want to get going?" Stazie said sweetly but shot a sideways look at her competition. "It's getting late."

"Yeah. Well, it's a bummer that you're working today or you could have joined us," Rey said to the salesclerk.

Emily sighed wistfully at him. "Yeah, too bad."

While Stazie briskly headed towards the exit, the clerk handed him the receipt. Next, she held up her extended thumb and pinky indicating a phone and mouthed the words "Call me" to him with a coy smile.

Rey smiled and nodded goodbye.

Since he knew the way, Stazie handed the keys over. She was just happy to get him out of that store and away from that predatory clerk. They wound their way through the forested highways and as they climbed mountain passes, he pointed out peaks and stopped at scenic overviews. She couldn't help but marvel at the spectacular scenery before her eyes. If he hadn't drawn her attention to it, she might have never noticed. When they had left the room this morning, she was less than eager but as they grew closer to the destination, she found herself actually anticipating the adventure. She had never done anything like this before.

As he drove, she kept stealing glances at him. She had never seen him so relaxed and carefree. Pretending to point her phone at the scenery outside his window, she snuck a shot of him with her camera. She wished they could drive on forever, being perfectly content just to look at him and the postcard view before her.

Eventually he pulled off onto a long narrow pullout on the side of the highway under some trees. It didn't look like much of anything except a wide spot in the road.

"Why are we stopping here?" she said.

He pointed to a wooden sign with the words 'Ashurst Trail' carved into it. "We're at the trailhead. From here, we get out and walk."

"This is *it*?"

"Uh huh."

"But where's everybody else?"

"Everybody else? Who are you talking about?"

"All the other people. You know, other hikers and picnickers?"

He glanced about the quiet road and parking spot. "Well, it looks like we're the only ones."

"That's not good, right? I mean shouldn't we wait until someone else comes along so at least someone knows that we're here?"

"No, this is when the trail is perfect. When there's not a bunch of other people around to screw it up."

"Oh," she said. She wasn't sure if he was right about this. It was daunting to be out in the middle of nowhere preparing to embark to even more nowhere with no one else around. "Uh oh! What about this?" She pointed to the poison oak and bear warnings that were posted by the path. "We can't go out there with poisonous plants and dangerous animals. We don't even have any weapons."

"Don't worry about it. I'll point out the poison oak so you can steer clear of it."

"And what about the bears?"

"I won't have to point them out. They're pretty obvious."

"You're kidding, right? Right? They eat people, don't they?"

He laughed as he donned his gear and camera bag and started out on the trail with a brisk stride. Once again, she found herself scampering to keep up. When her toes stubbed on roots and rocks, she found herself appreciating the clunky boots on her feet. As they walked along, she kept her eyes wide open for bears, feeling some trepidation. Although he said that they were pretty obvious, she figured that they probably could be pretty sneaky too and she wanted to make sure to have plenty of time to make a break for it if she had to.

Despite worrying about all the potential hazards, she couldn't help but look up and admire the canopy of tree limbs above her. She had never been deep in a forest before and didn't think trees could close in around her like they did. The woods about them grew dense and dark as they moved along the trail. The cool, moist scent of pine, oak, and other foliage filled their senses and the forest was serene. They struck an easy pace and soon, she felt herself relaxing a little. Rey was already there, a pleasant look upon his face. She envied how comfortable he was out in this wilderness.

They hiked for about a half hour when they started to hear a low rumble. As they entered a clearing, Stazie looked up into blue sky, trying to discern what was making the noise. There were no clouds present. The rumble was steady and intensified as they continued to walk.

Growing fearful, she said, "Rey? Do you hear that? What is it?"

He only smiled and continued walking. She grew reluctant to follow but then again, she was in the middle of the woods with no one else around. Except perhaps for some bears. She had no other choice but to keep up with him.

"Rey? What is that? Please stop . . . Rey?"

He continued his pace, as if he couldn't hear her. Her anxiety mounted. Within the next few steps, he disappeared around a bend and some foliage.

"Rey! Wait!" she called, but he did not return.

By this time, the rumble had crescendoed to a roar and she wasn't sure whether or not to follow him, or to turn and bolt. She decided to push on, just a few more steps. As she rounded the bend where she saw him disappear, before her crashed and coursed a magnificent waterfall plunging in a free fall from atop a ledge fifteen stories above and cascading down to the streambed below. Stazie gasped out loud, its grandeur and spectacle overcoming her.

Rey stood there grinning, soaking up the sight before him before raising his camera and firing off a few shots. He turned to see if she was enjoying it as well but her face was blank, her mouth slightly agape. Her expression was priceless, so he took a couple shots of her.

"So, what do you think?" he yelled above the water's torrent.

She shook her head and continued to stare, amazement washing over her face.

"How come there aren't any guardrails?" she yelled back.

"Why? This isn't a park."

She crept towards the edge and looked down to where millions of gallons of water went crashing to the rock bed below and flowed on. When she turned to him, her face was glistening from the flying spray.

"Where is all of this water coming from?"

"From snow runoff and rainfall, high up in the mountains."

"That's a lot of water. Doesn't it ever stop?"

He had to throw his head back and laugh. Then he said, "I guess it could, but it does snow and rain like hell up here. I don't think it's going to run out of water any time soon."

She nodded and continued to stare, her eyes filled with wonder. "It's so . . . beautiful. It's the most beautiful thing I've ever seen. Oh! And rainbows! Look at the rainbows Rey!" She pointed to the two brilliant arcs shining in the mist of the falls. "Why are there rainbows down here? Aren't they made up in clouds or something?"

He chuckled again. "It has to do with light rays being refracted by the water droplets."

So overwhelmed was she by the rushing torrent and the brilliant colors, she scarcely heard him. "Huh?" she said over her shoulder.

"Never mind. I'll explain later."

Impulsively she stretched out her hand, trying to touch the current racing past her fingertips. Suddenly, Rey was pulling her back.

"Whoa! Not too close. These rock faces get slick and you could slip right in," he said.

"But it's so incredible. I've never seen anything like it."

He wasn't certain if it was mist but he thought he saw tears in her eyes. He had rushed her out the door this morning before she had time to apply any makeup and he found her face appealing in the morning light. A smattering of freckles across her nose caught his eye.

"What is it?" she said, looking up at him.

"Freckles. I never knew you had freckles."

She patted her nose and frowned. "I get them from my mom. I meant to cover them up this morning."

"Why? They look fine to me."

"They do?"

"Come on. There's still a lot more to see," he said, turning back towards the trail.

She nodded. "Oh oh!" she said as a thought struck her and she fished around in her sequined purse. She pulled out her phone and aiming it towards the massive falls, she captured an image on the tiny screen.

Rey chuckled some more and shook his head but he was glad to see she was enjoying it so much. Before they set out again, she took one last lingering look at the falls and then turned to follow him.

As they hiked, her curiosity awakened and suddenly she wanted to know everything about what she was seeing and why—the aspen, the ferns, the animals, the geology. Rey found himself having to answer many questions in rapid succession, reminding him of the times he had taken Sela to the zoo. But he didn't want to squelch her desire to seek more, so he tried his best to answer what he could and wracked his brain over her more obscure questions.

The day had grown warm. They decided to take a break under a stand of tall fir. Stazie's stomach started to rumble. She remembered she hadn't eaten anything for breakfast. Rey reached into his pack and produced the leftover donuts and juice as well as the trail mix and beef jerky he had picked up at the camping store. Whereas she had turned up her nose at the items before, she now hungrily gobbled everything down, claiming it all seemed delicious now for some reason.

Rey, on the other hand, nibbled a bit, stretched out his legs and kicked back. He filled his lungs deep and relished the respite of feeling unburdened, even it was only for a few hours. He lay back on the bed of pine needles and stared up at the patch of bright blue sky that beckoned to him through the clearing of tree boughs above, the limbs unable to hold back its brilliance. Here, he felt far enough away that the world could not touch him.

Someday, he promised himself as he took another deep breath and let himself get lost in the sky.

Stazie tested the pine needles and within a minute or two had wriggled around until she was right beside him. When he didn't object, she snuggled in even closer, resting her head on his shoulder. He was so relaxed he let her be. Her hair was soft and smelled like the wildflowers that were in bloom around them. For a while they lie there, without speaking, soaking up the blue and the trees that stood guard above them. A sense of peace settled over them both.

It was odd to Stazie to feel so content. If she had had wings right now, she would've unfolded them to their full length to feel the warmth of the sun upon them. *Was this how a butterfly feels, coming out of a cocoon?* she wondered. And to have Rey by her side, it was so simple, so wholly satisfying, like no other time before, yet so much to ask for.

A high-pitched squeak shook her from her daydream. Another squeak and Rey sat up looking about. She wanted him to remain next to her but in another moment, he was on his feet and walked off. He returned shortly cupping his hands around something.

"Hey, take a look at this," he said.

She sat up. "What is it? What do you have?"

He opened his hands to reveal a baby squirrel, skinny and shaking. Its large dark eyes stared up at her.

"Stazie's heart melted. Oh my goodness! What is that? It's sooo cute!"

"It's a squirrel, a young one. It was just sitting over there on the ground. It must've fallen out of its nest somehow."

"Is he okay? I didn't know they lived in birds' nests."

"No, they make their own in the hollows of trees or sometimes brush. Poor little guy must've taken a tumble."

"Is it okay to pet him?"

"I don't see why not but probably not near his face."

"Will he bite?"

"He hasn't yet but you still have to be careful."

Stazie timidly reached out a finger to stroke the baby animal down its back. The squirrel continued to look up her but didn't show any fear. She held out her hands.

"Do you think I can hold him? Please?"

He looked at her expectant face, surprised at her request.

"Sure. First, cup your hands like this. Are you ready? Okay, here he goes."

Rey passed the squirrel to her. She opened her eyes and mouth wide in amazement, giggling at the feel of the soft warm little body in her hands. Then she loosely closed her hands around it and held it to her chest, instinctively cuddling the baby.

"Oh, he is too adorable!" Then she cooed, "There, there. Shhh, shhh! You don't have to be so afraid. I'm not going to hurt you."

Rey couldn't help but get a kick out of what he was witnessing. Was that a maternal instinct surfacing in Stazie Royale?

"Where's his family?" she said, giving all of her attention to the baby in her hands.

"I'm not sure. They're probably around though."

"What are we going to do with him?"

"In a few minutes, we'll put him back where I found him."

"Why? Can't we just keep him?"

Rey was surprised by her question. He never thought she would take to any animal.

"What? Are you kidding? What are you going to do with a squirrel? And how are you going to bring him back to New Jersey? It's probably not a good idea to take this kind of squirrel over there to those kinds of squirrels, anyway," he said, joking by affecting a heavy Jersey accent.

"Aww, but he's so little and so cute! I'm sure I could carry him in my bag. Or even get a little carrier or something," she said, cuddling it close to her cheek and looking imploringly at Rey.

"No, Stazie. It wouldn't be right. You don't have what it takes to care for him properly. He's better off here."

"But how's he going to find his family? He's probably an orphan."

"I'm sure his mother is looking for him right now. Let's put him back by the tree where I found him," Rey said.

Stazie reluctantly followed him to the tree but she kept the squirrel held close to her and spoke to it in soothing tones. She viewed the surroundings with a critical air.

"Do you really think his mother is around?" she said. "And don't you think that if she were a good mother, she'd be attacking us by now? He's so helpless. How could she just go off and leave him all alone like that? I mean, I could be trying to eat him right now and here he is so defenseless and all alone, with no one to protect him."

"C'mon Staze. Here's a good place for him right here," Rey said, indicating a secluded spot.

She pulled the baby closer. "No, seriously. You want to leave him there? All by himself?"

"Yeah, I think he'll be fine. He's close to his nest but out of sight of any predators. His parents should find him easy enough."

"Okay, so where is his mother? I can't believe she hasn't come back for him already."

"She's probably watching us right now, waiting for us to leave."

Stazie turned somber and resolute. "No, I don't think so, Rey."

He watched her clinging onto the baby, puzzled by her overly strong reaction. "Why do you say that?"

By now her eyes were clearly welling up with tears.

"If . . . if she were a good mother, she would have never let him fall out of the nest to begin with. And then when he was alone on the ground and searching for her, she would have come immediately to him and stay there with him. Not let some human take him away. No. She's a bad mother and we shouldn't leave him with her, even if she did come back for him. It'll teach her right if she were looking all over for him and worried to death," Stazie said. She hung her head and cradled the squirrel in her cupped hands.

It was obvious she was very distraught. Rey couldn't understand what the deal was over a squirrel she had just picked up not more than ten minutes ago. He approached her and held out his hands.

"Stazie," he said gently, "C'mon, you know it's the right thing to do."

Reluctantly, she opened her hands to look at the squirrel one last time and then she slowly handed it over. Once it was in Rey's hands, she turned and walked off.

He deposited the squirrel in the secure area and made sure to cover it up with some loose brush. He hoped the little guy would make it but he also knew the odds weren't all that great. However, there was no way he was going to mention *that* to her. He had enough to deal with at the moment.

He found Stazie by the stand of fir, sitting on the ground hugging her knees and looking up at the sky. She hastily wiped away her tears when he approached. Sitting down beside her, she looked so forlorn that he debated whether or not to put his arm around her to comfort her. He decided against it.

"Are you okay?" he said.

She wiped away more tears and raised her chin. "I'm okay. In fact, I really don't know why I was getting so upset over some squirrel anyway. There's like, a zillion of them all over the place."

"He's going to be all right."

Stazie's attempt at bravado crumpled away in an instant. "Do you really think so?"

Her imploring face was accentuated by the redness from crying. Rey didn't have the heart to tell her otherwise.

"Yes, I really do," he said definitively. "Animals leave their offspring alone a lot in the wild."

"They do?"

"Yeah. Think about it, there's no babysitters, no daycare. They learn to take care of themselves at a young age."

She stared off to the trees beyond and said quietly, "Yeah, but you never get used to it."

He looked at her confused but decided not to ask.

They sat for a few minutes more.

"So do you want to go on?" he said.

She sighed and then nodded. He rose to his feet and offered her a hand up.

"Okay. There's still a lot more to see."

As evening approached, they were both sorry the day was drawing to a close. No matter how much he tried to convince himself otherwise, Rey was enjoying himself in spite of how the trip started out. Although there was a little melancholia lingering after releasing the squirrel, Stazie seemed to relax into being herself, leaving behind any pretense. This person today was inquisitive, kind, funny, and even endearing at times. At first, old suspicions lingered but her behavior was so genuine that eventually he quit doubting her.

When they started the drive back, they exchanged stories and laughs on what they had seen and done during the day. Hungry, she rummaged around in his pack to see if there was anything else to eat.

She pulled out a brightly colored box. "What are these? It looks like little kid food or something."

"Little kid food! They're animal crackers."

"Animal crackers?" she said, turning over the box to examine the illustrations of circus animals printed on the sides.

"Hey, I just happen to like animal crackers okay?" he said.

"Okay, okay." She laughed. "I just never heard of animal crackers."

"What do you mean, that particular brand or—?"

"No. Animal crackers. Are they for feeding the animals out there? We could have given some to the squirrel, come to think of it."

"You're kidding. They're cookies! People cookies. I find it hard to believe that you haven't had them before."

She shook her head. "Nah uh."

"Then what did you snack on when you were a kid?"

"Oh, plenty of things. Pralines, éclairs, parfaits, blintzes . . ."

"But how about plain old cookies? You've had to have had cookies before."

"Sure, do you think we were cavemen or something? We had French twists, ladyfingers, macaroons."

"How about the cheap, run-of-the-mill, everyday cookies you sink into a cold class of milk and then pop into your mouth. You know, like Toll House? Peanut butter? Snickerdoodles?"

"Snickerdoodles? No, then. I guess not."

"Seriously?"

"Yes, seriously," she said. "When my mother lived with us, she didn't approve of a lot of things. Junk foods. Or me getting dirty. Or wearing old clothes. I guess my dad just continued with what she had set."

Rey puzzled over the unexpected socioeconomic differences between the classes. While he hadn't many opportunities to experience gourmet-prepared dishes of fine cuisine, he assumed that Stazie would've had access to just about anything she wanted, including things like snickerdoodles and animal crackers. He watched her out the corner of his eye as she turned the box of crackers over in her hands, studying the circus animals on the sides and testing the handle.

"Would you mind if I tried one?"

"No, go right ahead."

She opened the lid, pulled out a cookie and nibbled at it. Then she helped herself to some more.

"Rey?"

"Uh huh?"

"Maybe you should get your money back on these animal crackers."

"Why? Are they stale or something?"

"No, actually they are yummy. It's just that the lion tastes the same as the monkey. And that tasted the same as the zebra. In fact, all of these animals taste alike. You know, I think they screwed up on the flavors or something."

Once he realized that she wasn't joking, he had to turn his eyes away and force his hand to his mouth, trying to conceal his laughter.

"It helps if you bite their heads off first," he managed to say.

"Oh. Okay."

Stazie loved the little cookies although biting off the heads, as Rey suggested, didn't seem to make much difference in taste. She wasn't quite sure what he found so funny but she finally saw a smile much like the one she saw in the photograph.

"Are you sure? Nobody else is out here. Besides, aren't you getting cold? I know I am. There are still a few tables available inside. I'm sure we could switch," Stazie said as Rey lead her out to the open patio area of the resort's restaurant. "Why would you want to eat out here?"

"Because there *is* no one out here and they've got these," he said as he pointed to the large propane heater by the tableside. Then he gestured beyond the balcony. "But best of all, if you look right out there, you've got *that*."

For the first time since they had stepped out onto the patio, Stazie noticed the sweeping mountain range before her. She had seen mountains plenty of times before when skiing but never like this. In the twilight, the peaks were emblazoned in dusky purple and orange hues, their snowcaps radiating a pinkish glow, painted by the last light of the day. It was spectacular. She stood for a few minutes, awestruck, and then slowly settled into her chair, her eyes riveted on the mountain splendor before her. She didn't know why but she felt a knot forming in her throat. Why was it that she found herself so moved by everything today?

And how was it that he was able to see these things when she could not? Like the V-formation of geese flying across the sky or the quartz rock that looked like sculpted glass or the gold dust in the streambed they had waded in this afternoon? It seemed so effortless for him, as if he were a magician who could conjure up wondrous experiences on command.

Stazie considered her twenty-seven years had mostly been spent going from one social event to another—another party, another club, another shopping spree. It was as if she had lived in the confines of the cut-crystal bowl on the fireplace mantle at home, unable to see past the numerous facets of her lifestyle that changed angles, obscured vision, and blocked views. Instead, here was the world as it had always been; she simply had not seen it clearly before. And she knew now that she would never see it the same way again.

"I have to set something straight. Hold on a minute . . ." Stazie said, looking about.

"What do you mean?"

She signaled their waitress. "Miss, a bottle of champagne please," she said.

"Champagne? What's the occasion?" Rey said.

The waitress returned with a bottle and two flutes. She uncorked the bottle and poured out the bubbly liquid. Stazie picked up a flute and handed it to Rey. Then she took up the other one.

"Remember on the beach, when you tried to apologize to me with champagne?" she said.

Uh oh. Why was she mentioning that? Rey wondered. He swallowed and said cautiously, "Yeah, well, it's a little hard to forget."

Stazie looked at him sympathetically and with remorse. "Well, it's *me* who needs to apologize for the way I have acted. I know I was perfectly horrid when you have always been civil and kind. Please, forgive me?"

"Why bring this up now?"

"It's something that I need to make right. I don't think I could live with myself much longer if I didn't." She held up her glass to him.

He studied her, noting the sincerity in her eyes.

Then he touched her glass with his. "You know, you're all right. Apology accepted," he said and gave her a wink.

She heaved a sigh of relief. "Thanks."

Their dinner was serene, a contrast to the bustling restaurants she usually frequented. It was odd for Stazie to be quiet for once without feeling so alone. She found herself enjoying the pace and calmness of it all immensely. Rey's laugh came more easily now and his smile warmed her heart. What a day it had been. Her thoughts drifted to the waterfall, towering trees, and the baby squirrel she had held in her hands.

Suddenly, she felt a little embarrassed.

"I can't believe how overboard I acted today."

"What do you mean, how so?"

"I mean with the squirrel and all. You must've thought that I was an emotional nut case or something."

"You're a nut case? I'm beginning to see why the squirrel took to you," he teased. "No, seriously, not at all. I know you were anxious for the little guy but he's probably warm and safe in his nest right now."

"Well, it's just that he was so young and probably felt scared and abandoned . . . I kinda know what that is like."

"You were abandoned? What are you talking about?"

"Not *abandoned* abandoned. Never mind. It was just a slip. I don't know what I'm saying but forget I said it. Anyway, dinner was amazing. I wonder what they have on the dessert menu."

"No, go on. You were obviously upset when we had to leave him behind. It's not every day that someone loses it over a squirrel. So I know it had to mean something to you."

She glanced off at the stars and took a deep breath. Momentarily lost in her thoughts, she muttered, "Yeah . . . Ol' Hoppy Hops Right to It."

"Excuse me?"

"Oh, it's nothing. A slogan my mother came up with for the ad agency she worked for. They had thousands of these green plush frogs made up wearing little tee-shirts with 'Hoppy Hops Right to It' printed on the front. It was for an insurance company."

"Yeah, I remember that. Their commercials would always start with some kind of fender-bender and then that cartoon frog would bounce in out of nowhere saying 'Ribbet! Ribbet! Hoppy Hops right to it!' Which in-surance was that again?"

"Greenley and Pond."

"Right. So that was your mom who came up with that campaign?"

"Uh huh. I remember she was so happy. She even brought home one of the frogs for me. We went out to a special dinner that night, just the three of us. It was one of the few times I remember that we were all together. It's probably why I remembered it. But it was fun . . . Would you believe I still have that frog? A couple of weeks later, my mother left us. She just packed up, moved away, and never came back."

This admission surprised him. He noted the quiver in her voice and the way she scraped at her thumbnail. "Wow, that's rough. So it's just been you and your dad all of this time?" he said.

"Yeah, just Daddy and me. He never remarried, you know. He dates from time to time, but nothing ever becomes of it. The breakup with my mother devastated him. He knew nothing about raising a child, and sud-denly there I was. I could only imagine what it was like for him to chase after a four-year-old. I know that he still thinks about her but he doesn't ever talk about it." Stazie wistfully looked out across the balcony. "I tried to contact her when I was fifteen. Daddy never knew anything about it. I took money out of my savings and hired a private investigator to search for her. I guess I was hoping that once she saw us again, she would want to come back. At the very least, she would come and visit or I could visit her. We could maybe become friends . . . I don't know. It was stupid kid stuff. I had all these crazy ideas."

"So what happened?"

"It took a little over a year to track her down. My mother has always had the means to do whatever she wanted. Her family is extremely well off. Anyway, she was living in Rome and working for an ad agency there. After weeks of writing her, trying to tell her all about me and Daddy and what we were doing and how much I wanted to meet her, all I got back was a letter from her attorney informing me to 'refrain from any more intrusions' and that 'our client does not want her privacy disturbed.' You know, I always thought it was strange that they used 'our client' when they were talking about my mother . . . but . . . I guess that was that," she said, her voice was barely over a whisper. By the glow of the tabletop candle, Rey could see her eyes were misty.

He thought of his own mother and how she had always been there for him, Rick, and Gloria no matter what. And the nurturing way she tended to them, making sure that they had grown up feeling loved and safe. He could never imagine her leaving them like that. Reaching across the table, he laid his hand on top of Stazie's. She caught her breath at his touch.

Then she cleared her throat, straightened up in her chair, and said, "I don't want to talk about that anymore. Please, let's talk about something else."

Rey studied her for a moment more. She managed a small smile.

"Hey look—Venus is out tonight," he said pointing to a dazzling spot of light close to the horizon.

"Really? You can see another planet from here? Don't you need a telescope to see them?" she said, amazed. She gazed upward. It took her a moment to find it.

"Sure, they're incredible to see through a telescope but if you don't have one handy, you can just eyeball certain ones on nights like this when they are in view."

"But it's a just a white spot. I thought planets would be, I don't know, yellow or green or something. How do you know it's not a star? They kind of look the same."

"From this distance, it looks like a star. But see how its light is steady and not twinkling? That's how you know it's a planet. With any luck at all, we might even be able to catch Jupiter in a little bit."

"Oh! Isn't that the one with the ring around it?"

"Actually, Saturn has the ring but Jupiter is the biggest in our solar system."

Stazie turned back to him, her face filled with wonder. "Rey, how do you know all of this stuff?"

"What? About planets? I hardly know anything about them."

"About everything, all of it—like that dead-tail hawk you pointed out today. How did you know what kind of hawk that was?"

"The red-tailed hawk? Those guys can be found just about anywhere in the West."

"I've been to all of the Western states and I've never seen one. And even if I did, I wouldn't know the difference between it and a chicken. But not you. You seem to notice every detail. It's like you know everything."

He blushed. "That's a laugh. I'm far from knowing everything. And as far as noticing detail, it goes with the job."

"But how do you do it?"

"What? Notice detail?"

"No, where did you learn about so many things?"

"Well, I did pass a few of my classes in school," he joked until he saw her looking at him in earnest. "I don't know. I guess if something catches my interest, I'll look it up. Research it as much as possible in books, or the Internet, or TV. Whenever and wherever I can. And I'll ask questions, just like you're doing now."

"Oh," she said. "It's just that I've never met anyone like you."

"I hope that's a good thing?"

"A very good thing." She smiled and returned her gaze to the brightening stars. "Everyone I know is too wrapped-up in stock portfolios, their latest relationship, or drama. They don't ever see things like you do and they certainly don't talk about it. Most of the time they miss things that are right in front of their faces. I know I have."

Rey pondered this for a moment and then said, "Okay, now it's my turn to ask—given your upbringing and all, I've got to presume your father must have sent you to some good schools?"

"Uh huh. The very best," she said as she continued to star gaze. "Why do you ask?"

"Well, I just thought that somewhere along the line, they would have, you know, taught you at least some of this stuff."

"Oh, I'm certain that they did. But who ever pays attention in school? Except for maybe you," she said and giggled.

The sky was a velvety black, studded with stars in the clear mountain air. Never had the stars ever seemed this close to her. It felt as if they were winking directly at her.

"Which is the one they call 'The Lone Star?'" she said, caught up by their beauty.

"The 'Lone Star'? I'm not quite sure if I know."

"I'm sure you do. It's the one that points somewhere."

"Oh, you must be thinking of the North Star. Yeah, that's right over there." He pointed off into the dark canvas.

"Right over where? Which one?" she said, craning her neck.

"Here, hold on a minute."

He pulled her seat close to his. Pleasantly delighted by this, she settled in closer as she felt his arm across the back of her chair. She tried to follow where his finger was pointing upward but his very nearness was incredibly distracting.

"Do you see the Big Dipper?"

"The big what?"

"Okay, right there. See those four stars that make kind of a crooked box? That's the Big Dipper. It looks like the dippers with the long handles they used in the old days for getting water out of a barrel." He turned to find her intently staring at him instead of looking to where he indicated. Addressing her gaze, he then motioned back to the sky.

"Now if you follow the leading edge of the dipper, you'll see those two stars that make a perfect straight line. Let your eyes follow in the direction to where they point and you'll come right to the little bright one that marks north."

"Uh huh," she said breathlessly, as she let her eyes follow instead his cheek, his jaw line, and the soft pulse in his neck, until they stopped at where his shirt was buttoned.

She caught his faint scent and savored the warmth that he was radiating. It immediately took her back to that morning in the fishing shack. Her own pulse quickened at the memory of him lying there in the early dawn.

"That's why they call them the pointer stars, because they'll always point out the North Star for you."

She realized she hadn't been paying attention to what he was saying. He was close to her. *So close.*

"Rey?" she whispered.

He turned his gaze from the stars and met hers. Present in his eyes was that intensity she had grown to love. Quickly closing the gap between them she kissed him, her lips meeting his, her arms wrapping around his neck. She had been waiting forever for this moment and she didn't want him to get away.

At first she felt a little resistance but within the next moment, she could feel his mouth part and his lips yield to hers. It suddenly occurred to her that *he was kissing her back.* Her heart hammered in her chest as she felt his fingertips gently graze her cheek. But when his lips moved and pressed against hers, she thought her heart was going to seize. The moment was so perfect she didn't want it to end.

"Stazie? Is that you?" A male voice sliced through the cool air.

Rey immediately pulled away.

Stazie slowly opened her eyes missing him already. Her lips tingled where his had just been.

"It is you! What the hell are you doing here?"

Josh?? *Oh poop.* Stazie couldn't believe it. Out of all the people and places in the world, he runs into her here, now. *Why?*

"Josh!" she said with a forced smile.

"I thought it was you. I'd know the back of your head frenching someone anywhere," Josh said with a sneer.

Rey turned to face the intruder.

Stazie's cheeks flushed red, hoping Rey hadn't heard Josh's remark. However, there wasn't any reason that he wouldn't. She wished Josh would vanish or explode or shrink to something insignificant. In that way she and Rey could get back to where they left off. *He was kissing me,* she thought dreamily.

Josh remained like a stain, stubbornly fixed to where he stood.

"What are you doing here?" she said.

He nodded towards the restaurant. "I had to get out of that shit box to have a smoke. They won't let me have one fucking cigarette in there." He pulled out a cigarette and lit it. He inhaled deeply, tilted his chin up, and blew out a gray cloud that settled over them.

"No, I mean *here.*"

"Oh, I'm meeting Trish and Alec. They booked some kind of jeep tour-beer bash thing for the weekend and talked me into it." He pulled up a seat and sat down.

"Oh, Josh, this is Rey Natal. You may have met him at my Spring Fling. Rey, this is Josh Pinard."

The playboy threw Rey a bored glance.

To Rey, Stazie's friend appeared to be contemptuous and blasé but nonetheless, he extended his hand to him and said cordially, "How's it going?"

Josh ignored it and took another puff. Then he faced Rey and said, "Yeah, I remember you now. You were the guy standing in the surf with a tie and an apology."

Rey let his hand drop. "Yeah, I guess that would have been me." He studied the intruder more closely. *So this was the asshole she was talking to Gidge about while we were driving up North?*

Josh was dressed in designer leather slides, baggy trousers, and a long-sleeved white dress shirt opened three buttons down to expose a smooth chest. Expensive cologne cloaked him like a shroud while every hair remained in place under a four-hundred-dollar pair of sunglasses perched on his head, even though the sun had long set. Rey knew the type. One good hit to the face usually dropped them.

"Funny, our Stazie usually isn't one to forgive so easily. But by the look of it, she has not only forgiven but she's conceded as well," Josh said peevishly.

Stazie's cheeks flushed scarlet once more. Flustered, she said, "So when's Trish and Alec getting here? Maybe you should call them and find out what's up."

"What a brilliant idea!" he said, dripping sarcasm. "Did it. And texted too. Neither answered. I don't know why they even bother owning fucking phones. All I know is that they better get their asses over here or I'm going to be really pissed off." He paused a moment for emphasis, then said, "So, anyway, you didn't answer me. What the fuck ARE you doing here?"

Rey knew what he was getting at. The missing prepositional phrase was obvious: *with him.* He looked at Stazie who wore an odd expression on her face. Her cheeks were pinking up. And yet she still wouldn't tell this bozo off. *Could it be that she still digs this guy?* he wondered. He decided not to embarrass her but in the meantime, he concentrated on fighting the urge to turn Ol' Joshie's primpy face inside out.

"I—I just wanted to get away for the weekend. You know, get out of the City. Rey was kind enough to accompany me."

"I see. Everyone knows you sure love an escort."

An awkward silence ensued.

Josh took another drag off his cigarette, tapped the ashes into Stazie's water glass, and then scrutinized her as if something was out of place.

"So what's up? You look different," he finally said.

"I do?"

"Yeah. Are you sick or are you pregnant? Or both?" Josh said.

Stazie blushed deeply. "N-no, neither. I'm fine," she said.

Rey hated what Josh was doing to her. In another minute he was going to rearrange this prick. He kept reminding himself that this was one of her friends and she didn't seem to object to what was happening.

"Stazie, would you like anything else? Another drink?" he said, trying to intervene.

Looking dazed, she said weakly, "Huh? No. I'm good."

"Are you sure?"

"Yes, Rey. I'm sure."

Then she slipped a compact mirror from her bag, checked her hair, and dusted her nose with powder foundation, covering up the freckles he had pointed out earlier. A column of smoke swirled from Josh's pursed lips, as he sat looking satisfied and smug. He turned back to Rey.

"I hear that you are doing some work on their place in Pennsylvania."

"You heard right."

"So then, what is it that you do? Drywall? Paint? Plumbing?"

Before he could answer, Stazie butted in and said, "Yes, and you should see how amazing the cottage is going to be. I can't wait. Rey measured every-thing exactly and drew everything out. Oh and he also did some other stuff on the computer as well. But anyway, it's going to be great." She appeared nervous and jumpy and at a loss for words.

"Oh. I see."

Rey decided not to explain anything. This jerk simply wasn't worth the effort.

Just then, the waitress came over and addressed Josh, "Sir, anything for you?"

He ignored her.

"All right . . . And how about you two? Anything else to drink?" she said.

"No, thank you," said Stazie.

"Well then, did you save some room for dessert tonight? I have our dessert menu right here—"

"I said no. Is that so hard to understand?" Stazie snapped all of a sudden.

Rey looked at her perplexed. The waitress had given them excellent service all evening. Although he could also see that Stazie kept her eye trained on Josh.

"We're fine, miss. If you could get our check please?" Rey tried to be as kind as possible to compensate for their rude behavior, determined to leave her a big tip.

While they waited for the check, Stazie fumbled to fill the uncomfortable silence that returned once more.

"So Josh, tell Rey what you do. I can never get it right."

"I agree. You never can. International commodity trading. But don't ask me to explain. It would take too long," he said condescendingly.

"For you to explain or to get it right?" Rey said.

Just as the two men squared off, the waitress returned and the tense situation was put on hold. Rey pulled out his wallet to pay.

"Rey, I'll get it." Stazie took out her credit card and placed it on the tray. "I don't want you to go over your budget or anything," she said innocently.

Josh snorted and looked away, trying to conceal a spasm of laughter.

Rey coolly handed his card directly to the waitress and said, "Put it on this, miss." Then he picked up Stazie's card and handed it back to her.

"It's just that it's kinda expensive. I mean, I've seen you buy a week's worth of groceries on that," Stazie said, trying to explain. "Besides, I told you that I was taking care of this weekend. Miss, put it on this."

"No. Run it on mine."

Josh choked back another laugh that escaped him. By the look on his face, this had become the evening's entertainment for him. He sat back and took another drag, while chortling and shaking his head.

Rey concentrated on keeping his anger in check while he stared out into the darkness, determined not to let Josh get the best of him. One of these days he'd run into him again when Stazie was not around. Preferably soon. *Then we'd see who was so fricken' smug.* When the waitress brought back his card, he signed the receipt and promptly rose. "Stazie, I'm turning in for the night."

"You are?" she said, her face looking strained. "Don't go, Rey. It's still early. Besides, Trish and Alec ought to be here any minute and then we can—"

"No, I'm tired."

He lingered, hoping that she would say that she wanted to leave as well. But she remained seated, looking between him and Josh.

"I'll see you tomorrow?" he said, trying one last time, but she only appeared more confused. He had seen that look before in deer caught dazed in the headlights. "Stazie?"

"G good night," she said, hesitatingly.

It was pointless. He couldn't force her to go if she didn't want to. *Maybe she wanted to be with the prick,* he decided. As far as he could tell, she was obviously in her element once again.

As he walked away he could hear her say, "Please Rey –," but she didn't follow and he wouldn't turn back.

On his way back to his room, he decided to take a detour to the convenience store where he had bought breakfast this morning. He walked on in the darkness, his boots crunching the hard gravel on the shoulder of the road. He tried not to think but his thoughts shouted above the stillness of the woods around him.

What the hell was I thinking? he chided himself. Her face was before him—that bright smile, those imploring eyes. He knew she was completely wrong for him. He had never intended on getting involved from the start.

You can't change people like that, he determined. *Just finish the job for her father and get out. So what was that back there?*

Maybe it was those goofy questions she asked all the time. Or that sense of vulnerability and sadness that often took him by surprise. It could be that unexpected sweetness that surfaced from under the layers of makeup and pretentiousness. Or perhaps it was just a physical attraction, that knockout body and those long legs of hers. He recalled her lips against his were perfect and irresistible. Once she kissed him, he only wanted more.

He got to the store, bought a couple of six-packs, and then retuned to the cool air. Once he got back to his room, he flipped through the channels on the TV. A sexy lingerie show was on. He watched the models strut their stuff in skimpy attire one by one on the runway but none of them could divert his attention.

Restless, he grabbed a six-pack and went to sit out on the terrace with his feet propped up on the railing and a beer in hand. The stars had migrated across the sky from where they had been when he had pointed them out to her. The North Star was shining even brighter now as if it were mocking him. He knew if he had been smart, he would have just pulled away from her when she started kissing him. He should have checked out for the evening right there and then.

But those lips . . .

All of a sudden, a fifteen-year-old memory of Amy Korvitch came to mind. His finger went immediately to the scar over his left eyebrow.

"Shit," Rey said out loud as he popped open another beer.

❧

Stazie woke and immediately looked at the clock. *7:42 am.* She turned over and tried to go back to sleep but her eyes resisted and remained open. For some unknown reason, her brain was active. She didn't like being up this early and it was odd to be so wide-awake. She lie in bed in for a few minutes more but sleep wouldn't come.

Instead she rose, went to the window, and peered out on the new day. The sky was overcast and there didn't appear to be anything going on outside in the early hour. The parking lot of sleeping cars was devoid of activity except for a lone bicyclist checking over his bike, getting ready for a ride. Her thoughts went to Rey.

Why did he leave so abruptly last night? she puzzled.

She admitted that Josh was acting like an ass but Josh always acted like that, especially if he had any reason to be jealous. And not more than fifteen minutes later, Trish and Alec showed up after all. If Rey had stayed, they would have been alone once more and could have picked up where they had left off.

He was kissing me.

The memory of it made her sigh as she put her fingertips to her lips. She continued to stare out the window, feeling wistful. *But why wouldn't he stay?*

For some unknown reason, Rey appeared to be upset. If he had only stuck around for even a few minutes more, he would've seen her put Josh in his place, telling him off when he attempted another slam about him. Thinking about it, it was the first time she had ever corrected Josh on anything before. She realized her stupid infatuation with him had made her blind to his rude behavior in the past. She also knew now that what she felt for Rey was so much different. *This was the real thing.*

Stazie's eyes returned to the cyclist. It looked like he was finishing up and donning a pack. In a sudden flash of recognition, she realized the biker was Rey. She did a double take and wondered how she didn't readily recognize his lean frame.

Where was he going?

She tried to open the window but was hampered by the locks. Instead, she snatched up the resort bathrobe, slid on her flip-flops, and bolted out the door, running down the hallway in her short pink nightie. She had wanted to spend another day like they had had yesterday with waterfalls, rainbows, and stars.

Why is he going without me?

She hammered on the elevator button but it was taking too long, so she galloped down the stairway instead, struggling to put on the bathrobe while she ran. She tripped on the bottom stair, stumbled hard against the wall, regained her footing, and dashed out the exit door to the parking lot. As she came around the railing, she could see him swing up onto the bike and start to pedal off.

"Rey!" she cried out. Panting hard, she pulled one last breath to yell once more. "Rey!! Stop!"

It didn't seem at first that he had heard her but a few pedal strokes later he made a wide lazy u-turn and slowly returned. Relieved, she smiled through her panting.

While she struggled to get catch her breath, Rey stood silently before her, waiting. He didn't look at all pleased to see her when he lowered his sunglasses.

"Wh-where were you going?" she finally managed to say.

"Out for a ride."

Her heart sank. There was an air of detachment about him. In place of his usual open expression, his face was dark. Stazie felt confused.

"Oh, well, where did you get the bike? I don't remember you packing one along in your suitcase," she said teasingly while trying to look coquettish.

"Rental."

"Even the hel—"

"Even the helmet."

"But it's so early."

"They open at seven." He shifted his weight from one foot to another, looking impatient.

"Oh. Well . . . Where are you going?"

"Out for a ride," he repeated.

She wrapped the robe more tightly about her, trying to keep out the chill.

"No, I mean I thought that maybe we could go somewhere together again. I would love to see the rest of the places in your photos. And today is our last day here. Why didn't you wake me up?"

"I didn't want to disturb you. Besides, I wasn't sure if you'd even be in your room this morning," he said plainly.

It took a second or two for Stazie to understand the implication. Then her eyebrows went up. "Huh? Oh no. There's nothing like *that* between Josh and me."

"Maybe so, but it's obvious he knows what buttons to push."

"Excuse me?"

"Why do you let him treat you that way? In fact, why do you let any of them treat you that way?"

"I—I don't know what you mean," she said, lowering her eyes.

"Oh, c'mon Stazie, you know exactly what I mean. Your so-called friends treat you like dirt. They treat everyone like dirt. And they feel they could just dish it out and everyone is supposed to swallow it. The difference between you and me is that I won't stick around to take it. And if you had any sense of who you are, you wouldn't put up with it either."

She crossed her arms tightly, still refusing to face him. Then she said quietly, "Well, that's just the way they are. They really don't mean anything by it. You must've misunderstood."

"Bullshit. They mean it all right. They carefully choose every word and know exactly when and how they are going to stick it to you. They seem to get their frickin' jollies off of running people down."

"But they're my friends, why would they treat me like that?"

"Are they really your friends? Have they ever acted like friends to you? Think about it."

His words stung deeply. Stazie stared off, blinded by tears. She took a deep breath. When she looked back at him, her eyes flashed with anger.

"And what about your friends?" she snapped. "If your friends are SO MUCH better than mine, then where are they? You've seen my friends. Where's yours? How come they are never around? I haven't once seen that shaggy haired weirdo you call your 'best friend.' Is he *really* your friend? Why don't *you* think about it?"

By the expression on his face, she wished she could have instantly retracted every word she had said. But it was too late. Rey swung up onto his bike and pedaled off. He rode hard and within seconds, he disappeared out of the parking lot. Stazie tried to call him back to apologize but by then her tears were falling and her pleas were weak.

He didn't return until right before departure. She found him packed and waiting in the lobby for her to check out. The long flight back was a silent one. Stazie tried a few times to engage him in some small talk but he wouldn't respond. He slept part of the time and the remainder of the trip he listened to his MP3 player with his headphones on, read, and looked out the window. Once they touched down, he briefly thanked her for the trip, called a ride share, and was gone.

Her drive home seemed lonelier than ever. Colorado wasn't supposed to turn out that way. Everything was going so well—at first. Then she had to open her mouth and tell him all of that stuff about his friends. After all, she couldn't deny what he had said about hers. It was the truth. They were a hard group to hang with. But she knew nothing about his friends at all.

Rey was so remarkably special from anyone she knew. Her stomach twisted in knots knowing she may have just thrown that all away on one callous remark. Could it be that she was just as cruel as her 'friends' and never realized it?

When she arrived home, she wasn't expecting her father to be sitting in the living room talking on the phone. She didn't want to have to explain how her weekend went. It was ironic that of all the times he was working late or gone on those never-ending business trips, he had to be home tonight. When he saw her enter the hallway, he hastily said good-bye and hung up.

"Stazie, Honey! How'd your trip go? Did it work? Hey, where's Rey?" Doug called out cheerily to her.

Without a word, Stazie made a beeline for her bedroom and shut the door behind her. She couldn't face him to say that she screwed up again. It was just too painful to admit.

Seeing her slip by, Doug knew that things probably went south once more for his daughter. Otherwise she would've parked herself in the chair across from him and happily babbled his ear off with every single detail. He was about to knock at her door when he heard her sobbing inside. He listened for a moment and then laid his hand gently on the door.

"Aw, Baby," he said quietly, his heart breaking for her.

The criminal defense attorney always knew exactly what to say in court for any situation and to any client. As a father, he couldn't find the words to explain that she couldn't force a relationship to happen. No matter what. Not if you threw yourself at them. Not if you abducted them and drag them off to Colorado for the weekend. Not even if you wanted them so desperately it felt as if you couldn't go on living without them.

At the wet bar in the living room, he poured himself a double. Before he downed it, he looked towards her door once more, raised his glass, and shook his head in empathy.

Chapter 7 ~ The Night

He ran his hand over the smooth unfinished beams, satisfied with how it was all turning out. No matter the job, he liked bringing projects to fruition. Laying his cheek alongside a new section of drywall, he eyed its plane carefully, making sure there were no wobbles or warping. The work crews were doing justice to his designs. So far, the quality was high, and he was confident that Doug would be pleased with the progress. It never ceased to enthrall Rey to see the transformation from ideas in his head to lines on paper to finished structures. There was something so complete about linear relationships.

He even permitted himself a slice of pride as he strolled out onto the expansive patio deck that cantilevered over the pines below where before existed only a missing wall and flapping plastic. Now that this job was nearing completion within another two weeks or so, he figured on making only one more trip up here. By then, it should be the last. He could turn in the key that Doug had given him for access to the house.

It had been close to four weeks since Colorado. Rey had delved deeper into his work than ever before, putting in long hours and weekends. The only breaks he allowed himself were walks with Jack Tate and rides on either his mountain bike or the used motorcycle he had bought off of a former co-worker. Since then, he had been cruising, enjoying independence, and putting some real distance between himself and what was behind him. Although he knew it would be another couple of months before his driver's license was reinstated, he had grown impatient and decided to go for it anyway. He was fed up with having to rely on mass transit, ride shares, and favors to get him around.

His mother's biggest fear was that he would be thrown in jail for driving without his license and registration. But he reassured her that he didn't plan on getting caught anytime soon. Marcie and Rick at first exchanged looks when they saw the bike. Then Rey thought he caught Marce mouthing the word "reckless" to his brother while pointing at him behind her hand. Rick plastered on a smile while reminding him that *anytime* he needed a lift *anywhere* he was happy to provide it. Rey understood their fears and concerns but this bike was something he couldn't do without. The freedom it granted him once more was worth every bit of scorn and scolding.

As he inspected the deck from one side to the other, he wanted to get another perspective of it. He knew the best view was afforded from either one of the bedroom windows, where he could scrutinize the truss work and overall visual impression. He first headed to the master bedroom where more windows had been added to the north wall, providing him the proper angle in which to see a majority of the patio. From that vantage point, the anchors and beams looked sound and straight but he still wanted to check it from one more angle. As he passed back through the room to the hallway, a small photo sitting on top of Doug's dresser caught his eye. He hadn't noticed it before but now felt compelled to pick it up.

It was of an exquisitely beautiful woman. Personally, Rey had seen very few classic beauties such as her in life. He wondered who she was and why her photo was on Doug's dresser. But he knew the counselor's clientele included all sorts of people, some of them celebrities and models.

Lucky bastard, he thought, returning the photo to its spot.

He went down the hall and crossed through the sitting area to the other wing of the cottage. There he hesitated at Stazie's room. She hadn't wanted any renovations done, so it was the first time Rey would see inside. Feeling guarded, he slowly opened the door. Her fragrance that was now so familiar to him hung in the still air of the closed-off room. It surprised him to see a shag rug on the floor, and a doll and a couple of plush animals lingering on the shelves alongside a dozen or more romance novels. He didn't think a woman her age would keep any of that girlish stuff. Her bangles, earrings, and trinkets were piled in small boxes on her dressing table next to various makeup brushes and perfume bottles. To him, it was any wonder she had any baubles left at home.

Looking completely out of place in the middle of the table was a small ordinary rock. He picked it up to examine it more closely. Turning it over in his hands, he recalled it was a rock they had found together in the creek bed by the trail. She was so impressed by its colors then, not realizing how dull it would become later when it dried out. "I ♥ Colorado" was written in marker on the bottom of it. He was careful to set it back down where he found it. Tucked in behind her assorted treasures, he spied another photo. This one showed Stazie with her father when she was still a teen. Although her arms were linked around Doug's neck and he was smiling, Stazie's face looked unusually somber.

It clicked all of a sudden. Picking up the photograph, Rey returned to Doug's room. There he compared the two images before him, the girl and the beauty. Something in Stazie spoke of the attractive woman in the photograph and Rey started to see the resemblance in the shape of her face and fine nose. As he studied the two more closely, he could even see where Stazie got her smattering of freckles, the color of her eyes, and when she chose to employ it, that haughty superior look.

Without a doubt, the woman was clearly more beautiful than her daughter could ever be. But Rey felt that Stazie's face had a certain warmth and charm that was absent in the cold, dignified beauty before him. It became apparent that the young girl's somber expression was accentuated by a sadness in her eyes. Recalling their conversation at the restaurant in Colorado, he suddenly was aware of how much the woman before him was to blame for that sadness.

Rey returned the photos to their respective places. Checking the patio from Stazie's window, he was satisfied with the craftsmanship and locked the cottage behind him. As he wound his motorcycle down the mountain through the forested roads, he shifted into fifth and opened up the bike on a smooth long stretch. As he cruised, he couldn't help but think about his parents and family. Although they were meddling at times and overprotective, he couldn't help but feel grateful for the love and security they provided him. All the success and wealth out there could never come close to that.

The evening had turned miserable. Stazie checked her mascara in the rear-view mirror to find that it had run, leaving black tracks down her cheeks. She didn't want the others she left at the club to know that they had gotten to her. She didn't even have Gidge to turn to, her 'best friend' having been cool to her ever since the cake incident and refraining from doing anything with her or even returning her calls. The new guy Gidge was seeing had set her up in an apartment and bought her a car, so obviously she didn't need Stazie anymore.

She realized it was a mistake to go out tonight. It started when she had entered the dark club and sat down at their usual booth waiting for the others to arrive but oddly, not one of her friends was there. She had understood the plan this evening was to meet here at eight. At least that's what Trish had told her. Maybe they stood her up. Or she got something wrong like she usually did.

Fifteen minutes later, it was getting rather awkward sitting by herself in the crowded club and she was feeling pretty foolish. She was getting ready to leave when she spied Josh strolling in, strutting with his usual arrogance and stopping briefly at the bar. She sighed with relief. It was obvious that she had gotten the meeting time wrong. He greeted her with a kiss on the cheek and slid in next to her in the booth.

"Hi," she said shyly.

He tilted his chin up in the slightest of acknowledgment.

"How are you? We're okay, right?" Stazie said.

"What? Yeah, sure."

"I mean, I hope you're not still mad at me."

"Angry at you? For what?"

"Colorado."

"Nah."

He accepted his drink that the waitress brought over from the bar and sipped it nonchalantly. As they made small talk, she could see Trish enter. Stazie waved to her, but instead of joining them like she usually did, Trish took a seat by the bar.

"What's up with Trish?" Stazie said. "I thought we were all going to hang tonight."

"Ah, what is ever really up with Trish?" Josh said.

Within a few more minutes, several of their usual group trickled in one by one. They too, refrained from approaching and perched around the darkened bar, seeming to keep a visual fix on the booth. Although she didn't know why, Stazie couldn't help but be reminded of the gathering of vultures she had seen feeding on road kill in Colorado.

The conversation with Josh had been going well enough, better than what she expected especially after having told him off at the resort. She knew he typically didn't take things like that very well. They joked a bit and continued to chat. After a few more minutes, he slid closer to her on the bench. She smiled at him, puzzled by his move. While keeping his eyes trained on hers and not missing a word, his hand slid under the table to her thigh and moved deftly up her miniskirt.

Caught completely off guard, Stazie gasped, "Josh, what are you doing?" as she grabbed his hand to block its advance.

He laughed crudely. "Hey, c'mon, Staze. I'm just looking for what you seem to be handing out."

Freeing his hand from hers, he tried again. She squirmed uncomfortably and caught him once more.

He drew close and whispered, "I've seen you watching me and I know what you've been saying to everyone. You know you want me and man, do I really want to do you." He poked the tip of his tongue into her ear.

With alarm she pulled away and said, "Josh—Stop! I mean it."

"No, *I* mean it," he said as he roughly pulled her close and rammed his hand up her skirt again, his fingertips grabbing her panties. "You know you want it, bitch. Ever since I met you, you've been nothing but a little cock tease." He then lunged at her and sucked at her neck.

She slapped him in the face and pushed him away from her, her eyes large with fright. Her mind flashed through all the times she had flirted with him and tried to catch his attention away from the swarm of girls that always surrounded him. It seemed so innocent and fun then. But this was different and her instincts screamed danger.

Unaffected by her slap, Josh surveyed her with cold eyes. He reached once more for her thigh but this time he gripped it hard, his fingers biting into her flesh. He smirked as she winced from pain. With his other hand, he grabbed a fistful of her hair on the back of her head and yanked back. She gasped, frozen with fear.

"Go ahead and scream if you want. No one will care anyway. And don't fool yourself into believing that I've forgiven you over the little talk we had in Colorado. I lied. Next time you'll think twice about ever correcting me over some fucking loser. Understand? *Nobody* ever corrects me."

Her hands grappled at his powerful clench on her leg but couldn't pry his hand off while her hair felt as if it were being ripped from the roots. The agony grew more intense. Looking like a small animal caught in a snare, she nodded and acquiesced as tears squeezed out the corners of her eyes.

"Just remember, the next time you wag your ass at me or decide to have the audacity to undermine me, you're going to regret it, bitch. Understand? I'm going to ride you hard." He ran his tongue up her cheek.

He released his grip, poured his drink down the front of her dress, and shoved her away. Then laughing, he rose and joined their crowd at the bar. They greeted him with loud applause, whistles, and laughter at her expense. Back at the booth, Stazie felt stunned. Her face burned with humiliation, and her head and thigh ached. The bar was packed with people, including her friends, and yet no one came to her defense. The once vibrant, exciting club now appeared sleazy and vicious. She grabbed up her purse and wrap and left, blinded by her tears that blurred her way. She tripped in her heels and crashed against another patron who rudely shoved her back and yelled, "Hey! Watch it, you stupid cunt. What the hell's your problem? Are you drunk?"

She had to get out of there.

Inside the safety of her car, she leaned her head on the steering wheel and wept openly with feelings of fright, pain, and deception crashing together. Nothing made sense. It seemed that everything and everybody had turned against her. Suddenly, a sharp crash against her windshield startled her, making her jump and scream. When she looked through the stream of beer and glass shards trickling down her cracked windshield, she could see her group of friends with Josh in the middle, pointing and laughing from the doorway where they had hurled the bottle. She started the car and dismally drove through the cold, wet streets towards home. She had never felt as abandoned as she did at this very minute.

Rey.

Where was he right now? She longed to be with him, where it was safe and comforting. When she had called him the next day after they had gotten back from Colorado, he had accepted her apology over the remark she had made about his best friend. She considered driving to his place but knew if she ever wanted to see him again, it would be prudent to give him some time. She didn't want to botch up things even further with him.

In the elevator she hastily wiped at the tears that continued to fall. The apartment was empty when she entered, the foyer still. Her heart sank. *Daddy must be out of town again.* Even Beatrice had left for the evening. Stazie would have gladly taken the maid's company tonight but thought bleakly how she had never given the woman any reason to. She had always treated Beatrice as nothing more than a maid. Of course the woman would naturally want to be at home with her husband and two children instead of here with her mistress.

Stazie went straight to her room and shut the door behind her. The last thing she wanted to do was roam about the cavernous apartment that echoed the sounds of her loneliness. She cringed at the feel of Josh's handprint on her bruised thigh and his dried saliva on her neck and face, and headed to the shower. There she let the hot water course over her, hoping it would wash away this evening's events. It did nothing to heal the ache she was feeling to her very core.

It was becoming painfully apparent that this was all there was to her life. Nothing more than a series of endless, meaningless events that never changed. And above all else, she was perpetually isolated and alone. The worst part was she could not even begin to conceive what to do to alter this course she was on.

Hoppy, laying against her pillow, grimaced at her as always when she crawled into bed. She studied his red gaping mouth and little t-shirt that read 'Hoppy Hops Right To It.' She couldn't recall how many times she had read that slogan over the last twenty-three years. And the countless times she had done exactly what she was doing right now, curling up on her side and clutching him under her chin, holding him close until she could finally fall asleep.

A couple of hours later, she was awakened by a bump out in the living room beyond her bedroom wall. She strained her ears but it was quiet for the next few minutes. Believing she must have been dreaming, she was settling back into her pillow when she heard it again. Then she heard a low voice. Frightened there might be an intruder in the apartment or perhaps somehow Josh and the others had broke in to continue harassing her, she grabbed up her phone to call the police. Before she dialed, she listened carefully to the low voice again. She realized that it was only her father. He had probably just gotten in and was making one last phone call. Relieved, her heart felt lighter at his presence. She eagerly went out to greet him. Although it was late, she wanted to see him. Maybe he could make sense of her horrible evening.

She could hear him mumbling something as she entered the living room, but the lights were off and she couldn't locate him immediately. Puzzled, she glanced back down the hallway and crossed into the dining room but he wasn't there. He started speaking again and she traced the sound back to the living room. A high-pitched giggle stopped her short. She reached for the table lamp and flicked it on.

"Daddy?"

From his position on the floor, Doug Royale's head popped up, looking beyond the sofa. He appeared startled.

"Daddy, what the—?"

"Stazie! What are you doing home?" he said, but he wouldn't move from where he crouched.

"Where's your shirt? And what are you doing over there . . .?" she said.

She gasped out loud as she walked around the sofa to where her father was hiding. He was dressed only in his boxers and it was obvious that he was fully aroused. What shocked her more was what she saw on the floor beneath him, clearly the object of his desire.

"Gidge?"

Her friend lay on the carpet, propped up on her elbows, and clad only in Doug's tie and unbuttoned shirt. Her clothes made a trail back to the front door. Gidge made no effort to move or cover up. She only rolled her eyes and sucked her teeth in disgust at her friend's discovery.

"Stazie, Honey, I know what you must be thinking," Doug said as he grabbed a throw pillow to cover himself.

Stazie backed up a couple of steps, swallowed hard, and shook her head.

"No Daddy, you don't." Then she looked at her friend who eyed her with contempt. "There's no possible way you could know what I'm thinking."

Gidge sat up and sighed audibly. A sardonic smile twisted her mouth as she witnessed the conflict between father and daughter.

"I thought you said you were on a business trip until tomorrow," Stazie said to her father. Then she turned to Gidge and said, "And you told me that you were busy tonight, that's why you couldn't go to the club."

Wagging her head, Gidge said sarcastically, "Well, duh. I *am* busy tonight or haven't you noticed? And why the hell aren't you still at the club with Josh?"

"Because I didn't want to be there."

"Shit," Gidge said with disgust. Then she mumbled under her breath to no one in particular, "And he told me I had nothing to worry about because he was going to be screwing her brains out tonight. I'm going to kill him . . ."

Doug turned to her and said, "Hey! Watch your mouth. She *is* my daughter. And cover yourself up, for God's sake."

Gidge looked at him innocently and slowly pulled his shirt closed around her. But as soon as he turned back to Stazie, she rolled her eyes once more, popped her gum, and silently mouthed '*Well excuse me*' with a sneer.

"Listen, Baby, I'm sorry I lied to you. I just didn't think that you would, well, approve."

The loquacious counselor found himself grappling for words once more. He suddenly empathized with all the defendants that broke a sweat on the stand under interrogation. His own judge and jury—his daughter—stood before him, her lower lip quivering and her face crumbling with betrayal.

"Aw, c'mon, Staze . . ."

For the second time that evening, Stazie needed to flee from the chaos before her and bolted out of the apartment into the hallway. There she fell against the wall, overcome with emotion and confusion. A wave of insecurity suddenly gripped her. She had absolutely no one. Her father was the only person Stazie had in her life and if he didn't consider his own daughter, she didn't know what she would do. She would be forsaken. There was no one else to turn to.

The sound of the phone ringing jostled him awake.

"Hullo?"

"Rey? I'm sorry to wake you. But please, I beg of you . . . I just need someone to talk to right now," she said, her voice breaking.

"Stazie? Are you okay? Where are you?" Rey said as he sat up.

"Could you come get me? I don't have anywhere else to go."

"Sure, but are you okay? Are you hurt?"

"No, I'm okay. I . . . I just don't know what to do. First Josh and then Daddy with Gidge . . . I'm all alone," she said crying and barely comprehensible.

Trying to make sense of what she was talking about, Rey rubbed his face to wake up. The sleeping pills he had taken to get him through the night were making him groggy. "Wait a minute, what happened? Josh was with Gidge and then your father?"

"No! I can't explain right now. Just please come get me or if . . . if it's okay, I'll drive over there."

By her choking sobs over the phone, he knew she was in no condition to drive. There was no telling how many wrecks she would get into.

"Just tell me where you are. I'll come over."

"I'm in the lobby at my apartment. I can't go home . . . not with *them* still there."

"Okay, I'll be right over. Don't go anywhere, okay?"

He could hear her continue to cry.

"Okay?" he repeated.

"Okay," she said in a small voice. "And Rey?"

"What?"

"Thank you. You don't know how much this means to me."

He found her dressed in her silk pajamas and sitting in the lobby's phone booth for guests with the door closed, looking like a sad little bird locked in a cage. Her face was swollen from crying and her eyes were puffy and red. He had never seen her look more pathetic. When she saw him approach, she came out, buried her face in his chest, and clung to him. "Thank you so much for coming for me," she whispered hoarsely.

"What is going on? Do you want to sit down? And why are you in your pajamas?" he said confused as he gave her a few gentle pats on her back.

"No. Please, can we leave right now?"

"Don't you want to get dressed first? It's cold out there."

"No. We need to leave now."

"But I only have my motorcycle. Can we take your car?"

"I can't drive it. Its windshield is cracked. Please. Let's go now."

"Wait, who's in there?"

"Daddy and Gidge. I'll tell you when we're out of here."

He gave her his jacket and then led her out to his motorcycle parked by the entrance on the sidewalk. She stopped for a moment when she saw it, then looked at him.

"Is this yours?"

"Yeah. How do you think I got over here so fast? I thought you were in real trouble. But you can't ride in your pajamas. Let's call a cab. It'll be a lot warmer and safer for you."

Suddenly, she pushed him back against the building. An abutment concealed them as she motioned for him to be quiet.

"There they are," she whispered and nodded towards two figures that had just exited the building.

Rey could see Doug and Gidge walking towards the curb. As they waited for the valet to bring around the car, Gidge was chattering happily but Doug looked haggard and worried.

"What's going on?" he whispered back to Stazie.

She shook her head and put her finger to her lips, her hand still holding him back. They watched as the couple got into Doug's car and drove off. Then she took a deep breath and released him.

"C'mon. We can go upstairs now."

In the elevator, she wouldn't talk and only continued to sniffle. He had never seen her act so strangely before. When they entered the apartment, Stazie turned on the light in the living room and glanced nervously about. Then she picked up Doug's discarded shirt and tie off the sofa, balled them up and threw them into the wastebasket. Next, she grabbed a robe out of her own room, opened the terrace doors, and went outside. At the railing, she looked down the to the street below.

Rey followed her, still perplexed by her behavior.

"Okay, now will you tell me what's going on? If not, I'm going home and going back to bed," he said. "I've got stuff I've got to do tomorrow."

"I don't know where to start. It's been a horrible night."

"He did *what?*" Rey said minutes later when Stazie finally told him of all Josh had attempted. "Are you okay? That son of a bitch! I'll kill him—"

He jumped from his seat and started towards the door.

"No! Wait!" She grabbed his hand. "It's over."

"But that arrogant shitbag can't get away with doing that to you. It's about time I turn his face inside out. I should have done it back in Colorado."

"No. It's okay. I'm okay. Please, sit back down. It was my fault for ever trusting him. For ever trusting *any* of them. You were right. I have no true friends."

It was the first time anyone set out to defend her and she was touched by his valiant gesture. Stazie held onto his hand, pulling him back. "Rey, just let it go. I need you here with me now."

"Okay, but I'm telling you, it's not over between him and me. When I catch that bastard, I'm going to pound the living shit out of him. I swear to God."

"Please, sit down," she said.

"So, what's going on with your father? And why were we ducking him down there on the street?"

Stazie averted her eyes in shame. "He's been hiding it all along. *They've* been hiding it. He and Gidge. She was supposed to be my friend. Would you believe that? I mean, what do you do when you find your father screwing your best friend? Right there on the living room floor? But I didn't know what to do. I had to get out of there. I just went to the lobby and that's when I called you. I'm so confused."

She drew her knees up, hugging them tightly.

Rey would've rather dismantled Josh and regretted that she had held him back but this new twist came out of left field and threw him. Hearing what she was dealing with forced him to consider her situation and all of its complexities. He tried to imagine what it would be like to find his father with one of Glo's friends on his mother's rug on the living room floor. But Joseph Natal stubbornly refused to materialize in his mind's eye doing anything with any young woman. It was completely inconceivable and Rey felt very grateful for that.

"You sure have had one crappy evening," was all he could manage to say.

His inadequacy with words was enough to produce a faint smile that showed through her tears. It was only momentary as new tears sprung anew.

"Uh huh."

He searched around for some tissue and brought them to her. He knew she was emotionally spent and there was not much more he could do for her. As he put his arm around her to comfort her, she sunk against him. They sat for the next hour, looking out over the city lights until her weeping finally subsided to a few sniffles.

"Feeling any better now?" he asked gently.

She nodded. "A little."

"All right then, maybe you should try to get some sleep. You've had quite an evening. And it's going to take some time for you to get everything sorted out. But that can wait for morning. Right now, you look like you need some rest. Call me if you need anything. I can even come back tomorrow if you'd like," he said as he brushed her hair away from her eyes and touched his lips to her forehead.

She whispered, "Why did you do that?"

He pulled back. "I'm sorry. I was just—"

"I need to know— was it out of pity?"

He scanned the cityscape as if he could find the answer in the life on the streets below. Finally he said, "No. It wasn't out of pity."

"Then stay with me tonight."

"Uh, sure, if you need me to. I can sack out here in the living room on the sofa." She embraced him, put her lips against his, and kissed him deeply, wanting him to know her gratitude, her desire, her longing for him. Unable to resist the feel of her, he kissed her back. But suddenly he caught himself, broke off, and pulled away. This seemed all too familiar. Rey was immediately taken back to that clear mountain night when wanting her only led to being burned.

"Stazie, you don't know what you are doing. You've had a miserable evening and you said it yourself, you're confused right now."

"You're the only thing that makes sense. When I am with you, everything is right. I know what I feel and if you tell me you're not doing this out of pity, then I think you feel the same way." Wrapping her arms about him once again and pulling her body into his, she whispered urgently, "Love me."

"It wouldn't be right for me to . . . not now. Not tonight," he said as he reached for her wrists to free him from her hold.

"Please Rey. You don't understand. I need you."

"But things are all a mess now. Listen, I don't want you to have any regrets. And tonight is not a good night—"

"I am not confused about you. And my only regret would be if you didn't make love to me. Please . . ."

She kissed his neck softly and worked her way to his lips once more. Then she took his hand and placed it between her breasts where her heart was pounding.

"This is all I'm asking of you. Stay . . . And love me."

Rey tried to reason with himself, wrestling with whether it was right or merely the timing that made it so wrong. It had been a while since he had made love to a woman and her caressing kisses were igniting a fire within him. However, it surprised him to find that it wasn't just that. He wanted Stazie Royale. It was undeniable. He was losing his chance of getting out of there. His desire was taking over and he was growing weary trying to fight it. *Would it be so wrong?*

"Are you sure?" he said, closing his eyes as her lips softly grazed the base of his throat and then moved down to his chest as she unbuttoned his shirt.

She breathed, "Yes. More than anything. I need you."

Feeling him tremble, she then kissed him passionately, her full lips parting.

A voice inside of Rey's head screamed for him to stop but he couldn't. On any other night, he would have forced himself to walk away. But not tonight. At this moment, on this very night where he had been drowning in his own grief before she called, he found that he needed this just as much as she did. Together, they both might find the solace that they were seeking.

She rose and took his hand. He let her lead him back inside to her bedroom. There, by the soft muted light from the city through the sheer curtains, they undressed each other, slowly and deliberately, their clothing dropping to the floor, their arms encircling and embracing, their lips and hands continuing to explore each other. When her body was revealed to him, he could only look upon it in wonder. He couldn't imagine how he ever resisted her before. He laid her back upon the bed, gazed into her eyes, and caressed her cheek.

"Anastasia," he whispered low, "You're beautiful."

Stazie felt as if his voice saying her name was nothing more than a life-saving breath.

Then he pulled her to him. For those next hours, with their bodies intertwined, they made love, letting passion guide them to cling to one another and cry out, become one, part, and then become one again. Together, Rey and Stazie lost themselves in place where the world and all of its hurt and confusion couldn't reach them.

She studied his face in the soft light, lingering over its features as she had that morning long ago. So much had happened since then. Stroking his cheek, she could see him break into a smile.

"What are you thinking?" she said.

"I was just thinking about the night we met. Have things changed between us, or what?"

"Oh, how I hated you so."

"I know."

As she looked upon the man who had changed her life, she said, "It's any wonder you're here with me at all right now."

"There's something about you, Stazie. I don't know what it is—something in your heart, some quality in you—it's hard to explain."

"There is?" she said, astonished.

He kissed her tenderly. "Yes, Anastasia, there is."

She threw her arms about him and hugged him fiercely. She craved the feel of his body against hers. As her fingers caressed his back, they lingered for a moment on his scar.

"Rey, how did this happen?"

Stazie could feel him pull away. His smile retreated.

"Listen, I'd rather not talk about it right now, okay?"

"But does it still hurt?"

"It's been a long night. I'll tell you about it some other time."

His abrupt reaction surprised her but it was very late. She kissed him and then snuggled up to him, drifting off as the stars hung low in the sky. She slept heavily until sometime in the early morning, when she woke with a start. In the darkness, she reached out to feel him beside her. Relieved that he was still there, she clung to his arm.

"Is something the matter?" he asked groggily.

"No," she whispered. "Everything is fine now."

It was after 10 a.m. when Stazie awoke. As she blinked her eyes and stretched, she was hit by a twinge of excitement in knowing Rey was right besides her, resting peacefully. Would it be better to wake him or watch him as he slept? Thinking of their love making the night before, she only wanted more. Giggling out loud, she turned over to find his side of the bed was empty, his pillow crumpled and the sheets turned back. In disbelief, she patted the space with her hand as if somehow he had grown miniature and was hiding somewhere in the folds of the sheets. Anxiety sprung up inside of her until it was stemmed by reason.

He's probably in the bathroom.

Taking a deep breath and lying back on her pillow, she scolded herself for being so panicky. She reflected on their night together. Savoring the memory of the way he had touched and kissed her body, Stazie hugged herself and smiled. Unlike those selfish impatient guys who had only used her for their own gratification, Rey was an intuitive lover who had taken her to a height of ecstasy where she had never been before. He would soon come back to bed and they could return to where they had been last night.

However, there was no sound of water running. After a few moments, she got up to check. The door was slightly ajar. She slowly pushed it open to reveal an empty room.

"Rey?" she called out as she returned to the bedroom.

Remembering distinctly how she had unbuttoned his shirt and pulled it off of him at the foot of the bed, with his jeans laying on the floor with his boots nearby, she looked about for his clothes. In her search, she found nothing but her pajamas and panties, placed on her armchair by the window. They had laid among his clothes just hours ago.

Where is he . . . ?

Her throat tightened as she pulled on her robe and went out into the apartment. Could he be in the kitchen?

"Rey!"

Beatrice appeared in the hallway. "Miss Stazie? Is everything all right?"

"Beatrice, have you seen Rey? Is he still here?" Stazie said, anxiously.

The maid furrowed her brow. "Rey? I'm sorry. I don't know who that is."

"Rey Natal! Did you see anyone this morning when you came in?"

"Why, no. I've been in the kitchen most of the morning and before that, I was dusting in the living room. You're the first person I've seen here today. Is something wrong?"

"What time did you get in?"

"At seven-fifteen, like always."

Stazie could feel the old fear coming on fast. It returned as a tide, there was no stopping it now. She ran out to the terrace and looked to the street below. The city was on the move with morning traffic, but there was no sign of his motorcycle by the front of the building. Dashing back into the apartment, she bolted past the maid.

"Miss Stazie! What is the matter?" the older woman asked with alarm.

Stazie continued out the door to the elevator. As it carried her downward to the lobby, a million thoughts flew through her head. *Did he leave me? He couldn't have. He made love to me last night . . . Maybe he went for a walk? Maybe he left me . . .* Stazie balled up her fists and raised her chin, trying harder than ever to keep her composure. *No,* she thought with resolve. *He wouldn't do that to me. Not Rey. Not after all I told him last night. Not after we made love. He's not like the others . . .* The knot in her throat grew painful and tight and it felt as if she had been kicked in the stomach. *Maybe he went home to feed his dog. Yes! Jack Tate probably needed to be walked. He'll be back . . .*

The elevator door opened and she marched straight to the doorman.

"Mike, did you see a man leave this morning on a motorcycle that was parked right out there by the door? He's about this tall and has brown hair?"

The doorman turned around, startled not only by her quick approach and rapid questioning, but by the fact that she was barefoot and dressed only in a light robe with nothing else underneath.

"Good morning, Miss Royale. Motorcycle? Oh yes. I did happen to see that gentleman around, let me see, a little after six or so?"

"Did he say anything to you? Leave a message for me or anything?"

The heavyset doorman shook his head. "No miss. He went directly outside, started his bike and took off."

"Oh." Stazie was crestfallen. "Are you sure?" she asked, almost in desperation although she knew what the answer would be.

"Yes, Miss Royale. I am sure. Is there anything else I can help you with?" he said, perplexed.

Holding herself, Stazie walked away without answering. She would just go upstairs and call him. That is what she would do. And when she did, she would find that Rey had indeed, gone home to feed his dog and was on his way back over to be with her. *Maybe they would go out to breakfast and maybe he would stay the rest of the day or week . . . or even forever.*

Her thoughts couldn't convey enough reassurance to keep her heart from breaking. And although the elevator went up, she felt with no one around to hold her, she was falling down.

At 5:47 a.m., Rey had sat upright, gasping for breath. His eyes were wet and his mouth was forming the name he had been calling over and over. He looked around him in terror, not recognizing where he was, the surroundings unfamiliar. He wanted to flee but then he glanced down beside him. Someone lie sleeping next to him. Baffled, he couldn't make out who it was.

As his brain slowly relinquished the nightmare and he became fully awake, he recognized that it was Stazie. He was in her room and they had just made love hours before.

Shaken and disturbed, Rey gripped his head, hoping to clear the vivid sensations that replayed in his mind. The grinding crunch of metal filled his ears. He saw himself crawling out of the wreck and making his way to the lifeless body on the side of the street. He slammed his eyes shut and took a deep breath trying to force his thoughts to quiet. But it was black—so black—like when he was regaining consciousness from the crash and hadn't realized what had happened. Suddenly, he felt as if he were suffocating under all that blackness. He had to escape. He flung back the blankets and dressed quickly, heading for the door.

Outside, he started his motorcycle, his head still cluttered with thoughts and decisions. Last night, he had been weak. Why he had caved in, he could not determine. He cursed himself realizing that the ramifications of this mistake were going to cost *her* dearly, not him. He wanted to turn the bike west and ride away from here, roll the throttle back and put some distance between memories and potential tragedies. But before he could, there was another place he was compelled to go to first.

The phone continued to ring. He didn't have his answering machine turned on. *Or maybe he disconnected his phone,* she thought bitterly. *Why won't he answer? Why wouldn't he call?* She reminded herself that he could still be outside with the dog. *Give him time . . . Give him time . . .*

Beatrice slipped in with an espresso and biscotti thinking that her mistress might be hungry. As she turned to leave, Stazie hung up the phone. "Oh why doesn't he call already? It's been close to an hour and a half," she said out loud.

Beatrice stopped in her tracks with a sigh and resignedly turned back to face her. Not knowing what to reply, she just stood there. She had witnessed her mistress crying, calling, and moping about and thought a little breakfast might cheer her up. However now she was unwillingly being drawn into this private matter. It had all the makings of a one night stand in her opinion and she wondered how these young women, with all their sophistication, still fell for it. But the maid held her tongue, knowing it was best to mind her own business.

Stazie woefully stared out the window. "I can't believe he would just leave without saying anything to me. He said I had a certain quality in me that made him stay with me." She turned back to Beatrice. "Well why didn't he stay with me this morning?"

Regardless of what words were used, it sounded like a pickup line to Beatrice. She didn't think her mistress would be so gullible. And when she recalled Mr. Natal, she would've never figured he would act that way. He seemed like a polite enough fellow. *But, there was no telling these days.*

To her relief, there was a key in the lock and Doug Royale entered the apartment. With Stazie's attention drawn to her father, Beatrice excused herself and headed back to the kitchen. The last thing she wanted was to be any part of the Royales' family affairs. Their predicaments usually seemed overly complicated for her.

As he entered the living room, Doug cautiously surveyed his daughter.

"Hi Baby," he said timidly.

Her eyes narrowed. "Is Gidge there in the foyer?" she said.

"No, she's not here. Listen, I really want to apologize for—"

Before he could finish, Stazie went to her room and closed the door. She couldn't bear to hear any of his explanations or excuses right now. She stopped short when she saw her unmade bed, Rey's pillow still exactly as he had left it. Her eyes went to the photo sitting on the dresser. It was the one she had taken of him when he was driving in Colorado. She studied his bright face and dark mischievous eyes. The blanket of disappointment and heartbreak about her grew heavy.

Was he capable of hurting me like everybody else?

It was the first time he had been back to the intersection since the accident. He parked his motorcycle at the curb and walked to the corner. From there, he watched the lanes of traffic as they took turns stopping at the lights and then proceeded on their way. One year's time changed so many things, yet other things remained painfully the same.

Rey fought to get his thoughts under control but the past came rushing up in blinding speed and with complete randomness. In his mind's eye, he saw when he first met Ivan in high school chemistry class as lab partners in sophomore year. The freezing rain pounding them as they raced down a steep mountain bike trail, muddied from head to foot by the time they reached the bottom. The wild dorm parties where they would get ripped. The time they woke up in a dumpster with no clue of how they got there. The long afternoon they had spent at the recruitment office, scared and excited about enlisting. Celebrating their new jobs at Schuster and Mohlen. Countless other events, scrapes, moments, adventures, and dares down half-pipes. He could hear their stupid jokes and playful ribbing of each other. He could see Ivan shrug and grin, the way he always did in his laid-back, easy manner. These memories that had been suppressed for the last year, now flooded his mind, mixing in a jumbled blur.

He approached the telephone pole and examined it carefully. A few splinters had broken away from its surface but the scar in the wood was still evident. He recalled the awkward, unnatural way Ivan's limbs were bent beneath him and the thick dark blood pooling and running to the curb from the mat of black hair that hid his fractured skull. He noticed that the curb had a fresh coat of yellow paint that covered the bloodstain that had flowed off its edge. The grass beneath his feet was springy and green as if it had never bore the weight of Ivan's body on it.

At that very moment, a car ran the light, nearly causing an accident. The sound of squealing brakes and a blast from a horn transported him back to fateful evening.

It was a Friday and the end of the workweek had finally arrived. Rey threw down his pen, scooped up the plans and reports on his desk and tossed them into his in-basket. He never liked coming in on Monday mornings to find his desktop cluttered. He logged off his computer, put away more drawings, and then hunted for just the right piece of paper. Finding a legal-size sheet, he crumpled it into a ball and weighed it in his hands, knew it would have the proper mass to reach its target. Taking a look to make sure his boss wasn't around, stood up and lobbed it catty-cornered over two cubicles. The wad hit its mark because to Rey's satisfaction, he could hear "Hey! You asshole!" Next, he ducked knowing that return fire should happen shortly. Within a few moments it did, in the form of a pink eraser that landed at his feet.

He picked up the phone and dialed the extension of his attacker.

"That missed me by a mile, you weenie," he said and laughed.

"It missed you, dude, only because you hid like a little girl."

"No, it missed me, *dude*, only because you throw like a little girl," he said. "Are we still on for tonight?"

"Yeah, but I can't stay out too late. Rachel's not feeling real well."

"But we've got to celebrate, man. This is my second promotion this year and I'm buying."

"Well then, what are we waiting for bro? Hang up and let's blow this popsicle stand."

Before Rey could close his overhead cabinet and dig his cell phone out of his desk drawer, Ivan appeared at the doorway, his crazy hair sticking out in all directions. Although he was a CAD draftsman and didn't interface with clients, Schuster and Mohlen had a pretty strict dress code for all their employees that included personal grooming and appearance. Rey still couldn't believe how his atheist friend was able to keep such a straight face when telling the boss he needed to keep his hair the way he did for religious beliefs.

"Okay, who's driving?"

"Yeah, right. Like I'm going to choose my piece of crappola instead of your sweet ride?" Ivan said and smirked.

"Just thought I'd give you the chance," Rey said, feeling proud of his three-month-old Porsche Cayman. The bonuses from his first and second promotions were already well spent.

The best friends walked out into the parking lot, slipping off ties, and unbuttoning and loosening their collars. Rey opened up the moon roof and cranked up the stereo. They were ready to go. He drove to their favorite spot, Jon John's Bar and Grill where they ordered their usual: buffalo wings, double cheeseburgers with steak fries, fried calamari, and a couple of pitchers of ice cold beer. They had been going to Jon John's ever since they had tried to sneak into the place as teens. It was the meeting place for all their celebrations.

After dinner, Rey ordered a round of tequilas to toast his promotion. Ivan raised his glass and said, "To my best bud Rey, the smartest, craziest, luckiest son of a bitch to ever grace this planet. Listen up mortals, after this promotion, 'mere anarchy is loosed upon the world.' Skål, dude!"

They downed the shots.

Rey followed up by toasting his friend and saying, "And to my baldness-challenged friend, may he live long, scorch the earth, and father lots and lots of children with crew cuts. Salud!"

As his friend laughed and shook his dreadlocks in mock defiance, Rey reflected on how, no matter what happened, they always remained close. They only time they had been apart was when they had enlisted in the Navy, hoping to serve together. While Rey was selected for the Construction Battalion, Ivan drove a supply vehicle for ground support. In college, while Rey worked on his architectural engineering degree, Ivan switched his major from English to drafting. And as Rey moved swiftly up the ranks at Schuster and Mohlen earning prestigious awards and promotions, Ivan worked as a draftsman there, making half the pay. Ivan never thought twice about Rey's status and instead was extremely proud of him. Rey knew he truly *was* a damned lucky son of a bitch to have a friend like him.

Three more rounds and Ivan was calling it a night but Rey was in too good of a mood to let it all end so soon. He persuaded his companion to have one more round before they took off. Back in the car, they smoked a joint, cranked up the stereo, forgot their seatbelts, and tore out of the parking lot. The responsive sport car fishtailed on the slick asphalt as it took off.

The rain began to fall. Racing down the streets, it felt as if they were snowboarding again down the steep snowy slopes, seeing how fast they could go, daring each other, and catching a thrill. Both were so inebriated, they didn't realize how incapacitated they were.

At one curve, Rey spun out in a one-hundred-and-eighty-degree turn, enough so that it frightened Ivan a little.

"Whoa dude!" he said, "That was tight! Are you sure you want to go this fast?"

"Are you chickening out or do you need to change your panties?" Rey said.

He downshifted and smashed the accelerator, careening through turns and weaving through traffic, narrowly avoiding oncoming cars as he cut across lanes. The two friends howled with adrenaline when the car hit off rises and became airborne. They flew down hills and sailed through intersections, slipping through the crosswise traffic.

"Man! That was friggin' bitchin'!" Ivan yelled.

Rey laughed and shifted gears

At the next intersection, he failed to notice the red light when a delivery truck pulled out in front of them. At high speed, he slammed on his brakes and swerved to avoid broadsiding the truck but the car went into a spin on the road wet from the rain. He couldn't pull it out of the slide. The low sport car struck the curb and flipped, deploying the airbags. Rey could hear Ivan scream as he was ejected through the moon roof. The car continued to roll, smashing in the roof and shattering the windows.

As it rolled, the g-forces pulled Rey halfway out of his smashed window, although he tried to hang onto to the steering wheel. There was an excruciating pain to his shoulder and head as the driver's side made impact with the ground. The battered car rolled one more time before Rey went unconscious. He came to for just a few seconds, long enough to see through the smashed-out windshield to Ivan's body lying broken a few yards away. He blacked out again.

The impact of the memory forced Rey to fall against the telephone pole. His hand went to the scar in the wood where Ivan's head had made contact.

I'm sorry. Oh god, I'm so sorry . . .

He sunk to his knees, shaking as terror and guilt over the deed that he had committed overcame him. The burden of what had happened a year ago was overbearing, crushing him with its brute force.

He had killed his best friend.

Grief wracked his body and a strangled cry fled his throat. Oblivious to the traffic that drove past, he clawed at the grass in rage, trying to erase the bright green that concealed the evidence of his crime. He knew the earth beneath him still held some of Ivan's blood. It was this spot where his friend's heart had stopped beating. This corner was the last thing he saw.

Spent, Rey finally broke down, sobbing. He sat back against the pole, drew up his knees, and put his head down. Tears of remorse and grief poured from him.

Ivan was dead.

He recalled his friend's face as his breath left him, looking directly at him through half-closed eyelids. The look seemed accusatory—*or was it pleading?*

Rey turned his face to the overcast sky above, unable to understand exactly what had given him the ability to take another's life. Somehow he had been empowered with the role of judge and executioner. His friend had wanted to go home. But Rey made him stay to celebrate. And when he had spun out, Ivan had warned him that he was going too fast. Yet, he went even faster. What he out to prove something and why?

While his friend would never see another day, Rey had survived to see another three-hundred-sixty-four more. If he was the cause of the accident, it should be his blood soaked into the ground beneath him. He certainly deserved it. Ivan had died before he could see the birth of his son. And he would never hold his girlfriend and tell her he loved her again.

Yet, I had the pleasure of making love to a woman last night, Rey thought bitterly.

His thoughts suddenly shifted to Stazie, another person who trusted him. He was starting to feel something for her and the last thing he wanted to do was betray her too. He cursed himself for giving in and complicating things by sleeping with her. It was entirely wrong to ever get involved with anyone at all. He had already ended one life and screwed up three others, including his own.

He imagined her lithe body, twisted and broken, lying in the grass before him as her blood drained away. Could his recklessness possibly kill her one day? Deep within, he knew that he couldn't trust that it wouldn't ever happen again. It was obvious that he was nothing more than a selfish bastard who needed to stay far away from everyone.

"What's wrong?"

Rey raised his head to see a little girl no older than Sela, staring at him intently.

"Olivia, come away from that man," her mother scolded, scooping up the child and glaring at him as if he were a criminal. "I can't believe you drunks are out in broad daylight," she said with contempt.

He watched the woman storm off with her child, the little girl peering at him with frightened eyes over her mother's shoulder. Whatever that child thought of him, she would carry away with her.

There was only one thing the woman said that made sense. Rey was ready for that drink.

It had been thirteen hours since he lie beside her and the day was fast coming to a close. All that was needed to be different from the others would have been one phone call from him offering an explanation or apology. But just like the rest, the call never came. Initially, her mind went through possibilities such as an accident or some other unforeseeable illness or emergency. Although she didn't want any of those events to come true, she couldn't bear to think that Rey would just use her like that. Then again, he surely would've contacted her by now if had been some kind of emergency. By the late afternoon, she had called his place a dozen times. There was no answer.

It had happened again. Years of hurt and abandonment seethed to the surface, stinging her to the core and making it hard to breathe. Slowly, her tears dried from the anger that ignited from within.

How dare he do this to me? How dare any of them do this to me? But wasn't he different? Or so she thought. Apparently she was destined to have everyone treat her this way. She was so unlovable that no one would ever stay, she reasoned.

Her anger mounting, she seized his pillow left untouched on the bed and hurled it across the room. Then she opened the door to the balcony and flung it out to the street below. Next, the sheets in which they had slept in followed the pillow over the railing. Returning to her room, her eye fell upon her bottles of perfume and trays of bangles and makeup. Disgusted, she overturned her dressing table, dumping them to the floor with a crash. It was all garbage, all a façade. For who, exactly, had she been doing it for? She didn't even know who she was.

Nearing hysterics, Stazie felt wild and trapped. She grabbed Rey's photo and slammed it into the trashcan, breaking the frame and shattering the glass. Hoppy's red grimace glared at her from his post on her nightstand. She snatched him up and took a good look at him. He appeared ugly, old, and worn out, his beady button eyes scratched and dull. Stazie shook him hard and then her hands started working to pull him apart. She tugged and ripped, until threads popped and she tore his head off and shredded his tee shirt. Then she tossed him into the trash can on top of the photo.

The mixed fragrances emanating from the broken and spilled bottles on the floor filled her room with an overpowering sweet smell. There was a knock at her door.

Her father, summoned by the crashes and odor, called to her as he tried the knob, "Honey? What's going on? Is everything all right in there?"

"Go away and leave me the hell alone! You're good at that. Everyone is good at that!"

"Stazie, please. Unlock the door. Let's talk."

Within the next minute, she opened the door only to brush past the confused counselor without saying a word. She grabbed up her keys and purse and left. When she arrived at Rey's apartment, she stormed up the stairs and hammered on his door with her fist. She wanted him to face her directly and tell her the exact reason why he wouldn't return.

"Open the door!" she yelled with fury. "Open the door!"

She pounded some more and imagined him inside, scrambling around to think of some good excuse. *Was he inside laughing? Smirking? Hiding?* But he didn't appear. Although her anger had fueled her this far along, it wasn't enough to hold up her crumbling esteem. She was sinking quickly as despair engulfed her.

"Where are you?" she said when he wouldn't answer. She pounded some more. "Please don't do this to me . . . Where are you?" When silence prevailed, Stazie leaned her head against his door and sobbed. "Not you . . . not you too . . ."

He hesitated before scrolling through his contacts, put down his phone, and then picked it up again. Finally, after a few more minutes, he selected her name and dialed.

"Hello? I need to speak to Mei-Lin Fong, please."

"May I ask who is calling?"

"Rey Natal. I was one of her clients about four, maybe five months ago."

"I'm sorry sir, but Ms. Fong took a position in San Francisco last month. Didn't you receive her email?"

At the moment Rey couldn't remember if he had or not.

The answering service continued, "Ms. Fong's clients are now being seen by Kathryn Mears. Would you like to me to connect you with her voice mail?"

"Uh, no, that's okay."

"Is this an emergency, Mr. Natal? If so, Ms. Fong has left a forwarding number for emergencies."

The seconds ticked by.

"Mr. Natal? Are you still there?"

He hung up. Looking out the window of the bar, he could see that night was upon him. After downing a couple more shots of tequila, he made his way outside. The bright reflections of neon store signs on wet streets were a stark contrast to the skies made darker by clouds on the move. Feeling extremely agitated, Rey started his motorcycle and rolled out into the street. The streetlights passing over his head ticked off the seconds like the fuse to a time bomb. He let the miles roll by in a blur, the cold wind on his neck and chest doing nothing to quell the continuous burn of sorrow mixed with rage.

He decided to turn into a sleazy neighborhood full of bars and clubs, hoping to find the action he was seeking, scanning the lines of clubbers outside waiting to get in. He didn't know exactly why, but he wanted a fight. If they bested him, they would give him the beating he felt he sorely deserved. *If I can find just one asshole who is looking for it* he thought when suddenly he spied exactly what he was searching for. Under the singular blue neon sign of an exclusive hangout, stood Josh Pinard, talking with two giggling girls in tight short dresses who were obviously vying for his attention. Josh posed in a relaxed swagger, taking a drag off a cigarette, and looking bored as usual in his designer jeans and silk shirt. Rey could spot him anywhere. There was a score he had to settle with this asshole.

Bingo.

Slowing down, he turned the motorcycle around and pulled up onto the sidewalk. There, he shut it down, took his helmet off, and perched it on the saddle. Without removing his gloves, he walked towards his target, his long stride closing the distance quickly. As he advanced, there were no exact thoughts in his head other than a set of objectives for dismantling.

Josh took another long drag off his cigarette, pointed a pout toward the sky, and blew out a long stream of acrid smoke. The girls chattered excitedly while he looked disinterested.

"So, should we stay here to see if Raul shows up or should we check out Mars 'n Venus? I hear it's hot there since Robo Dat showed up to DJ. He's supposed to be on at 11:30. I want to go!" one of them said excitedly.

The other said, "Me too! We should. Let's go. Can we go?"

With the cigarette perched on his lower lip, Josh said coolly, "Chill, bitches. Raul should be here in a min—"

He was interrupted by a hard tap on his shoulder.

Annoyed at the intrusion, he said, "What the fuck?" as he turned to face Rey.

At that, Rey grabbed him by his throat and slammed him hard against the brick wall of the club, pinning him. The girls gasped and moved aside.

"What's your fuckin' problem, man?" Josh hissed through gritted teeth.

"You obviously don't remember me, do you, shit bag?" Rey said in a low growl as he released him.

"No. Should I?" Josh said with disgust, trying to regain his composure as he smoothed back his ruffled hair and adjusted his shirt.

"That's irrelevant. But if you ever lay a hand on Stazie again, I'll make sure you do."

"Stazie? What did she tell you? Oh wait— that lying whore. I bet she said that I did something to her, didn't she? I should file harassment on her ass. The fact of the matter is she's been throwing herself at me all along. I have at least ten people who are witnesses."

"Well, *the fact of the matter* is I have absolutely no reason to believe you."

Josh's face suddenly registered recognition. "Hey, you're that house painter they hired to redo the cottage. I can't believe Ol' Staze sent you to take care of me."

"And what is that supposed to mean?"

"It means that if you touch me again, I will slap you with an assault charge that will send your sorry peddling ass to jail where they will throw away the key," Josh said petulantly, getting into Rey's face and jabbing his finger at him.

"Wrong answer," said Rey.

His fist connected with the side of Josh's head, sending him crashing down on the sidewalk. Stunned, Josh shook his head and swung at Rey, glancing his chin. Rey was upon him in an instant with an onslaught of blows that exploded from pent-up frustration. The second hit knocked a tooth out of Josh's mouth, while the subsequent hits hammered his nose to a pulp, and then blackened both eyes. Unable to get in a strike in return against the continued barrage, Josh's arms instead went up defensively to block the punches but without much effect.

The two girls were screaming for them to stop but Rey couldn't hear a sound above the pounding of blood through his veins. He then grabbed the now limp Josh by his throat and was about to land one more final blow when the sight of his adversary's battered face made him cease, his fist hovering in mid-air, ready to strike. The girls' frightened cries begging him to stop finally reached his ears. He dropped Josh to the ground and stood over him, panting and catching his breath. Josh lie still, unmoving.

"You killed him! Oh my god, you killed him!" one of the girls cried.

Rey looked at her, then back at the bloodied jetsetter. He removed his glove and checked the pulse on the side of Josh's neck, where he found a steady beat. Then he checked his breathing to make sure that air was getting past the swollen nose.

"Call 9-1-1," he told the girl.

She only cried harder and wrung her hands.

"I said, do it!"

The other girl took out her cell phone and started to dial. Rey straightened up and took a good look at the unconscious man on the ground. There was no doubt that Josh was a prick and it was only a matter of time before he saw his comeuppance from someone he had tormented. But Rey knew he had gone too far and Josh was merely at the receiving end of something far more treacherous.

He wasn't fooling anyone. He couldn't help but hurt people and destroy their lives. There wasn't any point in thinking that it would ever get better. An invading sense of shame and self-loathing replaced fury as he returned to his motorcycle, started the bike, and rode away.

❧

Rick gulped down his coffee. He usually had it hot and black and liked to sip it casually while listening to Marcie talk in the morning. But she wasn't talking and it was getting late. A worried line crossed her brow today as she watched him, silently hurrying him along. He didn't want to linger either. They both knew what day it was. Rick had even taken personal time off from work in preparation. He was glad he did because so far, things didn't look good.

He hadn't been able to reach his brother for the past two nights. He and Marcie had stopped over at the apartment but Rey wasn't there. They knew he would take the anniversary of the accident hard and they wanted to be there for him. In fact, they had made Rey agree to spend the day with them after much talk and convincing him throughout the year. However, he hadn't called like he had promised and still wasn't answering his phone or his cell.

Carmen Natal had called earlier, asking Rick for a report. She too, was very worried when she couldn't reach her youngest son either. The only thing the older brother could do was to try to calm her down and promise to let her know immediately when they located him. He didn't have the heart to tell her that he had already been to Rey's place this morning but there still was no sign of him. It was all he could do, himself, to keep from combing each and every street to search for his brother.

The hot coffee was on the verge of searing as it went down. He winced but fought through it. As soon as he was finished, he would set off again. Marcie started to gather her stuff for work, already running very late from waiting to hear from Rey. She would have stayed home as well but there were two people out sick at work and they were shorthanded.

"Remember, Rick—"

"I know. I will call you as soon as I find him."

"It's just that—"

"I know. He's got that motorcycle now and there's no telling what has happened."

Marcie held her tongue. They had been over this a dozen or more times already. She knew Rick was worried beyond belief. She too, was anxious for Rey. But she also was concerned for her fiancé. The last time she had seen him so uptight was the night of the accident. Marcie turned away and said a silent prayer for both brothers. If anything happened to Rey, she didn't know what Rick would do.

Rick got up and encircled her in a hug. She felt small in his big arms.

He kissed her tenderly and said, "Don't worry, Babe. He'll be okay. Rey's always been lucky like that."

"I hope so. For the both of you." She patted his broad chest. "Call me."

"I will."

Within another fifteen minutes, he pulled up in front of his younger brother's apartment once again. This time his heart leapt when he saw the motorcycle parked by the entrance to the stairwell. He breathed out a sigh.

Thank God he's all right . . . I'm gonna kill that little shit when I get a hold of him, he thought.

He got out of his Charger and was walking towards the stairs when he heard a car pull up behind him and hit the brakes hard. Turning around, he saw a Mercedes that had partly driven up on the sidewalk next to the fire hydrant. Inside he could make out a familiar blonde head.

Oh, no. What does she want?

Yet when Stazie got out of the car, he hardly recognized her with her puffy eyes and angry expression. She wasn't wearing any makeup and looked as if she hadn't slept well. He blinked hard just to make sure he had gotten the right person.

"Rick? Is he in there? Is that his motorcycle?" she said urgently as she approached.

"Yeah, it's his bike. But I don't know if he's home. I haven't been up there yet."

"Well, he better be home. I have a few things to say to that jerk," she said as she made her way past him.

Before she could get any farther, he reached out and caught her arm. "Hold on a minute. Not so fast. What's the deal?"

He wanted to chew Rey out himself for not calling in but he also knew if his brother was in there, he was going through a difficult time right now. He could always put the screws to him later when he was feeling better. In the meantime, Rey didn't need this chick putting him through the grinder again. Not today.

"What are you doing? Let me go." Stazie pushed against Rick but it was as futile as pushing against a wall. He outweighed her by at least seventy-five pounds.

"I said, what's the deal?"

"I don't have to tell you. It's none of your business. Now let me go or I'm pressing charges."

"Okay. I'll let you go but can we talk first? I mean, before you go storming up there?" Rick said.

"Talk about what? If you are trying to cover for your pathetic brother, save your breath. He deserves what I have to say to him."

"If I read you right before, you have a thing for him, don't you? Well, if you give a shit about him at all, I can tell you, he's not in any condition right now for any chewing out, from anybody."

"So what are you doing? Standing guard and stopping anyone who wants to talk to him?"

"If I have to go that far."

"I have to let him know that he can't do that to me. He can't just use me like all the rest and then dump me and think that he can get away with it. I trusted him. I confided in him. I . . . gave myself to him." She lowered her eyes and embarrassed, looked away for a moment. "And then he just walked away."

"Listen Stazie. I really don't know you and you don't know me. But you've got to believe me, Rey's not like that."

"He hasn't called! I haven't seen him since we—oh, why am I telling you this?" Her eyes brimmed with tears and she looked away once again.

"Hey, don't do that." As much as he hated what he was going to say next, he knew it was imperative to get this woman straight. "Listen, how about we talk about this in my car, okay?"

"Why would I want to get in your car?" she said, wiping at her eyes.

"Okay my car, your car, a coffee shop. Whatever. I just thought you might not want to be out here crying in public and all," Rick said.

A few people walking by were already giving the arguing couple strange looks. As he said it, she noticed it too.

"All right. We'll go to my car."

When Rick got in and closed the door to the Mercedes, he took a second to note the leather interior and state-of-the-art amenities. *This ain't half bad*, he had to admit to himself.

"So. What is it that you want to tell me?" Stazie said.

"Rey, like I said, he's not like that. I know you find it hard to believe but he'll come around. He just needs some space right now. That's all."

"Oh really? And why couldn't he tell me this himself? Did he put you up to this?"

"No. He doesn't even know that I am here."

"But space for what? What is so important that he just disappears without saying anything to anyone?"

Rick took a moment to look out the window and gather his thoughts. Whether Rey liked it or not, he was going to have to tell Stazie what was going on.

"You may have noticed a scar under his left shoulder blade that runs along to his side when you two were, uh—you know."

She rolled her eyes at his statement. "Yes. I've seen it before. In fact, when I asked him about it, he wouldn't tell me how he got it."

"Yeah, well a year ago today, Rey was in an accident. A major one. He was almost killed, his car completely totaled, and his arm nearly severed off. It was pretty touch and go. He ended up in intensive care for a couple of weeks."

"Okay, but what does this have to do with his behavior now?"

"His best friend, Ivan, was killed in the wreck."

Stazie was stunned. Her thoughts went first to the photo of Rey and Ivan that she had seen in his apartment. Then back to Colorado and what she had said to him about his friends. Her guts wrenched with guilt.

"Oh," she said quietly. It was clear now why he was so evasive about his scar. "But it was an accident. He can't blame himself for it."

"He does. And I guess in a way, he should. He was drinking heavily that night, smoking pot, driving too fast, and ran a light. The car rolled and Ivan was ejected through the moon roof. He hit a telephone pole ten feet away with his head. Poor guy hit so hard, he was killed upon impact."

"Oh my goodness . . ." she said, working the incident through her mind. "Is that why Rey doesn't have a license?"

"Yeah, the judge decided to go easy on him because he had no priors and a clean record. His company also vouched for his behavior. He did a month in the slammer, six months community service, went to counseling for seven, and had his license revoked for fifteen months. That's why this whole motorcycle thing is nuts. He still has another couple of months to go before his license is reinstated."

"But if his company stood up for him, why isn't he working with them anymore?"

"He had a hard time adjusting back to working there. Ivan had worked there too, as a draftsman. Everyone knew what had happened. But it's not like they held it against him or anything. In fact, they tried everything they could to convince him to stay. You heard my mom. He was one of their top designers. They had given him all sorts of awards and promotions before it all happened. Yeah, ol' Rey was doing pretty well for himself. Big apartment downtown, top-of-the-line sport equipment, state-of-the-art electronics, travel, clothes—you name it. He even had a sweet turbo Cayman. *Man,* what a car."

Stazie tried absorb it all. She thought of how Rey lived presently in that cramped box of an apartment with not much else besides a sofa, a bed, and a stereo, the skimpy cupboard with a handful of breakfast bars and chipped coffee cups, and bicycling through the streets in all kinds of weather. Then she thought of how she must have appeared to him with her antics, posturing, and bragging. Suddenly she felt very foolish.

"But his status never changed him. Rey was always himself. His head never got big like some people's do. He always took care of friends and family. Whatever anyone needed, he'd get it for them. Real, you know what I mean? And happy too. He was always up. But once he got into that accident and Ivan was killed, it really messed with him. I'm not sure if he'll ever get over it, to tell you the truth."

"Okay. But you said that he'd come around, eventually. Now, I'm not talking about this situation with his friend, but do you think he'll ever see me again? It's just that. . . I'm in love with him. And I can't stand to think of what it would be like if he closes himself off to me."

Rick sighed heavily. She had to bring up the "L" word. He shifted uncomfortably and wondered how Marcie would deal with this. He had no idea that this conversation would end up going in this direction. He wasn't much for talking to begin with, let alone this 'baring of souls' stuff, especially with Stazie. If she had a problem he could fix with a wrench or some motor oil, he could have dealt with it quickly and with ease, but not this.

"Well, you're going to have to decide what you are going to do and how you are going to handle this. I'm telling you that right now, he can't," he said.

Stazie furrowed her brow at Rick's oversimplification of the situation. Besides, it wasn't that easy since it was Rey, not her, who needed to reach out. She looked out the window at the Three Fortunes Asian Market. The shop look neglected. Its ornate letters on its once-gilded sign were faded and peeling.

Still, Rick had a point. She had never considered what Rey might be going through until now. With regret, she realized that she hadn't ever asked him about his life. Their conversations usually centered on her. When she thought about it, how much *did* she really know about this man she professed to love? He had never been forthcoming with much personal information.

Just then Stazie took notice of a tall, willowy redhead who exited from the stairs leading to Rey's apartment, her colorful peasant skirt flowing about her legs.

"Oh crap. Get down," Rick said, sitting low in the seat. He raised his head just enough to spy over the lower edge of the side window.

"What? Why?" she said.

The woman looked like she had been crying. Stazie and Rick observed as she took out a tissue to dab at her eyes and blow her nose. Next, she produced a wad of cash from her pocket and hastily counted it. As she did, she instantly brightened up. They could see her mouth form an enthusiastic "Yes!" as she shoved the money back into her pocket and proceeded down the sidewalk past them.

"But who is that?" Stazie whispered. "And what are you doing?"

"It's Rachel."

"Holy bunnies! *That's* Rachel?" She sat up to get a better look.

Rick stared at her in disbelief. "Holy *bunnies?*" he said, cocking an eyebrow.

Stazie looked sheepish and shrugged.

"Get down. She might see you," he scolded.

"So? She doesn't even know who I am. And why are we hiding from her in the first place?"

"Because, wait a minute . . ." He trailed off as Rachel crossed the street behind them and headed to a large new pickup truck parked there. "Here it comes . . ."

Rick continued to watch as she climbed in behind the wheel next to a guy who was obviously waiting for her in the passenger seat. In excitement, she embraced him with a passionate kiss, and then pulled out the cash to show him. Both grinned and talked animatedly.

"Uh huh. There," Rick said. "I KNEW it!"

"Knew what? What's going on?" Stazie said as the couple drove off.

"I knew she was bullshitting him all along. But would he listen? NOOO-ooo. Look at that thing she's driving. It still has the dealer stickers on it and everything."

It suddenly occurred to Stazie that Rachel had come from Rey's apartment. *Had she been with him all night long? Did he leave* her *bed to make love to this woman as well?* she thought. Before reasoning it out, her anger erupted. She opened the door and hopped out, catching Rick off guard. Then she beeped the remote over her shoulder, locking him in and temporarily detaining him. She wanted to speak to Rey all by herself with no interruptions.

"Hey! What are you doing? Wait a minute!" Rick called to her.

She could hear his muffled yells through the glass as he tried the door handle. She ignored him and climbed the stairs. Trying Rey's door and finding it unlocked, she walked in. The apartment was dimly lit and looked like it had been ransacked. Mixed throughout the papers and clothes strewn about were numerous empty beer, tequila, and vodka bottles. There was a scent of pot in the room. Rey stood with his back to her. He apparently hadn't heard her come in.

Seeing his lean frame, Stazie hesitated for a moment. He was dressed in the same clothes she had last seen him in. Her mind flashed back to unbuttoning that shirt and sliding it off of his shoulders, exposing his chest. But her anger kept her in check. He had obviously been here all along, not answering her calls and partying with Rachel.

She marched up to him and said angrily, "You jerk."

When he turned around, she immediately slapped him hard. He took it with no response, slowly rubbing the red mark left on his unshaven cheek as if he had expected it all along and deserved it. Then he looked at her without saying a word.

She was taken aback by his appearance—he looked haggard and beat. His hair was uncombed and dark circles ringed his bloodshot eyes. There was a droop to his shoulders that he usually carried so straight. And instead of his familiar aftershave, he reeked of alcohol. She had never seen him look so demoralized. Unwillingly, her heart went out to him and she struggled to stand her ground.

"Well, aren't you going to say anything? I've been waiting for over a day and a half for you to show up," she said.

Rey stood silent. He swayed a bit but held his stance. Outside a car alarm went off but neither of them reacted.

She grew frustrated with his stony demeanor. She expected an explanation; at the very least, an apology.

"Say something! I need you to tell me why you wouldn't even call." Hot tears filled Stazie's eyes. "Is that all I was? Just a one-night stand for you? Is that all anyone ever thinks I am? Good for the sack and then gone in the morning?"

He wouldn't answer.

She said, "You weren't supposed to be like the others. But you abandoned me too. Why? Answer me! I needed you." Not being able to stand his silence any longer, she shook him and then started striking him on his chest, face, and neck with her fists, as he did nothing to defend himself. "Answer me!" she sobbed.

As she broke down, she was unable to see the pained expression on his face and then its return to a look of determination.

"I have nothing to say except for I'm sorry for hurting you. But I . . . couldn't come back," he finally said.

"Tell me, Rey—was I only a diversion? You'll return to Rachel's bed, won't you? She'll wake up in the morning and find you there."

"What? What the hell are you talking about?"

"The woman you were with last night. I saw her leave here just now."

"I'd rather not talk about her." He swayed some more.

"You're drunk and disgusting," she said.

"Tell me something I don't already know."

"You know, you're no better than all the rest—trying any line, any means, any act—just for a piece of ass. I can't believe it. I fell for it . . . I trusted you." She averted her eyes . "Now I feel like such an idiot."

"It wasn't like that. I didn't mean for it to appear that way."

"Then what was it? Why did you make love to me?"

Rey held strong. He knew he had to refrain from going anywhere near her or he might take her in his arms. He had already done enough damage. She had to get so angry with him that she would just leave and never come back, in that way he could be sure. This was not a time for more weakness. He mentally shored up and faced her, hating himself for what he knew he had to say to her to make her leave.

"First of all, you came onto *me*, remember? I was headed out of your place when you dragged me back. Listen, I don't know what you expect of me. Some hero from one of your romance novels? A prince who rides up and saves the day? You think just because Daddy's little girl wants it, you get it? Let me tell you. It's not going to happen, okay?

"Yeah, I know your mother treated you like crap and your father was never around. But *get over it*. There are so many people who have had it just as bad or worse than you. Except unlike all those others, you have millions of dollars to keep your mind off of it. It may sound heartless to you but most people have a hard time feeling sorry for the spoiled rich brat driving around in her ninety-thousand-dollar sport coupe, vacationing at five-star resorts around the world, while being waited on hand and foot."

Stazie's mouth dropped open in indignation.

"What? How can you . . . Why are you being such a . . . such a . . . poop?" she said.

"See? That's another thing. It's *shit*, Stazie. Just say it—SHIT. When are you going to drop the little girl act? How old are you? Twenty-eight? Twenty-nine?"

"I'm twenty-seven!"

"Then I'd say that's plenty old enough to get over whatever it was that Mommy did to you, stop living off of Daddy, and grow up. I can't be the mommy, daddy, and pet pony you never had."

"Now, wait a minute. That's not fair," a deep voice from the doorway said.

Both Rey and Stazie turned to see Rick standing there. Neither of them had noticed when he slipped in and how much of the conversation he had witnessed.

"Here you go telling her to let things go, yet you aren't doing too good of a job of it yourself." He picked up a used joint from the counter and held it out towards his brother. "Like this. You dumb ass. I thought you gave this shit up. And look at this place. It's a total disaster."

"Oh great. When did you come in? And why does everyone feel the need to invade my life?" Rey said as he walked to his kitchen, opened up the refrigerator, and pulled out a beer carton. When he found that it was empty, he angrily slammed it against the wall.

"Hey, not just me, but Ma, Pop, Glo, and Marcie are all worried out of their minds about you. At least now I can call and tell them ol' baby Rey is right here safe and sound, having himself a pity-party and not splattered on the road somewhere."

Rey's eyes narrowed at his older brother. "You ass."

"C'mon Rey, get off it. There are people who care about you whether you like it or not. It's called *concern*. So why do you keep pushing everyone away? This woman right here told me that she is in love with you. And what do you do? Dump her like everybody else?"

Upon Rick's remark, Rey looked at Stazie to see if it was true. By her expression, he could see that it was. With regret, he knew he had gone too far.

"You know, as Marcie was saying just the other day about this thing with you, and I quote, 'Rey can't go on living his life as an apology.' End quote." Then Rick shook his head and said admiringly to no one in particular, "God, is she smart." Refocusing on his brother, he continued, "But she's right. And you know she's right. It's been too long and you've got to give it up. We all know you're sorry and I'm sure Ivan knows it too."

"Goddamnit. Have you ever killed someone, Rick? Have you? Not to mention someone who was engaged to be married and had a child on the way." Rey's voice grew ragged as tears formed in his eyes. "So what do I do? It wasn't enough for me take my best friend's life, I fucked up two others. What I don't understand is why did I ever have that power? And when I did, why did I make the stupid choices that I made? And how is that I can take life away but I can't give it back? *Why!*"

In rage, he struck his fists hard upon the breakfast bar. There was an audible crack from a support under the counter giving way to the force. He stood there, panting, his face twisted in grief.

For the first time, Stazie felt his crushing anguish to the core. Her anger and frustration toward him evaporated as her heart grew heavy in pity for him.

"You say it like it was intentional. It wasn't. It just happened," she said. "It was an accident."

"What are you talking about? You don't even know what the hell happened."

Rick said, "Well actually, I told her everything."

Rey threw his hands up in the air and shook his head. "That's just great."

Stazie said, "Don't you see? Ivan made choices too. He chose to be with you that night. It was a choice *he* made. Just like I chose to be with you."

"Yeah, well if it weren't for the choices *I* made, Ivan wouldn't be dead right now, would he? His biggest mistake was that he chose me as a friend. He should be the one living and going on with his life, not me. He should be with his fiancé and son instead of scattered ashes somewhere out there in the ocean. But because of me and the stupid ass stunts I pulled, he's not." His eyes blazed with conviction as he looked directly at her. "All I know is that I can't trust that my reckless choices won't get in the way of someone's life again." His message was clear.

She started to protest and said, "But how can you be so sure that something like that will happen again?"

"I can't, that's the problem."

"Maybe . . . maybe if Ivan were here he would have forgiven you. In fact he'd probably even want you to forgive yourself, if he was your best friend, like you say he was. If I was your best friend I know I would."

"You don't know what you are talking about."

A syncopated ring tone broke the tension as Rick fumbled for his cell phone. Sheepishly, he answered it, his voice lowered. "Yeah? Oh hey, Babe. Yeah, he's here . . . Uh huh. He's all right . . . Yeah. Tell Ma, Pop, and Gloria will ya? Oh, and Marce? You owe me a crab shack dinner . . . Yeah, she was here not twenty minutes ago. Didn't I tell you? But hey, I gotta go." Rick ended the call when he felt his brother's eye upon him.

"So now you're taking bets on me? Shit. You're really a piece of work, you know that?"

"It wasn't a bet on *you.* It was a bet on—"

There was a light knock at the door. Recognizing it, Rey immediately went to answer it. There stood Rachel, wringing her hands and looking as if she had forgotten something.

"Rachel, come in," Rey said.

"—her," Rick finished his sentence, dumbfounded at her audacity to return.

Surprised to see his older brother and Stazie there, Rachel said slowly, "Hi Rick, it's been a while." Then she sized Stazie up and down without a word. Regaining her composure, she said, "Rey, I forgot to mention that I need to take Tristan for his checkup next week. I don't think I have enough to cover it."

"I gave you all I had for now. But by Tuesday, I should have more."

Rick butted in and said, "Hey Rachel, if you need assistance, I can have Marce have some of her buddies at State look into it for you. They have all sorts of programs for people in your situation. In fact, they'll check out your taxes, your income, your assets, your accounts, and what you are reporting. Yeah, *especially* what you are reporting. I bet they can fix you right up. And fast too. In fact, I'll call her right now. She's at work." He took out his phone and started dialing.

"No! Um, I mean it's okay. You know, on second thought, never mind Rey. I'll be fine. I forgot about my, um, bonus I just got."

"But if you need it, I can—" Rey started to say.

"No. Really, I'm okay. Listen, I've got to go. Sorry to bother you," she said hastily, heading for the door.

Rick couldn't resist saying, "Yeah, you don't want to keep your squeeze waiting out there too long. He may not be there when you get back especially if something more lucrative comes along."

Rachel threw him an evil look before she exited.

"What are you talking about?" Rey asked his brother, as he closed the door.

"Her boyfriend, out there in her ride. He looked pretty happy at the cash you forked over to her when they were counting it together. And that new truck she drives sure is sweet. She must've paid some real coin for it. I'm guessing fifty-thou at least."

Rey looked at him in disbelief.

"I saw it too. They were both there in a new truck. It still had the stickers on it and everything," Stazie said.

He took one last look at the two of them and walked out.

"Where are you going?" Stazie said, trying to follow.

Rick blocked her way. "Just give him a few minutes. He's probably going to see if what we said is true although I think he knows that it is. It's a lot for him to digest, finding out someone he trusts has been using him all along."

"Yeah, well, I kinda know how *that* is," Stazie said with a frown.

Rick choked. Marcie always told him he had a natural born gift for putting his foot in his mouth.

"No. What I mean is using him for the wrong reason. Not that Rey dumping you was a good reason. But what I mean is that Rachel used the wrong reason for taking him for all that he's worth," he said, trying to salvage his claim.

Stazie put her hand on her hip and blinked at him. Then summoning up some patience, she sighed and said, "The wrong reason?"

"Yeah, like cashing in on Ivan's death. She's been a regular bloodsucking leech."

"You mean *that's her*? Rachel is Ivan's fiancé?"

"Holy shit, you mean you're just getting that now?"

She looked bewildered and shrugged. "Well, I didn't know—er, I mean, I couldn't be sure."

After another moment, when his brother didn't return, Rick looked out the window to the street below. He swore softly under his breath.

Stazie came over to the window. "What is it?" she said.

"He's gone."

When the phone rang, she picked it up immediately but before she would press the talk button she caught herself for a moment. She shouldn't appear so eager. Glancing at the caller ID, she could see that the name read 'Natal,' although the number was not the same. While she was sympathetic to what Rey was going through, another day and a half had passed and he still had left her hanging.

Right before her answering machine picked up on the sixth ring, Stazie hit the button and said coolly, "Hello?"

"Miss Royale? This is Carmen Natal, Rey's mother. Hello, how are you today?"

His mother? Thrown completely off guard, Stazie replied, "I'm fine, thanks, Mrs. Natal. How are you? . . . Oh, and please call me Stazie." *Why was she calling?* she thought. If Jack Tate had called her it wouldn't have been as much as a surprise. *Rey wouldn't have possibly put his mother up to this, would he?*

"I'm all right, Stazie. Thank you for asking. I am terribly sorry to trouble you and I hope you don't mind that I took the liberty to look up your number in my son's things but . . ." The older woman hesitated then went on. ". . . I need your help. I'm sorry. I don't mean to be a bother. And I certainly don't want to impose."

"You need my help? What do you mean?"

"It's my Rey . . . I just don't know who else to turn to," Carmen said as she started to cry.

Alarm spread through Stazie. She said anxiously, "What happened? Is he all right?" So this was it. She *knew* he had to have a good reason for why he hadn't called or returned to her.

There was a sniffle and then Carmen said, "He crashed on that motor-cycle of his. I knew it was going to be trouble the minute I saw it. He doesn't have his license yet! He's in jail now. The police picked him up. They said he was DUI but he swore to me that he wasn't. And then there was men-tion of some kind of assault charge. But that couldn't be my Rey. No, not my Rey." Her voice broke into a cry. "They'll lock him up again! Ohhh . . . my poor boy."

"A crash and assault? Is he hurt? How am I supposed to help?"

"He said that he's not injured but he won't always tell me if he is. And he won't say a thing about the other. You see, he doesn't want me to worry. But he's in a lot of trouble right now. Your father—he's a lawyer. Would you please ask him if he knows of someone who handles these kinds of cases? We would be eternally grateful. We don't know the first thing about retaining attorneys. We'll pay anything . . . Please, Stazie. They can't lock him up. Not my Rey. All we need is a name. Do you think your father could possibly do that for us? Someone who is good at these matters?" Carmen said.

Although Stazie was perplexed by this change in events, the kind jovial woman who had warmly welcomed her into her home moved her with her sorrowful pleas.

"Sure. He knows lots of people. I'll talk to him and see what he says. He'll find someone. Then I'll call you back, okay?"

"Thank you, Stazie. Thank you. God bless you . . . And one more thing—I never got to thank you for saving my son's life."

"His life? What do you mean?"

"When you went upstate, in the snow. He told Rick that he had almost froze to death except that you were there to help him out."

"He said that?"

"Yes. So once again, we are grateful. You truly are a wonderful person."

I am? Stazie thought with amazement. "Well, um, thanks. I'll call you after I talk to my dad."

When she hung up, internal conflict erupted as resentment, confusion, and hurt continued to simmer. Yet, there was also an ache and concern in her heart that wouldn't go away.

DUI? An assault charge? What was he doing?

Earlier that morning, a lone motorcycle had zipped along the highway. Rey downshifted to third and opened the throttle. The engine screamed as the needle on the tach spiked towards the red zone. Shifting up to fourth, then fifth, he continued to gain speed until the road appeared tapered before his eyes, the dotted yellow line a solid blur beneath him, the trees and buildings on either side of him a continuous streak of colors. He had the urge to go faster and faster, the need to outrun what was behind him. But at one hundred thirty-two miles per hour, it still wasn't fast enough.

His mind ran through some quick scenarios. Maybe if it looked like an accident, his family would be spared some heartache. None of them would ever forgive themselves if it were determined to be a suicide. Looking for the right moment and the right spot however, there was always something or someone in the way. The last thing he wanted to do was to hurt anyone else. Perhaps if he headed out to the rural areas he would find winding roads with guardrails hiding sheer drop-offs.

Rey felt angry and betrayed. Rachel had been exploiting him all along, manipulating him with the memory of Ivan. He couldn't believe that she would ever use their friendship as a ploy. *Or maybe it was a form of revenge for killing her fiancé and the father of her child?* As he reasoned with himself, he realized he had no right to be angry nor could he blame her for what she had done. With Ivan gone and a baby to support, maybe it was her only way to survive.

He always told her he would be there for her, for whatever she and Tristan needed. He gladly sold everything he owned and handed over the proceeds to her. And whatever money he made from freelancing, he always made sure to set aside as much as possible for her. Rick had dropped numerous hints over the past year, short of telling him directly, that enough was enough but he wouldn't listen.

Veronica Patel. It was ironic that her name and face came up after all these years. He leaned hard into the turns, the footrest scraping against the asphalt and sending off sparks. He wished he could have bought a faster bike. Lit only by the beam of the single headlight, the road was dark before him and seemed to swallow up all other light and sound, leaving Rey alone in his thoughts.

And now Stazie was involved. It seems that he had played her for a fool much like he had been played. He knew that he honestly couldn't help her. Yet he let her believe that he could. His moment of weakness ultimately ended up hurting her. After what Josh and the others did to her, he topped it all off. She was right. He was no better than any of the rest. All too aware of her fragility, he wondered how she would fare after this. And he would be the one to blame. Again.

The blind turn he headed into was too tight at the high rate of speed he was going. The rear wheel broke loose of its traction on a patch of gravel from an unseen pothole. The motorcycle wobbled crazily as he tried to correct but he knew he was losing it. He ended up laying it down and sliding, his hip and knee taking the brunt of the impact upon the roadway. Managing to roll onto his back within fractions of a second, both machine and man skittered across the road until they came to a stop a few hundred feet away. The bike narrowly missed hitting him. Rey lay on his back for a moment, his legs and back hot from the friction of his jacket and pants against the asphalt. He thought it odd how someone who was contemplating suicide just a few minutes ago was suddenly grateful for his helmet and leathers. When he sat up, shaking from the adrenaline that was still pumping through his veins, the flickering flash of red and blue strobe lights danced across him as a patrol car approached.

Doug looked sheepish when his daughter walked into his office. He had been trying to keep out of her way until this whole episode with him and Gidge blew over. But when she strode up to his desk and sat down directly across from him, there was no avoiding her.

"Hi Honey. How are you today?" he said cautiously.

"Rey's been picked up on a DUI. His mother claims that he was sober. She is worried because he doesn't have his license reinstated yet. I'm sure there's probably some vehicle registration issues too."

"Oh? Is that right? I would have never expected that of him."

"There are things I would have never expected of you either," she said simply. "He is also facing an assault charge for putting some sleazebag in the hospital. I need you to get them to drop all the charges and let him off."

"Assault? Now that's a whole different matter—"

"I did some checking. He was defending my honor, just in case you wanted to know."

"*Your* honor? I don't understand. Did you put him up to it?" said the counselor, thoroughly confused.

"Yes, my honor. And no, I did not put him up to it. Josh Pinard practically attacked me at the club the night that you and Gidge . . . Anyway, I still have bruises to show for it."

"Attacked you? Are you okay? Oh god, Honey, I'm sorry I wasn't there for you."

"You can do something now if it bothers you so much."

"But Stazie, I can't just waltz in and demand his release if that's what you are asking. It doesn't work that way. There are multiple charges here—DUI, licensing, assault—"

"I *need* you to get him out. You have connections. I'm sure there's some D.A. that owes you a favor."

"But it's not that easy to—"

"You OWE me," she said, her demeanor turning dark. "Mrs. Natal had only asked for a reference but I figured that someone like the famous Attorney Doug Royale, Counsel to Jocks and Stars, Cradle Robbing Back Stabbing Best Friend Humping When He Should Be My Absentee Father, Esquire, should be able to handle a simple insignificant case like this. You've definitely have had much tougher ones than this, am I right?"

Acquiescing, he nodded. She had said it with such finality that there was no argument from him. The counselor also noted with a bit of pride, that she was beginning to sound just like him. Maybe there was something more to her behind that bright smile and big eyes.

"Okay then. He's being held at the Twenty-Fourth Precinct. I'm heading down there right now to see if I can get any more information. I don't believe this whole thing should take terribly long to get him released, am I right?"

Doug nodded.

"Thank you, Daddy."

Despite what she had told herself, her heart leapt when she spied him exiting the door of the precinct where she was waiting in the parking lot and yearned for him to hold her once again. Rey was favoring his right leg but other than that, he looked okay. Maybe he would accept her offer of a ride home.

When she approached and he saw her, he turned away. She was crushed.

"Rey?"

"Please Stazie. Don't start into it all over again. I'm truly sorry for what I said to you. I was a drunken ass. And I'm sorry that I never called and that you were hurt and worried about me. In fact, I'm sorry that you ever got involved with me at all. I never intended for that to happen. I hope you accept my apology and also my gratitude for getting me out. And thank your dad for me too. I will reimburse the bail money to you as soon as I make some funds. But you should have really just left me there."

"But it's going to be fine now. Daddy got Josh to drop the charges, and—"

"Please, I've got to go."

She blocked his way. "You mean home? I can drive you. It's no problem. It looks like your leg hurts and I can help you."

"No Stazie. I'm leaving. There's no point anymore. I have to get out of this town, maybe even this state."

"Leave? But why?"

"There are too many demons for me here, too many memories. And I can't keep hurting people I care about. I'm tired of all the apologies I constantly make."

"Am I someone you care about?"

Rey kept his eyes on the parking lot, not answering.

She drew close and touched his cheek. "Please tell me because for at least once in my life, I need to know that someone truly cares for me."

His eyes met hers for a moment. Then he lowered his gaze.

"I can't," he said.

"You can't what? Feel anything for me?"

He took her hands in his. They felt small and fragile.

"You are going to go on with your life. Everything will eventually work out and after a very short time, you'll meet someone who will care for you and you'll care for him, and I won't even cross your mind. This will all be behind you and you'll be fine. Believe me, Anastasia, it's going to happen for you."

"I know I was really angry at you but I've gotten over it. I forgive you. But please don't go," she said plaintively. "I love you."

"Can you be so sure? You were going through a rough time the other night and may have said and did things unintentionally. I'm not sure if you are still thinking clearly. Emotions can make you do some really strange things."

"Yes they can. I know that now. But emotions aside, you've changed my life, forever. I am different because of you. Despite everything that has happened, I feel alive now. I can love now. And it's because of you, don't you understand that? I love you, Rey."

Stazie could see him swallow hard and clench his jaw.

Then he turned to her and said, "You underestimate yourself. You are different because of *you*, Stazie, not me. You are the one who changed your life. Oh, I have changed lives all right but not for the better. I want to be a different person but I can't."

"Are you sure your emotions aren't making *you* think 'really strange things'?"

"It's time for me to go. I've put it off way too long."

"Listen, I know you know more than I ever can. But what I'm saying now is right. It's probably the only 'right' thing I'll ever say in my life. Wherever you are running to, how will you know when it is time to stop? And when will you know that you are far away enough?"

His eyes filled with pain. "I'll know it when I get there."

Before he could walk away, Stazie threw her arms about him and planted her mouth firmly on his, kissing him and holding him close, determined to convince him to stay.

He pulled away one last time. Then he kissed her gently on the forehead and said softly, "Goodbye, Stazie. Have a good life."

"Please take me with you. Please."

He walked past her, crossed the parking lot, took the corner, and was gone.

Chapter 8 ~ The Arrival

"I don't know. He looks so depressed."

"Has he eaten anything?"

"No, it doesn't look like he's touched a thing."

"Not even the bagel with cream cheese? That's his favorite."

"No, Sweetie, not even that. I just don't know . . ."

Rick sat down beside his girlfriend on the sofa and patted the unhappy Jack Tate who rested in her lap. The little dog sighed, shifted a bit, but wouldn't move from Marcie's lap.

"He really misses Rey. I know he likes us and all, but Rey is his boy," Marcie said as she stroked the pug-mix's ears.

"Yeah . . . Hey, I wonder how what's her name is doing?"

"You can say it—*Stazie*. And why don't you cut that poor girl some slack already? After all, she did get him out."

Rick sighed. "I know. I guess she's all right."

He rubbed his beard and stared out the picture window behind them. He didn't know what got into him from time to time and he knew it was unfair to keep picking on Stazie. However, he was feeling depressed as well. It had been three months already since Rey left. Things weren't the same without him and he couldn't help but feel out of sorts.

The calls from the road had been sporadic. His younger brother had little to no coverage on his cell phone and the pay phones he happened upon were few and far between. Rick knew Rey was probably okay out there somewhere but he had to fight his instincts to go after him to bring him home.

"Marce?"

"Ummm, yes?"

"Marry me?"

Marcie's eyes opened wide as if she couldn't believe what she had heard. "What did you say?"

"Will you marry me?"

She studied him for a few moments and as she did, the surprise slowly faded from her face. "Ask me again when Rey comes home, okay?"

"Huh? What do you mean?" Rick said.

"Ask me to marry you because you want to. Not because you want to use it as a ploy to lure your brother back."

"What? But I—"

"I miss him too, Rick. And you know he's been bugging us to get married for the past few years and he'll be the first one at the church as your best man to see us get hitched. But he's got to have time, okay? He'll come around."

"But he's—"

"He'll come around. I promise you."

Rick sat back and rubbed his beard some more as he contemplated her. Then he shook his head and said, "God, how did you get to be so smart? Hey, you're not mad at me, are you?" he said with a sheepish grin.

"No. In fact, I think it is very sweet that you miss your brother so much." Marcie leaned close and kissed him. Then she poked his chest hard with her finger. "But if you try that again, I'll break your neck."

The doors to the terrace were open, letting in the Autumn chill of the late afternoon. Stazie wandered out to find her father sitting in one of the patio chairs, gazing at the setting sun beyond the skyline. She noticed more gray hairs on the back of his well-groomed head. Usually he had a Scotch in one hand and a document in the other or a laptop by his side. Today he sat quietly instead, occupied only by the scenery and his thoughts.

Although she tried to remain angry with him to make him pay for what he did, after Rey left, she couldn't muster enough energy. And after more time had passed, she even began to wonder why she had been so pissed off at him. In retrospect, she realized that Gidge had been playing them both.

And here was her father, alone once more. They both were hopeless.

She slipped into the chair beside him. When he turned to her with a cautious eye, she smiled warmly at him. Breaking into a grin of relief, he reached over and patted her hand. At his touch, she felt a sensation deep in her chest, as if her heart was expanding. Despite his downfalls, absences, and faults, she loved him. She thought it odd that she had never given it much consideration before and that it had taken her so long to realize it.

"Daddy, about Gidge—"

His expression turned apologetic. "Honey, I'm very, very sorry about all of that. I know that I—"

"Do you love her?"

"Love her?"

"Yes. Do you honestly love her? I mean it's okay if you do. I was wrong to assume that you couldn't. I've been thinking a lot about it and if you do love her, it's all right by me. I know I've held you down all these years. Maybe you would have found someone by now if you weren't always looking after me. And I want to thank you for doing the best that you could for me. What I'm really trying to say is that you are the one who chooses who you want to love, not me. And I should never interfere with that."

It was a totally unexpected admission. Doug raised an eyebrow and studied her closely. "Stazie? Is everything all right, Honey?"

"Yes, fine, Daddy. It's not that. It's just that I was unfair and I want to apologize."

He looked at her in surprise. "*You* want to apologize? To me?"

"Yes. Can you forgive me for the way I acted?" she said as she laid her head on his shoulder and hugged his arm.

"There is nothing to forgive, Baby. And you're sure you are okay?"

"Uh huh."

The perplexed counselor was pensive for a moment. His daughter's newfound compassion and understanding was going to take some getting used to. Then he sighed and said, "I'm the one who needs your forgiveness.

Not for this thing with Gidge. You know I'm sorry about that. No, I'm talking about the years in which you've been left alone to fend for yourself. Oh, I've always made excuses—'I'm working,' 'I'm busy,' 'I'm a single dad,' and all that other nonsense. So I made sure to get the best nannies, the best schools, the best of everything for my little girl. Yeah, well big deal. I know now that I was never the best father to you. If I had been, I would have been there for you.

"Instead, I ran away, just like your mother did, from my responsibility. Hell, maybe that's the only thing the two of us had in common, when I think about it. But now, after I hurt you and came close to losing you, and for what? Another empty distraction in my life? It was just some other thing that kept me from being a true father to you. And for that, I am sorry, Stazie.

"As for your question, I can honestly say that I don't love Gidge. In fact, I don't even like her when it comes down to it. It all boils down to nothing more than an impetuous infatuation from an egotist who is getting old. So, imagine how flattering it was when a young attractive woman flirted with an old fart like me? I was a total cad. I know she is your best friend."

Stazie halted him by raising her hand. "WAS my best friend. But it's okay. To tell you the truth, I'm not sure if I ever liked her either."

Father and daughter broke into grins that erupted into chuckles.

"We've been through a lot together, haven't we, Daddy?" Stazie looked at her father with tenderness.

Doug smiled back with love and cupped her chin. "Yes, Sweetheart. We certainly have."

She settled back to snuggling and watching the sunset. He seized the moment to say, "I received another check from Rey today. I believe that settles up the bond money. I just thought you should know."

She didn't answer but Doug could feel her hug his arm a little tighter.

"I wish I knew what to tell you, Babe. Sometimes you try to hold onto someone but they still slip away from you all the same. Other times you have to let them go. I should have let your mother go but I couldn't. I tried everything to make her stay but it didn't do any good. She left anyway. And unfortunately, it's like you said, 'you choose to love a person.' However it doesn't necessarily mean that they will choose to love you back."

"But how do you let go?"

He leaned his head against hers and sighed deeply once again.

"I don't know, Honey. I honestly don't know."

❧

The roads, the names of towns, and the many faces blurred along the way. Rey had been riding for the past few months, not in any particular direction, having been up the coast, around the Great Lakes, and across the Midwest. He thought some rambling would clear his head, but in fact, it made him feel uneasy. It reminded him of being on unfamiliar trails on his mountain bike where he didn't know where the sharp turns or drop-offs were. With his fast-dwindling resources, he knew he was going to have to land somewhere. The proceeds from the few day jobs he picked up along the way went to paying back Doug. And with only five hundred forty-six dollars left in the bank out of his entire savings, he was feeling the crunch.

The needle on the gas gauge pointed to empty. Rey switched to the reserve tank and thought about the high price of fuel and grumbled. Although the bike got excellent gas mileage, it still needed to be filled. After he gassed up in the next small town he found, he started the bike and pointed it toward Colorado. Fall was waning and the weather was getting colder. He hoped any chance of snow would hold out just a little bit longer. Thinking back to that night in the fishing shack, he didn't want to ever get that cold again.

The Truck On Inn he arrived at was hazy inside with cigarette smoke, although on the door was clearly posted, "No Smoking." Coming in from the pitch-blackness of the night outside, Rey blinked against the fluorescent glare inside the small busy restaurant. The scrawny young hostess with the nose ring glanced up from behind the counter where she was refilling the napkin dispensers.

"I don't have a table clear yet, so I'll be with you in a minute, sir," she said.

"Uh, no problem. I have to make a phone call first. Do you have a pay phone?"

Holding a stack of napkins in her hand, she pointed passed the counter stools towards the back of the restaurant. He found the shabby pay phone, long forgotten since the advent of the mobile, its tattered phone book hanging like it had been lynched. Taking some of the remaining quarters from his pocket, he inserted them into the phone and dialed.

Rick answered and upon hearing his brother's voice, grew excited. "Rey? Hey Bro! How's it going? Where are you?"

"I'm somewhere in Kansas right now. I should be making Colorado in about five more hours."

"And then what? You sticking there? I know how much you like Colorado."

"I'm not sure yet . . . Hey, is that Ma and Pop?" Rey said, hearing his parents' voices in the background.

"Yeah, they're over for dinner and Glo and Sela and Grandma are here too. We're having your favorite stew. Here, I'll get Ma—"

"No, that's okay, Rick, not right now. Tell them all I said hi."

"What? You don't want to talk to Ma? She's been worried sick about you."

"It's not that, I've got to go . . . I, I left my helmet outside and the place is closing up right now," he lied. "Tell them I'll give them all a call when I get there, okay? I was just calling to let you know where I was, but I got to go."

"Uh sure, man. Okay. Hey, can I at least reassure Grandma that you don't have a 'ho' with you?" Rick said and chuckled.

"You're a real riot, Rick."

"All right, all right. Hold on . . . Glo says hi . . . What? I told him already, okay? Ow! Geez—don't hit!"

The thought of his sister landing her usual sucker punch on Rick's arm made Rey smile and shake his head.

"Okay, I'm back. Hey listen, you take care of yourself out there or else I'll have to fly over and kick your ass, you hear? You think I'm joking? I'm serious."

"Yeah."

"Hey Rey?"

"I've really got to go, man."

"Love you, Bro."

Rey was taken aback by his brother's rare expression of sentiment.

"Love you too."

Thinking of his family seated around the dinner table made him feel that much more alone and hollow. The only things filling the emptiness inside of him now was a knot in his throat and heaviness in his heart. He decided to skip dinner and ride through the night, partly to save money but partly because he couldn't find solace in his restlessness. There was a place that came to mind and he had to get there.

By noon, he was north of Purgatory when he turned off a side road that took him to a local ski spot. There was no snow yet after the end of the long Indian summer and the lift wasn't running but that didn't stop him from hiking up the steep descent. The area looked so different in the late fall without snow covering the slopes but he knew this mountain well with all of its pits and turns. He couldn't recall how many times he and Ivan had raced down these slopes on their snowboards, daring and challenging each other.

When he got to the right area, he hiked further on back, off the main slope to a winding, narrow black flag run tucked behind a row of trees. Rey climbed a few more hundred feet in altitude and then centered himself in the middle of the run. Turning around, he looked down the slope. He remembered kicking it on this course on their boards. The sprawling Rocky Mountain range lay at his feet, the clear day vista stretched on for hundreds of miles. This was the spot. He plunked himself down on a tuft of grass and gazed at the world around him. Soon, his thoughts retrieved a memory from long ago.

It was the first time Ivan and he had taken on the slope for the day. The morning dawned bright and sunny, the sky a deep blue, crisscrossed with white puffy contrails from planes flying high in the jet stream. Fresh powder had fallen the night before and they were the first in line on the lift for the day, so spread before them was an untouched winter paradise. Not many took on this black flag run as it had a reputation for being an ass buster. He and Ivan took it as an invitation. At the summit, as they always did at the start of a fresh course, they stopped to contemplate their run.

Rey turned to Ivan and said, "Okay, since loser buys all, I want to make sure you get this straight. I'll most likely be pretty damned famished and pretty damned thirsty by the time we break for lunch. So I hope you brought enough bills for at least three dozen Buffalo wings, two pitchers, and two bacon cheeseburgers. Got that?"

He grinned and pulled up his goggles as he laid down the challenge.

"No worries, Bro. I don't need to carry that much green on me 'cause you should be pretty full after eating my powder!" Ivan shot back as he laid down his board and hopped on it with a war whoop.

Rey followed and the two of them slalomed and jumped, veered and twisted down the steep winding slope. They were neck in neck for several hundred yards. Anticipating a jump that Ivan missed gave Rey the lead while his friend wiped out.

He was almost a thousand feet down and far ahead of Ivan when a terrific roar grew behind him. The ground trembled beneath his feet. Before he could react, a cloud of icy mist engulfed him and within another second, the advancing wall of snow slammed into him from behind like a bulldozer, tumbling and tossing him in a turbulent slide of white blindness.

He couldn't count how many times he was flipped and rolled. When it passed, Rey found himself entombed. It was pitch black and the only sound he heard was his own rapid breathing. He tried moving, but the weight of the snow on his splayed limbs pinned him in place. His yells were muffled under the layers of snow. He wasn't sure if Ivan had been hit too. If he had, who would ever find them? Although he thought he would never need one, he now wished they had purchased avalanche transceivers. Instead, he and Ivan had both opted to spend their four hundred dollars on ski lift passes and beer.

After trying to free himself for a while and just when panic was feeling like an option, he heard a sound from the surface above. Suddenly light poured in from a small hole that was punched through the snow alongside of his stomach. Another hole resulted in a finger grasping at the toe of his boot. At that point, the digging commenced and Rey found himself being liberated scoop by scoop from his icy prison.

"Holy sweet mother of asteroids, Rey! There you are, man! I thought you were toast!" Ivan cried out in relief as he uncovered his friend. "Hey, are you all right?" he said as Rey sat up. Ivan looked his friend over for injuries and brushed off the snow from his shoulders and head.

Rey shook off his gloves and spat out some snow. Then he took in a deep breath, stretched out his arms and took in another. "Yeah. I think so. Was it an avalanche?"

"More like a baby avalanche, dude! But still a freakin'-A gnarly avalanche. I was just getting back on my board after wiping out when I saw the whole thing. This big ass shelf of snow broke away and started sliding like a total beast. I veered to the tree line and looked down. And there you were, dude, this little speck with this humongous mother of a snow pile barreling down on you. It was bitchin'! I saw you get plowed under. BAM!"

His hands danced in rapid motion as he demonstrated the scene.

"You had this sticking up out of the snow or I'd have never found you," Ivan said as he wrestled Rey's board from the snow. "It was most fortuitous, dude. Would you believe that all I saw was just the friggin' tip? Is that straight or what? Thank you, Burton," he said as he kissed the board. "I guess those avalanche transceivers aren't just for weenies, huh? I know what I'm getting tout de suite when I get home."

Offering his hand, he pulled his friend from the snow and the two of them sat on the slope for a moment, slowing their pulses and catching their breaths. It occurred to Rey how odd it was, on a clear sunny day, when all was tops and you felt totally invincible, that things could happen within mere seconds that change everything. If he had been on the slope alone, he would have been buried alive.

He clapped Ivan on the shoulder and then grabbed him in a bear hug. "Hey, thanks man, for finding me and getting me out," he said gratefully. "I would've died in there."

"No problemo. I'm just glad that I was able to get down to you so fast. I just can't get over that fricken' ass wall of snow. I've never seen anything like it before. Up close, I mean. It was like this pile of the white stuff was out to seek and destroy. Luckily it wasn't one of those freakishly huge avalanches like the ones I've seen on the Discovery Channel that bury whole towns and shit. You lucked out, man. It was good sized, but any bigger than that and I would've been digging 'til Christmas."

"I wasn't sure if you were toast too. Lying there, it was so quiet and dark, like a tomb. It was like God had stopped thinking about me all of a sudden. I really was beginning to think 'Game Over' for me—for both of us. You know the crazy ass stunts we pulled when we were kids. And you remember some of the hairy shit we did when we were still 'boots.' But you know, for the first time in my life I wondered what it would be like to be dead, to be totally gone off this planet. I had never considered that before. You know what I'm talking about? You stop being. That's it for you. Nothing you ever did on this earth really matters then."

Ivan contemplated Rey's words as he stared out to the horizon that was jagged with white mountain peaks. Then he nodded and said, "Dude, I'm thinking it's like this board tip sticking up out of the snow."

"Huh? WTF, over?"

"Okay, straight up, I respectfully concur we've been through some hairy-assed stuff and have taken it all for granted. People think they're all god-like in what they feel they have power over. Like we're all invincible supermen who don't have to worry about the consequences. But sometimes that stuff comes back to bite you in the ass and then you find out the cruise control you were counting on had failed all along and you are totally and woefully powerless."

"Oh yeah, so what are we supposed to do when that happens?"

"I say, bite back, Bro. Bite back and hold on like a mother fucker. There's not a whole lot we can do about it except never give up or give in and most of all, never forget where you came from."

"Wait, what does that have to do with my board tip sticking up out of the snow?"

"Don't you get it, dude? People have always been philosophizing that if God stops thinking about you, you will cease to exist. Personally, I don't believe that load of cheese. I believe that if *others* stop thinking about you, if there's no one out there worrying about you—you know like wondering about, caring about, remembering, and crying over your ass—*that's* when you cease to exist. Sayonara and goodbye.

"But just like this board tip sticking up out of the snow, if someone's got your back and cares about you, they can dig you out no matter how deep it gets. You *do* exist. And even if you manage to get your ticket punched anyway, when they remember you, you'll exist forever."

Rey pondered Ivan's philosophy carefully. The small patch of light peering through the darkness in the snow came to mind. He slowly nodded his head in agreement then closely studied his friend. Ivan always did have a unique perspective on things. Under that thatch of wild black hair and pilly woolen cap was truly a profound mind.

"Why, you magnificent bastard, I never knew you cared," Rey said, half teasing, half in appreciation.

"Hey, the infinite cosmos saw it fit only to give me Gina for family. She's hardly a sister to me, let alone a brother. You're my brother, Rey."

"Back at you, Bro."

They sat for a moment savoring the sentiment.

Then Rey said, "But if you say, 'I love you, man' then I'm going to have to put the hurt on you."

"Hey, just because I love you, man, doesn't mean we're going to be picking out any curtains together, so don't get your hopes up, see?" his friend joked back.

"Well I'm outta here. Last one to the bottom is buying."

"Yeah, that's what you said last time. And you ate a lot of snow."

The best friends scrambled up on their boards and raced each other down the hill.

Summing up that memory, Rey remained on the mountainside thinking and recalling his past and present. Even after Ivan had graced him with the wisdom of a harbinger, he had taken life and the people in it for granted. He wondered what Mei-Lin would say to him right now. He took a pretty good guess. *Your guilt is there for as long as you own it. But in the meantime, open up to others. Don't shut them out. It is the only way you will get through this.* Rey realized he had stopped going to see Mei-Lin because he wanted to handle things his own way. It was the same treatment for Rick and the rest of his family. For Stazie. He was growing weary of being by himself and, like Ivan rescuing him from the snow, wondered if he could ever be found again.

He reconciled it was time to bite back and hold on.

❧

"Are you sure you want to do this, Honey? You know I can still sublet the place across the way from me if you want. It's not too late." Doug had called Stazie while waiting for his flight at O'Hare. Checking in was a new habit he had developed whenever he was out of town.

"No, Daddy. I've already put a deposit down. I'm moving the rest of my stuff this afternoon."

"But *there*? Are you sure you're going to be happy there? It's kind of small."

"It's cute. With a little paint and fixing up, it will be perfect. And please don't worry. I'll be fine. In fact, you can drop by anytime you want. Except when I'm studying. But I'll let you know when that is. Oooh, I can't wait!" Stazie said and giggled. She hadn't felt this excited about anything in what seemed a long time.

"Okay, Babe. Sounds like you're going to have fun. Oh, and buy yourself a housewarming gift. Anything you want, on me. I wish I could be there to give you it myself but next stop I've got a deposition in Boston for the next couple of weeks."

"I know, Daddy. It's okay. Just wait until you see it. And remember to take care of yourself, okay? And call me when you get there. I love you."

"I love you too, Sweetheart."

"So *you're* the new renter?" Rick said, dumbfounded. He and Marcie peered in through the doorway at the stacks of boxes and clothes that already filled the tiny living room.

"Uh huh. Surprised?"

"Yeah, you can say that. But why here?"

"Oh. You must think I'm some kind of stalker or something, renting Rey's old place," she said and laughed.

Rick didn't join in. Instead, he eyed her curiously and nodded. "Yeah, you can say that."

Catching his drift, Stazie opened her own eyes wide.

"No, it's nothing like that. I knew that this one was vacant. I just needed some place quick and there are not too many places available in the vicinity. Believe me, I've checked! And I also needed some place that wouldn't chew up all of my savings or be too much to take care of. Of course, Daddy offered to help me out but I wanted to do this one completely on my own.

And since Rey . . ." She hesitated mid-sentence as she brushed her bangs back. ". . . well, it seems like he's not coming back anytime soon, so I didn't think he'd mind."

"It makes perfect sense. And I don't think he'd mind at all," Marcie said, reassuring her. "We were told someone was moving in by this Friday, so we came over to make sure we hadn't left anything behind. We just didn't expect to find someone here today, let alone you!"

"Well, I couldn't wait. I'm really excited. It's the first time that I'll be on my own."

"Good for you! How's everything coming along?"

"Great, so far. Do you want to come in? Nothing's set up yet but I've got so many ideas and I've just been itching to share them with someone."

"Sure," Marcie said.

She linked her arm in Rick's and gave him a tug. He still looked skeptical and she knew he was going to have a lot to say about this once they left.

They entered Rey's former home to find it transformed, influenced by the personal belongings about. Stazie had most of the place filled already with furniture, rugs, throw pillows, curtains, and a few plants.

"See, over here, this window? I'd like to replace it with glass tile instead. It'll let in light, but it'll get rid of that awful view of the brick wall across from it. And this wall here, I want to do in stripes. What do you think? Kind of a madras look? I think it will be a lot of fun. And a hanging chair there in the corner and wicker baskets to hold things. I've already ordered a bunch of stuff from Pottery Barn and IKEA. Oh, I can't wait to get it all finished!"

Marcie listened and nodded in agreement while Rick wandered about, poking his nose into a few piles of stuff here and there. He picked up one of the romance novels stacked in a box, snickered out loud at its cover, and shook his head. He let out another snort when he came face to face with a pink poodle plush dog.

"Man, ol' Rey would never recognize the place," he said. "It looks like Barbie's apartment dream house in here. Suddenly I feel the need to wrestle a bear or rebuild an engine or something." He moved on to assess what she did with the bedroom and bathroom.

Stazie felt a little annoyed at his remarks. Pulling Marcie aside, she said, "Ugh. How do you put up with him?"

The brunette glanced at her boyfriend and smiled. "He's harmless, mostly all bark with just a little bite."

"But what makes you stay with him?" Stazie said earnestly. "You're smart and pretty too. You can have just about anyone. Why him?"

"Rick? He's a funny guy. It may surprise you but under all of that rough exterior, he's the sweetest man I know. He has the biggest heart though not always the most sense or tactfulness. But he's worth the effort to me. I guess sometimes you just got to love them, warts and all."

Just then Rick re-entered the room, pointing a thumb over his shoulder. "Hey Marce, you know she's got four hair dryers in there? And like a bazillion shoes," he said and snickered.

Marcie blushed at his statement, raised her eyebrows, and sighed out loud.

"Yup, warts and all," she said under her breath.

The weather had turned bitter cold. The bright mountains in the daylight were now dark icy spires against the evening sky. A light snow began to fall. Rey wondered if he could ever get use to this unpredictable mountain weather. He still had another twenty-three more miles to go before he reached the small motel room that he had secured this afternoon with his dwindling funds. Although he loved riding his bike, at times like these he missed the luxurious warmth even the simplest car could afford. But then again, he wasn't feeling himself.

En route, he stopped at a cozy pizza place that had been converted from an old school house. While he waited for his order, he half-heartedly looked at the clutter of graffiti and numerous photographs lining the walls that were posted by patrons that frequented the place. His eyes drifted over the photographs tacked to the wall—the shared family grins, the encircling arms of friendship, the loving kisses between couples, the inside jokes known by those laughing in the photos that left the observer guessing the punch line. Usually, he would have gobbled down half a pizza especially on a cold night like this. Tonight, he could barely get down one slice. As for beer, he just didn't have any taste for it now, staring at the full pint he had ordered and opting instead for a glass of water.

Finally it was closing time and Rey knew he couldn't hang around much longer. He slowly rose from his seat, gave a wave to the guy at the counter, stuffed some cash in the tip jar that read 'Those who do not tip are shit bags,' and stepped out into the cold night air. After his eyes adjusted to the darkness, he found himself staring up at the stars where he easily located Orion's Belt, the Seven Sisters, and the Big Dipper. The pointer stars remained faithfully fixed showing the way to the North Star. He couldn't tell if it was just him or were they shining brighter than they ever had before.

Back on the road when found he couldn't control his chattering teeth any longer and his hands were numb inside his gloves, Rey pulled over to get on warmer clothes. He opened his saddlebag to remove a few things and balanced them on his seat. Then he extracted his leather jacket that had been rolled up tightly at the bottom. Opening it, he recognized her fragrance immediately. Its floral note still lingered in the lining and drifted up from the folds. Rey slowly slipped the jacket on, thinking of how she looked in it, sleeping in the cab with it wrapped securely around her.

Oh poop.

Marcie read her phone's screen. 'Meet me @ the park under r tree as soon as ur able to get away' the text message said. She wondered what Rick was up to again.

"Who is it?" said Gloria from across the table where she, Carmen, and Marcie were having lunch.

"It's Rick. He wants me to meet him."

"Is something wrong?" Carmen said with a bit of alarm. She stopped with her dessert fork poised mid-air, a little more nervous these days.

"No, I don't think so, otherwise he would have called me direct. He knew I was out to lunch with you today, so he probably wants me to come on over as soon as we are through."

"I still don't understand these phone things, these texts. If he needs to speak to you, why doesn't he just call on the phone? Or wait till he sees you again?"

"Well, Ma, it's a way of getting a message across without interrupting our meal," Glo said.

"But he interrupted our meal anyway, didn't he?"

"Yeah, I guess, in a way."

"He was raised better than that."

"I know, Ma. I know." Gloria stole a glance at Marce, smiled, and rolled her eyes.

"Maybe you should go, Marcie. Just in case he needs something or something is wrong."

"Oh, he'll be okay for ten more minutes," Marcie said. "We're just about through with our dessert. It's probably something up with Jack. Rick dotes constantly over that dog."

"All right, Marcie. You do what's best," Carmen said.

The worry crease across her brow was enough to change Marcie's mind. Carmen had been through the wringer with Rey out on the road. Perhaps it would be better if she didn't push it too far and have the woman worry about her older son as well. "On second thought, maybe I'll go check," she said as she packed up her things to go.

Gloria caught on. "Don't worry about this, Marcie. I got it."

"Thanks, you two," Marcie said as she rose and hugged them. "I'll let you know what's up as soon as I find out."

When she found her boyfriend at the city park under their favorite tree, she knew something indeed was up. Still dressed in his greasy coveralls, it was apparent that he had come directly from work. As she approached, she could see him pacing back and forth. When he saw her coming, he froze in place. Rick wore a strange expression on his face, one she hadn't seen before. She couldn't tell whether it was anxiety, happiness, or a stomach ache.

"What's up, Sugar Bear? We were just getting through dessert," she said.

"I hope you finished. That's why I texted."

"Well, you know your mom . . ."

He sighed. "Yeah, Ma. But listen, Babe, I'm glad you came over right away anyway."

"What is it? Are you still at work?" She tugged at his coveralls.

"I took off early. See, I couldn't wait."

"But isn't Stan going to blow a fit?"

"It doesn't matter, Marce. Now if I can just get through with what I have to say before I throw up."

"Are you ill? Here, why don't you sit down?"

"Marcie!"

She stopped abruptly and looked at him with surprise.

"What I want to ask you is . . . well, see we're under our tree? The one where we first met when I accidentally clobbered you when I was catching that football."

"Yeah, Ricky, I know. Go on."

"Well, I . . . I . . ."

He dropped to one knee, pulled out a clean folded rag from his pocket, and produced a diamond ring from its folds.

Holding it up to her, he continued, "Marcella D'Annato, please, will you marry me?"

Marcie gasped as her eyes welled up with tears.

"Oh Rick! Of course I—" Suddenly she turned stern as she placed her hand on her hip. "Wait a minute. This isn't another one of your ploys to get your brother back is it? I told you I would break your neck if you ever tried that again!"

Still on one knee, Rick looked up into the fire in her eyes. "What? No Marce, this is for reals. I mean it. Will you marry me?"

"What about Rey?"

"What about him? I just saw him at the garage. He stopped by. I told him what I planned to do. He's stoked about us."

"Wait, he's back in town? Is he here to stay?"

"Yeah! As far as I know. Anyway, he says hi. He had something else he had to do right now and he's kinda in a hurry, but he said he'll see everyone tomorrow night at our place. That is, if you don't mind. He doesn't have a place yet and I said it would be all right if—"

"Rick!"

"Huh? What?"

"Aren't you down on your knee for a reason?" Marcie said as she laid her hands on his broad shoulders and looked down at him tenderly.

"Oh yeah." He grinned. "I repeat. Marcella D'Annato, please, will you marry me?"

"Yes, you big loveable lug. Yes, I will marry you."

Stazie picked up the chip bowl and empty soda cans, and decided to eat the last remaining half of bologna and cheese sandwich on the plate as she cleared her small kitchen table from lunch with her study group. They had just made it through the eighth chapter of introduction to textiles. Her classmates were a lively, friendly bunch and they had all quickly bonded over homework and labs, and the comfort of oversized tees, sweatpants, and slouch socks. Stazie enjoyed having them over to her place for study sessions and coffee. But today she looked forward to a quiet afternoon, maybe to read or go out for some air. She did a lot more walking these days.

Despite her excitement over her newfound independence, the apartment and living completely alone with no servants took some getting used to. She disliked the way that housecleaning took up so much time and cooking was a challenge. She wasn't ever sure if she was doing either right but the pride in having her own place and calling her own shots compensated for her lack of skills.

Although her trust fund included investments to keep her supported indefinitely, she was planning a career. Too often she looked at people on the move in the city around her who all had things to do, schedules to stick to, and places they needed to be. Everybody seemed to have a role in the big world. They had jobs. Although she had never given it much thought before, it started to play on her mind. She wanted one too. It was another thing she could call entirely her own.

Doug was naturally surprised by his daughter's sudden interest in schooling and career and offered to pay her tuition to the finest college. It floored him when she declined his offer, wanting to apply at the local university on her own. He was proud of the way she pursued it but stunned when she was accepted and worked out every last detail on her own.

Just as Stazie was settling down with a cup of tea to peruse her DIY small wood projects book she just got, there was a knock at her door. When she opened it, she found she couldn't move. It was all she could do to hold her fingers to her mouth and stare back at the person who stood before her. Jumbled emotions and thoughts crowded her head instantaneously, leaving her dazed.

Before she could react, Rey held out his leather jacket before him. As if in a trance, she reached for it.

"Rey? What are you—?"

"Don't worry. I'm going," he said. "But I just rode over two thousand miles to give you this. It's more yours than mine, these days."

He lingered, waiting for the sting of a well-deserved slap or worst yet, her coolness. At first, when none was forthcoming, he was relieved. There was still a chance to correct a wrong that had been done. Maybe he hadn't thrown it all away after all. However when she remained quiet, he started to believe that perhaps it was too late after all.

As he turned and headed down the flight of stairs, she snapped to as if she had just awakened. "Wait! Don't go yet," she called out.

He hesitated for a moment and then returned to her doorstep.

Looking at him as if she were trying to solve a difficult puzzle, she said softly, "You actually came back . . . to see me?"

Not knowing what to say, Rey stood there with his hands shoved into his pockets.

"How are you doing?" she said.

"I'm doing okay . . . Better. How about you?"

"Better."

The moment grew awkward but Stazie didn't want to him to leave just yet. She opened the door wide.

"I'm sorry, please come in. I guess it must seem weird to find me here. I hope you don't mind that I, um, leased your apartment."

"No, not at all. Rick told me that you had moved in. My lease was up and it was open. I'm glad someone could use it."

"Well, I've made a few changes."

"I'll say!" Rey said when they entered into the living room, coming alongside of the baby grand piano planted in the tiny apartment. "Wow, how did you get this in here?" The piano dominated the room, leaving little space for much else. "Is this the same one?"

"Uh huh, the one from the cottage. Daddy said I could have whatever I wanted for a housewarming gift, so I chose this."

"This? Why? Do you play now?"

"No," she said shyly, "But I'd like to learn. I remembered how you looked at it when you first saw it and I guess it started to look different to me."

He cleared his throat and then glanced around the room looking at the window sashes, throw pillows, and flowers.

"I know, it's all kind of girlie and frou-frou now," she said, a little embarrassed.

"It may surprise you but that was one of the things I missed about you." He added under his breath, "I know it surprised the hell out of me."

"Really?"

"Uh huh. . . Hey, what did you do to your hair?"

"I decided to go back to my natural color and shorter. I got tired of blonde," she said, but self-consciously her hand went up to scrunch her honey colored curls. "Why, does it look bad?"

"No, it looks great. I don't know, I think it fits you better."

"Oh." She smiled, pleased.

She showed him the rest of the apartment—her paint schemes, fabrics, even the pet goldfish she kept in a bowl. She held back when she showed him her bedroom but caught herself and directed him to the tidy kitchen, instead.

"The place looks awesome. I always figured something could be done with this shoebox. I guess I just never felt the inclination. Maybe all it needed was the right person."

"I've been having lots of fun experimenting with all the things I've been learning in class."

"Class, huh? So you're going to school? Right on. Hey, are you taking astronomy?" he said pointing to the star chart poster that hung on the wall next to a small telescope in the corner.

"Huh? No. Not astronomy. I just decided to take your advice and start looking things up. I wanted to know more about stars after the ones we saw that night. One thing led to another and I found that telescope and well . . ."

"Cool. So what are you taking?"

"You know, at first I thought about nursing after tending to you when you were hypothermic," she said.

He looked sheepish.

"But I settled on Interior Design. I think it suits me better."

"I agree."

"Hey, would you like a piece of cake?"

He tried to conceal a wince as he swallowed hard and said uneasily, "Uh, no thanks, I'm good."

"Don't worry. I made it from a box mix this time for my study group. It didn't turn out half bad. Look, we ate a few slices of it already."

"Well, in that case. Sure."

They ate their cake in silence. Neither knew the right words to fit comfortably in the moment.

"Rey?"

"Uh huh?"

"Seriously, why did you come back? You didn't ride all this way just to give me a jacket."

"I'm not sure. But I know being there just wasn't right. I love Colorado and I have every intention to go back and live there permanently, one day. But not now. Not under the pretenses that I showed up there. When I go back, it will be for the right reasons and at the right time."

"Well, do you plan on staying here for a little bit then?" she said tentatively.

"Long enough to make things right, I hope. I'm not sure how long that's going to take."

"Oh, you mean regarding your accident with your friend and all."

"Ivan had squared things away with me a long time ago. I was just too dense to listen to what he had been saying to me all along. It's still going to take some time to work it all out but I think it'll be better now. No, I need to make things right with my family. They're always there for me and all I did was push them away and worry them needlessly."

She tried a smile of encouragement but wasn't sure how reliable it was.

"Most of all, I need to make amends with you. That is, if you are willing. Or you can kick my butt out if you want and I'll totally understand if you do. You know, I was really surprised that you even let me in. I thought you would never want to see me again," said Rey.

"A lot has changed. With me . . . with everything."

"Well, is there a possibility that we can start over again?"

Stazie thought about her life at present. It was odd to think that after all the time spent in pursuing him, it looked like he was finally willing. But now she didn't know what to do. She was independent for the first time and enjoying every minute of it. She had friends—true friends—now. Her near future held graduation and a career. She and her father had a better and stronger relationship than ever before. What would it mean to have Rey around? Although her heart skipped a beat at the thought of it, her new-found rationale reminded her it was purely out of habit and calmly put it in its place. He was the only remnant left of what her life used to be.

"I don't know what I want right now. I wish I could tell you but I'm very conflicted. It's been over half a year already."

"Right. I can understand that."

They sat for a few minutes more, the silence hanging like a curtain between them.

"Listen, I better get going. I know I dropped in on you unannounced. I'm sure you have other plans," he said.

She nodded.

He paused for a moment at the door to say, "Take care of yourself, Staze. The place looks great. You look like you're on your way. I'll be seeing you."

Rey descended the familiar flight of stairs one last time. Outside, he took in a deep breath and looked around at his old block. There wasn't anything left for him here. The sky was heavy with clouds and rain began to fall. He was getting ready to climb on his motorcycle when he felt a light touch on his back. Turning around, he found Stazie, wrapped in his leather jacket, her cheeks wet.

"Was there any other reason you came back? Besides the jacket and making amends, I mean?" she said in a small voice.

Tenderly, he held her face in his hands as he stared into her eyes. "A long time ago, you told me that you failed to see things that were right in front of you, things you took for granted. I know now I was guilty of the same thing. Maybe I was worse because I had family and friends, people who cared about me, and I still couldn't see it. No, it only took me getting flattened by an avalanche on a ski run years ago and thousands of miles since then to finally open my eyes.

"You may not believe me, but I came back for you, Anastasia. I came back for *you*. It's the damnedest thing, but I think I love you."

He took her up in his arms and holding her close, kissed her. With her in his embrace, he felt at ease for the first time in months.

Touching his forehead against hers, he said, "I can't say what is going to happen from here. I'm far from figuring everything out. But I am willing to work at it, as long as you want me."

As she kissed him back, the sky opened up releasing a downpour on them. They didn't notice.

Stazie woke with a start. The sun through her window told her that it was already late in the morning. She lie on her back and stared up at the ceiling, knowing that his side of the bed was empty once again. Once before, she would have felt anger and betrayal. Now, when she searched within, these emotions were absent. Gone was that desperation of feeling abandoned.

 It wasn't that she didn't feel disappointed. When she woke, she had hoped that he would be there but knew most likely, it wasn't meant to be. With a sigh, she reached for his pillow and held it close, hoping to catch his scent. He loved her, she was sure of that. The uninhibited passion in which he made love to her the night before attested to it. However, she had come to accept who he was and what he had to do. If he needed more time, she was willing to wait. If he needed more space, she would give it.

Stazie put his pillow back in its place and turned onto her side. She faced the wall and looked at the photo hanging there of the waterfall she had taken on that bright day, long ago.

I'm going to be all right this time, she thought with confidence.

She turned her attention instead to her list of things to do that day: food shopping, laundry, and studying for a test she had on Tuesday. She would call Beatrice later to chat and get some more recipes. She would also email her father to remind him of their lunch date when he got back. With energy and peace, she smiled to herself, stretched, and wriggled her toes.

It's going to be all right.

Suddenly, she felt the bed jostle. Rey slipped in behind her. The feel of his arm encircling her middle made her gasp with pleasure.

Pleasantly surprised, she turned to face him and said, "What? I thought you were gone."

"No, just putting on some coffee. I hope you don't mind."

With delight, she snuggled against him as he pulled her closer and kissed her.

"No, I don't mind a bit," she said and smiled.

"I couldn't find that Sula-whatsis coffee in your cabinet though. Only some instant French roast."

"Sulawesi. That's okay. Instant is fine."

"Really? I thought Sulawesi was a must-have for any 'complete kitchen.'"

"Sure it is. But it is also kind of expensive."

He laughed. "Uh huh. I guess a lot *has* changed."

She nestled for a moment, enjoying the way her body fit against his.

"And Rey?"

"Uh huh?"

"Remember how yesterday, you had asked me if we could start all over again?"

He nodded.

"I'm ready now."

X-Mas Tree

978-1-7333609-2-0

Novella

In this coming-of-age tale, 15-year-old Peter gets his first glimpse at the responsibility and commitment it takes in being a provider. X-Mas Tree is about a father and son's love for each other that is tested by the challenges of progress overshadowing tradition and the transformation of a boy to a man.

Like Us, The Polar Bears

978-1-7333609-4-4

Young Adult Novel

Seventeen-year-old Molly needs to figure out how to get her brilliant plan to save polar bears into action while dealing with a few … challenges:

☑ Phobias + self-doubt

☑ Anxiety + more anxiety

☑ Loss of BFF

Hope arrives in the form of Sig, the last-available lab partner, who has an audacious idea for saving the polar bears and—a secret. He accepts Molly as she is, problems and all, and challenges her to follow through on her polar bear rescue plan. She accepts his challenge, putting her well outside her comfort zone. But as Molly and Sig set off to raise funds for the cause, complications threaten to melt the thin ice that keeps Molly from drowning in her own problems.

Just like the polar bears she is trying to save, her world is rapidly changing. Can Molly hold on long enough to survive?

About the author

Tess Marset is a freelance writer and educator who resides in Edmonds, WA with her husband and two sons.